A SECRET LIFE

A SECRET LIFE

Gillian Nelson

GUILD PUBLISHING
LONDON

To David
my dear companion

'When the children are asleep, I can put off the light and open the black-out curtains. I see stars, the rim of a hill, that's all. When I try to think of our old London there is nothing but darkness and flames. How I wish you were with me, Tikki! I have a sense of impending desolation like a dry wind blowing in and out of my soul.'

Part of Lucille's letter to her husband,
November, 1940

The hills are shadows, and they flow
  From form to form, and nothing stands;
  They melt like mist, the solid lands,
Like clouds they shape themselves and go.
Tennyson

1

ALFRED

When Alfred let his memories sink down to their lowest, most watery, most childish point, he came up against a green cloth. His face was found pressed to it, giving him relief and pleasure. His mother was there too, but he could not make out anything of her appearance.

His only knowledge of her looks came from a studio portrait kept in the front room. The flourish of the photographer's signature and the silver mounting lines diluted some of Mrs Tickener's personality, which she could ill afford. She looked timorously out of the frame, seeking approval, holding her baby son uncertainly, as if she feared to drop him. The picture also showed how sweet and pretty her face was.

Alfred has another memory of her. It is the day of his sister's birth and he is taken in to see Mother and baby Ida. Again the face is not there, only an arm in a flannel nightdress curved round the baby whose mouth is open in a scream, though the room, in his memory, is entirely silent, even the clock makes no sound. He is led away again.

From that time on, his Aunt Maud lived with them and his mother spent whole days upstairs, resting. The little boy scanned the cliff of stairs, peered into the shadow above, then sat himself on the bottom step as guard or watchman. At the age of five he was sent to the Board School. In the infants' class were forty other boys and as many girls, sitting in pairs, writing on slates, wearing rags and boots without socks. These children called him Fred, which made him two boys – Alfred learning manners from Aunt Maud, and Fred picking up how to fight. He accepted this without comment even to himself. His only problem with school was that while he was there Ida scribbled on his book. This had a blue cover and alternate double pages of pictures and reading. On the fly-leaf was written: *To my dear little son, Alfred, from his loving Mother.* The pictures were of animals such as he had never seen – foxes and asses and cranes. He wanted to learn to read simply to find out what they were doing with grapes to eat and wearing clothes, and so why Mother had desired him to have this book; but Ida's crayons blotted out the words.

He never played with his sister, left her to sit on Maud's knee. In school the two sexes were separated and he had noted in the streets how the men walked down the middle of the pavements while the women, in their long, dark clothes, slipped along close to the walls and the shop-fronts. To some extent he feared them.

One day he came back from school to see all the blinds in the front windows drawn right down. While he stood surprised at the gate, Mrs Bryant from next door came up to him, her face swollen. She took the puzzled child into her own house and told him his mother was dead.

'She has gone to Jesus,' was how Mrs Bryant put it.

'When will she come back?' asked Fred immediately.

'When she's better,' replied the woman with equal speed. 'Jesus makes people better. You have learned that, haven't you, Alfred?'

He did not answer. He was thinking about how the house would be without Mother. Although he cannot now remember any word or look of hers, he can to this day clearly recollect sitting then in Mrs Bryant's parlour and imagining the kitchen in his own home next door – the range, the copper with a wooden lid, the knife-grinder on the wall, the enamel pots, the cabbagey smell, the soap, slippery yellow – all without his mother's hands and without her height against the tiny window. So, when he speaks in old age of remembering his mother, it is her absence he is reaching towards.

'You know Jesus takes poor ill people away to make them well,' Mrs Bryant repeated.

When the boy was allowed to go home, he found it was not true that his mother had gone. She was still in her bedroom. He did not see her, the door was locked and father had the key, but Aunt Maud told him she was 'laid out very pretty'. Alfred sat down on the floor outside the room with his back to the door. The adults were scared by his stony face and there he remained until his father ordered him to bed. Then he went, like a sensible boy.

The next day Mr Tickener cried at breakfast and told Maud to take away the eggs uneaten. Alfred dared not ask about Jesus, but set himself to wait. In a sense, he is waiting still.

All the relations came in black clothes and then his mother's door was opened and a long box was carried out. She was in it, said Maud, who was holding Ida in her arms. When he heard this, Alfred went to hide in the outside lavatory and so missed the funeral. It seemed a horrible way to make someone better, to put them in a box and bury them.

Alfred went on waiting for her to return; although naturally Fred was soon taught in the playground that dead bodies are eaten by worms, and by the teacher that those who have departed are in the sky with God wearing crowns like stars.

Alfred used to dig in the garden with a spoon. He found a few pale worms and inspected them curiously. Even when placed on his hand they had no apparent wish to eat him. As for the stars – they were far away and cold. On the nights when he could see from the window, cats were usually yowling on the outhouse roofs. His mother had hated cats (so Aunt Maud told him) and their noise made the boy's skin go gooseflesh. He pulled the curtains on the stars.

All Fred's childhood, Mr Tickener sat in the front room with his paper and cigarettes, while Maud was a presence in the back kitchen and scullery. Ida and Fred were mostly in the street. Apart from their waspish teachers, the only women they knew were their aunt with her dull face and creased white lips, and Mrs Bryant next door, who, smelling of sweat and mothballs and full of curiosity, was unpleasant in a different way.

At twelve Fred was tall and strong with a thick body. His teacher was pushing him to go to a higher school, and Fred was keen to sit the scholarship, but Mr Tickener said the family needed his wage and fixed up a position as errand-boy at the grocer's on the Broadway. It was considered a good opening. 'Stick to it, my lad, and you'll be a manager one fine day,' said Mrs Bryant jovially.

Fred stuck to it with his usual patience, but he loathed it. He knew he did not want a life of petty jobs, and old women in felt hats finding fault, or the sickly smell of ripe cheese when he took down the shutters in the morning, or the mice in the bottom of packing cases which the men stamped on. It was not money he wanted, but someone's kind smile and the assurance that he would not become old, bent and humbled like the ancient assistant whose rheumatic fingers could hardly fold the blue packets of sugar any longer and whose legs would not hold him steady on the ladder to the highest shelves.

He was saved by Mr Bryant who spoke to him of joining the navy, describing the life in rosy and manly terms. Mr Tickener did not care either way so long as Alfred sent home his pay.

It was a dull day when Alfred first arrived at Chatham. The sea gave no hint of power or beauty but something in its still grey levels appealed to the boy and eased the accumulated distress of his childhood. In moments of leisure he watched it from the barrack windows as a boy on a street corner watches a girl, broodingly, with promises to himself.

At first he was buffeted by discipline, drill and the tests of lower deck life. He put up with it. The navy at least offered him a man's world and he took it, grateful to Regulations for delivering him from the grocery.

When he was posted to a ship, he experienced the sea at close quarters and knew joy for the first time. Whatever the water did he was at one with it, and he loved the sweet battleship for sliding through the waves.

The slipping, rolling, arching heavy waters which maintained his ship buoyed up his spirits. A glance at the water and its sky-meeting would compose him for any fatigue. He learned every appearance, colour, sound and movement of the oceans, but never saw them in a romantic way. It was never for him an angry beast or a blue field; the wake did not fold and cream like ribboned lace, nor did the roar of the waves speak to him of anything but themselves. His mind was simple and literal, which caused his passion to be all the stronger for it was unfragmented by imagination, of which he had none.

For twelve years he drew all his nourishment from the sea.

2

HOLLY

For some time Holly had been sitting on the edge of her parents'
bed and staring into an empty wardrobe. Curls of fluff and one
shoe lay inside on the dull wooden floor; a hanger with a belt
dangling from it hung crookedly on the rail. Each time her mother
passed she banged one or other of the doors shut, and each time it
swung out again gathering speed until the ratchet at the top
stopped it with a jerk: thud. Whenever her father came into the
room he took hold of both doors to close them, and even got as far
as lining up the latch with its socket, but never managed to
complete the job. Distracted by his wife or his thoughts, he
wandered on with an aimless look of mystified purpose, and the
doors swung out again, at different speeds: thud . . . thud.

The bedroom was hot, flickering with sun shafts and shadows
that confused Holly. Curtains had been pulled over the open
windows but a sticky wind flapped them continuously and
sometimes one blew right up sweeping across the dressing-table.
The yellow sunlight came and went on the mounds of clothes on
the bed and the litter on the floor – scraps of paper, a vest of
Hugh's with a hole in, old newspapers for wrapping things and the
lace mats brushed off the dressing-table and kicked aside by her
mother, who usually took such care of her things. Holly had been
told to sit still, so she remained scissoring her legs in a frenzy of
anxiety and distaste. Beside her a nightdress, pyjamas and the
satin case for them had been thrown down on the sheets with
gloves and scarves her mother had pulled from the bottom
drawer.

The street outside was full of people, adults in a hurry, carrying cases, shopping bags, parcels, calling out in sharp voices to children who hung back, subdued like herself.

It was only three days since the family had come home from Sandalcliff. As soon as they had arrived, Daddy had taken her to the shop on the corner and bought lots of sugar, flour and soap. Piles of butter oozing greasily in the sun had been stacked at the door of the shop. Daddy had bought some and several tins of the powdered milk for Hugh's bottle. The place had been crammed with women filling their baskets. When they got home, Mummy had been crying. She held a piece of paper in one hand and a bright orange envelope in the other. Holly had hardly conceived her mother could cry like this, bawling as a child does, and she was frightened by the ugly red face.

Over the following days things had become worse. Her parents kept listening to the wireless with angry faces, refusing to play with her, or going into their room and shutting the door on her. The trunk full of beach clothes had been unpacked, yet nothing properly put away. Her sandshoes and chipped bucket remained on the landing. Now the trunk was being filled again. Armfuls of winter clothes had been dumped in it, sheets and a spare rubber square for Hugh's cot. Back and forth her mother went, impatiently pushing past the wardrobe door. Thud.

Her father came in with two pairs of shoes, polished and held taut by trees.

'Why on earth bother with cleaning your shoes at a time like this! Haven't we enough to do?'

He said nothing, placed the shoes beside Holly on the rucked coverlet. His wife put her hand to her temples. Her blue dress had lost a button and was stained with damp under her arms.

'There's all those stairs from the Underground at King's Cross. How'll we manage the trunk?'

'It's Euston. But we'll go by cab, and the cabby can get us a porter.'

'If there are porters – or cabs!'

Fred, just about to close the wardrobe doors, was trapped by this new worry and let them go again: thud . . . thud.

Lucille followed her advantage. 'You just don't think at all what it'll be like for me and the children.'

'Yes, I do.' He put out a hand to her.

'And the expense!'

'The money doesn't matter a damn.'

'That's fine, that is, coming from you.'

'What do you mean?' he asked firmly, yet tired of it.

'I've not had two pennies to rub together for years and you tell me money isn't important.'

'Well, is it?' he asked softly, putting his arms round her. Holly watched them keenly. 'So long as you are safe and the children.'

Lucille's head dropped on to his shoulder.

'What shall I do?' she wailed.

'It won't be for long.'

After a moment their restlessness separated them and the desultory work continued, piling clothes, opening drawers, looking under beds and cupboards, finding forgotten articles behind the hot water tank. Fred took his cuff-links from a china box and jinked them up and down in the palm of his hand before dropping them back.

'No need for those.'

'What about your uniform?' Lucille asked, stiff with a fresh anxiety. 'Is that issued to you?'

'Officers buy their own,' he replied proudly. Then, seeing her face, parried quickly, 'It's a great leg up to be recalled *and* promoted.'

'It doesn't affect me now, your being an officer.' Visions of tropical stations flew through her head, aggravating her misery with their lost opportunities. For years she had dreamed of escape from Mitcham.

'The pay will affect you.' Fred could not hold the remark back.

She countered, 'How will I get to Ida's at the other end?'

'We'll send her a telegram when the train time is certain.'

'Telegrams! At a time like this! The lines will all be kept for official things.'

'Keep calm, little flower.' Fred's smile wrinkled his dry, sunburned cheeks.

'Calm!' She burst into tears, and Holly shrank down against the bedclothes not wanting to see, yet already somewhat inured to her mother's distress.

'There, there, darling. It'll be all right, you'll see.'

Lucille's indignant reply was muffled in Fred's chest.

'It won't last long,' he repeated. 'Until Christmas, they say.'

'What won't last?' asked Holly in a small, sharp voice.

He looked at her over Lucille's head and a tremor passed over his broad face, but he did not reply.

Lucille pushed him away. 'I must get on. There's so much to be done.'

The baby, Hugh, wailed from the back bedroom and Fred went out of the room, knocking past both the wardrobe doors.

'Mummy, what is going to happen?' Holly was almost too frightened to ask, and this in itself was frightening for she was a child ever ready to speak up. Little Miss Bossy-boots, they called her.

Lucille replied flatly, 'A war's going to happen.'

'What's that? What's a war?' Earnestly she brushed her fringe up off her forehead with both hands.

'Men fighting.' When Lucille spoke to Holly she used a different tone, much more matter-of-fact.

'Like boys fighting at school?'

'No. We are going to be bombed.'

'Now, now,' interrupted Fred, standing in the doorway with the baby in his arms. 'Don't frighten her, darling.'

'She'll be a lot worse frightened soon.'

'Time enough then. But if we can get you away to Ida it will be all right.'

'Stop saying "all right" like that!'

'I'll make us some tea,' said Fred. He took Holly's hand and led her out of the bedroom away from the jaw-like thudding doors.

The kitchen was home still. Nothing here was altered. The cupboard doors were closed and it was full of the correct things showing through the glass panels; and the big drawer that would not run easily held the box of cutlery with the tablecloth folded on top as usual; and the kettle was on the gas stove with the piece of quilted felt for holding its handle hanging from a nail in the bumpy painted wall beside a calendar of London Bridge. The smell of soda and steam was the same as ever, not like the rest of the house full of something new that had to do with change and Mummy crying, being cross all the time.

Fred poured Holly a cup of milk and found a chocolate biscuit in the coronation tin. He lit his pipe and let her blow out the match. Then snuggling her to him with one arm, while he held Hugh in the other, he began to tell one of the stories about Mrs Willoughby's cat. Mrs Willoughby lived next door and, as far as Holly knew, had no cat. This was the essence of the stories about him. They were the thrilling adventures of a cat so mischievous that he was invisible. As Fred usually told them at night, before Holly fell asleep, it was a treat to have one now in the afternoon. She leant confidently against him, holding his hand to her side with one of her own.

Daddy's hands were large and square with short, clean nails. They smelt of Lifebuoy soap and had rather wrinkled skin across their backs with a few large, grey veins. These hands were reassuring to Holly. If she thought of her father when he was away at work, she visualised his hands not his face, although she loved that too, especially the way he could furrow his brow like corrugated paper and hold it while she rippled her fingers against the rubbery ridges. Sometimes he let her brush his hair, and most mornings she watched him shave, adoringly. His face half disappeared under foam, then his hands moved about round his chin, one pulling and stretching as his mouth twisted out of shape, the other finely slicing with the blade, and the whole face emerged again, pink. Then Fred took off his dressing-gown revealing vest and braces and trousers underneath, and put on his shirt slipping the braces over the crackling linen. Holly was always glad when this stage was reached. She much preferred her father fully dressed, and was, for all her love, slightly wary of him in his night clothes. There had been a few times when, going into her parents' room, she had been met by anger, dismissal, or just coldness flowing towards her. Mother in her nightie Holly liked, she was gentler and sleepy-kind; Daddy in his stiff pyjamas she hesitated before, the antennae of her devotion picking up a strangeness, even a withdrawal, he would vehemently have denied.

But with his shirt and jacket he put on a total normality and received the unimpeded torrent of her love. At breakfast she sat by him on a piano stool. They had shredded wheat. On the packet was a drawing of a large building with small people streaming in and out of it. Underneath in red letters was written: BRITONS MAKE IT IT MAKES BRITONS. This was one of the first things Holly read by herself. The fact that she could make no sense at all of it doubled its appeal.

Daddy filled her bowl.

'That's the ticket,' he said every morning as she began to eat, trying to keep pace with him, mouthful for mouthful, and copying Fred's way of holding the spoon, of tilting the bowl to scoop up the last drops of sugary milk dotted with specks of wheat.

'Good Lord above, what are you doing sitting here with so much still to do?' Lucille had come into the kitchen. She jerked Holly away from Fred and took the baby.

'For pity's sake,' he said.

'Yes?' She faced up to him, cheeks red.

'Have a heart, Lucille. The child's scared.'

'Aren't we all?'

Fred gave her a look, then went out into the garden. Holly could see him among his sweet-pea canes as if it were a perfectly ordinary day. The smoke from his pipe rose over his curly head.

Lucille took Hugh into the front room to give him a bottle and Holly trailed after her. When the last few drops of milk were gurgling down, Fred came in.

'Darling, I'm sorry. You're upset – and who wouldn't be.'

At his softened tone Lucille began to cry again. Holly watched as the pale face crumpled and pouted, and the eye rims reddened. She felt detached now, not afraid.

'There, there, little flower,' said Fred tenderly, and kissed Lucille in a special slow way.

Mummy put Hugh down in the corner of the sofa, propped by a cushion.

'Look after him, Holly,' she said and the pair of them went out, shutting the door with a click.

Holly looked at the panels of the door and the unmoving handle. She wanted to open it but dared not. She listened, and heard voices of people passing in the street and a dog barking. Things far away she could hear plainly, but her parents, just in the passage, she could not hear. Neither of them wanted her. Hugh's baby gaze went past her to the shining mirror on the wall.

Once she had stood outside their bedroom door and listened to the solid silence inside, then, unable to bear her lonely ignorance, she had rushed in and Daddy had been very angry with her. She would never risk such anger again. She sat down on the floor and folded her arms across her cotton dress, and waited, her cheeks hot, her hands cold.

So this was war.

Next day was a hurried, early awakening and breakfast standing up in the kitchen. The trunk was in the hall strapped down in heavy secretiveness and two bags on top of it, one with three full bottles of Hugh's milk. Mummy put on her best hat and peered at herself in the little glass in the hatstand. Her eyes were watery.

In the taxi Holly sat beside her parents, hands planted palm down as if ready to spring up. Hugh was in his mother's arms, and his pram strapped beside the driver. No one but Holly spoke. She did her best to keep up a commentary on their journey, for she was known as a chatterbox as well as Bossy-boots, and tried to play her roles in an effort to keep the world as normal as possible.

The station was packed with travellers straggled across the forecourt in long, bulging lines. Women who looked like her teachers were standing by lines of two-by-two children wearing labels tied to their coats. Holly had travelled so little she hardly knew the crowds were unusual, but she hated the noise, the smoky air, the tearful faces, the grey faces and all the hurry which threatened to drown her. She kept up her piping questions, why is this? what is that? but no one gave her any answer, so she began a monologue to herself.

'All these people, you see, are going on holiday to their aunties or to the seaside some of them, and their mummies want to go too but they can't, not yet, and so they are crying, but soon they will be able to, when the daddies have got a bit more money. The children have labels because – well, they are not sure where their aunties live and the men will look at the label and say "This is the station, ducky," and auntie will be there. I can't remember what my Auntie Ida looks like but Daddy knows because she's his sister, like I'm Hugh's, only she's older and we live together. We live at home with Mummy and Daddy and so we don't have to have labels or to stand in lines.'

She looked with pity at the queue of boys all carrying small cases or draw-string cloth bags bulging with clothes. One boy put out his tongue at her as Fred hustled his family through the barrier.

The train to Inverness lay along the platform like a segmented iron worm, two red lamps in its rear, its head bent out of sight. Holly peered at the black wheels down in the oily damp below the platform, and at the hoses and chains which hung at the back of each coach. The sounds of people talking and shouting, of barrow wheels rumbling and engines hissing made walls round the child, isolating her. Above, steam and smoke poured silently to the glass roof and mingled there in the sunshine, where a few birds fluttered through the dun and white clouds which muffled the incessant cries from below as they floated up in confusion.

Holly sniffed the soot. She had stopped talking aloud, for her brain could make no coherence of this scene. Faces looking out of the train's smeared windows were all worried, cross, or had tears streaking down them. No one seemed pleased to be going on holiday.

'Well, I am,' she told herself defiantly, and clung even tighter to Fred's hand.

The Tickeners walked the whole length of the train and half-way back without seeing a single empty seat.

Lucille lifted both hands off the pram handle and dragged her hat down her forehead. She said in a loud, tragic voice, 'I can't go!'

'You must, darling.'

'I am not going to stand up all the way to Inverness, Fred, so it's no use your expecting it. We'll go back home.'

'Lucille, darling –'

'How could I possibly feed Hughie standing in the corridor? Just tell me that, will you?'

At that moment a woman tapped on the window and, although the sound was inaudible, they noticed her agitated movements. She indicated with signs that the man beside her was not travelling. Fred bounded into the train and was hidden from Lucille and Holly, then he appeared in the carriage sliding into the seat as the man left it. He beckoned them in. Lucille picked the baby up out of his pram, left it and the luggage, propelled Holly up the high steps of the train and down the crowded corridor. She was pale, stiff and angry, taking the seat as if she had been done an injury rather than a kindness. The woman whose husband was leaving patted Lucille's knee understandingly and tried to take Holly on her own lap but the child jumped away and clung desperately to Fred's legs. The two of them could stand together, she thought, all the way. None too gently he prised her fingers loose.

'I have to fetch the luggage, Holly. Don't be childish.'

Through her shocked tears she saw her father out on the platform again.

'Ay, that's the idea,' said the woman, who was also watching Fred, 'the bairn's pram and the trunk can go in with the guard right enough.'

Holly was outraged. What her Daddy did was not this person's business, and why couldn't she talk properly?

Fred passed the two bags through the window. There was no space for them in the racks, so they were put on the floor and Holly sat on one. Then Fred leaned in through the window and, with an embarrassed glance round, said to his wife, 'Goodbye, darling.'

'No, no!' cried Lucille, looking angrier than ever. In a bout of frenzied movement she leapt up, put Holly on her seat, and pushed her way out of the train, climbing over suitcases, laddering her stockings.

'Have a heart, missus,' someone said.

Holly intended to go with her mother but the woman had a firm grip on her arm.

'No, lassie, you bide here a wee while.'

'No!'

A man sitting by the door slid it shut and held it closed with his foot extended. Holly struggled with it, her chest heaving, her head full of confused darkness. Defeated by the door, she turned to look at the carriage full of people, all staring at her. She squeezed shut her eyes and wished them away. Perhaps it was one of those dreams that went if you told it to.

When she opened her eyes she saw Lucille and Fred on the platform hugging each other. Holly was now in terror lest the train start and carry her away from them for ever.

'Come in! Come in!' she cried.

Doors started slamming.

'Your mother's no going,' said the woman.

'Daddy! Daddy! Come in here!'

The scream filled her body with its vibrations but Fred heard nothing. He was seen to unclench his wife's arms from round his neck. They moved out of sight.

Holly screamed again, and Hugh began to give out the wide-mouthed piercing fear cries of a baby.

'There, my lassie. Be brave.' said the woman, but this time to Lucille who reappeared silently in the carriage in the midst of her children's cries. Holly saw her and stopped her noise at once, her

– 13 –

heart expanding with relief. She waited for Fred to appear. Then she saw his face pressed to the window.

At that moment the train jerked violently throwing Lucille and Holly down on top of the woman and Hugh. When they stood up again the platform was moving, faces were flicking past, quicker and quicker, all straining eyes turned one way.

'Where's Daddy?' Holly whispered, her throat sore with screaming.

'He's gone home to get his things,' replied Lucille in her most down-to-earth voice. 'Then he's going to sea.'

Sandcastles and donkey rides came to Holly's mind.

'Without us?' she asked, not believing it.

'Children can't go in battleships.'

'He's going *on* the sea?' It wouldn't be the Southend paddle-steamer that he had once taken her on. Probably one of those big ships, only smudges on the horizon.

Her next thought was of Fred sailing far beyond the edge of the sea away from her. 'Where to?'

'Where to what?' asked her mother impatiently. She was uneasily aware the other passengers were listening. Fred should have explained all this to the child. She was so obsessed with him.

'Where is Daddy's ship going?'

'Heavens, how should I know? To fight.'

'Is this all the war, then?'

Lucille did not reply. She cradled Hugh back to sleep again. Holly found she was, after all, sitting on the strange woman's lap. For once she had nothing to say, lost in the terrifying not-understanding of a child, knowing only that in this extremity she must cling to her mother whom usually she ignored, even faintly despised for being so silly with Daddy.

After half an hour's travelling, Lucille propped the baby between herself and the Scotswoman. She took out her compact to repair her face, and delicately tucked back loosened strands of hair.

'That's a brave lass.'

'I've got to make the best of it, haven't I?'

'At least your bairns are safe.' She peeked at Hugh. 'My, what a lovely child.'

'I'd never have had him if I'd known this was coming.'

'Little pitchers?' said the woman warningly, arching her eyebrows at Holly's back, but the child was used enough to her mother's bitter remarks. She had heard her say at different times that she should not have married Fred, let alone have had the kids. In fact, Holly had once asked her, innocently, why she didn't sell Hughie back. 'You got him from the baby shop, and some shops take things back – for a bit less money. It's called second-hand.'

'I know that, thank you, Miss Bossy-boots.'

'Well, why don't you?'

'You better look out it's not you I take back.'

'Daddy wouldn't let you!'

'You and your precious father may have a surprise one of these fine days.'

Her mother's threats meant little to Holly. Most of the seven years of her life Holly had not taken much notice of Lucille. She was slapped sometimes and her heart was hot and swollen for a few hours; then occasionally she was given a treat by her mother, like taking her up to Town to see the illuminations for the coronation but Holly had spoiled that by becoming over-tired and telling everyone the lights were horrid. It was Fred her being homed on.

The Scotswoman and Lucille were chatting about all the usual grown-up subjects, and Mummy was using her talking-to-strangers voice that made Holly think of jagged bits of glass, but whoever Mummy spoke to she always made them smile and lean towards her with their mouths a little bit open, as the stranger was doing now.

'The boy's heavy for you,' she said. 'Let me nurse him for you.'

'Well, thank you,' said Lucille, and, taking off her hat, shook her small, gold head, freeing herself. She stood up to smooth down the folds of her skirt and saw herself reflected in the rectangular mirror flanked by advertisements for Cornish havens. She was a woman without a husband. Her lips trembled. She sat down and took Holly on her knee, reaching into one of her bags for some pencils and paper.

'Let's draw Daddy's ship,' she suggested, but Holly pressed close to her breast and shut her eyes. She had no one to cling to but her mother while her thoughts were brimful of her father. Daddy gone to sea.

He was always happy at the seaside, or the river, or even sailing her toy boat on the pond in the recreation ground. Holly did not say 'happy' to herself, but she felt overwhelmingly secure with Fred at the sea because his mood was buoyant, he indulged her, was never at all cross. He'd roll up his trousers and paddle for hours along the tideline with her, keeping shells in his pockets, carrying her bucket of little crabs tangled in slimy, fuzzy seaweed. Early in the mornings, the pair of them would leave Lucille in bed and go to the pier before breakfast. In the sunshine the streets and the prom and the rattling planking of the pier were peculiarly renewed, as if the night had scrubbed them, leaving them out to dry tidily, ready for the new day. Fred and Holly shared the newness and promise with a man who had a small white dog which did tricks for biscuits. These could be obtained from a slot machine and came in two flavours, orange and chocolate. The tea shack man was just hanging out his bunches of balloons rubbing squeakily together and his bundles of paper flags for decorating castles. His unused spades glittered red and the smell of the gas boiling his urn was pungent on the clean morning air. Fred had some tea – Daddy could always drink a cup of tea, was a remark Mummy made most days – and Holly had a packet of biscuits in crackling cellophane. Then they walked to the pier end, past a few fishermen whose lines wavered slackly in the dark green sea which smacked the piles lazily, sloshing to and fro, dandling violet jellyfish in its swell. If you looked inland you saw the deserted beach, the diamond flower-beds on the prom and the rows of houses up the cliff with red roofs and unwinking eyes. It looked like a painting quietly facing the sun until a tram went along the front. Daddy looked out to sea, pointing out the buoys marking the channels, explaining currents, tides and weather to the child who, holding his big, thick hand and gazing in turns at his face and the counterpane of water, shifting and sparkling in the sun, was taken up in love for him.

Now in the train she imagined Fred on his ship, sailing out past the markers to the navy blue edge of the sea and over it into the sky. Emptiness invaded her body; her inside was a hole and she crouched in her seat becoming as small as possible.

'Why, she's only a baby really,' thought Lucille as her daughter tucked into the curve of her arm. 'Poor little Bossy-boots.'

*

Fred was confused by his feelings as he made his way back to Mitcham by tube and bus. He hated to leave his family, the only three people in the world for whom he had any affection, but was excited at the prospect of returning to the sea. From the moment the telegram came, the sense of excitement had been sprouting and springing in his heart, threatening to smother his sadness at leaving Lucille.

He had left the navy when he married her, at the very moment when his career had seemed about to take off. Having become a Petty Officer at twenty-four, the idea of going for a commission had been put to him. Solemnly, he had gone on leave, promising himself to make a decision about this, but knowing already, in his depths, what the decision would be. He had taken a holiday with his sister, Ida, and his old father. Ida paid her own way. She had changed in Fred's absence from a downtrodden skivvy-schoolgirl to a smart, hard, city typist, and Fred was greatly impressed by her until he met Lucille in their boarding-house. Lucille was fair, thin, with spun silk hair in plaited coils over her ears. She wore dresses the colours of flowers and satin shoes dyed to match.

She re-named him Tikki. The name suited her up-to-the-minute style, the style of a poor girl from back streets with nothing but looks and youth. She had a sprightly way of dancing and twirled her cocktail stick with gay flourishes, the blob of cherry on the point, sucking it delicately with pale lips, laughing. She was as different as could be from Aunt Maud and the grim women he had served in the grocer's shop; he was soon possessed by her as only a virile man who has held himself in check all adolescence can be. She was his girl, with all that implied to his honest, straightforward mind. When she and Tikki stood by the fairy lamps on the prom watching the wrinkling sea (at least he was) his heart was huge and hot in his chest. Lucille whispered 'Sub-Lieutenant Tikki' to test him out.

But it would not, he saw, be possible to stay in the navy because that would mean being apart for months on end. It was a husband's job to protect and cherish and he then asked nothing of life but to look after Lucille. Fred made his decision at a stroke, without soul-searching. Husbands and wives should be together; there were no two ways about it.

A few days after their wedding he told Lucille he had sent in his papers. Her pretty face turned white, then violet with fury. His heart could still twist at the memory. Her anger not serving, she had dissolved into weeping and pleadings without end until even steady Fred's thoughts had nudged the idea that she loved his uniform more than himself, but he did not blame her.

'What will you *do*?' she wailed.

The cry had reverberated at the back of his mind all the years he worked as a car salesman, the years when he reverted to being Fred, except when Lucille was in a particularly sunny mood, if he had brought home roses or perfume for her. He knew she deserved the very best, such a stunning and sweet girl as she was, like a stick of rock in her striped beach dress. He pitied her weakness and it bound him to her all the more closely. Though he hated the work of selling cars he did not let on to Lucille. After a bad day at the showroom he arranged his face to cheerfulness and put a spring in his step as he turned the corner of their street. He never considered it had been a mistake to leave the navy; the greater his wife's distress the more she needed him there.

But war had come, and a summons back to sea. Now it was his duty to leave his wife. Images of waves and ships filled his mind, drowning Lucille's tear-stained face. When he remembered her it was with a stern sense of doing right, and a submerged thrill of delight.

*

It took them all that day and half the night to reach Inverness. At first for Holly the train was this one, crowded, dusty carriage; then Lucille took her to the lavatory and she saw other children, other piles of luggage, other little rooms with people jammed so tightly their knees touched. There was a boy with white mice in a cage. Another stared forlornly into the corridor.

'In there,' said Lucille and pushed her into a tiny, horrible room with a barred window. When Holly pulled the chain the bottom opened and she saw the pebbly ground rushing past underneath. This was the most terrifying thing she'd ever seen. It made her shake so much she couldn't open the door to get out.

'Turn the little knob,' called Lucille. The train rattled and bumped. Holly leant against the door, fearing the whole floor might open and drop her through.

At Crewe they ate their sandwiches and a man fetched Holly a paper cup of orangeade.

'Buck up,' he said. 'It's not the end of the world.'

'Not yet,' remarked someone else, dolefully cheerful.

'Listen to the wheels. They talk, you know. "We'll soon be there, we'll soon be there, we'll soon be there."'

Some passengers left the train at Carlisle, more at Carstairs. Holly was able to lie down on half a seat. The cushions were crisp and dirty, pricked her cheek. The train said to her: 'Daddy has gone, Daddy has gone, Daddy has gone.' The hole inside seemed big enough to swallow her. She might dive down into it, just as Daddy jumped off the pier into the sea. She slept.

At Perth a trolley came along the platform and ladies handed hot drinks through the window. By then, there was no one in their carriage but Lucille, the two children and a soldier who had slept the entire journey.

What had begun with drama and unbearable anxiety dragged itself out so long with the monotonous clackety of the wheels that it ended with nothing more than sagging, weary boredom. Holly slept, woke to see the carriage with its dirty floor had not changed, and slept again. She understood that this too was war.

The journey remained in her memory as a tunnel. It led back to home which already she hardly believed in. Nor, without Daddy, did she want it.

The tunnel opened out into daylight at the farm.

*

She woke in a double bed beside her mother who was snoring gently. Lucille's head had slipped off the hard bolster and rested on the mattress. Her lower cheek was puckered. When she had watched her mother for a few minutes, Holly sat up. The room was large. Hugh was in a cot between two windows covered by thick curtains round which light was creeping. There were some tall, dark cupboards and a treadle sewing-machine. Holly cautiously let herself down from the high bed and her big toes reached a floor covered in linoleum. There was a heavy, sleepy stillness in the room. She crossed to the window and slipped behind the curtain.

Her imagination went blank at what was beyond the glass. It felt like being at the bottom of a green bowl. There were no tiled roofs or back gardens, no chimney-pots or lamp-posts standing up, only a grass slope leading away and away, rising above her.

Below was part of the farmyard, grey stones, grey sheds, a wall with a faded blue door. Beyond some spiky trees made to seem tiny by the hill climbing into the sky like a wave – smooth, rounded, overhanging. Holly's heart rose to meet this sight as if it were something long known and recognised.

A man with a hooked stick came out of a door in the house, crossed the yard with two dogs running beside him and, passing through the blue door, began to go up the hill. Soon he looked small as a toy although he had gone no distance up. She noticed white objects scattered like beads among the green and grey of grass and rocks above him. They moved along slowly in strings but, as the dogs came near, collected into groups.

Another man appeared in the yard and a girl in trousers. She left the blue door open and Holly could see a stream beyond, which the girl crossed, balancing on a stone. Holly wanted to be down there.

She put on her clothes and left the room with her mother and brother still asleep. On the landing she had another moment of surprise, faced with a second unexpected view of the unknown. Here was a hill wrapped in Christmas trees, dark and still, and water glinting silver down a crack of rock. The farm road led away through a gap in the hills towards the village of Balchraggan, and the morning sun blinded her as she looked after it. Near at hand grew pears and cherry-plum trees, while rowans and birches and hazels stood with their roots in the river bank beside the track. All trees unknown to Holly.

She went down the staircase, slippery without a carpet, holding tight to the banister, every sense alert to pick up and understand this strange place. The hall floor was of stone and there was a huge oak sideboard with some birds on a branch under a glass cover. On the ground was an animal's foot with umbrellas and walking sticks in it. Over each of the six dark doors stags' antlers were fixed. Holly stood, very uncertain which way to go, then was guided to the kitchen by a sharp food smell.

It was barley mutton stew. Her aunt's kitchen always smelt of barley stew, or lentil soup, or leeks, or potato scones, or fresh brown bread. Ida was forever cooking; she had to with Hamish, Maud and the shepherd to be fed, Meg the land-girl, Bob and Bruce the evacuee twins newly sent from Glasgow, and now Lucille with her two. Trust Fred to have dumped his family on her!

Holly went into the kitchen and stared around her, noticing first the large table set with many places and silver spoons, then the black range crowded with long-handled black pots, with two china dogs on the shelf above, then the windows that had no curtains but narrow door-like panels half folded back. Below one window were two white sinks, one very deep, and a wooden draining board. Under that was a row of polished boots. Several worn rugs were placed at certain spots on the stone flags – at the stove, the sinks, the back door and by a wooden armchair. Each mat had a worn patch in the middle. No one was in the room which was indistinct in shape with shadowy corners, alcoves, cupboard doors ajar. Then another door opened giving a glimpse of a shelved larder and Aunt Ida came out. When she had folded back the shutters, she saw Holly in the doorway.

'Hullo. First up?'

'Yes, Aunt Ida.'

'Come and have your porridge then.'

'What's porridge?'

Ida gave her a sharp glance through her round spectacles. Then she called up to the evacuee boys. They had been at the farm two days already and she considered they should be prompt for breakfast by now. Hamish came from the yard, letting in a shaft of sunshine and kicking off his boots on the step. The land-girl followed him, wearing a red scarf to match her cheeks. Finally, Aunt Maud rattled at the door handle before fumbling her way in. Holly saw the old woman's fingers were bent down against her palms with knuckles jutting out.

The porridge was strong tasting and hot. Auntie put a mound of brown sugar on Holly's and a moat of milk round it, but Uncle Hamish scattered salt on his and no milk. He ate standing by the stove, rising and falling on his stockinged feet. He was a small, sinewy man with a large head and a big nose.

No one spoke much. When milk ran down Aunt Maud's chin, which had bristles, Ida stretched across and wiped it for her. She did this with a tight, blank expression as if not wanting to notice what she did.

Then they had round slices of something called white pudding, fried and eaten with fatty toast. Bob and Bruce were obviously used to it. They finished up the last crumbs from the frying pan, getting up from the table to do so at a nod from Ida. Holly ate experimentally and slowly.

The windows of the room faced north-west across the valley to the Balchraggan hill, dark green now against the morning sky. The kitchen was dull at all times and often cold except close to the range, but in September, with the yard door open, it was cheerful enough, a place of wonder to the child from London.

'I like white pudding,' she announced, 'but it makes my tongue furry. Can I have a drink, please?'

'You can,' said Aunt Maud, in a croak, 'the question is – may you.'

'Now, Aunt,' warned Ida, pouring Holly a cup of tea which she had never had before.

'Mummy gives me milk,' she said.

'Please Auntie Ida,' said Maud, rapping the handle of her fork.

'I wasn't asking. I was just saying.'

The old woman blinked rapidly several times.

'You can have milk if you like,' said Ida, amused.

'Daddy always has tea, doesn't he?' Holly put a hand on her aunt's arm.

'Well, I should say Fred is just about made of tea by now.'

'Tea and tobacco,' said Hamish.

'Like his father,' remarked Maud, seeming to approve.

'Did Daddy have a father?'

Everyone laughed, especially the two boys.

'That would be a grandpa. They've never told me about him.'

She had thought grandfathers were what other children had, like sisters and nannies. She began to think about relations, and under her fringe, as she sipped the bitter tea, hallowed by Fred, she inspected Aunt Maud. Her hair was so thin that her shiny skin beneath showed, and her neck was spotted mauve. Holly studied with curiosity how this colour edged up towards Maud's cheeks where there were several moles with bushy sprouts of hair. She had big bony arms ending in the horrible twisted, knobbed hands. Holly thought she looked like a man with a lady's dress on.

'You'll know me next time you see me, miss,' said Maud, returning Holly's look with eyes like prunes, dull and black.

Ah, she is ratty, thought the child. Ratty was a word the children in Mitcham applied to any grown-up without authority over them. There were ratty ladies whose garden walls they walked on, and ratty shopkeepers who liked you to buy more than one big aniseed ball at a time. Holly, having placed Maud, mentally dismissed her.

'Auntie Ida,' she began again, 'when you were little was Daddy the baby?'

Bob and Bruce laughed again, for any mention of babies was likely to make them snigger.

'Everyone has been a baby,' said Ida.

This could not possibly be true of Aunt Maud.

'The lassie means are you younger than Fred,' Hamish explained.

'Oh, I see, yes, I was the baby.'

'Poor motherless mite,' croaked Maud.

'But you are older than Daddy now.'

'How do you make that out?'

'Your hair is grey.'

Ida flushed slightly.

'The Tickeners go grey early,' Maud informed them, stirring her tea so erratically that it slopped out of the cup.

'Take care, Aunt, let me help you.'

As Ida raised the cup, the old lady said, 'Your grandfather was white at thirty. A handsome man was my brother.'

'Handsome is as handsome does,' commented Ida, tipping the tea down her aunt. Holly could make no sense of this cryptic remark.

'And what's that supposed to mean?' asked Maud, when she could.

'Dad was mean and arrogant,' said Ida loudly. 'As you very well know. He kept you as little better than a slavey.'

'Now then, my girl,' cautioned Maud, but mildly.

'Though what he had to be so stuck up about I'll never know – working as a porter in an auction room all his days.'

'There was more to my brother than that.'

'Yes, a thoroughly nasty temper for one thing! Heavens above – you suffered enough with it, Aunt.'

'Was he my grandpa?' asked Holly.

'He was.'

'Mummy doesn't tell me about him.'

'I daresay not. She would rather have had a father-in-law in a better line of work.'

Hamish pushed back his chair. He did not like Tickener spite.

'Will you come outside with me, lassie?' he asked Holly.

Delighted, she put her hand in his.

The air was milder outdoors than in the house, and full of the damp sweetness of moss and of resin from the pines. Two collies lying by the byre wall stood up to follow their master. Hamish spoke to his shepherd and called out an instruction to the land-girl who had also come out of the house, then he led Holly through the gate in the wall that she had seen from upstairs.

Here was the stream. Holly knew magic, like that of a picture coming to life. She was through the door and by the water. It had pinkish pebbles on its bed, and the plants growing at the edges were half in it, floating, jewel bright.

Hamish led her past a row of oaks, powerful, squat, hill country trees with umbrella tops and the ground at their feet rubbed bare and dusty by cattle. Dried cowpats could be kicked aside like old pancakes, others out in the meadow had bright blades of grass growing through them. Small quiet birds flicked up out of the ground as Hamish and Holly walked steadily in a diagonal line from the blue gate, towards the cattle who were grazing in a marshy dip at one end of the big field. They watched Holly with bulbous, luminous eyes, grass hanging from their lips, legs in mud up to the knee. She observed their fat tongues and the way their noses dribbled.

'When do you milk them, Uncle?'

'They're steers.'

'What's that?'

'Boy beasts. See – they have nothing to give milk with.'

Holly pushed up her fringe, staring and puzzling. She put together the pictures of cows with udders, usually seen jumping over the moon in her books, and pictures of milkmaids on stools, and the lady next door who had fed her baby not using bottles, which Mummy had said was disgusting, and understood her first lesson in sexual anatomy.

'Why do these ones, these steers, have things like Hughie then?'

'For the same purpose,' Hamish answered. He thought her very babyish for seven and blamed Lucille. 'Now – let's look at the pigs.'

He took her about the farm all morning, helping her to straddle the burns ('You'll be needing rubber boots, lassie'), showing her the climbing places on the dry stone walls, letting her roll in the hay barn. Never once did she feel sad about Daddy.

They went in late to the midday meal and found their barley mutton stew kept hot in the oven on two blue plates. Lucille was sitting on a bent wood chair holding herself as tight as possible, feeling completely out of place.

She had known before ever she came she would not like the farm at Upper Balchraggan; and she had never much cared for Ida. The stew was not to her taste. A nice piece of plaice with some tinned peas were Lucille's preferred lunch. As for that old witch Maud who had terrorised her Tikki with her stories when he was a boy! Lucille had forgotten she would be here, might not have come if she'd remembered.

When they were first married Tikki, strong, brave man that he was, had sometimes had nightmares in which he had shouted and struggled. She used to wake him and cradle his head on her breast. How sweet it had been to be his protector for once. When he was calm, she had asked him what the nightmare had been about. He had mumbled and gone all sheepish, but, in the end, she had made out that his Aunt Maud had told him dreadful stories to make him be good. She had actually said that down below the gratings let into the city pavements lived Roman Catholics, dreadful, wicked people who stole little boys and tortured them, and that if he were naughty she would drop him down to them, let him slip between the bars.

Lucille had not been able to keep from laughing just a little. 'Oh Tikki, darling, such nonsense!'

'Well, of course I knew they kept barrels and coal down there, but at night, you know, when I was in the dark and thought of hell and the martyrs – '

'What martyrs for heaven's sake? Oh Tikki!'

'Foxe's *Martyrs*. That was the book Maud made me read on Sundays by myself in the parlour, all about tortures and chains, racks and fires.'

She had kissed him tenderly.

'There was nothing kind when I was a boy,' said Fred. 'My father kept out of it. On and off I believed Maud. I had to.'

'Poor you. Poor darling.'

Lucille had often thought how she would like to be able to punish the dreadful aunt for making her boy suffer so. Now here she was actually sitting beside the old horror, who made sickening noises as she ate.

On her other side was a man in dark clothes with a silk muffler wound loosely under his chin. He had a short upper lip and a chin that trembled as he chewed. He was the Minister who regularly came to lunch, Maud's friend.

Never had Holly sat at a table with so many people. Not in the least abashed, she launched into an account of her morning with Hamish.

'Be quiet, Holly,' said Lucille. 'Eat your dinner.'

Holly put down her knife and fork to push her fringe off her forehead and say earnestly, 'Oh, I can eat and talk, thank you.'

Maud clicked her dentures, getting them into position for an onslaught on the child's behaviour.

'Ay, so can we all,' interposed Hamish, 'but it's no good manners.'

Holly was silenced. She already respected Hamish highly.

'Has the child not been to the country before?' asked the Minister, gently.

Lucille favoured him with her widest smile. 'We are Londoners, you know,' she said with a shade of superiority.

'Ay.' He waited for more.

'We go to the south coast sometimes or into Surrey, down to Windsor or Hampton Court –'

'Do we Mummy? I don't remember.'

'Holly, be quiet. My husband and I just love walking by the river, but since we had the children –' wistfully, her voice died.

'They must be fine places.'

'Quite lovely, yes.'

'All I can remember of Hampton Court are crowds pushing and litter all over the gravel paths,' said Ida.

Surprisingly the Minister laughed. 'Your sister-in-law, Mrs Tickener, is a realist.'

'What else should a farmer's wife be, I'd like to know?'

Ida and he exchanged a smile as she left the table to pull treacle scones, dark and crusty, from her oven, setting them out on the slate-slabbed dresser and moving on to her next job. Lucille glanced at the scones and remarked that her speciality was angel cakes.

'They'd make one bite for a hungry man,' said Ida dismissively.

The scones were served with thick, tepid custard. Lucille toyed with hers. Everyone else had a large helping and then another. Meanwhile Ida was rolling out another batch, sleeves furled, apron taut across her flat stomach. She rarely sat down for a complete meal.

Ida looked as if she had never been anywhere but the farm at

Upper Balchraggan. She had met Hamish Fraser in Glasgow where she was visiting a married friend from her office and he was giving himself his annual pre-Christmas leave from the farm, a week in which he was always, more or less deliberately, looking for a wife. Ida had fitted his bill. She was healthy, strong, intelligent and wanted a husband to escape from her father. He had not reckoned on having to take the old lady too, nor had Ida. When she married, old Mr Tickener coolly announced he did not need his sister any longer and she must go. Maud had given her nephew and niece the better part of her life; Ida discovered she felt loyalty to her, despite the straitened and darkened childhood she had suffered. Hamish admired Ida for this. It made her a finer person. He thought so whenever he saw her help the crippled old woman, looking aside if she could, but with gentle hands. When he found in his wife traces of Maud's superstition and ignorance, he bore it, hoping for a son or a daughter to loosen Ida's tight spirit, but in six years she had not conceived. A tall, dark, plain woman with considerable dignity, she was beginning to face the possibility of being barren.

Lucille could hardly have been a sharper contrast; the very way she sat in her chair and lifted her fork proclaimed her wilful apartness from the Fraser household. She had from the very beginning faintly despised Ida, a gauche girl who had to sit dances out, partnerless, while she and Tikki flirted under the fairy lights. When Ida had married this backwoodsman, Lucille had imagined them living somewhere tumble-down and cold, perhaps with a tap outside. Upper Balchraggan was quite a surprise to her, though she was trying not to show it.

She knew she had come dashing up to the Highlands in terror of the bombs. Everyone expected them to fall on London in relentless outpourings from the first day of the war onwards.

For the next six weeks she sat near the old-fashioned wireless, which was wedged on a bamboo table in the kitchen, to listen to every news bulletin. The others were equally concerned. Maud's chair was pushed up to the wireless until she could place her ear against its fabric mouth. Hamish drew close with a face creased with apprehension, Ida paused in her work with stilled, floury hands, the children were hushed, but there was nothing – no air raids at all, no fires, explosions, epidemics, terrible wounds, panic-stricken mobs, nothing. Instead it was reported that many were returning to the capital. Ida looked significantly at Lucille, but both Hamish and the Minister thought she should not dream of going back. The bad times must surely come.

Lucille tried to make the best of it, hiding from everyone that she was scared by the open sky and enormous vault of stars. The mud, the farm smells seeping into the back regions of the house disgusted her. The cold wind sliced at her body in London clothes, and the grey stones everywhere, houses, walls, barns, the hillsides themselves, intimidated her. She was a town dweller, every inch. A person whose feet were made for pavements, whose eyes liked to be confined by brick terraces, pressing close. When she could smell petrol, soot, dust, horse dung, girls' perfume all making a faint dry scent in the street Lucille was invigorated. She loved shopping and the small luxuries she could afford – pennyworths of pleasure.

At Balchraggan she was as brave as she could be, and attempted bright conversations. Usually only kindly Hamish responded. Ida's manner was impatient and scornful, especially when Lucille sat by the range in her fluffy jacket buffing her nails or changing the collar of a dress from lace to pleated georgette. Ida was forever busy about much weightier matters, and old Maud read her Bible in silence for hours on end, swaying in her chair as if it were a rocker. Sometimes she would look up and say, 'You had better look after that baby of yours,' as if Lucille were an uncaring mother.

In fact she had more sympathy for children than for adults. When the twins spoke, casually, of their life in a slum tenement Lucille's hands clenched and for a moment she looked ugly and did not care. 'How dreadful! How terrible!' she would say, and take one or the other twin on her lap. The child would soon wriggle off. This hurt her. Most things about Balchraggan were hurtful. She hadn't wanted to come and was doing her best not to show she didn't like it. Why was Ida so unfriendly? After all, Tikki sent money for them.

The Minister observed the cross-currents. He came to read to the old lady but usually talked more than he read, of Maud's past, the days when she was bringing up 'my boy and my girl here'. When Ida came near, Maud leaned over her chair arm and patted her aproned thigh with the deformed, arthritic fist. Ida just smiled grimly at her aunt.

The Minister admired them both, and Hamish, another hard worker, one of life's realists; but for Lucille he developed a fondness. She was crisp and cool and wounded and never, he saw, looked out of the window.

One day he said to Ida, 'Lucille tells me she is famous for her angel cakes where she comes from.'

'In Mitcham?' asked Ida ironically.

'Shouldn't you let her try her hand?'

'She's welcome,' said Ida and left the room.

'You go ahead, my dear. Poor Ida suffers from the old man on her shoulder sometimes.'

Because it was the Minister who had said this, Maud made no response other than clicking her dentures. Lucille was already taking flour and scales out of the cupboard.

'She'd love some bairns,' he continued.

'More fool her, then!'

'Oh, come now.'

'You know I don't really mean it.' From the egg basket she took two eggs and stood beside him with one in each hand. 'But having kids is not exactly a bed of roses. Tikki and I had such fun before . . .'

'Salad days.' He stroked her hand, just one stroke.

Lucille baked her feather-light cakes and Hamish did indeed eat one in a bite, but he asked for more. Then she preserved an assortment of leaves in glycerine and arranged them in a copper pan with some dried flower-heads. They looked handsome on the sideboard in the hallway.

'I've never done anything like that before,' said Lucille in wonder at herself. Ida did not believe her. It was just the sort of things women who lived in towns did do.

All September and into October the greens of pine and grasses, the purple heather and the feathery, yellowing bracken clothed the massive shoulders of the hills, and the peaty water of the river poured like beer over pale rocks, foaming slightly and filling Holly with pleasure all the more intense for coming on top of her sorrow for her father. She let the beautiful strangeness soothe her. Invigorated and released by the wild country, her imagination expanded, changing her internal world at the same time. Her mind took leaps forward almost daily, making up for too long years of babyhood. She went with her uncle as often as he would take her to the sheep on the moor, or way up beside the river to what he called summer pastures beside a grey gleaming loch overhung by a precipice dotted with scrawny pines and birches letting fall their golden discs of leaves. She was permitted to pick flowers wherever she liked and soon the house was decked with paste-pots crammed with heather twigs, devil's bit scabious and a few, late, weedy honeysuckle sprigs dropping their trumpet petals to make marks on Ida's polished tops.

She learned the farm rhythm based on the needs of animals and the consequent weariness and hunger of men: the duties in byre and fold-yard before breakfast, big meals, boots left on the step, slippers in a box by the hearth, farm work from six to twelve, one to five, and evenings too at busy times like potato harvest, other evenings round the kitchen table with Hamish doing accounts at one end, Ida sewing or darning, early bed in unheated rooms. They had one bath each a week, otherwise it was cold washes of top, then bottom half. Wet gloves were always to be dried on a string over the range, never left to sog on the mat. Children helped with the dishes in turns, and had as many pennies for pocket-money each Saturday morning as they had years of age, and for Hughie a halfpenny in a piggybank.

Indoors, Holly was confused by the tensions between the ... women, the way her mother seemed not to like Aunt Maud, the fact that when the Minister talked to Mummy it annoyed Auntie. It was troubling, and she managed by taking her mother's side. It was the only safe way, and, in any case, she loved it when Lucille gave her a warm smile of secret gratitude over her teacup. For the first time Holly was finding her mother a solid and important person. Even so young a child saw the lostness and aloneness of Lucille, whose only armour was the absent Tikki, her prettiness, and the blue airmail letters.

She made as much as she could of having a husband at sea, and Fred's letters were her main ploy. Before she read fragments aloud, she held them pressed to her throat for some minutes, stroking the writing with her forefinger. In fact, there was not a great deal to them. They were fond, rather sentimental, always beginning 'My dear little flower', and dwelling on the past and the future rather than the present, but the way Lucille handled the letters gave the impression of daring and self-sacrifice.

She replied to him very publicly. First, she went to the Post Office in the village to buy her airmail form, wearing her heeled brogues which never failed to make Hamish growl, 'They're no better than slippers, woman, for these tracks.' She bought only airletters from the shop, not fancying anything else from its muddled and faded stock. Once a week she took the slow bus to Inverness and collected Hugh's milk from the chemist there. Each time she brought back something for herself, a whiff of home and luxury to see her through the next week. 'I can afford it now that Tikki's getting an officer's pay,' she told anyone who enquired. At first she bought small things like bath cubes which scented the austere farm bathroom with its monstrous geyser rose geranium or violet, then face creams, chocolates, lace hankies, and a bunch of carnations in the dead of winter that must have cost the earth, as Ida muttered to Hamish, then a diamanté clip for her hair on Christmas Day, and many magazines, all with women who looked like Lucille on the front: pale and wistful with wide mouths and smoothed hair.

'Why do you waste Fred's money on this rubbish?' asked Ida. 'There's no one here to admire you.'

'I think it's important to keep oneself nice.'

'The children would like a few treats,' said Ida to her stove.

Next Friday Lucille returned with toys for all four children and a chocolate cream cake in a gold box for Ida, who was no better pleased.

*

Long before that Holly and the two boys had been sent to the village school which stood between the kirk and the old graveyard on the shore of the loch. The schoolmaster, whom the children called Dominie, lived in a house attached to the school building and the Minister lived in the manse opposite. Both men were grey haired, dressed in black coats and trousers and coarse grey sweaters knitted by Ida. The Minister's sweater cuffs were neatly tucked up inside his jacket sleeve, but the Dominie's hung down, picking up dust and chalk. He also had fingers whitened by continually twisting and twirling the sticks of chalk. He spoke in a sing-song voice like everyone else at Balchraggan, and at play-time he might walk the class down to the pebbly shore and point out the waterbirds, or the clouds gathering at the far end of the loch and sailing majestically down, brushing the hills. The Dominie's bony fingers plucked at the air.

The school Holly had gone to in Mitcham was nothing like this.

There had been hordes of rough, smelly boys, and a white tiled cloakroom where these boys tried to catch you and kiss you for a dare, or twist your arm if you would not. There had been many teachers, all ladies, all perpetually cross, and inscrutable school happenings, like forming lines and numbering alphabetically, standing in height order, always answering 'Yes, Miss', or risk a ruler across your palm. Holly took some time to believe the homely one room at Balchraggan was a school at all.

She saw she must change, forget about arm twisting, and words like BUM scratched on the lavatory door. Here you had to wait until you went home, or, in an emergency, could go to the Dominie's house but emergencies were not thought the thing at all. She must even forget what she liked about her old school, things such as sitting in the hall on Empire Day while the big children did a pageant, and singing a hymn on Mondays which said:

> Daisies are our silver,
> Buttercups our gold,
> This is all the treasure
> We can have or hold.

When, timidly for her, she asked the Dominie for this he said no, it was sentimental. Were daisies silver? Had she looked? Was that all the treasure she had? What about books? He'd seen her reading. As for Empire Day, 'We are not over fond of that particular day in Scotland, Holly. Now, when it comes to Robbie Burns' day we will sing and recite his poems.'

Bob and Bruce, bold little pugilists, came to terms with the school soon enough. Holly took longer, but from the first day she liked it. In fact she revelled in the atmosphere of learning. The room was warmed by a stove and had windows looking both ways, towards the glen and the loch, so that whether storms came sailing up from the sea or down from the mountains the children could watch them flow past, throwing down on the wind rain, hail, snow, while they were warm in the room and the page under Holly's hand was dry and faintly uneven to the balls of her fingers because of the ink.

By the time of Hallowe'en she had become friendly with Donald and Chrissie, who asked her to their home. She went to a cavernous, candle-lit kitchen, glowing with turnip lanterns. She ate apples, roast potatoes, gingerbread men and, as a prize, won a bag of aniseed balls. Chrissie sat with her arm round Holly down on the hearth among ash and shadows while Donald lit indoor fireworks. You put a match to a certain dot on a piece of green paper and a flame, green and blue, crept along like a sleepy snake until it reached a picture of a treasure chest where it gave a little pop and a flare.

Donald was scornful, spoke of bangers and rockets, which they were not allowed because of the black-out.

'It's girls' stuff, this. Do you two like it?'

Holly nodded. It was lovely to sit by the fire with her friend and watch the looping fireworks. When Donald teased her for being a girl she did not mind.

The children and their mother walked Holly home, and she wondered at the brilliance of the stars, turning up her face. So many and so shining white. She pulled the freezing air into her lungs as she and Chrissie walked with their arms round each other. Donald and his mother were ahead, their long shadows probing each bend in the path, then being swallowed by the woods. Frost was thick on the fir branches. Some wild creature cried in the wood, sending a shiver of pleasure up Holly's spine.

'My Daddy's at sea,' she said. The words had popped into her mouth.

'Stars must be marvellous at sea,' Mrs Chisholm turned her head to say.

Holly imagined them: the sea frosted white and Fred's pipe smoking in the moonlight.

'Does the sea freeze?' she asked.

'Of course not, silly!'

'It does too. In the antarctic,' Chrissie told her brother.

'Yes, you're right,' he admitted – and Holly secretly thought this rather magnificent of him. 'Ships can even be trapped in the ice. Then the sailors get off and have games of football. I saw pictures of them.'

Holly gazed at Donald's back in wonder as he casually threw these scraps of information over his shoulder to her and Chrissie. This was a new fact to fit into the endless story of Fred's life she told herself in bed at night.

'What do they eat?' she asked.

'Oh, fish, seals, whales.' Donald's voice went squeaky with the effort of imagination.

'They melt the ice in huge saucepans, chunks of it,' Chrissie added.

'Sometimes their fingers or toes drop off with cold, you know.'

'Even their noses.'

'Children that's enough! You don't want to alarm poor Holly.'

'Och, Holly's tough. Aren't you?' Donald turned at the gate to Balchraggan and his eyes glinted at Holly, who nodded proudly.

Aunt Ida came to the door and spoke for a few minutes to Mrs Chisholm. She addressed Ida as Mistress Fraser; it was still the custom then.

'What do you say, Holly?'

'Thank you for my nice evening. And the walk home was lovely.'

'Goodnight then, lassie.'

'Goodnight, Mistress Chisholm,' said Holly.

When the door was shut, Ida remarked, 'You can say Mrs. No one expects you to act the highlander, any more than me.'

'But I'd like to be, Auntie. I love it here.'

'Don't let your mother hear you say so.'

Holly dreamed that night of Fred running, running with a ball at his feet, gathering snow, becoming a huge snowball. In the corner of the field where he ran stood a snowman wearing the Minister's spotted scarf. The snowman was watching Daddy who was taller than the other men chasing after him and the ball. This finally flew into the net and became a fluorescent blue snake.

She thought of her father a great deal; he was in her head all the time, unremarked upon but comforting like a friendly shadow going everywhere with a body. She rarely felt sad by then at his physical absence because she possessed a mystical sense of his being with her, knowing whatever she did and approving it, in some strange way taking part. She spoke to him in her mind, held his hand going up the hill, listened for his laughter when Donald told a joke. This man, to some extent fashioned by herself, was more real than any of the people around her. He grinned comfortingly at her when Auntie was cross, wrinkling his forehead in the way she loved. She drew him into everything she did, at times hardly able to realise he was invisible to others.

When wild December storms blew down the loch and she discovered all the country children's snow and ice games, Fred enjoyed them with her. The wind carried ice to sting your cheeks like gravel, and the snow, feathery light, piled wrappings over the fields, concealing hollows, smoothing crags, levelling hillocks until the world around Balchraggan was a billowy whiteness as if an enormous sail had fallen from the sky's mast. It was a soft, cold, deep, stumbling whiteness with blue shadows, sea-blue crevices. It squeaked under your feet – eek, eek, eek.

The children built barricades and had prolonged battles. Holly was employed as a ball roller, since her aim was poor. She moulded and stacked snowballs until she could have cried with the pain in her hands, only Donald would have called her 'Sissy', which was unbearable, worse than the cold.

The land-girl helped them make a snowman in the yard. Then it snowed again and half-buried him. His hat had a bun of snow and his red scarf was white. Holly filled her nails with ice scratching frost leaves off the bedroom window to look out at him.

After the early dark which was coming on as they left school, the children tobogganed down the hill, madly careering, screaming with delightful fear, and rolling off head over heels. Crumbs of snow worked right through to their skin, where it melted and stung.

They slid on the playground's ice and on the frozen ponds. Gingerly they trod on the river. In the ice, bubbles and leaves were caught. Once they saw a silver fish sandwiched there. When they chipped away to reach it, they found a stiff, jewelled, glass fish. 'A grayling,' Hamish told them.

Christmas, which came at the same time as a thaw, was quite an anticlimax, one more way in which Holly's new life differed from her old.

In January, the Dominie told them about Janus who looked back and forward. Holly tried to see down the slope of the winter and autumn to the last summer days at Mitcham, and found she could not. Her old home was a blur, just a few unrelated objects still clear – a certain door handle she could at last reach, her cereal bowl, a velvet curtain and a toy monkey on a stick, the sweet-peas, the golden rod clump beside the coal-shed. 'Before the war', which Lucille was never tired of talking of, meant for Holly nothing but her father's presence. 'After the war', which all the grown-ups constantly invoked like a charm, meant for the child Fred's return; and it was to Balchraggan that she imagined him coming because life anywhere else had no appeal to her.

'On September 3rd last year this war began,' the Dominie reminded them, and asked what each child could remember of that day. Suddenly as falling down a hole, Holly was back in the station surrounded by noise and shadowy light and strangers. And there was Fred's face hanging unhappily at the train window before the jerk that separated them.

'Those of you with fathers away must try to be especially kind to your mothers,' the Dominie said.

Instead, Holly grew bitterly jealous of Lucille who received pity and attention, and also letters from Fred, which she guessed were full of the sort of secret things which her father sometimes whispered to Lucille when they sat together on the sofa while Holly was told to look at her book, or dress her dolly.

She was even more jealous of the letters Lucille wrote back on the blue airmail sheets which the child imagined had been made specially for her mother because Lucille loved blue. She chose things in that colour whenever she could. Most of her dresses were blue, her nightdresses too, winter and summer ones, even her hankies which she dabbed with scent from a blue glass bottle and tucked under her bracelet.

Lucille liked to make an event out of writing to Tikki. She spread the sheets of his letter on Ida's walnut bureau and wrote her reply carefully, with a tender smile. She was aware this irritated Ida and charmed the rather uncharmable Hamish. The Minister, if he were there, watched with his small smile and, when she had finished, drew her to the fire for a little chat about London and home. But she was quite unaware of the effect on Holly.

One morning Lucille gave a letter to her to post on her way to school. Holly held it as if it were explosive, and felt the words wriggling and fattening on the paper like the firework snakes. What was it that they murmured to Daddy from Mummy? and what right had they to say things which left her out? when Daddy was always with her, knew everything she thought, *agreed* with her. And what happened when they shut the bedroom door on her? She ought to know. It wasn't fair to shut her out. The words on the page in her hand and the two figures linked together were almost one.

Holly stopped in the lane and opened the letter.

'My own darling,' it began. Well, that was nothing. Holly read on, making sense of the joined grown-up writing as best she could. Lucille was only telling Daddy what she and Hugh and the other children did, how she'd broken a vase of Ida's (why did Mummy need to say that?), and how Hamish had lost his shepherd to the army and what would he do, and the new dress she was making. And she missed him. (But she did not say she missed him gallons, and tons, and miles high as Everest as Holly would have done if she'd been Fred's wife.) That was all. The letter ended, 'Love from your own Lucy.'

Holly was scornful of the poverty of this letter, and she sensed that her father walking beside her was unimpressed too. If she could write about love to him she would say – well, all about kissing probably, though it was not kissing Fred she enjoyed but walking hand-in-hand up the pier with him.

She heard the footsteps of Bruce and Bob coming after her, and saw she was holding the opened blue sheet in her hand. Guilt pounced on her. The form was torn jaggedly along its edges, impossible to re-seal. She clambered over the wall and tore it into shreds. The wind scattered them and some blew back into the lane.

'What's that?' asked Bruce, picking one up.

'Nothing!' Holly raced down the track to school, but Bruce gathered up a few pieces and saw what Holly had done. He told Chrissie who talked to Holly about it at playtime. By then Chrissie had some of the torn scraps in her pocket. Holly did not mind Chrissie knowing. She was her best friend. They sometimes speculated together about love.

'I thought it might tell about in bed,' she explained. 'But there was nothing about that.'

'What was it then?'

'Mostly being cross with Auntie. She is a lot, you know. But I think Auntie's nice.'

'I think your mother is much nicer!'

'Do you?'

'She's ever so pretty.'

'I expect that's what Daddy likes,' said Holly gloomily, thinking of her own dark, straight hair. 'What *do* they do in bed, Chrissie?'

'Cuddling, I expect.'

'But that's not secret.'

'Really tight cuddling.'

'Honestly! You are stupid. It must be something else.'

'Stupid yourself.'

'I am not!'

'You are, and rude. It's very rude to talk about kissing and that.'

'Chrissie Chisholm! You're always doing it.'

'I am not!'

'You are, too.'

Chrissie decided to send Holly to Coventry, which was the favourite weapon of the little girls and deadly effective. Over her dinner she told her mother that Holly Tickener had torn up a letter to her father instead of posting it. (She didn't mention the reading of it, not wanting to be drawn into these topics by her mother.)

Holly was challenged as soon as she arrived home at teatime. Lucille leant her fists on the kitchen table to question the child who stood in her stockinged feet with hat, coat and gloves still on. Ida watched from the sink, Maud from her chair, the land-girl from the stove where she was warming her bottom, and the two boys from the back door.

'What did you do on your way to school?'

'Nothing.'

'Did you post my letter?'

'Yes.'

'What is this then?' asked Lucille, putting a damp rectangle of blue paper on the table and holding it there with her index finger.

Holly studied her mother's face to see if it was useful to go on lying.

'Who told you?' she asked.

'Chrissie told her mother, and quite right too.'

'She's a sneak!' called out Bob who liked Holly better than Chrissie.

'How did you dare to destroy a private letter?' asked Lucille.

'It wasn't private. It was only things I knew about us all.'

'You mean you read it?'

Holly was amazed. Why else open it?

'You read my letter to Daddy? My private letter!'

'He's my Daddy,' Holly said. 'He's not yours.'

'Being rude will not make things any better,' her mother said coldly.

Holly was conscious of the witnesses all round the room. She was afraid but also angry, and her mother's coolness doubled the turmoil in her heart.

'You always interfere between Daddy and me!' she cried.

Lucille's face became, if anything, more expressionless. 'Holly, be quiet.'

'You do, you do! You tell him things that aren't true about me.'

'That will do.'

'That time you stopped him reading to me!'

'Don't be any more childish than you have to be.'

'And you wouldn't let him say goodbye to me on the station.'

'Holly, be quiet! I forbid you to say anything else. How old are you, I'd like to know? Just a great baby, I can see.'

'Not a word of apology to your mother,' interrupted Ida.

'If she were my child,' said Maud, 'I'd –'

'Well, she isn't and I'll thank you not to interfere. Holly go up to bed.'

Holly was beginning to cry, half-choked with emotion.

'Go along,' said Lucille. 'We don't want to see you down here for quite a long time.'

The next day was Saturday and Holly had to remain in bed. She lay idly on her back. After a night's tears, which Lucille had ignored, and hours of sleep that had partly been spent in her mother's arms, Holly's mood had changed. There'd been nothing secret in the silly old letter. No need to tell her never to do it again, because she wouldn't want to. Grown-ups wrote boring letters.

Her father was back beside her again, in thorough agreement with her opinions. He was not at all angry. She had only done it because she loved him. He knew that.

The woman who cleaned for Ida came into the bedroom.

'You've been a bad lass I hear,' she said cheerfully. Holly pulled the sheet over her mouth so that the woman could not see she was grinning. She went round the room dusting, moving small objects and flicking behind the cupboard. She sang 'You are my sunshine' as she went.

'What's for dinner?' asked Holly.

'Toe-nail pie,' she said, picking one up from the floor. 'Your mother's upset.'

Holly smiled behind the sheet. She thought her mother daft to make such a fuss about a silly old letter. It was daring to belittle the tall figure of Lucille, but irresistible.

Before she was entirely forgiven Holly was made to write to her father to explain what had become of her mother's Friday letter.

She did not mind this for she was on the best of terms with her Daddy, who, in fact, watched over her shoulder as she wrote to him, on the lined paper with a cat in the corner that the land-girl had given her.

When this childish thing arrived on Fred's cabin table, he was not troubled by the contents, which he dismissed as some womanish nonsense of Lucille's, but disturbed by vivid thoughts of Holly. He was off duty for the following half hour and gave himself up to dreams of his little girl. He imagined telling her a goodnight story as she sat on his lap in her blue-dressing gown; then he thought of the pair of them out together in the early morning at the seaside, her feet in white ankle socks and brown sandals pattering eagerly beside him. She would climb on the bar above the beach and swing on her tummy while he held her waist, both of them looking across the ribbed sand to the flopping waves of a calm tide.

'Does the sea go on for ever, Daddy?'

'Yes, all round the world and back again.'

'When I've learned to swim properly, could I go that far?'

'I wouldn't be surprised.'

But the war had come before she had given up the rubber ring which held her bobbing in the pool each morning while he sat smoking in a deckchair for the time of her lesson. He remembered in his cabin the smell of suntan lotion and the greasiness of her back, the chlorine, her sticky, wet hair as he towelled her dry, polishing her small limbs, then carefully helping her to put on her clothes, stretching the vest wide for her head, buttoning the straps of her skirt. All this gave him intense, innocent pleasure to recollect.

Fred was an innocent man. No matter that he was married and had heard countless lewd conversations on board ship, no matter that he issued contraceptives to men going ashore and dealt with buggery cases at defaulters, his private thoughts were not much different from a lad's.

From his mother's death onwards he had slept in his father's room, no allowance being made for his youth. Old Mr Tickener's double bed took up most of the space. His collar box, brushes and stud tray, hair oil and coiled razor strop crowded the dressing-table; his threadbare suits hung over worn shoes in the wardrobe out of which seeped the stink of mothballs. The only light was over the bed, the only rug beside it. Fred lay listening to the unvarying sounds of his father's preparation for bed, then the creaks of the springs as he rolled into the central hollow of the mattress, followed by complaining sighs and snores like the rasps of a blunt saw. The boy fingered the spots on his chin, the back of his neck. He felt over his muscles and the hairs in his groin. He was outgrowing his strength, Maud had said in her condemning voice, and he was made to feel weak, dirty, pushing and childish. Eventually from his confusion he slipped to join his father in sleep, with his face pressed to the green stuff of his mother's dress.

He could have loved only someone like Lucille, for a fully adult woman would have challenged him too much. Lucille, pretty as a sweet-pea, liked everything kept fresh and pure. 'Common' was her most damning epithet, a word for her associated with brazen, blowsy women.

A bewitching girl, a manly husband; between them a love which was for the most part a pastime, a thing of tender jokes and sentimentality. Each cared for the other, as it were, in spite of sex. They shrank from the act even while performing it, driven by urges they both thought crude, unfairly placed in them by nature. Immediately afterwards they avoided each other's eyes, and in the morning Lucille took care to be especially flippant, Fred jolly.

He did not know that he feared women. It was obvious they liked him, flattered him, and he believed the feeling was mutual. He knew very little about himself or other people, because he shrank from any thoughts that might stir up uncomfortable feelings. His total love for Holly arose partly from believing that she could never hurt him, that he knew her through and through.

His reply to her letter was a long one for him – over two pages about Sandalcliff, Mrs Willoughby's cat and how she used to help him in the garden. When he came home again, would she like her own set of little tools? By then Holly used some farm tools with handles cut down to work with Hamish and the land-girl; and Mrs Willoughby's cat was as nothing beside the wild cats that lurked in the woods above the bridge. Because she felt him always with her, she had overlooked the fact that the real Fred did not know about her life at Balchraggan, that he had never been there, never crept into the wood with her and the boys to track the cats or the pine martens. It gave her a twinge of superiority and a stronger sensation of disloyalty. To make up for this she began to talk to his photograph stuck beside her bed. He had sent this with his letter. In it he faced the camera full face, with his cap on.

'Only one of those dreadful passport things,' said Lucille, who had taken it from Holly but then gave it back. 'Hideous!'

Holly thought it very like her father, and discovered that if she winked at the photo he winked back, quite clearly, under the shade of the cap's peak. Holly believed that as long as Daddy winked at her, he was safe. When the evenings were dark she kept a torch beneath her pillow and flashed it on the photograph from time to time. She always caught Fred smiling to himself, probably thinking of her.

Lucille grumbled about the torch, especially when it rolled to her side of the bed, but half-heartedly. She sympathised with the child's longing for Fred. A good deal of her own time was spent wishing him with her, imagining 'after the war', that magic time that was coming, that must come, to make up for these barren years, to rescue her from the cold countryside and having to live in someone else's house.

When she and Ida quarrelled it was a dour affair. Ida would contain her temper for several days, then let it out with a few stiff, hard words, bending furiously over her work at the same time. Maud would join in and hold out her hideously buckled fists as if in salute to Ida or perhaps with some notion of seizing Lucille and shaking her. The old cripple's intervention always silenced and quietened Ida who did not want such an ally. Between her sister-in-law and her aunt she felt, in her own way, as embattled as Lucille did. The row died away without really getting going, and Lucille left the room with pointed dignity, but in her room crumpled and wept, longing for Tikki. She remembered how he had said 'not long'. Outside the black hill was freckled with late snow. Hamish was marching across the yard with two buckets of pigswill. 'Tikki!' her faint heart cried.

'Look, Mummy, I've been making a surprise for your birthday, but you can have it now because Auntie is so horrid, isn't she?' Holly held out a box covered in flowered paper, crudely made.

Lucille blinked, embarrassed to be caught with tears on her cheeks. Holly took off the lid and showed pink cotton wool inside.

'You can keep something in it.'

Lucille blew her nose.

'What about my naval brooch?'

The little pearl crown was Lucille's most treasured piece of jewellery. She took it out of the blue leather box in which it had come from Gieves – sent by registered post just before Tikki went to sea – and placed it on the cotton wool.

'Doesn't it look pretty?' said Holly, entranced with her present.

'Yes, darling. It's a dear little box.' Lucille put an arm round Holly and they sat down on the edge of the bed together.

'Aunt Ida's ever so strict, isn't she?' Holly enquired, wanting to help.

'She's got a lot to do.'

'She's not very like Daddy, is she?'

'No one is like Daddy.'

'No,' agreed Holly fervently.

They both looked at his photograph in a silver frame on the chest of drawers – not the despised passport snap which was on Holly's side of the room, but Lucille's beloved equivalent, in which the stripe on Tikki's sleeve showed.

'After the war,' said Lucille, 'when we go home again –'

'Will we go back?'

'Just as soon as ever we can, darling.'

'Oh.'

This was a blow. Holly looked up from the little box and saw the view outside. Although it was March, the wind was brooming snow across the hillside as white dust. Her mother was talking about their home at Mitcham and holidays at Sandalcliff. Fred, in his two pictures and from beside Holly's shoulder, watched them. Perhaps somehow it would be all right. She turned back to Lucille who smiled, wanly.

From then on Holly began to look after her mother. It was a conscious purpose of the child, to take her father's place. In their double bed she would hug her mother, curling up against her back and resting her cheek against the rounded shoulders. Lucille slept hunched up, often cold despite the pig, an earthenware hot water jar Ida provided for each bed. (They stood in the day on the back of the stove with their stoppers upside down on their curved tops.) If Holly's hand came round her mother's waist, Lucille would take hold of it and give it a few, quick pats, her mind far away. To help herself get to sleep Lucille told herself stories. In most of them it was peacetime and Tikki was a captain, sometimes the youngest admiral in the history of the navy, and she was packing her days with parties and dinners against a background of sunny waters and palm trees, flowers in her hair. As she danced her feet pressed on the china pig. Holly knew from her breathing that Lucille was asleep. Hugh was bubbling through his mouth as usual. Ida said every day that the child needed his adenoids out.

Holly slipped out of bed and, with difficulty, tugged open the black-out curtains so that she could see the stars. Then she lay on her back, holding Fred's hand, and thought what she would do next day. She might go with Hamish when he went to inspect the sheep up towards Glen Livet. If so, should she persuade Donald to come and they would explore the big waterfall up there? Or would he want her to help with his tree house by the burn? Or Wishart's dad might let them have the boat on the loch if the weather was calm. At the moment there were no clouds, or wind. The stars bloomed down, the hill shouldered them up.

Soon the summer would come back, and all sorts of new things to do would be discovered. She couldn't imagine what, but knew they would all be marvellous. At Balchraggan each day held treasure of some sort. You woke in the high bed, you scrambled down and looked out of the window, had a sniff of the morning – wet, windy, dry, sunny, misty, whatever it might be – and a sight of the farm work and then you got dressed and things began. That's how the day was, that's how a year was, here.

She smiled broadly to herself and tucked her hand more securely into her father's. She slept.

3

HOLLY AND FRED

After their second Christmas at Balchraggan, in January 1941, Fred at last came back on leave. He had been in the Mediterranean and beyond, and the sight of London, broken and grey under winter skies, was a raw shock, different from the shock of battle and violent injury, but no less painful. His polished shoes crunched glass on pavements, his eyes were assaulted by jagged buildings split open, with gas and water piping hanging in the air and remnants of cosy wallpapers flapping over piles of rubble. Men in overalls and tin hats were climbing over cascades of brick and stone. Their white faces had gritty dust in the creases. When they saw Fred's tan and his uniform they gave him a thumbs up sign.

'God bless the navy,' called out one man. 'You been giving them hell, mate?'

Fred was appalled that while his back was turned this had been allowed to happen to his city. The civil defence workers seemed futile as ants.

He went into a post office with shattered windows and a roughly patched hole in the ceiling to telephone Lucille but he could not get through, so sent her a telegram and went to catch a train. The station was brown with soldiers' uniforms. Hundreds of men with kitbags and rifles were sitting and standing with a hopeless patience in winding columns, smoking, hardly speaking. Fred could find nothing to eat. All the little kiosks were boarded up, and the station hotel, awash with army officers, could offer him only watery tea and a hard currant bun without currants.

Everything was colourless and comfortless – no homecoming. His ship, the ruddy faces of his companions there seemed doubly alive by comparison.

When he eventually sat wedged between two other men in a train, he summoned up the oblivion of a sailor's ever-ready sleep to carry him through the journey. He had no wish to speak to these people, or even to exchange glances with them.

His telegram arrived at the farm next day, only an hour before Fred himself. Lucille hardly had time to change herself and the children into best clothes. She and Holly both felt sick, and their breath came in shallow pants. Hugh was put to have his afternoon nap in his pram in the garden. Holly was turned out too, and hung herself over the gate, swinging it in a passion of expectation, entirely undefined. The Fred who had been at her side for months fled, the real man in his office suit that smelled of the train – he was unimaginable here. She swung in limbo, backwards and forwards on the gate.

A man came up the lane in a long skirted overcoat and carrying a green case and a wicker basket of oranges. When she saw who it was, Fred was already level with her. She sprang off the gate and stood ready to jump into his arms, but he walked past as if she were not there.

Lucille was in the doorway. Fred put down his burdens, took two strides, like a giant, wrenched off his cap and seized hold of his wife who disappeared into his coat. Daddy just lifted her up and swallowed her.

Holly felt a void open inside her. The world went still and quiet. She turned to Hughie's pram and stared down at the little boy with prickling eyes. Then she had Daddy's hand on her neck, his arms swinging her up to carry her indoors and hold her on his lap, while Mummy sat in the armchair. Now her body was dissolving in joy and tears were pouring down her cheeks, dribbling down her neck, soaking her collar. Now and for ever it would be all right.

There was excitement all afternoon. Maud, Ida and Hamish came in. Fred unloosed a cascade of oranges. 'I've been in the Med,' he said. How jaunty he sounded! Everyone had an orange, cut in half, with a lump of sugar melting on the top and using Ida's best apostle spoons. Then left-over Christmas cake, and whisky, and presents from inside the green case – lace hankies, fans, black lace scarves. 'Very Spanish,' said Ida draping one over her head, 'Quite the signorita!' Suddenly the old woman cried out, 'Ooh-la-la!' and tried to heave her crooked arms into the air. Everyone gaped at her. 'Castanets,' she explained, her grin revealing her imitation orange gums. Holly and the two boys began to giggle so hard they had to stuff their faces into cushions.

Then they had supper with a Christmas pudding and some old crackers and everyone wearing funny hats. The boys squeaked and squirted feathered whistles, and Fred sang to Lucille, 'Daisy, Daisy, give me your answer do!' She kissed him first on one cheek, then the other while he fixed his blue, blue eyes on her. 'I gave you your answer long ago,' she said, 'Romeo!'

At bedtime it turned out that Holly could no longer sleep with Mummy. That was Daddy's place.

'But why?'

'Because, darling.'

'Because what?'

'Fathers and mothers always sleep in the same bed. Holly, darling, you know that.'

'Yes, but why not me too?'

Her stocky body became rigid with determination.

'I want to stay in your bed.'

'No, Holly.'

'That's not my little girl,' said Fred, as jovially as he could. In reality he disliked her red, contorted face.

'I *have* to be in your bed with Daddy.'

'Oh, don't go on, Holly.'

Fred coughed and rustled the pages of a story book he had been reading to her.

'I have to.' Holly stamped her foot.

Lucille, overwrought herself and ashamed, slapped her face. Fred went out of the room.

'Where's Hugh going?'

'Nowhere. He can stay in his cot where he is.'

'That's not fair!'

Lucille could have cried. All she wanted was to be in bed with Fred in the dark and privacy, where she could pretend Balchraggan did not exist, and here was this difficult child making one of her bothers and Fred looking cross.

'It's not fair. Why should Hugh stay and not me?'

Holly knew she had lost the battle from the moment Fred left the room, but had no idea how to conclude the scene she had made. Ida released her.

'Because you are a growing-up little girl, not a baby,' she said and took her hand to go upstairs.

'The kid's a bit out of hand, isn't she?' Fred asked of Lucille who came timidly towards him in the hall.

'You've no idea what a handful she is, Tikki.'

'My poor darling girl.'

Holly, when they reached the bathroom, asked her aunt, 'Does she mean I'm naughty?'

'Yes. Turn round and I'll undo your buttons.'

'Why am I?'

'There was that letter. Hands up.'

From inside her dress, Holly said, 'Daddy understood.'

'And then you broke my vase. Now your vest.'

'That was an accident, Auntie.'

'That's not an excuse. Come on, in the bath.'

'I didn't mean to let the sick ewe out, the catch broke.'

'Give me a leg. Yes, Uncle Hamish knows that and he forgave you didn't he?'

'Uncle is kinder than Daddy,' said Holly, immediately appalled at herself.

'Don't talk like that,' said Ida, calmly and rubbing Holly's back with vigour. 'There's no sense in comparisons.'

Before going to her new bed in what had been a maid's bedroom, Holly took the snap of Fred from the wall in her mother's room and placed it at the bottom of her bottom drawer, underneath the lining paper. She got into bed feeling a stranger to herself. She ran her hands over her stomach and chest, and then brushed her fringe up with the heels of both hands, staring fiercely into the darkness.

*

Fred's leave was short and the weather turned cold again. The Tickeners hardly went outside the front room of the farmhouse, which Ida and Hamish tactfully more or less gave up to them. Holly could not persuade her father to go out of doors with her, except to the village shop for tobacco or to the hotel for a drink, and then she had to wait in the hallway for him. He didn't watch her climb her pine by the bridge, and she wasn't sure he believed about the wild cats, or the deer coming down to steal hay from the byre in the coldest weather.

Nor would he tell her about the sea or his ship. When she, or anyone else, asked him, he put them off with something else. To the loving and watchful child it was as if his uniform had altered him. It hung on two wooden hangers behind the bedroom door, and the cap was on the antlers in the hall. Yet Daddy without it, lounging by the fire in an old jersey of Hamish's which was too small, was not quite the Daddy she remembered. He was not very polite to Aunt Maud, and he wouldn't play with Holly.

*

In March when the fields above the farm had been ploughed and harrowed, Hamish employed the children to help him collect the boulders lying on the surface. They put them by twos and threes in buckets and lugged them to the field corners where mounds of stones from other years were half buried in blown leaves and dead weeds. The larger stones were put aside for wall repairs. It was cold, harsh work.

So was lambing which happened just a little later. Hamish and Meg were up all night for a week or more. When she took them mugs of tea into the sheds, Holly saw their hands were swollen blue-grey with cold, noses red, woollen hats beaded some mornings with ice.

By late April the lambs were frisky in the fold-field, some already on the hills, and daffodils bloomed, secretly, green-yellow, in clearings among the pines where once there had been homesteads, before hunger and greed drove the people away.

In one ruined cottage near the farm Holly and Chrissie set up home with dollies' china, a battered saucepan from Ida, old cushions from Mrs Chisholm, and even a broken primus that Donald got to work. He pretended to scorn the little house, which was still called Lurgann by the locals. It had been a handsome building with dark pink sandstone sills and lintel and chimneys, one at each gable end. Donald climbed up and stood where the roof had once rested spying out the valley which was still brown with winter but misted with purplish birch buds, and hazed olive by sprouting larches. Straight ahead the boy could see the far side of Loch Ness with fields and behind and above them the peaks of the Monadhliath. From time to time snow showers moved across the distant sunny sky like grey screens. The girls chattered below him, making primrose wine with stolen sugar and burn water.

When the spring really came, the late, quick, overwhelming spring of the north when trees fountain into leaf, flowers are stars in the tender grasses, and the sun persists till eight at night striking through the veils of foliage like x-ray beams that show the anatomy of newly leaved trees, then Lucille burst into liveliness. Through the Minister she had met the wife of the commander of the local RAF Base. She began to go there for formal entertainments, then casually to play tennis and to dance. One afternoon, she had her hair cut off and came home from Inverness with a halo of wispy curls.

'How do I look?' she asked, turning this way and that.

Ida glanced once and clattered her pans.

'Verra charming,' said Hamish.

'You had no call to shear off your crowning glory,' Maud told her tartly. 'Fred likes long hair. All men do.'

'What do you know about it?' muttered Lucille.

'You are quite the faery of the glens,' said the Minister.

'No doubt they will like it at that Base.'

'Well, that's the general idea,' agreed Lucille.

Lately she had been adopting a casual, slangy way of talking which Holly, for one, greatly admired. Lucille had two especial men friends at the Base, called Doug and Pete. The farm heard quite a lot about them, how fast they drove their cars, how splendidly they danced, how modern they were, and their ability to loop the loop.

'Why don't you bring them home, Mummy?'

'Doug and Pete! They'd die of boredom here.'

'I could show them Lurgann. Anyone would like it there.'

'What's Lurgann when it's at home?' asked Maud.

'It is a sort of home – for me and Chrissie,' replied Holly, laughing. 'We could make tea for Doug and Pete, we could Mummy, easily.'

'Good heavens, what would they think!' said Lucille her small face puckering in dismissal.

Two or three nights a week she caught the six o'clock bus into the town. There she picked up the station bus which jounced along the concrete roads to the point where the aerodrome was set with the waters of the Moray Firth brushing it on three sides.

Lucille did not go straight to the mess. First she called on Milly, the Commandant's wife to hear the news and find out the mood of the Base. It altered from hour to hour depending on what missions the men had flown, or not flown because of the scarcity of spare parts or bad weather. Milly was a local girl and was living in her parents' home. She was smart, gay and rather daringly bold, picking up the RAF slang almost as soon as it was minted, and passing it on to Lucille. The pair of them, both from quiet homes, revelled in the excitement of wartime, without realising it. The spice of danger, the fleeting thought of 'Perhaps I'll not see him again' greatly enhanced the looks of the pilots, navigators, gunners and bomb-aimers with whom they danced, smoked and chatted into the long, light northern nights. The opposite shores darkened from green to grey to almost invisible before a tinge of primrose appeared over the sea and the hills stood forward again from the colourless sky.

Lucille was happy. She lay back in a low chair and closed her eyes to savour the pleasure of cigarette smoke, deep voices, the meandering, out-of-tune piano, even the faint swish of breakers on the beach. If Doug or Pete were there, she let them hold her hand. Once or twice they kissed.

She knew that Milly and the men had enjoyed this sort of life before the war. They were only catching at something they owned in normal life. For Lucille, it was the first time she had been with socially assured people with some money and sufficient education. Marvellous it was – the way they made light of things! If only Maud and Ida could see these casual manners. Here were no heavy hints, hissing breaths indrawn, no condemnation. If you wanted, you did; if not, nobody minded. Heaven!

After the war when Tikki was back with her, when perhaps he would be a captain at least, their life would always be like this, gay and easy, full of jokes, tears. Lucille was struck by how readily these new friends of hers wept, even the men sometimes and the girls frequently, but prettily and not for long. Their surface emotions fizzed over. She thought it part of their charm but could not copy it. Inside herself tears were hard and painful, a lump in her chest like a hastily swallowed lump of green apple. And the idea of Tikki crying, was just quite impossible to imagine.

In every other way she took on the manners of the Base, in her jaunty dancing, her cheeky replies, her slang, her smart, casual clothes and her yearning, yearning to belong, to stay there, for time to stand still between dusk and sunrise with no missions to fly.

*

Maud's room was on the ground floor. Ida used to help her undress and leave her in the chair reading her Bible.

Ida loved the summer nights. She pulled open the black-out curtains to let sweet, moist air flow into the upstairs rooms. The hill rounded softly against a white sky and below her each flagstone of yard was plain, yet the middle distance was featureless, dim air, dim ground. There was nothing in detail to be seen, all colourless and vague, and the sound of the stream running. Ida remained at the window, breathing lightly. She had no wish for bed. It was rest enough to stand here absorbing the space and quiet.

It seemed impossible now that she had ever endured the close-packed noise and dirt of London. There everyone was jostled up against his neighbour, even in solitude overhearing the shouts and footsteps, the lavatory cisterns of others. Here each person was separate, alone in a landscape that ignored them.

She heard the distant car come up from the village and stop at the lane's end. Maud heard it too and began the process of standing up, reaching for her sticks and shuffling across the room towards the door. Her folded hands fitted over the sticks like clamps. The skin was ivory, so smooth it shone faintly in the half light when she opened the front door.

Lucille's coat separated itself from the trees. Her heel taps came in an irregular beat as she walked partly on stone, partly moss. Then the click of the gate and the whole girl was visible swinging her handbag by its chain. Maud loomed in the doorway with two grey plaits hanging down her worsted dressing-gown, her face malevolent and shrunken without her teeth.

'You've no need to get up, Aunt Maud. I've got a key.'

Lucille squeezed sideways past the old woman, avoiding the scandalized eyes. Painfully Maud turned after her. With the door open the hall was lit sufficiently. Lucille flung down her coat with a stagey gesture and walked into the kitchen to draw herself a glass of water.

'And Alfred at sea, fighting for you!' burst out Maud, as if a conversation were in progress.

Lucille challenged the old woman over the tumbler's rim.

'Tikki likes me to have a good time.'

'Aren't you ashamed?'

'Not in the least.' She put down the glass, and walked back to the hall with precise steps.

'Coming home after midnight with a strange man.'

If Lucille was enjoying her own nonchalance, Maud was appreciating the drama.

'Doug is my friend, not a stranger. Tikki wouldn't want me to walk up alone in the dark.'

'The Lord's hand will come upon you.'

'Oh, fiddle-de-dee!'

This silenced Maud. She stooped heavily over her sticks, her head settled between her shoulders. Lucille picked up her coat.

'Goodnight, Aunt Maud.'

Maud took a few shuffling backward steps, trying to block the way upstairs. 'I only hope that we can keep all this from the innocent children.'

Memories of Fred's childish miseries fuelled Lucille's anger like twigs thrown on embers. His fear of the pavement gratings.

'For heaven's sake, you old black crow you! Leave my children out of it. I'll not have you blighting their lives too.' She was shouting.

Ida appeared on the stairs in her nightdress. 'Aunt, you should be in bed.'

'And you should put a stop to these goings on, my girl.'

'Lucille does as she pleases.'

'In your house! It's not right.'

'She isn't a child.'

Standing with the two Tickeners, both in long, old-fashioned nightclothes, Lucille almost felt she was a child, and resented it.

'All the village will know,' said Maud.

'If they choose to sit up all night to spy on me, I expect they will. So what?'

'Dancing. Gadding about,' mumbled Maud, her anger losing momentum in tiredness. 'Jezebel.'

'To tell the truth,' said Ida, 'it is not quite what Hamish would like.'

'He's always talking about ceilidhs. That's dancing isn't it?'

'Hamish likes a ceilidh well enough, but there's dancing and dancing.'

'It is not right,' Maud told Ida. 'A married man should stay at home with his wife.' She seemed to be losing the thread.

'Come on, Aunt. Time for some shut-eye.' She took the sticks from her hands and supported her, capably, towards the open bedroom door. 'We'll talk about it all in the morning.'

Like hell we will, thought Lucille going upstairs.

Crouched on the top step was Holly, pressed sideways to the banisters. 'Mummy, what have you been doing?'

'Having a nice time – just as Daddy would want,' said Lucille in a loud, defiant voice to carry down to Maud.

She bundled the child into bed and quickly joined her.

'Why doesn't Aunt Maud think so then?'

'Old fusspot, fuss, fuss, fusspot,' said Lucille, tickling Holly and hugging her. Sleepily giggling she fell asleep again.

Old crow, thought Lucille. Cawing old black crow. Look what you did to my Tikki. Perhaps you'd like to throw me to the Roman Catholics. But you shan't.

It was lunchtime before Lucille came down next day. The Minister thought she looked as fresh as the pink campions her little girl had put on the windowsill. His smile was luckily unobserved by Maud, already sitting at her place at table with a napkin tied like a bib.

*

In June the burns were brilliant with gushing brown water, delicious for paddling, with dipping hazels, rank ramsons in the undergrowth, primroses fading in the moss, bluebells thick. Donald fished for trout over the sandy bottomed pools where fat spotted gentlemen snoozed, silver shadows, and refused his worms. Holly and Chrissie lay reading or dreaming, passing each other the bag of Horlicks tablets. Above their heads was a patch of sky fringed with leaves, perfect, high, serenely protective.

'Your Dad been in many battles?'

'I don't know. 'Spect so.'

'Whee – boom!' Donald planed his arms and made what he believed to be the noise of a shell.

'Shut up,' commanded Chrissie. 'We are reading.'

The war hardly troubled them. Holly was at home in her world and, as her father had been part of it for only one brief leave, he was not missed as he would have been in Mitcham. It was with an effort that she could call to mind the back garden there, shut in between other gardens, with her sandpit and Fred's sweet-peas, the dustbin by the door lined with newspaper and a gigantic clump of golden rod.

She was growing fast and becoming strong, developing her tall body so like Fred's. Whenever not at school, she was outdoors playing with Bob, Bruce, Donald, Chrissie, Wishart – all the local children but mostly the boys – climbing, building dams, helping on the farm, improving their house. She wore shorts, aertex blouses, jerseys, wellingtons or plimsolls. Lucille called her a tomboy, rather disparagingly. (Milly's little girl was petite and delicate with pretty manners.) So now, thought Holly, I am a chatterbox, a bossy-boots and a tomboy. Well, Daddy had never minded her chattering, so probably he'd like a tomboy too, someone in trousers, like him, not a fussy girl. She extended her skills to paring sticks, tying knots and diving.

When two years had passed and then a third winter, Balchraggan had become the only home she knew, though her mother still spoke ominously of London. So, when in 1942 the news came that their house at Mitcham had been destroyed by a landmine and Lucille cried, Holly felt only relief from the worry that her mother might decide to go back there one day when she quarrelled worse than usual with old Aunt Maud.

That summer she stretched her body and her imagination, making the highland landscape her interior world. She wandered all hours up the glen bottoms or over the moors, watching, listening, comparing shape with shape, colour with colour, buds, leaves, twigs, flowers, grass with moss with lichen – learning her chosen world. She would throw herself down and stare for minutes on end at the sky as cloud outliers detached themselves from a creamy mass and drifted free towards the sea; or, perched in her pine tree, would endure the sudden pelting of a short storm, the branch swaying, the clouds massing in grape purple towers. Sometimes she was with Donald and the others, sometimes alone – solitary but friendly, and always conscious of the invisible Fred who went beside her.

In the autumn he came back on leave. He was by then a Lieutenant-Commander.

Now Holly did not make the mistake of thinking she was first with him. Lucille went to Inverness to meet the train and Holly at the farm instructed Hugh, who was three and a half, what Daddy would be like. Ida was cooking a special meal, suet dumplings with mutton and button onions. As farmers they were not badly off for meat, but rarely had it not filled out with pulses or potatoes.

'Look what Tikki's brought me!' cried Lucille, before she was in the door. It was a fur coat. Fred could not say where he had been but, wherever it was, fur was plentiful. He had a fur hat for Ida, slippers for Hamish, for the children hats, gloves and slippers, some white, some tawny, though Lucille's coat was black lamb. Fred poured out these treasures as soon as the door was closed. Holly did not have the endless hug she was expecting, nor did she she cry this time.

Fred also humped in a gallon jar of honey. He had a stamp album half filled with stamps, some triangular, for Holly. Also a doll in queer clothes with a pigtail. For Hugh he had a lifesize pink fur rabbit which made the timid boy cry at first. When his cases were opened, Lucille was also given strange embroidered blouses and little mats, some long grey feathers in a cardboard cylinder, beads, gloves, a ring with a purple stone, and perfume, and fresh flowers that he had bought in Inverness and presented to her. Lucille told them several times with golden delight that Tikki had stopped the taxi and gone into the market, emerging with this sheaf of lilies and chrysanthemums. Bronzed, tall, smiling, everyone had noticed Tikki, and for Lucille the moment was one of the sweetest of her life. He handed her the bouquet and kissed her in front of the crowd, one or two of whom gave a faint cheer.

Holly had hoped her father might bring a penknife or some rope or even a hammock – all good naval things. Fur gloves were actually a nuisance if you wanted to climb trees or make snowballs, and fur hats pricked your forehead. As for stamps! Only sissies collected them.

'Well, chatterbox, you're quiet,' said Fred in a new loud voice.

'Yes.' She smiled at him lovingly.

'Glad to see me, are you?'

'Yes.' Of course, she thought, of course. Fancy asking!

'Good! Good!' Fred stamped heartily.

Holly watched. There was something different about him. She had picked it up from the first moment with the fine-tuned sensitivity of love.

Ida said the meal was ready and everyone moved to the kitchen table.

'Once more into the breach,' said Fred, rubbing his palms together.

Before Hamish had said grace Fred was breaking open his home-made bread roll. Reaching for the butter dish he smeared on half the roll a good part of one week's ration. Everyone noticed, but, of course, no one said a word to the sailor just safely home. Perhaps the twins thought it only his due. Fred was a figure of enormous glamour to them.

After the soup, Hamish carved the meat, tenderly cutting it into thin slices. His sinewy hands worked methodically, not fast and before he had finished Fred passed up his plate for a second helping. Hamish looked quickly at Ida, who shrugged slightly, and gave his brother-in-law one more pink wafer of meat. Everyone was watching except Lucille who was admiring her new ring and placing her hand on Fred's arm. Heavy handedly, Ida brought the conversation round to the subject of rationing.

'We only have a small weekly allowance of most things.'

'Scandalous,' said Fred equably. 'Don't you think it's scandalous, Holly, my puss?' He took some more butter to finish up his roll. 'The government wants a kick up the pants.'

Lucille giggled.

But when, at teatime, Fred took spoonfuls of jam and piled it on his plate, it was Holly who took it on herself to say, 'Daddy, we have to make a pot last two weeks, because of the sugar you see.'

'Do you indeed?' His voice lacked interest.

'Yes, we do. So you shouldn't take all that much.'

He barked with laughter. 'Miss Bossy-boots in person!'

'It's greedy, Daddy,' she told him earnestly.

'What the devil's happened to your manners?'

'Don't talk to Daddy like that, Holly,' Lucille intervened.

Holly's face burned, her heart more so.

'I suppose,' said Hamish carefully, 'you have pretty short commons on your ship, Fred?'

'Lord, no. Excellent grub. Bags of it too. Fighting men, you know, and all that.'

'No ships biscuits?' asked Ida.

'We make our own bread with white flour,' he replied, poking his jammy knife into Ida's pale khaki wartime loaf.

All the people seated at the table were thinking something similar, and Holly had no doubt her father was greedy. He also boasted, talked too loudly and didn't sit still – things forbidden to the children. She went up the hill to think about it. Up there in the heathery sweet harshness of rock and boggy pool, her memories of Fred took over from this recent shock. She smiled trustfully into his imagined face again, and ran her finger ripplingly over his furrowed forehead.

'Where've you been?' he asked, when she came in.

'I went up the braeside.'

'Speak English, Holly. Now, where did you go?'

'Up the hill.'

'That's better. You should be proud of being English.'

'I'm not proud of what they did around here.'

'*They* did! For God's sake, Lucille, what's this kid been learning?'

'Don't ask me,' she answered, with a little shrug she had learned from Milly. 'You sent us all here, Tikki darling. Lord knows, I didn't want to come.'

Fred turned back to Holly. 'Tell me, what did the English do here that was so terrible.'

She stared at him mistrustfully, hating herself.

'Come on. Let's hear what you've been spoonfed at school.'

She tried to tell him what the Dominie had said about the clearances, the burning townships, the fertile ground handed to sheep and ultimate barrenness, the cutting down of fugitives from battle, the firing of crofts that had sheltered them, but inevitably it came out in the schoolmaster's patriotic terms, and with words Fred had never heard. When she finished his face was red, and she felt afraid of him. Her voice tailed away as he twisted on his heel and presented an angry back to her. To fear Daddy was a terrible thing; it meant she must be really bad. The fact that she wasn't sure how she was bad made her guilt all the worse.

She went up to her room, and, resting her head on the window pane, stared, unseeing, at the yard.

'Where've you been this time?' he asked when she went down.

'In my room.'

'Well, stay down here. Bedrooms are for sleeping, not mooning.'

This became a feature of Fred's second leave – he had to have them all with him, even though he did not seem to enjoy their company much, Holly noticed. He spent a lot of time reading the paper, or rather folding and re-folding it, rustling and hemming, and a lot of time walking up and down the kitchen or the hall, stopping to poke his stubby forefinger into the works of the grandfather clock, or Ida's bowl of pot-pourri, or turning the egg-timer over and over. The red sand running through fascinated him. What was he thinking as he stared at it? or paced up and down the hall? Holly no longer knew the answers to questions of that sort.

On the second day he organised cricket in the fold-field. Holly, the tomboy, was expected to be good at games but annoyed Fred at the outset by not knowing the rules of cricket.

'We play shinty here,' she explained.

'What?' he asked, red-faced.

'It's like hockey, only the sticks are – '

'Holly, stop blethering,' ordered Donald who could see Commander Tickener wanted to start playing.

'Good lad!'

Fred organised about a dozen children into two teams and set them to play. He bowled most of the time, which Holly considered unfair but no one else seemed to mind at all. Nor did the boys resent being given out – or didn't show it. Chrissie took several catches, but Holly dropped or missed every ball that came her way.

'Butter-fingers!' shouted Fred in a jolly voice at first, but then more and more angrily as if cricket were not a game at all. Nor for fun.

'Keep your eye on the ball.'

'How can I when I don't see it coming?'

She was also afraid it might hit her and side-stepped. Then the boys all chanted 'butter-fingers', and even Chrissie gave her pitying smiles.

When cricket palled, they played rounders which was worse because the bat was narrower and round like a rolling-pin. Holly, told by Fred to run on, and by Donald, her team's leader, to stop, became confused, ever more clumsy and eventually tearful.

Instead of risking being called 'cry-baby' – the very worst thing – she sneaked away from the game and climbed into the hayloft. From there she could glare down on the others, put a spell on them. She knew this was childish, but her misery made her feel babyish again. She hated them all.

Hamish found her in the loft. 'What's the problem, lassie?'

'Nothing.'

'Your father been coming His Majesty's officer with you?' Hamish meant this kindly, he was smiling, but Holly wasn't going to take sides against Daddy with anyone.

'No. I came up to read my book.' She had a book on the hay bale where she sat, but in fact she kept it there. The loft was one of the places where she 'mooned'.

'Well, get away down to your tea, then,' said Hamish sharply.

That day Ida provided only toast and dripping.

'Rather thin, isn't it, girl?' asked Fred of her.

'It's what we have to make do with.'

Fred asked for salt and sprinkled it with great care on his slice.

Another thing the watchful child had noticed about her father was that he had become what Lucille called finicky over food. He prepared each forkful elaborately for eating – a shred of cabbage, a cube of potato dipped in salt, the meat, a touch of mustard and a smear in the gravy pool on his plate, then in it went and he masticated it with pleasure. When they had shrimps one day after a trip to Inverness, Fred peeled himself a small plateful before eating any, and then he luxuriously chewed them up. The rest of the family, quicker and less systematic than he, watched.

'Can I have one?' asked Holly, who loved shrimps.

'Didn't you have your share?'

'Yes.'

'Well then – one.' He handed her a tiny pink curl, so small she hardly noticed swallowing it. She told herself that the old Daddy would have fed her more than half his plateful.

Fred did not often eat at the farm. He and Lucille were out a great deal. She introduced him to her RAF friends, whom Fred referred to slightingly as 'those flying johnnies' and seemed to have not the least idea of being jealous of Doug or Pete, although Maud by her hunched shoulders and mutterings tried to nudge him into it.

His leave ended with a week in Edinburgh. Lucille was vibrant and pink with pleasure. She sat in the train, legs crossed, lamb coat over her shoulders, party-dresses in the case over her head, holding Tikki's arm. He was hers, not just for today, or a week, but for ever. He looked so handsome in his uniform and his wallet was so full of notes it would hardly fold over. Best of all was the way he looked at her. She knew he would hold her hand at their table in the hotel, buy her carnations if they were to be had, let her choose her favourite cocktail, what show they should go to, and press her close to him in his strong, clumsy way as they danced. Probably, he would want to do *that* in bed every night, he seemed extra keen on it this leave, but, poor Tikki, with the dreadful war to go back to, she really couldn't refuse him.

Edinburgh in wartime was not pre-war London. The buildings were like unscaleable grey cliffs and the wind skirled round corners carrying grit. There were no flower-sellers, nothing pretty in the shops, no lights; but they were asked out by men Tikki mysteriously knew, invited to cocktails, to lunch, to a 'hop' at the North British Hotel, even to a show at the Empire with Henry Hall top of the bill. No, it wasn't London, but still . . . She saw with pleasure that Tikki never so much as glanced at another woman although the bars were full of them in short dresses with drapes, fox furs, and hats on the sides of their heads. Thanks to Milly she could easily hold her own – she knew the slang, the gestures. She felt she had come of age socially during the fallow time at Balchraggan and her eyes were luminous with self-satisfied pleasure, even a sort of arrogance that could so easily have tipped into timidity. Fred watched her tenderly. He knew her modern manners were a put on, no more part of her than the rhinestone brooch with which she pinned his flower to her shoulder, but her success in assuming them touched him, without pleasing him. He could not tell her it was the girl who quivered in his arms in bed and cried out 'Oh, please – no. Oh Tikki!' that he really loved.

*

When Fred had been gone a whole day, Ida broke a silence she considered tactful and told Lucille to pull herself together. Half the women in the country were in her shoes, and at least she had her children safely away from the bombs. And Fred was all right. Not like Donald's mother, poor Mrs Chisholm, whose husband had been posted missing.

By way of answer Lucille resumed her visits to the RAF Base, where she helped organise a party for local children, then a dance in aid of SSAFA. Her requests for tombola prizes were effective, even the Minister giving her a bottle. Doug and Pete were mentioned frequently, and came sometimes to call for her, one in a taxi ('Think of the cost', hissed Maud), and the other in a red sports car all the boys thought smashing. Holly wished her mother would not jump into it quite so lightheartedly. Sometimes Mummy kissed the man on the cheek.

'Are they sweethearts?' asked Chrissie.

'Of course not,' said Bob, before Holly could answer.

'She is a shameless hussy.' Maud squeezed out the words.

'Och, there's no harm in the lass,' said Hamish. 'It's wartime pleasure that's to blame.'

'All the same,' said Ida to Hamish when they were alone, 'it does make me feel sorry for Fred for once.'

'He's well enough satisfied with her. You ken that.'

She sniffed. He caught hold of her.

'No, you are to stop it, do you hear?' He gave her a small, loving shake. 'I dinna want discord in the house. I tell you – there's no harm in the girl.'

'Girl!'

'Aye. And you're the big sister who understands, aren't you now? Aren't you Ida, my lassie?'

She softened. She kissed him. He rubbed his stubbly chin against her face.

*

In February the station was much busier, and Lucille went there on only one weekend. Then, on the 19th, both Doug and Pete were killed. They flew together, and their plane crashed as it came in to land, half shot away as it was. The two wives came up for the funeral. Lucille also attended and returned to the farm looking dreadful.

'Mummy!' cried Holly when she saw the shrunken face under the black hat's veiling and the way her mother was stooping in the doorway.

'My dear girl, come away in by the fire and warm yourself,' said Hamish.

Silently, Ida stirred two spoonfuls of sugar into a cup of tea and placed it in Lucille's shaking hands where she sat by the fire with the fur collar of her coat drowning her thin shoulders.

'Mummy what happened?'

Lucille's face was made of soggy tissue paper.

'What happened, Mummy?'

'Holly, be quiet,' commanded Ida.

'You know about burying people. You're old enough,' said Lucille with a feeble spurt of crossness.

'Drink up the tea, lassie.'

'Did you, did you love Doug and Pete such a lot?' asked Holly, timidly.

'I didn't love them at all.' Tears began to run after each other down Lucille's cheeks and to drip off into the fur.

Holly cast about for what to do. She fetched Hugh and sat him in her mother's lap but he was pushed away to Ida. Then she brought Fred's photo from the bedroom and a chocolate biscuit. When nothing worked, she crouched beside her mother and stroked her shin with her finger-tips. Gradually Lucille's leg stopped trembling, but she still stared at the fire and hunched up in her coat. Everyone else was painfully conscious of the silent woman who seemed unconscious of them.

'Soon be time for spring cleaning,' remarked Ida in her positive way.

'Like *The Wind in the Willows*?' asked Holly, also keen to make things normal. 'Can I help you with the whitewash, like Mole?'

'We'll see.'

'Let's have a game of Ludo,' suggested Bob.

The land-girl sat at the table to write her weekly letter home. Family life went on haltingly around the figure of Lucille.

*

After that she began to occupy herself more with the children, taking Hugh for walks and playing board games. That summer she saw something of the beauty of the countryside. The hills she could never like, but the shallow rushing river where the children found her a seat on a big stone was pleasant. Sunlight dappled through the hazel and birch trees, throwing down coins of sun and shadow. There were ferns with thin black stalks and silky grass and pale, woodland flowers with drooping stems. Chrissie showed her and Holly how to plait rushes into little baskets. She kept one to put her hairpins in. Donald and the other boys larked and swam in the pools, while Hughie paddled and splashed her skirt.

The children all liked Lucille and envied Holly. Their mothers rarely went out and wore their hair in curlers and scarves all day. Lucille had a brown linen jacket and a small, brown straw hat worn over one eye that she put on even to go to the woods.

'She is quite ridiculous,' said Ida.

'Not over sensible, I grant you, but happier now,' said Hamish.

What chiefly galled Ida was Lucille's developing cleverness in the house. Because of shortages caused by the war, they had to 'make do' all the time. Lucille was better at making pretty garments from unpicked clothes. What Ida sewed was serviceable and tended to have square corners. It was Lucille's idea to patch loose covers and then embroider the plain fabric to match the worn pattern. This was considered very clever by all their visitors.

Now angel cakes were not the only thing she could cook well. Her shepherd's pie, flavoured with grated raw carrot and with a layer of baked beans, which were off ration, was better than Ida's. She even invented a sort of wartime trifle made of all sorts of leftovers which the children named abracadabra, because it was so magically good.

*

In the summer of 1944 the chief thing that happened to Holly was that she and Chrissie began to talk a lot about boys, especially about Donald and Wishart. Holly was said to be Donald's girlfriend and Chrissie was Wishart's. They hardly knew, to begin with, what they meant by this, but it was grown-up, part of the bigger children's talk, all the muffled giggling and the squeaks of 'Oh, you never did!' from the playground corners.

They went self-consciously for walks as a four, then split into twos.

'Has Donald kissed you?' Chrissie asked, and her pink tongue poked out between her white teeth.

'No.'

'Wishart has me.'

'When?'

'Last evening he came round. We went in the hay loft.'

'What was it like?' Holly asked earnestly, her eyes round.

'Oh,' replied Chrissie, airily, 'just a kiss. *You* know.'

Holly pushed up her fringe in an effort to imagine. She thought of Fred and his kisses which were rather moist on her lips (closed) and sometimes inside her elbow.

She and Donald went for long walks in the woods, but kept a space between them. Up the path that climbed between the fir trees up and up, then, with a blaze of sun or a swipe of wind, depending on the weather, let you out on to the moor, dark, pitted with lochans, stretching to the flanks of the mountain, rimmed by sky, treetops below.

There was something in the way Donald talked that utterly engrossed Holly. She had always got on well with boys by joining in their pursuits like tree-climbing and fishing, but Donald liked to do other things. He collected and pressed leaves and wrote beautifully neat labels for them. He read lots of books and told her the stories and even if she had read them already herself, the story was different told his way. He had some old binoculars of his father's and they watched birds, entering with them into the centres of trees.

It didn't seem to make any difference that Donald was a boy, except he was stronger than her and said things in a way she would never have thought of, but liked and agreed with all the same. He confided in her that he meant to be an actor. A few weeks later he began to bring copies of plays for them to read aloud. There was a little pool, edged with red and green mosses, where they shared a rock seat and from here came the astonishing sounds of St Joan defying Cauchon or Gwen cheeking Algernon – except there was no one to be astonished, only the grouse grumbling, the rock pippits tweeting in the heather roots and the dishcloth, munching sheep. Holly thought Donald marvellously clever to be so different from everybody else. She had this extraordinary sensation of knowing him almost as well as herself, and yet feeling he was exciting because he was different. This did not make sense to her, and yet it was so.

The two talked often of their fathers. Holly could explain to Donald how muddled her thoughts were. The boy told her that he feared his father was not a prisoner, as Mrs Chisholm still desperately hoped, but would never come back. He said this with his eyes fixed on the topmost pine plumes jerking in the wind. Holly felt ashamed that her father had been appointed to a shore post and was safe. She needed to share risks with Donald.

*

For earlier that year Fred had been given a desk job at Portsmouth. His war record was outstanding, first on converted trawlers laying depth charges, then in the Atlantic, and most recently on the Russian convoys with a carrier. In the eyes of some he was the perfect officer – loyal, responsible, painstaking, with a friendly yet authoritative manner, neither ambitious nor subservient, equable. But some of the senior officers, particularly those who had belonged to the pre-war navy, were somewhat critical of Tickener. Not for what he did – that was copybook – but for his lack of a certain air. They all possessed a lofty, social manner verging on superciliousness. Even those in no position to know that Fred had begun at sixteen on the lower deck, sensed and resented a difference in him. He never put a foot wrong. You couldn't fault the chap's manner in the wardroom, his prompt payment of messing bills, his willingness to drink anyone under the table and yet be alert on duty. Nevertheless, there was something; hard to put your finger on, but there all right.

Fred himself was as aware of it as anyone. The shock of his arrival on his first wartime ship as an officer had been extreme, a body blow. He knew he was an outsider and always would be. He had come innocently to table and been thrown into the currents of class, rank, birth, schooling that ran there. His superiors had wives who were titled, or uncles who were admirals, a grandfather who had been a general; even, in one case, a prime minister. Of course, in wartime it all mattered less, the social layering. To some conscripts it meant nothing at all. Secure in the outside world they shrugged it off. Not Fred. He became known as a glutton for work, the steadiest gunnery officer under fire anyone had met, a man whose whole nature seemed a coiled rope of authority well exercised and discipline well received. His excellence made no whit of difference to the opinion of those who looked down on him, perhaps it even confirmed this opinion. He tried too hard. A direct and frank manner is not greatly useful in dealing with prejudice and snobbery, especially when it is concealed behind uniforms and service regulations. Fred, sitting at table, sensing some message being flashed down from man to man like a signal he could not read, felt goaded and cornered without knowing whom or what to blame. The navy was not to be criticised. His superiors were just that. He was a fighter with nothing to square up to.

His response was to strengthen those parts of his character that could defend him. Certainties became dogmas, self-pride verged on arrogance, and his high spirits, once his most charming characteristic, were channelled into heartiness.

On top of this were the horrors he had to encounter almost daily – deaths of shipmates, burns, mutilations. Injury to himself did not bear thinking about (as the phrase went on board) so Fred did not think of it. His own death was not allowed near his consciousness, however much it may have sapped his inner vitality.

He went home on leave in July, meaning to put away shipboard manners; but it was his loud, hollow laugh that Holly noticed first.

*

Donald made her lie down in the long grass in which tiny birch saplings were growing and a hawthorn, their branches tangling with the grass which grew tall, bleaching at the top because it was August. The smell of it was warm and dry; the seed heads dropped grains of white pollen on her hands. Higher in the sloping field was a rose bush long returned to briars whose probing stems infiltrated through the undergrowth of moss and tiny plants. Behind the rose was the stone wall of Lurgann, the children's house. The sky was cloudless; the sun glared in it so that Holly must shut her eyes if she looked up.

Donald kissed her on the mouth. She waited, tingling, wondering, and was surprised at the dryness of his lips, their soft warmth, as of tissue paper, smooth.

Donald was overcome with this kiss, their first. The space between him and Holly, as he sat, knees hunched, beside her seemed to be shimmering. He felt sweetness and a kind of awe. The boy and girl inspected each other's face, solemnly. They were for a long while content with one kiss, drawing mentally apart and considering it, happily. After a long pause, they turned, as if to an unheard signal, and he pressed his closed lips firmly on hers again, only parting his lips slightly as he drew away with a soft, smacking sound.

'Do you like to kiss, Holly?'

'Yes. Do you?'

He flung himself down on his back.

'Yep.'

She thought this a very manly word.

'You smell nice,' he told her, after staring at the treetop and squinting at the sun for some minutes, 'like sweeties, a bit, and soap.'

Donald thought Holly very pretty, and had inspected her frequently that year to see if her breasts were growing. Lately he could make out small swellings under her aertex blouse.

'I'm growing hair,' he told her.

'Where?' She was astonished.

– 67 –

'You know.'

'No, I don't. Where?'

He dragged down his shorts and indicated a faint fuzz.

'Is that what happens when boys start to be men?'

'Yes.'

'Like girls get –'

'Yes.'

'Is that all that happens?'

'No, your johnny gets stiff sometimes.'

'So it can go inside someone, you mean?'

'Yes. One day,' he added with an anxious glance.

'Oh yes, one day,' she agreed willingly.

He put his arm under her shoulder and together they stared and winked at the leaves overhead and the sun beyond.

'Lurgann could be our home one day,' she said.

'Yep. I could mend it all right. Then I'd go to work and you could stay here and do the cooking.'

'No. Ladies who stay at home complain too much. I want a job, like you.'

'What sort of job?'

'I could be an actor like you, couldn't I?'

'Actress. Yes, you could. Then we'd travel round all the theatres together.'

'And come back to Lurgann sometimes.'

She arched her neck and tipped back her head so that she could see the roofless cottage upside down. She imagined the door painted blue and cups with rosebuds on.

'Shall I kiss you again?'

'Yes please, Donald.'

Holly's eyes remained wide open and she saw his face come down and be distorted by nearness. The smooth dryness of his lips surprised her again.

When it was time to go, they went by different routes, although a hundred times before they had been alone at Lurgann and returned together.

She met Fred as she came into the farmyard and felt a cold hand grip her insides. Why is it, she asked herself, that grown-ups can spoil things just by the way they look at you? She found no answer but a guilt she hadn't known she possessed.

'Mooning up at that ruin again?' he asked in a hostile voice.

'Yes – no!'

'Make up your mind, Holly.'

*

Fred had three weeks' leave and the family spent a fortnight of it at St Andrew's, recommended by Hamish who had a cousin who ran a hotel there.

Holly observed that war altered holidays as well as everything else. Like Sandalcliff, St Andrew's had a long sandy beach but there was no other similarity. The stone town was withdrawn, its back to the sea, and the inhabitants provided no donkeys, beach huts, sand races or toy boat regattas. Indeed there was no park or pond or promenade and the swimming-pool was built into some hollowed rocks and fed by the tide. There was seaweed to tangle her thrashing legs, crabs to catch toes and salt mouthfuls for Hugh when he went under despite his water-wings and Fred's exasperated, imprecise instructions. Shouting, he ran awkwardly on the slimy rocks.

The Tickeners stayed with Hamish's cousin, a Mrs Spens, whose house was in South Street and called itself a private hotel.

'But it's only a glorified boarding-house,' said Lucille.

The bedrooms were crammed with extra folding beds and cots, and the guests ate at long tables. A fat waitress struggled between the chairs and the walls, trailing a smell of sweat a few paces behind her. Her trays were stacked with plates of wartime food – sausage and potato pie, onion and cheese mash which was brown on top so you were lucky if served one of the first, also haggis which tasted only of oatmeal, and woody beetroots in a watery white sauce. Pudding was either spotted dick or jam roly-poly with custard that had a foam on top due to the powdered milk it was made from. The smell of these meals clung to the downstairs rooms with an acidic greasiness. The upper rooms were scented with mothballs and damp and cheap soap.

From their windows the Tickeners had a view of the wide street and the gateway to a ruined abbey. It was often raining and the children looked down on red and green segmented golf umbrellas. They spent a lot of time in their bedrooms, either reading or playing snakes and ladders until the rain stopped, when they would go out to the khaki sand which was dented with footprints of all sorts – boots, sandals, brogues, dogs, seagulls – and flourished with trailing messages like 'I Love Lucy'.

– 69 –

It was a beautiful beach fading into a silvery blue flat distance but marred by wooden posts planted all over it to stop gliders from landing. Limpets and velvet seaweed stands clung to the bottom of these posts. They never walked right to the end because Lucille would not take off her high-heeled sandals to walk barefoot. The sand was cold, she said.

On the other side of the town, below the abbey ruins, was a harbour and cliffs. Holly liked the way the waves slapped the rocks and sucked back on themselves pulling in little stones and slippery broad ribbons of seaweed.

It could have been a nice holiday, if only Daddy had been Daddy or she had been herself. They had both looked forward to St Andrew's and thought of each other there with love, imagining something like Sandalcliff, in mood at least.

When Fred thought of before the war his memories flipped back to Holly's birth that had helped him endure the worst days of his marriage and the loss of the sea. Like the turning pages of a photograph album the years sprang from past to present, showing him her babyhood and early childhood, the chubby cheeks, the wet kisses, the abandoned giggles as she rolled on the floor playing bears with him, the first words and the earnest, commanding looks that went with them imploring him to understand and make the contact last, then her first questions and the adorable acceptance of all he told her, the little female's steady blue gaze. He could run over too, her first days at school and the teacher's commendations of her intelligence, his pride in her which was fierce and renewed his love along with his ambitions. To deepen and balance Holly's childhood, he had indistinct memories of his own – his father's face concealed behind a newspaper, Maud in a fury of piety, the soft cloth of his mother's dress pressed to his face. He loved Holly the more because he had saved her from any experiences like that.

For her part Holly could see only an interrupted spool of memory pictures mostly drawn from the last summer at Mitcham. Fred stood there in the sunlight, enormous, full-faced, smiling at her like a kindly tower, wrinking his forehead, holding out his hand. He was the mainspring of her life. Donald was nothing but the palest copy of Fred and in the train going to St Andrew's the boy's image had faded away. She chattered all the way, whether the two grown-ups listened or not. For the most part Lucille, wearing her most composed expression, looked out of the window, twisting her head this way and that with slightly flared nostrils.

'Pretty little place,' she said from time to time, when the train stopped at a country station with a few geraniums in old buckets painted red. She was less happy with the hotel.

'I could write my name in the dust under the beds,' she said.

'Why should you want to write there?' asked Holly.

'Don't be pert!' Fred, irritated by Lucille's ability to find fault, turned on the child. He looked under the bed and saw a gigantic violet chamber pot furred with grey fluff.

'Well,' continued Holly, used to several years' licence at the farm, 'I can't see any reason to write your name on the floor. Especially not under a bed.'

'Shut up, will you, Holly,' said Fred calmly and coldly.

'And the window cord is broken,' went on Lucille. 'If you pushed the bottom up it could easily come down on a child's head.'

Anyone sensible would notice the broken cord, thought Holly, and not dream of sticking their head out, but she said no more, inspecting her father under her eyelashes. He was looking baffled.

He continued that way, baffled and cross but aiming in fits and starts for jolly holiday manners. Fred, the unselfconscious man, the patient forger ahead, the drowner of all that worried, was being edged towards some sort of analysis and fighting back. Lucille too, was aware her life was changing and not only because with their Mitcham home bombed and Tikki an officer she would never resume her pre-war life. The loneliness at Balchraggan, and, more, the unbearable cheated look of the widows' faces, had altered her, developing a sharpness, a shallow disillusion. Holly, entering adolescence, faced without knowledge many changes and yet was tied hand and foot to her father. Of the Tickener family only Hugh was not in a period of transition. His mild, friendly nature and lack of passionate wants protected him as he sat on the outskirts of their squabbles.

One rainy afternoon Fred shouldered depression aside and suggested they go out for a nice tea somewhere.

'You can't have cream teas just for the asking nowadays!' It pleased Lucille to underline the nastiness of civilian war.

'We'll see what we can do,' replied Fred easily, secure in his ability to manage his wife.

Lucille was really glad to go out. She put on her hat with a veil and smiled at Fred who was wearing a grey tweed suit with a blue shirt and a blue tie, brown lace-up shoes and brown leather gloves. He had never had such good clothes or been more well-set, in every way. She was proud to be with him.

'Ready, Daddy?' cried Holly, rolling off the bed where she had been reading.

'Holly can't go to a tea shop in shorts,' said Fred.

'Why not, for the Lord's sake?'

'Hasn't she got a frock?'

'Don't call it that,' said the child, rudely.

'Isn't it a frock you wear?' he demanded icily.

'No. A dress.'

'Good God! A frock, a dress, what's the difference?'

'Frock is a horrid, horrid word.'

Fred's bright blue eyes bulged. He could not believe this.

'The only dress she has is the green silk I made over from Ida's,' said Lucille who was quite used to Holly and her vagaries. 'There's no real need for dresses at Balchraggan.'

'I don't agree at all. Little girls should be in frocks. To tell the truth, Lucille, I have been quite upset since I came back at how the children look.'

It was clear from his face that this reproach had been simmering in Fred for days. His jaw was flushed, and he wriggled his shoulders impatiently. 'They look grubby, down-at-heel, common.'

'Common!' Nothing could have offended Lucille more.

'I want my children properly turned out, at all times.'

'Per regulation,' she mocked. 'Don't come the three stripe officer with me, Fred Tickener.'

Holly felt a piercing pity for her mother.

'Shorts are perfectly OK for all I do,' she said, helpfully.

'And that's another thing. There's too much slang. And playing about with boys.'

'Boys are a damned sight more interesting than girls,' announced Holly, defiantly using one of Donald's better expressions.

'Holly, will you stop interrupting?'

'Yes, darling, don't interfere.'

'Children should be seen and not heard. That's what I was taught. Don't you know that?'

'I think that's a silly old saying and –'

'I don't care a tinker's arse what you think, my girl. Shut up!'

This was much worse to Holly than a slap. For Daddy to say

such rude words to her! She curled up inside her defiant body.

'You are being a bit old-fashioned,' remarked Lucille mildly. 'Seen and not heard is rather old hat.'

'None the worse for that. Ida and I learned more manners from Maud than Holly has forgotten.'

'Please don't criticise the way I have managed,' said Lucille with dignity. 'I didn't ask to be dumped at Balchraggan – and I notice you don't get on so famously well with Maud yourself.'

There was a pause which crackled with the painful thoughts of three people. Hugh was humming gently to himelf, shaking the dice of his snakes and ladders set, then tracing down the snakes with his finger, sucking a thumb.

'Come on, old prickly-puss,' said Fred to Holly. 'Say you're sorry.'

'Sorry for what?' she muttered.

He looked at her, sadly summoning up the child he had imagined at sea in his cabin, pretty and docile.

'It's you should be sorry, for calling me and Hughie common.'

'What does it mean, common?' asked the boy, taking his thumb out of his mouth to ask and jamming it back again.

'It means sucking your thumb, you baby you! And barging through doors like Holly does, and not saying thank you. As for those torn jerseys they play in!' He added to Lucille.

'They tear them playing,' she said in a heavy voice, contemptuous of how little he understood these children she had been left with. 'They don't put rags on every morning. What an idea!'

'All I know is they look like street arabs.'

'What's that?' asked Hugh, imperturbably.

'Are we going out or not?' Lucille wanted to salvage the afternoon. Eventually Holly changed into the green, smocked dress she hated and they found a real hotel which gave them a tea with a saucerful of biscuits, and pallid icecreams for the children. The hotel was beside the links and Holly stared forlornly at the view of grey waves coming in sideways, and marram grasses arched down by the wind.

Fred regained his hearty voice, for there was no use dwelling on things. 'Shall we pay a visit to the toy shop on the way back?'

This was a sort of saying sorry, thought Holly scornfully.

'Yes, please,' said Hugh.

'What would you like?'

'An aeroplane.'

'Not a ship?'

'No.'

Fred stared pointedly at him.

'No thank you, Daddy.'

'Can I have a book?' asked Holly.

'You can. The question is *may* you.'

'May I have a book please, dear Daddy.'

Fred ignored, or did not notice, her sarcasm.

'Bookworm,' said Hugh, taught by Bruce and Bob.

'What about a dolly?'

'Daddy!' Contempt for dolls filled her childish face. Fred remembered he had brought her one home.

At the shop there wasn't much choice of books or toys. Hugh found a paper cut out of a plane and was approximately satisfied although he knew he could not make it alone. Holly chose a book with a dark blue cover and silver writing on the spine. She sniffed the lovely clean smell of new paper and print. It seemed to be about a girl and her horse.

Fred took it in his lordly, overseeing way, and put it down.

'Three and sixpence! For a book!'

'I think they mostly are,' said Holly, helpfully.

Fred inspected a few others. 'I meant a comic really,' he said, 'not a book. *Sunny Stories*, how about that?'

'You didn't! You didn't mean a comic. You said book, distinctly. Didn't he Mummy?'

'Oh, don't drag me into your quarrels.'

Holly was hot with anger, not so much at losing the book but at Fred being mean. 'You just spent three shillings on a measly tea.'

He was affronted. 'What the bill says is my business. Do you want *Sunny Stories*?'

'It's for babies.'

'Then you'll have nothing. Put that down.' She was hugging the book. 'I'm getting very tired of your manners.' This was said not in a tired voice, but in one charged with held down energy.

Holly slammed the book on the counter and raced out of the shop. Fred gave an angry shout. She belted ahead, eyes full of tears, and butted a man, who was strolling along with his dog, full in the stomach causing him to stagger backwards and knock against some vegetables displayed outside a shop on upturned wooden boxes. One after the other, they toppled, scattering cabbages, turnips, potatoes which rolled into the gutter swimming with muddy rain water. The shopkeeper, with the man and his dog, stared after Holly in angry disbelief. She was unaware of what had happened, only mortified by the accident of plummeting into a man's squidgey, fat tummy.

Fred was obliged to apologise all round, and to help set up the crates again. Hugh picked turnips out of the road and was smacked for getting water on his best grey shorts. Lucille stood aloof in the bookshop. Very quietly, when the bookseller was in the doorway giving Fred advice on shaking mud out of cabbages, Lucille took the book Holly wanted and put it in her handbag, the big one Tikki had brought her from – wherever it was he'd been.

Eventually Fred looked round for his wife and saw her standing in the bookshop in her brown linen jacket and pert hat, leaning on her furled umbrella. She looked so ladylike and untroubled, it almost removed his bad temper, until he remembered how out of hand she had allowed Holly to become.

Holly had stopped running, and managed to control her tears. As she came to the boarding-house, Mrs Spens was just letting herself in carrying an oilskin bag of onions. She invited the child to come down to her basement kitchen, then to help her peel the onions. She offered her a pair of goggles, and put some on herself; they helped to stop one crying over the peeling, she said. Holly found they gave the kitchen a look of being underwater, green and dim, with darker patches in the corner. Was that a giant crab lurking behind the rocking chair?

'That's pretty smocking,' said Mrs Spens, tying an apron under Holly's armpits to protect her clothes.

'I think it's babyish.'

'Oh, I don't know.'

'It is. when you are nearly twelve you don't wear baby's dresses or read *Sunny Stories*.'

'You read a lot?'

'They call me a bookworm,' she said, half proudly, half resentfully. 'If I'm not reading I'm helping Hamish or climbing my tree.'

'Tomboy, are you?'

'That's what they all say. And chatterbox.'

Mrs Spens smiled in agreement.

'And butter-fingers.'

'Why that?'

'I can't catch balls and I drop things when I help wash up.'

'Everyone does.'

'Do they?'

'You watch. Just see how often a grown-up drops a plate.'

'Yes, I will.'

Holly felt better. She was experiencing a remission from unhappiness.

'What are the onions for?'

'Our meal tonight. I fry them with potatoes and a bit of liver, minced. Liver's off ration, you see.' She spoke brightly enough but looked tired.

'It must be a lot of work feeding all of us.'

'It's my job, dearie.'

'Where is Mr Spens? Is he at sea or a soldier?'

'He has passed on.'

Holly was uncertain she understood this, so she waited.

'He was gassed in the first do, and died of bronchitis the year after the Abdication.'

Holly, who had a gasmask, had never thought about gassing. 'What did the gas do?'

'Filled the poor fellow's lungs up with muck.'

'Did the Germans do that?'

'We did the same to them.'

'I thought British soldiers didn't do bad things.'

'Fought clean, you mean. You should've seen my man when he came back from the Somme. He went out tall as an oak tree, and strong! He could lift me over his head. When he got back he was like a bit of rubbish on the high-tide line.'

Holly pushed her fringe off her forehead with both oniony hands. She had never had a grown-up conversation before. Her hair stuck up in spikes from her head, increasing her air of astonished intelligence.

'What was the Abdication?'

'What? Oh – nothing to do with us folks. I just remember it were then my Fred died.'

'Fred?'

'To tell the honest truth, I'm not sorry he went when he did. He couldn't have borne to see this lot, not after he'd given his lungs to that one what was to end war. So they promised us.'

Holly peeled the brown skin off another onion. She said, almost to herself, 'My Daddy is all right.'

'You thank your lucky stars.'

'I do. Except – well, he's changed, Mrs Spens.' Holly expressed this awful fact absolutely plainly for the first time.

'Ay, people change and that's a fact.'

Holly saw Mrs Spens was too tired to waste words putting you off, as Mummy did.

'I don't know your Dad, but he seems a nice man from what I can gather.'

'Oh yes! He's strong and clever and brave, and everyone likes him, Mummy says.'

'Well, then.'

'Yes.' Holly brooded. Already the clear details of what Fred had said and done were fading. She was left with a sick feeling. Was it because Daddy had let her down? Or was it because she had been rude?

The onions were finished. Holly took off the goggles and the kitchen reappeared in harsh grey detail. Mrs Spens began to peel a box of potatoes, sitting comfortably with her knees apart. She was a large, fat lady. Mr Spens, if he were alive, could not have picked her up at all far.

Holly was calmed by the quiet noises of the kitchen, a kettle simmering and singing, a cat's tiny yawn. Out the back a drying green could be seen, a seagull perched on a post.

Mrs Spens told her she had once visited Balchraggan when Hamish's father had been alive. Holly flushed with pleasure to share what she loved. They began to speak of the farm.

The door opened with a crash that jarred the plates on the dresser. 'Holly! go upstairs at once,' said Fred. He turned to Mrs Spens, 'I am sorry indeed that she should come barging in like this.'

'That's no matter, Commander Tickener, I like the child fine.'

'My apologies all the same.'

Holly was sent to bed for running out of the shop, for butting the man, for spilling the vegetables, and all her accumulated rudeness of the day. So she had no onion, liver and potato pie, only a tummy ache of misery. She heard Fred say to Lucille, '– with a

– 77 –

dirty great apron tied round her sitting with that gross woman chatting like a fishwife!'

'Tikki, must you?'

'What the hell does that mean? Don't you care about Holly's manners?'

'I just can't understand you this leave. It's as if you didn't like the child.'

'Nonsense. She has to learn what's what and who's who.' Then, slowly as always with Fred, the meaning of her words came to him. 'How can you say such a thing? Not like my own daughter! Not love Holly!' He fixed her with a glare of extreme seriousness, and warning. 'I think you must be feeling off colour, Lucille.'

'Just tired of it all,' she said, as if casually, and ran the tap to wash her hands.

Fred had noticed these moods of wilful weariness that came over his wife, and disliked them, though he did not admit as much to himself just felt a grudging resentment.

'Holly means no harm,' went on Lucille. 'She's only little.'

'As to that – I'm not so sure. Have you noticed her – er – figure, lately.'

'Surely not? Nothing's happened yet.'

Fred flushed and so did Lucille. Both were embarrassed at any mention of sexuality, however veiled.

That night Holly hardly slept. She lay in the ugly bedroom watching the shapes of the furniture emerge with the light, feeling round the horrible misery that was inside her, ugly and half-hidden as the cliff-like wardrobe with its eerily reflecting panel of mirror. She loved Daddy with all her heart, and it wouldn't be possible for her to think bad things of him. (She forgot she had condemned him already for greed and meanness.) Yet he stood up against her and she couldn't catch hold of herself any more. She seemed to fade away. If his approval did not support her, she was not there. She should not be there.

Very early in the morning she dressed and went out, creeping down the worn beige carpet on the stairs and along the linoleum to the front door. She passed through the gateway of the abbey and into its grounds which were half-park, half-railed off enclosure. In the centre was St Rule's Tower, not a ruin like the rest, indeed climbable on payment of two pennies. The man, however, was not there and Holly had no money in any case, so she climbed instead to the top of the boundary wall, and lay on her stomach half under an overhanging tree and gave herself up to the channelled grief of a child, which is not the less bitter for being based on ignorance.

Her thoughts revolved a handful of images again and again – those of Fred in a nasty temper with her, Fred despising her way of thinking and her likes, imposing his on her. He spoke rudely, calling her dirty, and butter-fingers! But Mrs Spens had been right. She remembered he had broken his pipe stem in the train. In fact, Fred's breaking pipe stems was quite a frequent happening. He had a drawer of broken pipes as well as a rack of usable ones and a best one wrapped in chamois leather. This one had a little hinged lid, punched with holes, to stop the wind getting in at sea on the bridge. She knew and loved everything about him. If he did not like her – she shouldn't be here.

She jumped down from the wall and went back to the tower which fascinated her, rearing up so clear and dark red into the morning sky. The doorman had arrived.

'If I bring tuppence later, can I go up the tower now?' she asked in the bold way that came naturally to her.

'Children's free,' he said without looking at her as he set out his postcards.

The staircase turned round and round in the square tower. Her knees felt trembly and she panted, yet hardly noticed this she was so preoccupied with the flinty misery inside her. On the top was a new world – a cold, flat sea and small town, the ground below spotted with gravestones and litter baskets that looked squashed. She saw and noted in a disconnected way, saw and did not see because for the first time in her life she was grappling with a self-consciousness grown so monstrously guilty it stood beside her much more real than anything, rather as an imaginary Fred had stood at her shoulder for years, only this personage, instead of reinforcing and helping her, was destructive.

'I am not happy,' she whispered to herself. A terrible fact. It was her childish way of saying, more accurately, the pettish adult's 'life is not worth living.'

She was completely alone, as if the world below her was as empty as it looked.

Donald had once written a composition about pirates that the Dominie had read to the class. The final scene had described the villain thrown off the cliffs. Donald had written, 'he looked like a meaty pancake, not cooked.' This had secretly amused the teacher and impressed the class, but Holly now dwelt with horror on the bloody flat object with arms and legs sticking out like a trodden starfish. As she leant over the parapet there was a misty hole in her head to balance the stone in her chest. If her head grew heavy again, as normal, she was sure she would topple over, but it would not matter. Her unhappiness muffled her, cutting out time, space, reason.

*

Fred had also woken early, before Lucille, and had gone for a stroll to find a newspaper. He was glad to think that the holiday was working for him, relaxing his over-tensed nerves. For the first time for months he was in surroundings he could bear to observe. It was a nice enough town, a bit unreal in its distance from the war. The sun on the stone was pleasant but he much preferred the warm bricks of London. He lifted his head to sniff the air, as if he might catch a whiff of the city, for he only felt quite at home there. The sea no longer soothed him; he was too likely to see wreckage or bodies floating in the troughs of the waves. His eyes ached with the thousand days' scanning of tipping horizons in the arctic half-light, through snow or mist; if he closed his eyes, he saw jagged holes torn in the sides of ships, the metal bent inwards and fire-blackened, hoses snaking over pitching decks, dead bodies in heaps against the bulwarks, slithering in blood pools as the ship rolled.

He opened his eyes now on the sunlit harbour. Although nothing like Sandalcliff, it reminded him of early morning walks there with Holly. Silly kid! What had got into her? He walked round the harbour, planting his feet down with a sailor's steady gait that looks slow and lazy but is neither. The cottages climbed the hillside and the abbey tower rose above them. At Sandalcliff the houses had been red and cream and hadn't there been some sort of fun-fair helter-skelter at the top one year? He had taken Holly up and come down on a mat with her on his lap, her firm body lying trustfully against him even while she gave yelps of apprehension. His arm muscles tightened now as if to hug her.

Well, what did she want?

In his cabin he had thought almost as often of Holly as of Lucille. No. That wasn't true. Couldn't be. The truth was he censored his thoughts about his wife.

It was one of his tasks to go through the men's mail, censoring any mention of their position – although, God in heaven, the Huns knew to a bloody furlong where they all were, the poor devils in ships consigned to convoy duty, sitting ducks, forced to go at the pace of the slowest merchantman. But it was his job to erase with blue crayon all mention of ice, Ruskies or midnight sun. His steady, pale eyes skimmed the awkward handwriting of the sailors, expertly picking out the facts but also being forced, however briefly, to read what the men said more intimately to their wives and girls. His own letters were as chaste as Maud's might have been; his thoughts were hardly less puritan – where Lucille was concerned. He saw no harm in cuddling little Holly. Sometimes he bathed her and held her in the towel afterwards, or played games with her toes and fingers, making the teddy bear run up her thigh or her arm.

His broad face softened. He walked up towards the tower happily remembering how Holly used to meet him from work on her tricycle, furiously ringing the bell so that he noticed her as he came off the bus in a press of men wearing bowlers like himself. As if he could have missed her! a little girl with a fringe, black as coal, and a masterfully loving smile.

'Did you guess Mummy would let me come today? I was sure she would because I got a pair of cherries in my bowl.'

'Is that lucky, my puss?'

'Extremely.' (A new word, proudly said.) 'Don't you know *that*? I hung them on my ear and kept them to last.'

He had taken her thick little hand and she had steered with the other occasionally making believe to run the front wheels into him, though nothing in the world would have made her hurt him in reality.

At home, tie loosened, jacket off, he'd gone to look at his sweet-peas. In the early summer they found dead fledglings on the concrete path fallen from sparrows' nests in the gutters. These had distressed Holly until Fred told her that, if he put them in the golden rod clump by the coal shed, their mothers would find them and make them well.

'Look Daddy – put the poor birdy in the golden rod,' she'd cry and give satisfied nods as he did so. Good kid!

He used to be able to talk to Holly, he told himself, better than to many adults. She listened. She never got him wrong. In his mind's eye he saw her loving, upward glance as they walked along hand in hand.

'Daddy, if the earth is turning round, why doesn't the window go round to where the door is?'

He had bought a cheap tin globe and, using the table lamp for the sun, had explained to her. He could see now the flower blue of her eyes (what flower? borage perhaps, he thought), and smell the hot tin, and feel her body pressed confidently against him. A deep breath of love for her filled him.

A few more paces brought him into the abbey grounds, sharp with morning sun and shadow. The grass had recently been cut. There were stripes between the beds of salvias – not a plant Fred cared for. The man who sold the tickets for the tower sat by the door on a folding, slatted chair, stroking a cat.

'That your kid?' he asked, jerking his head. Fred looked up and saw Holly standing on the parapet against a sagging wire fixed in loops to leaning stanchions. She was looking down, head drooping.

He knew immediately that he must not startle her or she might be catapulted through the wire. He started to pelt up the steps, getting slower and slower but forcing, forcing himself on. Holly must have heard him, heard someone's footsteps, for she had got down from the edge and was standing watching the doorway as he emerged from the roof.

'Holly, dar-ling! you mustn't – climb – up there. It's dangerous.' Pants cut up his words.

She stared, in a state of shock herself.

'Don't you – realise – you could – fall?'

'Yes. I might fall.'

What an odd look on her face. Where'd he seen that sort of look before?

'A fall from here would be no joke,' he said more easily.

Holly saw he had no idea. His face said only worry and love. She watched almost with pity.

Fred meanwhile was taking in her colourless eyes and the taut muscles of her cheeks. He remembered where he'd seen the look – in a pilot on the carrier who had refused to fly after one bad mission and then – Ridiculous! Children didn't . . . did they?

'Come on Holly, little prickle-puss, you're not still angry are you? New morning: new deal.'

He wrinkled his forehead at her, and pink ridges sprang on the smooth brow. She could not help a tiny smile.

'That's better. Now, what's the matter?' He put his arm round her and together they looked down on the town. He knew he must go gently. 'Aren't you very happy?' he asked.

Fred meant this to signify only an understanding that Holly was a little out of sorts with the world, but the child had until now considered happiness an obligation – Happy Christmas, happy holidays, happy birthday, many happy returns of the day – and would never dream of saying she wasn't happy without the worst of punishments following. How kind and wonderful of Daddy to guess! She twisted into his chest and admitted fuzzily, through tears, 'No, I'm not.'

Now something would happen and Daddy be himself again. All the painful heaviness in her chest and the arrows of dislike she had shafted for him would fall to the ground, harmless. He would follow up her admission with some answer – but what could it possibly be? – some marvellous, father's explanation. His forgiveness that would make the world bright again.

'There, there,' said Fred.

She waited expectantly. He fished in his pocket for a clean handkerchief with a blue **A** in the corner and tucked it in against her wet face.

'Come on now,' he said, 'what's the trouble, puss?'

But she had told him. She was not happy. Nothing was worse than that.

'There, there.'

She leant against him, her sobs subsiding. She grew still and her cheeks prickled uncomfortably against his jacket. But she did not want to draw away, to face him, to go on as before without the marvellous relief she still faintly hoped he could give.

'Look at the sea,' said Fred.

She did so, avoiding his eye.

'Remember Sandalcliff and the orange cream biscuits?'

'Chocolate usually,' she corrected, rather unwillingly. Daddy was making everything ordinary again without curing her pain.

'We'll go back after the war.'

Red spades shining in the sun came fresh as their paint to her mind, and the purplish jellyfish wavering in the green water, the smell of tar melting between the planks.

'You'll like that, eh?' Tenderly he kissed her forehead, pushing up the damp, crumpled fringe.

'It isn't the same here, is it?' he enquired.

'Nothing's the same,' said Holly, bitterly.

'Is that the trouble?'

Eagerly she scanned his face in case he had understood after all. He wore his usual friendly, open expression, the blue eyes like her own in the deep shadow of their bushy eyebrows. No, he didn't know.

'Sort of,' she replied.

'It's changed for me too,' he told her. 'That's what growing up is.'

'But you grew up ages ago!'

'I am not sure when a person really grows up, Holly,' he said heavily. This was about as far as Fred could go in analysis. 'It's more like things change around you but you stay the same.'

'Oh.'

'Yes, I don't think people change much, Holly.'

'Things get finished though.'

'Yes, a lot is finished.'

A feeling of doom struck her as he spoke. Did Daddy need help and comfort, just like Mummy did sometimes? She rallied her forces.

'A lot's to come though – good things. It'll be exciting after the war.'

'Yes, and to start with – breakfast,' said Fred with an attempt at lightness, but his look was still strained. He and Holly communicated wordlessly for the space of time it took a seagull to rise from the buoy at the harbour mouth and fly to perch on the flagpole of the tower, then they began to go slowly down the steps, Holly leaning from above on Fred's shoulders testing out his strength and balance, pressing down, then drawing back. Both of them liked this feeling, the mutual protection, the ambiguity of support.

4

INTERLUDE

After the summer holidays another autumn, winter, spring climbed into the distance. Lucille survived the long year by concentrating on each moment and her placing in it. After five years she still painted her nails and made up her face for breakfast. The way her heels tapped on the stone floors irritated Ida but was a tonic for Lucille; it announced she knew where she was going – even if she did not no one would guess. It was true the family were mostly taken in by her smart, gay, brisk manner. All the same they were glad when she sat down to read and stopped projecting herself at them.

She read a lot, having no false pride in taking books Holly brought into the house. They discovered many things and this drew them together. Holly liked to sit beside her mother reading. Under her consciousness taking in the story, was a deeper apprehension of Lucille, partly a protective adult, but much more a vulnerable friend.

In the spring of 1945 the war faded out of their lives. V E Day sent a surge of excitement through the Highlands but it was an ebbing tide. The fighting on the other side of the world was hard to believe in or remember, the May sunshine fell so complete and whole across the hillsides, and probed deep the golden, glassy rivers. Forests, which could seem sinister in winter, were then newly leaved and cut through by glades of light, places of green and quiet simplicity.

Lucille began to dream of the home she would soon have in London and the foreign stations she would visit with Tikki. She went to furniture auctions, picked up new ideas from magazines, and talked colour schemes with Milly who was similarly planning a new home with her returned husband. Lucille hardly noticed the summer pass lost in her effervescent future.

When the new bombs were dropped and *The Scotsman* was full of diagrams and technical explanations, Donald, then fifteen, was at his lordliest. Even Hamish listened when he explained to them how atoms were split, what heavy water was, and so on. But on the day when there was a celebration meal at the farm for the final end of war, an argument flared over the ethics of nuclear power. Those who understood least, said most. Maud was hot against all science. She had dressed herself that day in royal blue satin with strings of jet. Her pendulous cheeks were damp and scarlet.

'If God had wanted us to –'

'You said that about aeroplanes,' Ida interrupted her. 'I remember clearly. You said, if God wanted us to fly he would have given us wings.'

'And was I wrong, my girl?' asked Maud, her chest heaving. 'With London bombed to pieces.'

'I can see all kinds of good coming from this,' said Hamish. 'There'll be cheap fuel, atomic motor cars running almost for nothing, central heating for us all. Think of that Lucille!' he added slyly.

Lucille came out of her daydream enough to smile at him. She was thinking intensely of Tikki's return. Her fingers were rasping on the woven metallic ribbon on his sleeve, four rows of it; she was seeing his face beneath the peak of a cap with oak leaves on.

When the actual day arrived she was dizzy with anticipation. To savour the moment when her proper life began again, she stayed upstairs. Outside the windows hung the overbearing green slopes, and she dared a small, triumphant grin at them – you can't get me now. Downstairs the children were running in and out of the door, and Maud sat hunched watching for her boy.

'Come on down, Mummy,' Hugh called.

But she was the princess in the tower, waiting.

When the taxi appeared at the lane end she even went into the bedroom and shut the door. It was absurd to feel shy of Tikki, but for an instant the future hung so huge above her head that she feared it. If only she could stop time, hold this moment forever in her hands – she alone, but his voice in the distance, happiness just about to shower around her. It was like her wedding day.

Fred took the stairs two at a time and caught his wife in an iron hug. His dear, sweet, precious little Lucie! How fragile and pretty she was! How he needed her! Thank God, thank *God* this war was over.

Lucille pulled gently away from him, kissed his dry brown cheeks, looking at him with demure and luminous eyes. Here she was at last! In all her beautiful freshness and into her brown eyes creeping that hint of criticism that was, for him, the spice to her tenderness.

'You are not in uniform,' she told him in a shaded voice.

'No,' he agreed firmly. He added a bold smile. 'I have put that away for ever.' He drew a deep breath as she went suddenly still. 'For ever, Lucie love.'

She had understood at once.

'*What?*'

She walked backwards away from him until she came up against the window, where she put her palms on the cold glass.

'You have played me the same trick.'

Anger flooded through his body and drained away again as they stood apart. Then familiar, soothing pity for her returned.

'You are throwing away all I have ever wanted,' she said clearly.

He had known she wouldn't like it, had hoped to break it more gently. 'It's my life,' he said and tried a wary smile.

'And mine,' she flashed. 'How about asking me?'

'Well, naturally, I took everything into consideration.'

'Like hell you did!'

He took a pace back, affronted by this sort of language from her.

'A man has to come to his own decisions,' he said in a grandiose voice.

Lucille slumped back on the window while he walked up and down the room a few times. Then, as he passed her, she held out a hand, 'Tikki darling! Let's not quarrel. You've only just got home.'

He grasped her tight, only too glad to bury the moment. She fluttered her eyelashes against his cheek and murmured, 'Butterfly kisses. Remember?'

Fred relaxed. She was going to be sensible. No scenes. 'How I've missed you.'

She let him lead her to the bed where she lay in his arms, apparently soft and compliant. After a while they spoke of never being separated again.

'There's a possible house I've seen in Norwood,' he then ventured to the top of her head, half-expecting an eruption.

'Oh no,' she replied calmly, luxuriously, 'I need to be somewhere much more romantic.'

She propped herself on an elbow and smiled down at him as beguilingly as she knew how. Fred kissed her for some time, utterly charmed by her all over again, this fragile, childish, flower girl.

'Yes, somewhere much more romantic,' she repeated.

'Such as?' he muttered.

'Well, if you decide to stay in the service – '

'Get that idea out of your head.'

He sat up, slipping awkwardly against the bolster. She sat up too, steadying herself, knowing this was a crisis point.

'Listen for once to me,' she commanded.

A mulish expression settled on his face and he folded his arms with a discourteous show of patience.

'You love the sea,' she began. 'Your letters are full of nothing but the sea and the navy.'

'The war – '

'Is over. And look how well you've done! A captain after the start you had, Tikki darling. It's miraculous, even Ida says so.'

'Fat lot she cares,' he muttered like a sulky lad.

'Not only that – just think how you hated selling cars.'

He frowned, his arms fell to his sides.

'I remember you coming home smelling of the train and sweat, and that ugly red rim on your forehead where the bowler cut in. It used to last half the evening. We never had enough money for anything nice.'

'Well, hang it, Lucie, I used – '

'Nothing really nice, Tikki. And that dreadful little house. How glad I am it was blown to smithereens.'

'Norwood is – '

'But I don't want to live in the suburbs and be a salesman's wife again.'

'Who said anything about a salesman?' he asked. 'I have several other leads to follow. Now I'm an officer in the R.N.'

'I'm so proud of you! You are so handsome and young still. And so am I. Look at me, Tikki.'

He did, fondly.

'I don't deserve to be buried alive, not after all these years here. We can go abroad and have fun, have some real life now!'

Foreign places had never appealed to Fred. It was the sea he loved and England.

'I've had enough of abroad,' he told her.

'Not with me you haven't. You've never had a wife on foreign station with you.'

'Oh, Lucie,' he sighed gently.

A year after the war's end most of the wartime men would have gone and the regular officers would be reasserting their codes of etiquette, probing all Fred's social weaknesses, and, worse, his huge, stiff pride. 'What was your old man, have you said, Tickener?' 'A porter at an auction sale room.' How would that go down in the wardroom? 'Were you at Oxford or Cambridge?' 'Neither.'

Why did he care? He knew of men like himself who answered boldly, 'Chapel Street Board School was the only university I ever had,' and carried it off too. But not Fred. He cared too much. His ambitions were higher than anyone's. Too high to be put to the test. If ever he heard of an honour, a medal, an accolade of state he always felt: That could have been mine – had I cared to compete for it.

And then of course, in a peacetime navy, there would be other wives, hard and snobbish ladies who terrorised Fred. Lucille was his sweet flower but he feared for her in such surroundings.

She snuggled closer to him. 'You've not actually sent in your papers have you?'

'No.'

'Say you won't! Oh please, Tikki, say you won't!'

Fred gazed at her, all but helpless. Superimposed on her pretty face, he saw sights that were always recurring. Men running in smoke, and, as they ran, dissolving into blood; a man frozen in the water; charred bodies bobbing in burning oil; flesh spattered in gobbets on steel; and, sliding into the greasy depths, innumerable flag-draped bodies consigned there by himself. He did not summon up these images, he had no imagination for that. They presented themselves to him whenever he glanced through a scuttle or from the bridge – even here now on his wife's bed. They pursued him, and the only way he knew to avoid them was to leave the navy, even though that would mean leaving the sea he still loved.

'What do you say, Tikki?' asked Lucille, pecking kisses below his ear.

Her scent was sweet, her flesh soft, her voice longing. For her sake he wavered.

'What about the children,' he said, as his last throw. 'They need a father.'

'Boarding schools!' she said triumphantly. This was what Milly had arranged for her kids. 'We will be able to afford it and the discipline will do them both the world of good. They can come out to us for holidays. It will be such fun!'

Blue tropical waters, white cap covers, the silken water parting smoothly round the keel. There the dead men might not lie so thickly, he thought, filled with longing despite his judgement.

It was at that moment Holly came into the room.

'When's Daddy coming down to us?'

'We're having an important talk. About where we shall live.'

'Oh yes,' she agreed with enthusiasm. 'There's a super house for sale up the glen.'

'I have probably got a house in Norwood,' said Fred firmly, shooting a blue flare of a look at Lucille.

'Where's that? Near the naval base?'

'In London.'

Holly understood at once all that Fred meant, just as her mother had.

'You can't,' she said in a voice that squeaked. 'You absolutely are not allowed to!'

Fred fired another glance at Lucille to say, the child needs a firm hand. I need to be at home.

'Now, my darling,' said Lucille, as kindly as she could, 'don't get upset. Nothing is decided.' She took Fred's hand.

Holly's face was scarlet, her eyes buttons. 'It would kill me to leave here!'

'Don't be more childish than you have to be,' Fred told her frostily, leaving the bed and twitchily adjusting his clothes.

'Children know what is good for them just as well as anyone else.'

'I decide what is best for my family.'

'Don't be pompous.' Holly pumped this out, feeling the truth and the dare of it.

Fred was by then standing very straight and lofty, removed from both his wife and daughter.

'I have said we are moving back to London and there's an end of the matter.'

Holly was unquelled.

'Why should it be? There are four of us to consider. I –'

'Be quiet Holly,' he said with a senior officer's calm. 'I have made up my mind. When you came bursting in, in that ill-mannered way, I had just been telling your mother.' His eyes dared her over Holly's head to contradict. She was still sitting on the bed, her legs straight in front of her. 'I am going to leave the navy and we'll all be together.' He looked from Holly to Lucille's unresponsive face. His sturdy shoulders relaxed, he warmed, he tried to kindle them. 'We'll have good times again. You'll see. The Tickener family at home.'

Like electric shocks flighting through her, the idea of screaming, or of battering made Lucille rigid, then empty. She was experiencing knowledge without thought: this was the end of her lovely life. Bodily she knew it. Unhappiness was being wrapped round her. She was weak, helpless, alone; even to herself she seemed a dim, fading personality.

Fred was still talking to Holly. She heard the child burst out, 'For us to accept like slaves?'

'You need your backside tanning.'

Nothing like this had ever been said to Holly. Her head rocked with its vulgar enormity as if he had fetched her a blow. After a few moments her eyes filled with tears of outrage and self-pity.

Fred was pleased to have found a way to silence her. A touch of plain speaking was needed was it? Immediately, he felt kinder.

'Come on, Holly,' he said encouragingly. He offered her his handkerchief. 'Be my good girl.'

Forcing the tears from her eyes with the heels of her hands, she stared at him defiantly. I hate you, her look said, but she dared not say the words. She feared his anger, his raised hand, and the fear increased her hate, the hate the fear.

'Oh, be a bloody obstinate little ass for all I care! What a welcome home I've had from you two.'

He slammed the door behind him. The two left inside inspected the room and the shut door. As they looked around, their eyes passed over each other.

Lucille did not know what to do, was afraid there was nothing to do but conform to Fred. She had no skills, no money, no self-confidence; and she loved him. These weapons she handed him for use against her.

Holly was held motionless by violent thoughts knocking about in her head, resentments, love gone sour, quick firing plans. She must go with her parents now, but in time she'd escape. Let him just watch out! She'd wait a few years and then be grown up and free to come back. Perhaps she would be an actress, as Donald and she planned, but in any case she would come back.

Lucille sat down suddenly on the bed, folding her arms on the brass rail at the end, turned her head away from Holly, resting it on her hands. She felt her wedding ring against her cheek, and a sick weariness inside her.

Holly was left standing against the treadle-machine. The familiar bedroom looked all wrong, a strange, dingy place she had strayed into by mistake, everything gaunt and dull.

Outside, the evening sky was pale behind the hump of darkening hill, and the pines around Lurgann stood like stiff feathers in a bunch.

5

CARSTEAD

They moved to Carstead, which was a good deal smarter than
Norwood, farther from London. At first glance Lucille was
pleased with it. She approved the expensive half-timbering and
the countrified names of the roads – Farm Lane, The Acres, The
Oaks. The Tickeners lived at number 4 The Warren, a house with
blue shutters pierced by heart-shaped holes, and with a conservatory at the back, entered by french windows from the sitting-
room which was consequently rather dark. It had mirrors set into a
high oak mantelpiece. Lucille placed there two china statuettes of
girls in long dresses. They were presumably standing on a hilltop
or at least in a wind for one was holding her hat and the other's
ruffled skirt was streaming out behind her. The one in pink had a
wolfhound pressed to her side, the lavender one held a white
flower. The mirrors reflected them both charmingly. They
cheered Lucille a little, but not much. Carstead was the best class
place she had ever lived in but the social life she wanted did not
happen.

She began to see how the roads branched and spread, netting a
thousand, thousand houses like her own. Each faced, across its
gardens and hedge and the road, a mirror image of itself, or a
distortion of it that underlined the sameness. Shined blank
windows were turned inward on housewives busy as fierce little
mice. From the early alarm jarring them from dreams to the last
locking up of doors, their days were predictable.

She saw too that the women were the counterparts of their
husbands, travelling so obediently up on the trains to their offices.

– 93 –

In a crowd formed of disintegrating parts, those who greeted and commented did so in phrases prescribed by habit; those who kept mum, but observed, were a set piece on the worn upholstery of the battered train seats. Behind newspapers hundreds of minds per train took in three or four variations on a dozen topics. The coaches shudderingly rattled their loads over the points and blasted through stations where other newspaper readers stood a yard back, shoulder to shoulder, infinitely weary yet geared up to a day that, differing in no marked way from the preceding and succeeding ones, would merge with them so that life could seem both endless and brief.

Lucille saw all this, and then had to pretend very hard to herself that she had not. She did not want to have to give up altogether.

She looked to Tikki to amuse her, but he became surly if she mentioned evenings in Town. They hardly ever went anywhere. On Saturdays, of course, he drove her to the 'village' – that is the row of Tudoresque shops she walked to all the other days – and they bought doughnuts for elevenses, sausages for lunch, shrimps for tea, which were all his favourite things. The rest of the week-end Fred gardened if the weather allowed. To his neighbours he gave every appearance of satisfaction with life.

He was, however, a man fissured with discontents he could not name. Lucille did secretly admit her disillusion. Fred never could.

He often thought of the multitudinous appearances of the sea as he sat at his office desk. Its beauty and power pursued him down the hot, gully-like streets of the City, and when he caught sight of a boat on the river his heart twisted. He never questioned his decision to leave the navy; that had been right, his duty as husband and father, however hard. He sat at his desk and dreamed of the sea. His desk had two telephones and an intercom to Margie, his secretary. She was an ex-Wren and very sporty, her hair cut in a mannish style. Dashing, he supposed she was. When she was out of his sight, he never thought of her.

He brooded on Lucille who was disappointing him. She was so often bad-tempered, and she nagged.

'Let's go out,' she would say. 'Please, Tikki.'

The idea of the journey back up to Town and the falseness of sitting in a restaurant making conversation to his own wife appalled him.

'Or ask some of your naval friends round,' she would suggest.

In fact he had no friends, except Margie. His naval cronies had put on civvies and disappeared in the crowd. He did sometimes run into one in a bar, and they drank, reminisced, parted. Fred had never had a close friend. He'd had Lucille.

One evening in their second year at Carstead, he did ask Margie and her husband back for coffee and sandwiches. It was not a success. Margie seemed to make Lucille quieter than ever. She kept looking her visitor up and down, as if making notes on the scarlet two-piece she wore, but said little. Margie was her usual loud, unthinking self. When the war was mentioned, she said, 'Actually, my war was quite a lark, really! I mean – all those gorgeous officers.'

Without a second's pause, Lucille was back in the kitchen at Balchraggan, large, bare, cold, Maud croaking, buckets of pigswill under the sink. Oh why? she cried silently.

'I suppose I shouldn't say so, but I did enjoy it,' Margie went on.

'Have a spam sandwich,' offered Lucille.

After they had gone, she fabricated a scene, inferring Fred was having an affair with his secretary. Fred exploded. She pressed home sharper and sharper accusations: he was mean, he neglected her, he drank too much.

She discovered she felt better after a row and from then on they had them quite often, and Fred did begin to drink more.

Holly, in her room above the living-room, heard the sounds of conflict. Once, when Lucille came weeping up the stairs, Holly burst out to the dark landing and threw her arms round her mother.

'Don't mind him, Mummy. I love you. I'll look after you!'

Even to herself it sounded childish, but she kept a grip on Lucille, who, for an instant, leant into her embrace then, with her customary brisk coolness, pushed her away.

'Please don't make one of your scenes. Your father's quite bad enough,' she said and went into her room.

Holly glared down the stairwell towards her father. His maleness affronted her. She could hear the clink of his glass, smell his tobacco. Invisibly he seemed to be smiling at her.

*

Holly's reaction to Carstead had been mild. She surprised herself and delighted Fred by liking number 4, it resembled a doll's house, and she, Alice-like, had been made small enough to fit it. There were leaded windows, a red roof, a neat garden, a birdbath, two sentinel laburnums. She walked through streets of such houses to catch the train to school and there new studies filled and altered her developing mind, with facts, examples, reasons building a mental structure that hid the Highlands.

In dreams she re-entered her happy land, steep, flashing with silver waters, with purple clouds pressing like soft breasts on moorland slopes, curlews crying and drifting at speed up the wood's margin, grey on grey. There too was Donald full of plans and ambitions to climb this, construct that, and holding out to her on his open palm a leaf or an insect for inspection.

To waken in her slot of a room, made harsh by the orange street lamp outside, was to enter monotony and duty. The suburbs quelled her. They changed so little with the seasons because housefronts, laurels, traffic islands are not subject to transformations as are cottages tucked in a hill's fold, larches, and lanes that fill with snow or puddles.

She found for herself the occasional beauties of suburbia and made do with them. There was an almond tree in brilliant leafless flower against a blue sky one morning as she went for her train. For two days she missed the train from gazing at the tree. The third day it rained, on the fourth the petals were falling but the image lasted her as refreshment for weeks. She heard birdsong and lazy lawnmowers, watched lightning play over a city skyline and clouds cast shadows on cooling towers that rose like simple chessmen from the spillage of the streets. She discovered violets grew thickly on the downs in the bleached short grass where the couples lay among the icecream papers and cigarette cartons. She walked home in the rain, face tipped up, and dreamed down the avenues when snow weighted the hedges of *cupressus leylandii* with some faint resemblance to the pines of Balchraggan.

Once she wrote to Donald of all this. Letters between them seemed alien, part of her developing academic self not of the gipsy moorland life, but once she had begun to put on paper words intended for the boy to read she could hardly stop. She wrote and wrote about the past, then a little about the present. Having sealed the letter she kept it in her desk for several days. It seemed as if her happiness was wrapped up inside it. To send it away might be finally to lose the chance of a return to Donald and the wild spaces of the north.

No answer came and she never wrote again, but treasured him in her dreams and her daydreams, inventing a romance for herself.

For daily life she had Fred whose affection and friendship continued her firm foothold. She, more than Lucille, appreciated what he had lost in leaving the sea and how much he disliked the city job he had.

Fred drove his Standard saloon up and down to his office. He could not face the lack of privacy on trains. Detouring up through Mitcham and Battersea on his special route that avoided black-spots, he was moving through the scenes of his youth, but he did not reflect on this, except occasionally to call to mind some pleasant incident, such as the buying of a garden chair, a lounger with a canopy, and carrying it home for Lucille in a huge parcel. The shop where he had bought it was still there – all that was left in a bombed terrace. He tried never to think of the war; certainly put the office out of his mind the moment he left it. He thought a lot about Holly, whose figure was budding and character beginning to assume permanent adult shape. He usually hid from himself the fact that many of her ideas were in conflict with his own, and concentrated on visualising Holly at the times when she was being 'his little girl'.

She had polished oval nails and square hands like his. He glanced at them on the wheel, felt their easy strength so pleasant to him as he changed gear. As a small child Holly had often stroked his face with her dry-skinned hands. He thought about that for a mile or so, enjoying the feel, re-engaging his powerful and protective love for her. Coming in from school soaking wet from a rainstorm one night, she had peeled off her black stockings by the fire and rubbed dry her feet, ankles, calves and thighs. Fred had watched round his newspaper as she held her legs to the fire until the soles of her feet were as pink as a baby's. 'The fruit of his loins'. The phrase had returned from his childhood reading.

Warmed now by the car's heating, soothed by the habitual motions of driving, Fred thought of Holly with tenderness. Her black hair was no longer cut in a fringe but pulled back in a knot of curls that bounced like grapes on her neck. Her brow was fully exposed and from the wide sockets her brilliant eyes shone with a gaze steady as Fred's own. She had his straight nose and regular face, her mother's pointed chin and small pink lips which she licked meditatively when she was puzzled. It was a schoolgirl's face, open and unsure, the skin shiny from soap, the hair marred by dandruff. Fred could pigeon-hole her as a child needing his care, but not accept she might be diverging from him. All evidence of that he dismissed with the label 'growing pains' which Maud had once used of him.

The secret life of Fred and Holly continued on its own way without their conscious knowledge, just as an underwater current strongly flowing shows nothing on the surface but a ribbon of smoother sheen. Even to themselves, there was more to it than a father and daughter pair in a family. Fred's passion and Holly's identification with him were fathoms down. The daily life of meals, talk, putting on coats was all that showed. To have suggested anything else to Fred would have provoked shocked anger. In the face of such an insult he would produce the response the accusation warranted, automatically, by training. Underneath, there might be a half-comprehension of something to terrify him.

As a boy he had constructed a world room, and its furnishings did not include, not even dimly in the shadowiest corners, an item that resembled being in love with your daughter. There were cliff-fronted chests and cupboards labelled duty, manners, discipline, what is not done; there might even be seats of stiff upholstery named affection and courtship, which led to marriage itself, a bureau of secret compartments and drawers stacked with letters, bills and deeds held with indiarubber bands that snapped at Fred's fingers; and that was all. Nowhere in Fred's overstuffed morality was the sort of love he had for Holly allotted a place, so he did not recognise it.

She, knowing instinctively, half-loved, half-feared the knowledge, and for the most part buried it and concentrated on her upper life – being a schoolgirl, practising hairstyles, reading, building up Donald into a Romeo who would return to confound her school-fellows when they boasted of too-present boyfriends, and also quarrelling with Fred.

His possessiveness got under her skin. All the girls agreed fathers were the end – so fussy, with all this 'be in by 10.30' business and no nail polish – but Mr Tickener did sound the absolute end the way Holly told it. Her mimicry of his voice and gestures was killing.

'Of course,' said Pam darkly, 'Holly is probably like her Dad.'

'Perhaps that's why they quarrel,' remarked Cynthia, who read.

'You mean likes repel,' said Mary, who did not, but remembered her science lessons.

'Yes, it's psychological,' agreed Cynthia.

What maddened Holly most, she told them, was Fred's insistence on knowing all she did. She became adept at avoiding his questions, partly by using her rapidly increasing knowledge of how little he knew. She could induce a type of baited bear silence in Fred by using a French word.

'What film are you going to?'

'Je ne sais quoi.'

'Is that its name, Holly?'

'No, of *course* not. How could it be?'

'What is it then?'

'On verra.'

Fred was too proud to show again that he had not understood. Hugh and Holly shared a grin.

Or it might be: 'What's that you're writing?'

'Homework.'

'I know that, Holly. What subject?'

'History – the sumptuary laws of Henry VII.'

Fred's historical ideas were limited to Trafalgar, 1066 and some vague personal memories of Lloyd George, though these hardly counted as they had happened in his lifetime. He once had a furious argument with Holly about the Abdication. He knew positively about this because he had been an adult when it occurred. He considered the King should have remained on the throne and married Mrs Simpson and 'be damned to the whole crew of them!'

'But the constitutional angle –'

'What the hell do you know about it. How old were you? Four was it?'

'It's history now, Daddy and Miss Lewis says –'

'It's not history to me. I *remember*, I tell you. I read the newspapers and heard the poor fellow speak. It was an outrage. They hounded him out of the country, Baldwin and his bloody cabinet, his own country mark you.'

'In any case,' said Holly coolly, 'it wasn't just his wanting to marry her. There had been other issues. It was feared he would not quite fit the Bagehot mould.'

'The *what*?'

'Bagehot is the authority on – '

'Look, Holly, I don't need lessons from you. I admire and respect the Duke of Windsor and I don't give a tinker's cuss what your Miss Lewis thinks or this Baggit chap. Good God!'

But their main area for fencing was Fred's wanting to know exactly where Holly was at all times. He had docketed, as a matter of course, the bus and train times, the hours of school (lessons, breaks, lunch-hour, etcetera) so that he knew at any moment of the day, should he pause in his work, where she was and how occupied. Inside his briefcase was a copy of her timetable. Weekends presented him with problems. She went frequently to the theatre with girls from school, all of whose fathers' names and phone numbers Fred had listed. He must know not merely what play, but by what train, to which terminus, then which bus, or was it to be underground, to which theatre, and when returning and how, and would she stop for a snack, if so where, and *be careful*, do not speak to any strangers, go to the ladies' room with your friend. Holly usually started to answer but as the questions gathered pace, for the more Fred was told the more there was to ask, she was overtaken by a frenzy and cried out to him to mind his own business.

Fred was dumbfounded at this remark when she first made it.

'You are my business, Holly. You're my daughter. I have to protect you.'

'What from?'

'There are all sorts of dangers.'

'On Victoria Station? In the Old Vic?'

'Yes,' he replied with heavy earnestness.

'What – for heaven's sake?' Her scorn was measureless.

Fred said no more. He thought in terms only of sexual attack and was far too embarrassed to say so.

The girl's well-formed figure and the bloom of her cheeks caused him delight. He wanted, often desperately, to kiss her. He looked from Holly to Lucille's duller skin and avoided, somehow, the unkind comparison; but when he saw himself and Holly reflected in the conservatory windows as they came in from the garden on a summer evening, his heart was swollen with pain and pride in their joint beauty. She was his little daughter, his darling. He put an arm round her. Immediately, Holly stiffened, closed up, moved away.

Ah well!

He eased in the clutch, selected first gear, took off the brake, allowed his left foot to rise as his right pressed down, and moved away from the traffic lights. He was approaching the outskirts of Redbridge on a wet, darkening December afternoon. He turned on the windscreen-wipers and the side lights, and negotiated his way through thin traffic down various side roads. He was an excellent driver and prided himself on mastering his car with gentle strength. His hands seemed to move as if knowing their work. He guided the car smoothly into the gravel drive of Holly's school.

Redbridge Grammar was inconveniently accommodated in several adjacent town houses with prefabricated appendages built out at the rear so that the girls passed through what had been sculleries and servants' bedrooms, now used for lockers or games equipment, string bags of balls and grubby hockey pads looped by their straps to pegs on the wall, into bleak shed-like rooms lit by fluorescent tubes. However the front rooms retained a houselike air which threw Fred off balance. This was his first visit. He intended to put things straight with the headmistress. He was not prepared for the plants in brass pots which stood in the tiled entrance porch, or the large pictures and the polished floor. The building, called Main School, smelt of warmth and clean paper. There was an almost inaudible, yet melodious hum of children at work in the sewing and art rooms which he glimpsed one after the other through glass panelled doors as he was led to the Head by a stately girl. He was abnormally conscious of his footsteps and tried to quieten them. The girl walked ahead in the manner of a priestess, placing her toes down before her heels, her head up, and her ball-like breasts bounced gently under her prefect's tie and the silver badge. She provided the wide, high, shadowy corridor with a perfect focal point.

'Not very pleasant weather,' she said to him firmly. He was walking just a fraction behind her.

'No, by Jove.' The rain of the morning was beginning to turn to snow. He remembered noticing this as he drove down from his office. 'You like snowballing though, I expect?'

Her smile, though polite, was pitying.

'Mr Tickener, Dr Shaw,' she said, ushering Fred into the headmistress's room.

Dr Shaw appeared first to him as a crumpled face low behind a desk littered with photographs and small silver cups and papers, then as a short, fat woman untidily dressed in several clinging layers. As she was not smart or stately like her pupil, Fred relaxed. She wore round spectacles with flesh pink frames. Having come round the desk to shake hands, she seated herself and Fred on spindly chairs set either side of a table bearing a cyclamen. She did not look comfortable, overlapping the small seat, and he did not feel it, but managed some introductory chat about the weather and the school's surroundings. The now steadily falling snow, grey against the backs of houses, was beginning to pile up on the bicycle sheds outside. Fred was still most uneasy – this place of women and study was disconcerting to him. He kept rearranging his feet, putting his hands in different positions, and moving his body with convulsive lunges which he checked in mid-surge remembering the tapering legs of the chair.

'My daughter,' he eventually stated, almost belligerently.

'Yes, you wish to discuss Holly's future.'

'That's the wrong end of the stick, Dr Shaw. I want your support in stamping out this theatre nonsense.'

'Mr Tickener,' began the headmistress in a soft but ponderous voice, 'I am rather proud to be able to tell you,' she began to open out the fronts of the two cardigans she wore and to wrap them around her, 'that this school is one of the earliest foundations established for girls after the 1870 Education Act,' and then held them in position by folding her stumpy arms across her chest, 'and we have always prided ourselves on education without too much direction. Or, in other words, we believe that if a girl is well and comprehensively educated her own choice of direction in life, her career if you like, though, of course, not all girls need, want, or would benefit from the sort of careers men are more or less forced to undertake, not always with the happiest results, I am sure you will agree,' she smiled at Fred revealing the salmon pink gums of her dentures and took a breath, 'her own choice will be right.'

'The theatre is not a career.'

'Well, we've moved out of the nineteenth century, Mr Tickener. It *is* perfectly respectable.' She heaved lightly with academic humour, lifting up and supporting her floppy breasts on her folded arms.

Fred was suspicious of the amusement; he also had difficulty in translating nineteenth century into recognisable dates. He rocked dangerously on the chair and replied, 'That's as may be. It's unsuitable for my daughter.'

'Of course it happens that girls make wrong choices,' agreed Dr Shaw, earnest again. 'But sooner or later their own good sense, and, I like to think, our training make themselves felt and they abandon their false starts.'

She became aware that Mr Tickener was not giving his full attention to her. He was inspecting the snowflakes tumbling down the windowpane.

'What had you in mind for Holly?' she asked.

'Teaching possibly.'

Again she heaved with her private laughter. 'You fathers are inclined to imagine teaching is something one does to fill the gap before marriage. It's an honourable career, Mr Tickener, and it calls for a fair measure of dedication.'

Come off it, Fred said to himself, and aloud, 'Secretarial work?'

'Oh no. Holly has absolutely no leaning that way. No patience or method.'

'What about doctoring,' ventured Fred, with the air of a salesman sorting through samples.

'She'd not be up to scratch with physics and chemistry.'

'Holly is very bright.' He flushed with extraordinary speed. 'Her mother and I have always said so.'

'Parents do, parents are inclined to, Mr Tickener,' said Dr Shaw, bouncily heaving.

His pale eyes were as visionless as marbles.

'But in Holly's case you're right. She is a clever girl, but on the arts side.'

'On no account will I have her at art school.' His heavy shoes trampled the carpet in a tattoo of irritation. 'That's no better than drama.'

Again Dr Shaw made a business of arranging her woollens across herself. 'It appears you are unversed in our terms,' she said.

'An arts candidate is one who concentrates on arts subjects, that is to say English, History and foreign languages.'

'Why not say so plainly?'

'It is pretty generally understood.'

After a short silence, she loosened her hold on her clothing, stood up and pottered back to her desk where she shuffled through some papers, then sat down, turned on her lamp, and showed a serious face to him.

'Perhaps the best way forward would be for me to arrange for you and Mrs Tickener to visit the Drama College so that you – '

'Holly is not going there.' Fred stood up.

'Mr Tickener, we adults may propose, but our children often oppose us quite successfully. Might it not be better to accept defeat graciously?'

Fred did not appreciate being spoken to as if he were a pupil. And what did she mean 'our children'? She had none.

'Holly is my daughter. I think I know what is best for her, Miss Shaw.' He lightly stressed the Miss, which was not lost on her.

'May I ask you,' she said, leaning back in her chair and twisting a pencil round and round in her fingers, 'very tentatively, whether you would say your parents knew what was best for you?' Her stresses were even lighter.

This took him aback. He was appalled at her cheek, and for one dreadful moment afraid he might cry, for it was part of Fred's internal myth that his mother would, had she lived, have understood and approved all he did. Behind Lucille's face gleamed her potent and more loving one. On the other side of the matter, on reality's side, since she had not lived, was his arrogant father with plans for a life in the grocery trade. In Dr Shaw's study Fred was swamped by his memories of mice being stamped on in emptied packing-cases.

The headmistress saw her remark had not paid off as she had hoped. Sometimes this approach worked wonders with awkward fathers.

'It is just because I had to make my own way,' Fred told her with dignity, 'that I know it is a father's duty to guide and direct.'

'Give Holly a chance,' suggested Dr Shaw, who valued the girl. She even liked this clumsy but honest man who looked like her with the same square brow. His musical voice was a bass version of Holly's, which was sweet and warm and never heard without pleasure. 'Give her her head for a year or two, at least.'

'All the damage would be done. No. If you will not put an end to this nonsense about the theatre, I shall have to remove her from this school. From teachers altogether. She can leave now, I believe.'

'That is your prerogative, Mr Tickener.' She put down her pencil and sat up.

'I don't want to,' he said, conciliatory the moment he sensed a softening in her attitude. He placed himself in a chair which faced across her desk. This again helped him for it was an office situation. 'Quite frankly, we like the school and Holly is happy here. It's very impressive, what I've seen,' he gave a backward wave towards the door and all that lay behind it – polished corridors, prefects, sewing-rooms, libraries.

'We aim to give a thoroughly rounded education.' Dr Shaw perfectly realised she had lost the battle with Fred Tickener. Whether Holly also would lose it she would watch with interest. 'Now, with her abilities on the arts side, might not a try at Oxbridge be our best bet for Holly?'

Fred's china blue eyes rolled in an effort to grasp the meaning of Oxbridge; when he had, he beamed. This was more like it.

*

That afternoon was timetabled for games but because of the snow there were none. Holly phoned her mother at lunchtime and suggested they did some Christmas shopping and Lucille met her, coming into Redbridge on the two o'clock train.

Lucille said every year that Christmas was for remembering people and kept from season to season a list of dozens of acquaintances from years back to all of whom she sent, if she could afford it, something rather more than a card. She also believed that her gifts should come from the whole Tickener family, so she took Holly with her to the shops and involved Hugh and Fred by making them look at each purchase when she came home. Part of the pleasure of shopping for Lucille was this taking out of bags, inspecting, handing round that went on at home. The 'Don't you think he will like this?' and 'Isn't that just the colour for her?' extended for a whole evening sometimes the liberation she felt when standing at a counter, free to make a choice, to take for herself, and give to others.

Fracturing her wish to buy presents was her never-ending fret over money. She had sufficient but would have liked much more, and sometimes spent as if she had more. Then she had not enough and was forced to skimp, hiding her improvidence from Fred who would be angry. The end result was that she felt more or less permanently hard done by, and walked past the festively dressed shop windows with expectant eyes and pinched lips.

Her ideas of gifts were not out of the ordinary. She chose calendars, telephone pads, stockings, handkerchiefs, cigarettes and gloves. Holly was bored by the objects, pleased to be with her mother in the warm department store dressed as a child in school uniform with her satchel of books but feeling the secrecy of growing up inside the buttoned rain coat. She played the part of a child, trailing behind Lucille, standing just back from her shoulder at the various counters, staring at the hanging decorations, not listening to her mother's conversation until drawn into it by a 'What do you think, darling?' She did not mind being taken for a child still because she was so confident of her strength and power. If she wanted, when she was ready, she could throw off this disguise and be – whatever she pleased!

When Lucille arrived at the men's department for scarves and initialled handkerchiefs, Holly noticed a rack of tie-pins. One was a gold bar with a whip twirled round it. She knew Hugh would love this. He had just started riding at the stables down the road and had dreams of hunting. She took it to her mother who was standing happily at the counter while the assistant went for a scarf of a particular colour.

'Hugh would like that.'

'Yes, wouldn't he?' Lucille agreed, always pleased to please. 'See if you can find a calendar with ships on for him to give Daddy, will you. In there, look.' She pointed to the stationery through a tinsel draped arch. 'Sailing boats if possible.'

'Yes, a galleon or two.'

When that was done, they had tea and cakes in the fourth floor restaurant where Lucille sank prettily into a chair of green cane. She took off her hat, puffed up her hair with her fingers, and smiled happily at Holly. In the atmosphere of feminine self-indulgence Holly was less easy in her uniform. Her velour hat, white blouse and striped tie did rather glare at the room full of resting, flushed ladies. The pastry forks were too small for her inky fingers, the paper serviette useless when the cream spurted on her cuff. She solved her embarrassment by retreating into an imagined scene. She was a famous actress sitting in that empty seat by the window wearing a red hat, waiting the arrival of someone who had sent her a mysterious letter, signed 'A friend from the past.' It would, of course, be Donald. She watched the doorway, building up her fantasy. Donald appeared wearing black velvet, like Hamlet, but smiling joyously.

'We'll catch the five o'clock if we hurry,' said Lucille.

In the train Holly fished about in the basket among the presents they had bought, all made a little more interesting by their paper wrappings. The tie-pin was not in a box, or even a bag, but loose.

'That's a swizz,' she said.

'What is?'

'The man didn't wrap Hugh's tie-pin up.'

'We can do that.'

'It should have a nice little box with some cotton wool.'

'Let's check through the list, shall we?'

As her mother read the names from her list, Holly located the relevant item. She picked out various receipts. The one from the men's department was for two scarves and a pair of gloves.

'Mummy, did you pay for the tie-pin?' Busy-body, chatterbox.

'Holly!'

'No, but did you?'

Lucille compressed her lips, took the basket and said nothing. Holly remembered she had been sent to the next part of the shop, out of the way. Could her mother *really*? No.

'I'm sorry. I shouldn't have said that.'

'You should not.' Lucille pushed away from Holly's attempt at a kiss and the rest of the journey including the walk from the station to The Warren was done in silence, so was the hanging up of coats, the changing of shoes to slippers, the putting on of the kettle. Lucille was past mistress of such silent warfare which never failed with Fred or Holly. Hugh ignored it so she never used it against him.

On this occasion it revived Holly's suspicion. She didn't know what to think. More precisely, what she was thinking did not accord with what she wanted to think. It wasn't possible that Mummy . . . She was so crisp and cross with anyone who broke rules. Holly and Hugh had discussed it. 'Why does she mind so much every little thing?' the boy had asked. 'It's like her having to have the house absolutely neat.' 'Does it make her safe somehow?' Hugh wondered. 'What's she afraid of?' 'In the war, when I slept in her bed, she used to cry in her sleep sometimes. I'm not joking, Hugh.' 'Poor old Mum!'

So how could she have taken something and not paid? That was a huge rule to break. Yet there swam into Holly's consciousness memories of other times when she had been surprised by things Lucille had bought, things she had previously said she could not afford, and . . . Holly felt a little sick and rather frightened at her thoughts. How could she! She glanced at her mother putting on her apron with a shut face.

Then Fred arrived home earlier than usual and Lucille burst into talkative friendliness.

Holly began to put the things they had bought on the table for him to inspect, which was what her mother always liked to do.

'We got this for Hugh,' she said, forcing herself not to look at Lucille, 'but the man forgot to wrap it up. Wasn't that peculiar?'

'Was it, puss?' Fred asked vaguely. He was full of his interview with Dr Shaw and wondering about the best moment to choose to tell of it. Meditatively, he took off his walking-shoes and put them beside his armchair.

'How many times have I to tell you – don't leave your shoes there!' said Lucille, the cords on her neck standing forward.

'Why the hell not?'

'What does it look like if anyone comes in.'

'Who's likely to come?'

'No one, oh! no one,' she agreed in a meaning voice.

'Well, ask someone then and I'll put my shoes in the cupboard.' Fred was tired of this routine dialogue.

'Not until you've done the re-papering.'

'Have a heart, Lucie. I'm dead tired after a day at the office. Up and down step-ladders – it's a young man's job.'

'Shall I get the decorators from the village then?' with an edge of triumph.

'No.'

'So you –?'

'There's nothing wrong with the old wallpaper.'

'It's only pre-war, that's all!'

'Better than what you buy now, and that's a fact.'

'I won't argue,' she announced, gathering up her packages with hostile cracklings. 'Just so long as you know. No one is invited here until it's done. So the longer you leave it the lonelier I shall be. Fine Christmas we shall have, I don't think.'

Fred swung up his head like a baited bear. 'I could give Trevor and Margie a ring. After all, they have seen the old paper so it wouldn't matter.'

'Yes, suit yourself, do. Ask your lady friend by all means.'

'Oh, Lucille stop it! For God's sake! Sometimes you are infernally silly.'

Entering one of her silences, Lucille left the room with it, leaving a vacuum behind. Fred sat with his paper, not reading. There was a time when Lucille would never have spoken in that sort of way. She'd have called it common. Holly sat listlessly, having disconnected thoughts about her parents, their marriage, Fred's roughness, Lucille's stiffness. There was absolutely nothing between Fred and Margie. This was as clear as daylight to everyone concerned, so why, both Fred and Holly were asking themselves, did Lucille play the slighted wife? Holly had no answer, but Fred came up with the word 'unhappy'. This was always a goad to his conscience. He still had a naive assumption, never destroyed by experience, that people were meant to be happy. And if his wife wasn't he must do something, try again. He stood up.

'Leave her, Daddy,' said Holly. 'She only sulks for attention.'

He ignored her. He never looked for motives or hidden meanings. He felt it beneath him to do so.

In her room Lucille thumped the mirror with a fist. The face in there was shut off from so much it liked and wanted that she almost hated it. Then from her pocket she took a string of crystal beads she had slipped in there when no one was looking. Holding it by the clasp she twirled it gently so that all the facets twinkled as the beads swayed into and out of the lamp's beam. But not for long. Ennui and disappointment came back. She crept under the counterpane and lay there, completely covered, holding her arms across her chest with her knees drawn up, shivering slightly, patiently waiting for the mood to pass. Outside, the snow was falling, falling in grey moving soundlessness. Inside, the room was full of furniture and objects she had chosen but which now meant little to her, they were callous presences, not friends, observers of her loneliness. Her body trembled. She disliked its weakness. She disliked her whole self very often, but was stuck with what she had.

'Lucille,' called Fred softly from the door. With only one lamp the room was shadowy, the window a grey rectangle. He decided his wife was not there and went back to his armchair thankfully. He hated scenes.

Wearily, Lucille stood herself up and began to put away her purchases in a special cardboard box on top of her wardrobe. Her thoughts went ahead to Christmas morning – the work, the clearing up, the boredom.

In the back sitting room Fred found Holly. She had put on the outside light and was watching the snowflakes' endless, tumbling, feathery fall.

'Look how they are piling on the birdbath, like a wedding hat,' she said to him.

'Mm?'

'Or a cake.'

To him it was merely a mound of snow.

'A fantastic layer cake of finest spun sugar and cream.'

'You're certainly good with words. I could do with you in my office when I'm writing letters.'

'Is it hard?' she asked, surprised. 'You're so good at things, Daddy.'

'Work's a struggle sometimes. Can be.'

'Well,' she said largely, in her grown-up manner, 'I daresay all work is boring sometimes.'

'Not so much boring as – these young fellows don't see things my way.'

She turned round to him and slipped her arms round his neck.

'You're a young man yourself.' She kissed him. 'You are my young man. See?'

Fred flushed with pleasure and love. She leant against him and together they watched the snow falling.

'Remember Mrs Willoughby's cat?' he asked.

'Yes.' Through the snowflakes she saw the earlier garden. 'And the little birds in the golden rod. I believed their mothers would find them, you know.'

'That's because it was true.'

She gave a snort of loving amusement.

How she wished Dad could always be like this – kind and not demanding – for she loved him still more than any one else in the world.

'Dad, I don't mean to be awkward.'

'No, lovey, I know. It's just growing up.'

At that moment Lucille snapped on the light. 'What in the world are you two doing in the dark?'

'Watching the snowflakes how they fall,' replied Holly in a poetic voice.

'Well, if you've no homework you can help get the supper.'

When the meal was ready Fred came to the table rubbing his hands and saying as he always did when in a good mood, 'Once more into the breach, dear friends.' There had been a time when Holly used to ask him what precisely he meant; now she merely gritted her teeth, and signalled with her eyes at Hugh who nodded faintly.

Then, over the meal, more habitual remarks were made, remarks suitable for that time of day, that end of the week. Each member of the family, while taking part in a conversation, was also pursuing inner thoughts. Fred, particularly, was going over his news, deciding when to tell them. He waited until Lucille was breaking open the apple pie, letting out steam and an acid scent. Then he said, apparently casually, 'I had an interesting encounter today.'

'Oh? Hugh how many times have I told you not to do that.'

The boy, finding his pudding too hot to eat, was separating it into mouthful sized lumps and distributing them round the rim of his plate to cool.

'It burns my mouth.'

'Have some top of the milk.' She gave him the jug, and prodded a larger one of custard towards Fred.

'Yes, I had a highly interesting meeting.'

'So you said. Who with?'

'Dr Shaw.'

'Whatever for?'

'To discuss this young lady's future.'

Holly half choked over a wedge of pie. 'How could you!'

'She informs me you are doing well.'

'At drama?' Holly put down her spoon.

'No, your drama as you call it –'

'What else could I call it?'

'– is make-believe. You've a real life to lead. Dr Shaw intends to put you down for Oxbridge.'

'Oxford I'd like,' she said, 'but it's not as easy as "putting down".' Her sense of superiority overcame her caution.

'There you are! So you have thought about it. I might have known my Holly was sensible at heart.'

'I've thought it over, yes, because they speak of nothing else at school. Of course OUDS is good.'

Fred disdained to ask what OUDS was. He masticated a spoonful of apple and custard. Holly watched him, the memory of his recent tenderness strong. Above all things, even more than the theatre, she wanted Fred's approval.

'But I don't need a degree,' she said, to test him, 'to be a great actress.'

'Even less to be a third-rate walk-on.'

'Personally,' Lucille remarked, 'I don't see the point of degrees for girls. Milly didn't have one.'

'Who the hell is she?'

'Just the very nicest woman I've ever met,' she replied quellingly and he knew at once she was someone at Balchraggan in that part of life he did not share with her. 'Have some more Hugh?'

While she served the boy, Fred began to repeat some of Dr Shaw's comments on Holly. The praise was sweet. Nothing could be better than to do well in his eyes, to feel renewed the trustful approbation of childhood. On the other hand RADA was what she wanted and had planned on gaining by a campaign of softening Fred, getting him to take her to the Old Vic as a birthday treat, persuading her drama teacher to speak to him. Fred, it seemed, had outflanked her by going to see old Fanny Shaw.

Fred took her hand over the table. He wrinkled up his forehead and smiled, the skin round his mouth puckering in C-shaped curves.

'Eh darling? Aren't you proud?'

She had lost the thread but loved to see how pleased he was with her. 'Yes.'

'This calls for a toast.'

'I've nothing but cooking sherry,' said Lucille quickly.

'What needs a toast?' asked Hugh.

'My eldest unmarried daughter setting out for Oxford University.'

'Oh Daddy!'

'You finished the whisky last night.'

'Yes, but I had a sort of feeling a noggin might come in handy tonight so –' He took some bottles out of his briefcase.

He had a special relaxed, slow moving manner when he did things about the house. Holly loved it, and watched him now in a sort of trance. He fetched everything needed on a tray and cleared a space for it.

'Now then. Once more into the breach.'

Expertly, neatly, he mixed what everyone liked, or could be allowed.

'So. All ready? Is that how you like it, Lucie? Right then. To Oxford and Holly.'

'Oxford.'

'Holly.'

'Oxford and Holly going there.'

She could not fully grasp what had happened, or how. She was still determined to go to R A D A; the idea of Oxford was only a second string if she failed.

'Nice, pussy?'

'What? Oh yes.'

'Drink up then.'

'Daddy!'

'Yes?' Forehead rolling up into grooves, eyes beaming. What was it he had said when they were looking at the snow, something about being old and let down? She moved her chair closer to his and he rubbed the back of her neck. Whatever he was, old fox or old innocent, she was a child again, helpless and dependent.

Afterwards the rest of the evening was rather an anticlimax. Even Hugh and Lucille felt that. They settled round the gas-fire in the sitting-room and the flush of difference faded from the day. Fred took up his newspaper, and Hugh went to his meccano which was kept on an old tray. Lucille was mending socks. Holly sat doing nothing. Something momentous had happened yet everything went on as usual.

The fire was made of fat, perforated ceramic worms laid vertically side by side. The flame was first blue, then a steady red, except where a crumb of plastery stuff had fallen and stuck over the outlet hole where it jiggled in the flame and made a popping, whining noise.

The air in the room was sluggish with heat, fumes and a family's lassitude in each other's too well known company. Fred put down his paper and picked up his latest yachting magazine. Hugh then told him that a boy at school's father had bought a yacht. He said they were going sailing in the summer.

'Would you like a yacht, Lucie?' Fred asked in a tone both playful and lofty with possibilities.

'Chance would be a fine thing.'

'Well, and why not?'

'Because,' she replied scornfully.

'Look Lucille, if it's what you want, I will buy one.'

'They cost thousands, Dad!'

'I am aware of that, Hugh.'

'Take no notice,' said Lucille. 'Your father's talking through his hat.'

'His admiral's hat,' agreed Hugh, softly.

'Sarcasm is the lowest form of wit,' Fred told him. This had been said to him as a boy and had impressed him deeply.

'No. Puns are supposed to be,' Holly corrected him.

Fred looked pained but did not argue. If she was to go to Oxbridge perhaps she knew.

'Could we really have a yacht, Dad?'

'I'm toying with the idea. Yes. It's one of the ideas I am considering.'

Lucille fished the wooden darning mushroom from the heel of one sock, which she folded on the arm of her chair, then began on another hole.

'You would really like to, wouldn't you, Daddy?' asked Holly.

'It's certainly an idea that appeals.'

She was knocked by a sudden wave of pity for him. He loved the sea and had to drive up the City every day.

The room returned to silence and the gas-fire's whining pop, pop. Not even Hugh had any belief in Fred's scheme. He had these ideas every now and again. They never came to anything. There had been the plan for ski-ing holidays when none of them could ski or had any equipment. The sheer cost put paid to that. Then he had proposed a pony for Hugh with no place to keep it; then building a retirement cottage in Cornwall when he had no energy for wall-papering even; now a life afloat.

He tried so hard to bend life the way he wanted it, thought

Holly, and must feel let down by them so often. By her most of all, for he could not let her be and something in her compelled constant rebellion.

Hugh was not troubled by his father's smothering love. The boy joked, parried, ducked and was, in any case, endowed with a nature which went its own way. Fred seemed to assume that, as a boy, Hugh would have his own plans and pursue them. He scanned his school reports only cursorily and paid him £5. They had the easiest of relationships.

But Holly's life was built on Fred's love. Its arched vaults sustained her. She counted on him utterly to be there, a trust-worthy, trust-seeking counterpart to herself. She loved his solid body and strong face. Each wrinkle and fold was hers. As a child she had run her hands over his warm features; now with her sapphire eyes she checked him over, owned him and was owned. When she saw a photograph of her father, she might cover the mouth and chin, look only at the brow, eyes and upper cheeks and see herself – a nobler, manlier self.

And just as one may be self-critical and suffer moments of lacerating dislike of the personality one is locked up with and yet be in no way hindered from making all allowances necessary to keep self-approbation alive, so Holly loved her father deeply, pervasively, and without possible end.

6

HOLLY AND DONALD

There was a surge of life through number 4. Lucille took out her best black dress and a wisp of veiling beaded with chips of crystal. It hung to just below her eyes, drawing attention to their size and the softness like faded brown velvet. She and Holly took the train to town, and picked Fred up at his club, where they ate ham and salad on oval porcelain plates among other groups preparing for an evening out, the women in cocktail dresses of rustling materials. Holly was disappointed that none of the men spoke to her father. He had, instead, a cheery conversation with the barman, who had once been a steward on a ship Fred had served in. It was curious, she thought, how often he happened upon lower deck shipmates. Commissionaires, lift attendants, night watchmen – he had small links all over London.

Outside the theatre a group of young men were busking. There was a singer, a man with a washboard and a drum, another with a guitar. Holly hung back from her parents. The singer had a narrow face with stiff brown hair standing above it.

'Come along, pussy.'

'I don't think that sort of thing should be allowed.'

'Why ever not, Mummy?'

'It's quite a nuisance.'

They had seats in the second row of the stalls. Fred settled himself between the two women and placed a small, pretty box of chocolates in each lap. Holly's was round with a blue ribbon that she fingered as she watched the play, a farce, Fred's choice. He and her mother laughed a lot, and so did she.

In the interval, her parents went to the bar but she remained in her seat, slipping down and sprawling her legs out, observing the audience and picking up scraps of conversation. She saw a tall man come through the door marked E X I T among the gilt and maroon scrolls of the box above. He looked incongruous in an old raincoat and tall enough to be on stilts – that was her first impression and then she realized it was the singer from the group in the street. To her surprise he came right into the auditorium, moving easily along the edge of the pit, then began to step sideways along the row where she sat. She dragged herself suddenly into an upright sitting position and the box of chocolates fell.

'Holly! I knew it was you with one look.'

'Donald!' She could not believe it. Yet it was her dream come true.

'You didn't know me, did you?' His mouth widened, stretched and tipped up at the corners, breaking the long lines of his face.

'I see it's you now,' she said taking deep breaths to calm her thudding heart.

'Should hope so.' His eyes darted about her, with energy and intelligence. 'You are the same, but you're different too.'

Familiarity, strangeness and joy kept her silent, smiling.

'The difficulty is,' he said, 'you are always at Lurgann for me.' He might have added, looking into the distance and watching buzzards over the ravine with eyes blue and shining.

'That's what I was thinking – you belong there.'

'We still think alike,' he said smugly, and sat down in Fred's seat, bending his length in three at hips and knees, folding into the tip-up seat. She noticed his broad, flat wrists covered with dark hair sticking out from a too-short sweater sleeve. She recognized a white scar on his thumb. Close to he smelt of sweat and city soot. This was Donald and not Donald.

'Where have you been?' he asked. 'Holly, where have you been?'

'Here,' she laughed, immediately content with Carstead and London since Donald was there too. 'Living at home, going to school.' She found herself laughing loudly.

'You never wrote.'

'I did. Once. There was no answer.'

They were speaking rather unsurely, feeling their way.

'We moved down here when Mother was sure Dad was not coming back. She's a civil servant in one of those secret places.'

She was exposed to the shame of having forgotten about Mr Chisholm being missing.

'I hadn't remembered,' she mumbled.

'Oh, I forget very often. I was only eight when he went away.' She saw Fred's back going.

'Don't look so tragic. It's not all bad. Some of my friends have their old man on their backs.'

'But – your father!'

'It can be rotten.' He smiled and she saw the boy's face shine in the man's. 'The important thing is – I've found you and you're just the same.'

'Of course I'm not.'

'Deep down?'

'Oh, inside, yes.'

He kissed her on the cheek, then rubbed his face against hers expertly, fondly. She felt small and delicate. Since she lay in the grass with Donald she had only been kissed clumsily by boys taking their due at dances. Donald's touch transported her back to happiness and sureness.

'Kiss me, Holly.'

She did so – and was suddenly aware of the public place they were in.

'So what were you doing outside? Tell me.'

'Well, busking to help out the grant. I'm at music college. Nearly finished.'

'You're not going to act?'

'Sort of. I want to sing in opera.'

Now, after the wondering start, the two could not speak quickly enough, pouring out information, adjusting.

'I don't know about that.'

'I'll take you. Not to seats like these though. We'll have to go in the gods.'

'I usually do. This is Daddy's treat, because I've done well, got into Oxford.'

Donald sat up straight and put both hands between his knees.

'That's very good.'

'It's not what I care about. I want to act. You remember? He won't let me.'

'Does that matter, what he wants?' Deliberately Donald stretched out his legs right under the seat in front. 'How can he stop you?'

'Well . . .'

He looked at her with an edge of anger.

'Well . . . I can't just go away to drama school, just like that.'

'Why not?'

'He'd be so angry.'

'When did you mind what people say?'

'But your father . . . You don't understand.'

'No.' He shook his head and his body twitched. 'Just send for entrance forms, apply and, if they'll take you, go.'

'He says it's an uncertain life. Cheap rooms, he says, no work, what he calls "undesirable johnnies".' She laughed rather weakly.

'You don't really want to act,' he told her kindly, folding up his body again and twisting round to her.

'I do, Donald!'

'Not enough to annoy your Daddy.'

'It's more – not wanting to hurt him.'

'Good Lord, what about your own self?'

'Perhaps it wouldn't have worked.'

'You should have found out,' he said inflexibly. 'Mother didn't want me to be a singer, but I simply told her it was my life.'

'How extraordinarily simple!' she said, mockingly, enviously.

Her shield shaped face was a comical mixture of daring and inhibitions with her lips sucked inside her mouth, cheeks hallowed, eyes very round and blue. He kissed her again with softly pecking, promising kisses all round her mouth.

Fred and Lucille were seen round Donald's back edging back along the row. Lucille had her chin tucked in, her narrow shoulders drawn round, her hands clutching her pendant; Fred looked anywhere but at Holly.

Donald sprang up, seized hands, introduced himself.

'Donald Chisholm from Balchraggan. You remember me, Mrs Tickener. Our picnics up the river?'

'That time is very dim to me,' she said. 'Hadn't you better go back to your seat?'

'Oh, I'm not here to see this show. I came in to find my Holly. I'll go now.'

'You better had,' said Fred, jingling his money in his pockets.

'Can I have your phone number?' Donald asked. The lights were dimming, the people behind restive. Fred pushed him indignantly away.

From then on the three Tickeners sat unmoving and silent while the audience around them rocked and roared. Nothing was said leaving the theatre or driving back to Fred's club apart from tinny, unmeaning words. Finally, seated with drinks, Fred asked who the fellow was, with a ponderous casualness. Holly explained and Lucille looked in the other direction.

'What's he do?'

'He's training to be a singer.'

'A *what*?'

'Singer.' Here she was, already back in his net.

Fred turned half way from Holly, then back. He drank some whisky, smacked his lips, drank some more. He was a fair-minded man doing his best to mind his own business.

'What's the matter?' Holly asked in a thin voice.

'I'm only surprised at a daughter of mine having anything to do with a pansy.'

'Do you mean –' she stopped, not really able to imagine quite what Fred did mean.

'Anyone who sings for a living must be wet behind the ears.'

This was one of Fred's most condemning expressions, usually reserved for Hugh's scoutmaster and their neighbour's son who played no sport.

'However that may be,' said Lucille, 'he is totally unsuitable as an escort for Holly.'

'Escort! He's my oldest friend.'

'Well, in that backwood we had to make friends with whoever offered.'

'I don't know anyone nicer.'

'Standing in the gutter, singing, like a pauper!'

'Students do that, Mummy.'

'Students!' snorted Fred. 'Well, you're going to be an undergraduate at Oxford. That's what we're here to celebrate, eh?'

Holly had to get away from them and went to the ladies' room but her mother followed.

'I'm not sure if Daddy noticed, but I saw you kissing that boy.' Lucille avoided Holly's eye as she said this. Social outrage made her speak but she would so much rather not.

'I am eighteen.'

'As long as you live in our home you will behave properly.'

Lucille drew her under lip taut before re-applying her lipstick. She adjusted her veil and, in the mirror, gave Holly a little smile.

'Come on, darling. This is meant to be a happy day.'

Holly returned her own muted smile. It was, of course, a brilliant day for her, finding Donald, but they didn't want her to say that. So she said very little for the rest of the evening but allowed Fred to jolly her along. He was not seriously worried. After all, Holly had a marvellous future lying before her. Back at number 4 he gave her a special goodnight kiss, pulling her towards him firmly and very tenderly. His little girl, who had done so well! His big heart seemed to press against his ribs with the force of his love and pride in her.

In her bedroom Holly snatched out her handkerchief and scrubbed his kiss off.

*

For the next four months all Holly saw was Donald's face – either in reality or in imagination. His being filled hers to overflowing. What he had touched glowed with some of his glory, any subject he mentioned became peculiar to her, words of his had life and vibrated in her head. As for the look of him! She gazed, awestruck, at his height, his coarse, strong hair, his greyish, springy flesh and the eyes which communicated an equal awe. Neither of them could quite believe their luck, and yet it was not luck, but destiny.

'I always knew I'd meet you again.'

'You couldn't have!'

They smiled.

'I did too.'

Their thoughts appeared identical. When their hands were linked, finger lapped over finger, which was hers, which his? She was no longer sure. When they nibbled at a biscuit, bite and bite about, was it with his mouth she tasted or her own? The grey-brown skin of his forearm must be herself because she experienced the touch of her pink fingers on the responsive flesh. When they lay together on the short turf of the downs in the hollows of the golf course, the two hearts' double pumping were not two, but a fourfold one.

Holly had not dreamed love could be like this. It was not after all a matter of romance, of moonlit flower gardens, nor anything to do with withdrawals and pretence. It was ordinarily marvellous, like brown bread and butter with honey, or sunshine on the beach making each speck of sand glint and be itself. The world was not transformed by love, as poetry hinted; it revealed itself in splendour and she and Donald stood at the centre mutually revealing themselves not only to each other but to the world.

They were only two because an invisible mirror hung between them, dividing their wholeness into parts.

Fred and Lucille were making the best of Holly's changed state, her dreaminess, laziness, disinterest in books, refusal to talk things over in a sensible, adult way. It was, after all, only a phase. She would meet scores of much more suitable young men at Oxford. Holly would tire of Donald. He had no money, his poor clothes matched his plain face – big mouth, big nose, wiry hair like a flue brush, spots. One thing they were agreed on, as long as Holly lived in their house she would behave herself like a lady.

'Don't you care about me myself?' she asked furiously.

'You know we love you,' said Lucille. For her this was a passionate speech, and tears pricked Holly's eyes.

She sat half way up the stairs thinking it over.

Daddy was very kind to me when I was little. I really appreciated it at the time. But it's normal to grow out of one's parents, like animals do. Part of life really. In fact, it's unhealthy not to. Leaving the nest and all that. These old maids who live with their parents are pitiable. Really they are! I'm so lucky and glad to find Donald. Daddy'll soon get used to it. After all, it's natural. He must have known from the start that I would leave home and love some one else. It was only me that didn't know! How odd that seems now. Now I know I love Donald for ever and ever.

That afternoon Donald came to number 4, invited by Lucille who cooked a large meal and spoke of boys needing filling up. Fred talked a lot of the navy and the war. Donald was polite, but winked at Holly and held her hand quite openly as they sat by the fire.

When he had gone, Holly went glowing into the living-room.

'You must see, darling, he is quite an unsuitable friend for you.'

'Why?'

'That Scottish accent to start with! And he's no money and no prospects.'

'Students haven't.'

'Do stop using that word,' Fred commanded. 'You make the lad sound like a refugee from eastern Europe. Only foreign countries have *students*.'

Later, when she tried to explain to Donald how she felt about Fred, 'He's only your father, for God's sake.' His hardness was as little to be pierced as Fred's. She had to agree with one of them.

'You are right,' she whispered to Donald. 'Only you and me matter.'

It was not true, for she belonged to Daddy as well as Donald, but in a different way, of course.

Above everything else Donald was independent. His lack of a father, his intelligence and type of talent, an artist's, all ensured that, and gradually his spirit filled Holly. She was less and less able to take life at home with Lucille's meaning silences extending over several days, and Fred's self-consciously 'hurt' face, and the ever repeated, 'as long as you are in our house – '.

In late May Donald's course ended. There was no opening for him, just a holiday job singing with his group on the pier at Whitby. So he took that for the summer season, and Holly followed him after three weeks. She packed a case while everyone was out and left a letter but no address. Her mouth felt dry, her legs wobbled, but her hands moved busily enough.

Donald met her train at York and they travelled by bus over the moors, in sight of the sea, to Whitby. Because the Yorkshire hills were just a little like the Highlands, she felt she was going home with Donald, who loved her and talked endlessly, a chatterbox like herself, seriously and jokily, with fun and kisses and dreams of their future when he would be famous, a great singer.

It was a shock to see where he worked, not really a pier but a holiday arcade beside the harbour. The three men performed on a tiny stage without curtains. Propped up in front of it were crude notices advertising various other acts. Donald sang and the other two swayed about with their instruments. The audience simply stood in the open space in front of the stage, coming and going at will, and for the most part watched with expressionless faces, chewing gum, licking ices, and smoking. Holly tried to ignore the lostness and anxiety which crept up on her.

'It's not much is it?' asked Donald in a confident tone when he rejoined her.

– 123 –

'Just for the holidays,' she repeated his own words, bravely. 'Just a job for now.'

He took her to his room over a fish and chip shop. The dead, cold smell of it was appalling to her, a combination of fat, fish and the coke used to fire the fryers. The room was poky and bare, without a carpet and the shiny green walls appeared to have trickles of condensation marking them. Holly gulped and opened the window.

'We can buy some airwick.'

'What for?'

'This smell, Donald. It's awful!'

'You'll get used to it. We can't afford luxuries.' He looked round. 'We could make this room quite nice.'

The next day they were married. It should have been a happy day – was a happy day, Holly kept telling herself, but the face of her father surfaced again and again.

The ceremony was in a Registry Office squashed between the bus depot and a castellated house advertising Bed and Breakfast. There were no flowers, and, although two electric lights were turned on, the room was still dingily dark. In the ante-room a woman was vacuuming throughout the event.

The only guests were Donald's two companions and the man who was in charge of the pier entertainment, a red-faced Yorkshireman called Herbert, who took a fancy to Holly, liking the challenge in her eye and the creaminess of her skin. She was wearing a new, cheap cotton dress, blue speckled with yellow and rose buds, and with yellow ribbons hanging down the front. Donald had bought her a bunch of yellow roses at the florist's near the chip shop and the petals began falling while she was signing the papers. As they came out she looked anxiously for Fred. A bus came swirling into the depot, but Fred was not on it.

Herbert stood them what he called a slap-up spread in a hotel on the front, where the five of them sat in a bay window projecting into the street so that kids sucking lollies and their mums in crimplene two-pieces were as much spectators of the wedding breakfast as the other customers in the dining-room, most of whom were smarter and older than Holly.

Donald thought she looked spectacular in the cheap blue material, and when she pushed back her hair with both hands his memory dived back to Balchraggan and pulled out the bright child face of those days.

'We are going to be happy,' he whispered to her.

She kept involuntarily imagining what Fred and Lucille would be doing. Were they shouting or crying, trying to trace her or giving her up, selling her bed and tearing up her photographs? Anything was possible now she was on this roundabout of a new life in the strange, harsh, brash, cold but sunny northern town.

'What are you thinking about Mrs Chisholm?'

She looked round. Somehow they were back in the room over the chip shop. 'My father.'

'Don't then.'

'He has a right to feel that I've treated him badly.'

'Look.' He kissed her. 'You have only done what any normal girl does and married the man you love.'

But, suddenly ebbing, his own courage and high-spiritedness drained away. He was lonely and fearful, exposed to her.

'You do love me don't you, Holly?'

'Yes.' A small, timid word.

'Please tell me you do. Darling Holly. I can't bear it if you don't.'

'I do, I do, of course I love you.'

They fell together on the bed.

*

Safely married, Holly wrote to Carstead again and gave her address, then waited for Fred to arrive and the terrible scene there would be; but he did not come.

She had a lot of time to pass every day and could not stay long in their room. The fat smell was rather worse in the morning when the shop below was not frying and a breeze from the sea fanned the night's cold staleness up the face of the building and in the window, as well as up through the loose floorboards. Holly could plainly hear the sounds below of raking and sloshing the tepid fat, emptying out sacks of potatoes into buckets of water, the fishman's arrival with an ammoniac wave to crest the stink of fat for ten minutes, and the interminable chatter, screech and hack of the owner and his wife. He had a cough, she a raucous sense of humour.

Sometimes Holly watched Donald's show, which came on five times a day as the 'serious' item between two comics, but mostly she wandered about the town and along the sands imagining she had caught sight of Fred. Often she was sure she had – a tall, strong man with his trousers rolled to the knee paddling, just like Daddy had at Sandalcliff, or in a deck-chair with a child on his lap telling stories. When she came close, diffidently, these men turned on her blank faces. Fred's face she could not visualise. It was just a rosy blur with two blue spots for eyes.

She met Donald every evening after the last show, and that was the best part of the day, when they walked, arms linked, out to the end of the jetties, past the fishermen and the other couples. There the sea slapped softly at the stones, and an occasional bigger wave splayed a fan of broken water against the wall. If the tide were right, boats slipped out of harbour, their engines only muttering, their riding lights' reflections sinking and rising in the water. The sounds of the town had faded almost to nothing, and its illuminated frontages could be dismissed if you turned your back and looked the way the harbour light streamed, out to sea.

Hunger usually drove them back. Donald was perpetually hungry and ate from the stalls along the arcade. This was expensive and they had little money, so Holly tried to cook at midday. They discovered chitterlings and had these white flakes of used-up animal fat every day with potatoes and over-ripe tomatoes, sold cheaply. They had bananas for pudding, sliced bread and tea for other meals, sometimes jellied eels or an orange or icecream. Holly had no knowledge of nutrition, no skill at keeping a room in order, even had she had the heart to trouble with the crowded, ugly place. Donald could not help sometimes comparing Holly to his mother, or Chrissie, his sister. Cleanliness, order and good wholesome food seemed to spring naturally from their hands.

He grew thin and even paler than usual, but Holly did not notice the gradual change, being preoccupied with her guilt and when Fred might come.

On Donald's day off, which was Tuesday, they always went up to the moors. These were days of happiness and love. They took oranges and a bar of chocolate with them, and, as the bus climbed up out of the town, chugging, panting, protesting, Donald and Holly held hands, laid leg against leg, quivered and kissed. When they left the bus they stopped in the first hollow they came upon in the heather and bilberry blanket of the rocks to make love, thankful to be free of the chip impregnated bed, and, in Holly's case, her father's looming presence. He did not exist on the moorland which stood in for Balchraggan. It was not the same, it was bleaker and smaller, lacked the tremendous gorges, the matted woods, the waterfalls, the buzzards, and you could, if you listened hard, hear the hum of traffic on the roads which skirted and crossed the moors, but still . . . Donald and Holly were happy and free there, free to love each other.

In Whitby, although neither would have admitted it, the other seemed less real and compelling. Donald sometimes saw Holly from the stage and then she was just another girl in the audience, looking bored. And she, snuggling close in bed, was appalled to find the aroma of cold frying in the folds of his pyjamas. She suffered jabbing thoughts that he should not have brought her to this room.

But on the moors, they were happy and could speak freely. His face became transparent to her again and revealed their loving dual unity.

It was a poor summer that year and for several Tuesdays in a row it rained. On the third, the pair went to the moors, despite the rain, and ran in it, kissing with the water running down their foreheads and cheeks. Donald rumpled and pulled up her hair until she looked like the Highland child. When he hugged her as tightly as he could, the rain seeped out of their jerseys.

In their room again, the animal smell of wet wool mingled with the frying and Holly's poor cooking on the flaring gas ring, but Donald would not eat. He said he felt cold and sick. The next day he had a temperature and did not go to the morning show. Herbert arrived at lunchtime.

'Get up, young fellow me lad, or else – '

'He's not well, Herbert.'

'Either he comes or I telegraph for a replacement and that's final. No second chances.'

'I've only got a cold, Holly. All right, I'll come.'

'You are not fit to go out, Donald.' This was the very first time Holly had felt wifely. She must look after and defend Donald.

'He must come, or – ' repeated Herbert.

'That can't be legal.'

'No, well, there's nothing very legal about holiday pier work, darling,' replied Herbert, easily. 'It's casual, see?'

'Doesn't Donald have a contract?'

'A course not.'

'You should have,' she told him.

'What's the point?' asked Donald wearily, and pushed his bony legs out of the bed.

'Hey up! You're thin, lad,' said Herbert.

Donald dragged on his trousers without a reply. He was shivering. Herbert, when he'd seen the boy into his clothes, left. He found the clogging oily smell very unpleasant. Holly made Donald a hot drink of cocoa, but he was sick just after drinking it.

All that week he performed at the amusement arcade, and lay in the chip shop bed fully clothed between acts. He'd have kept his clothes on all night too if Holly had not pulled them off him.

She wanted to fetch a doctor but they had two worries. One was that he would forbid Donald to work and in that case they would have no money; the other that the chippie owner would say he couldn't have a sick man in his shop – well, almost in it, Donald's cough could be heard below – and they'd have to go. Both were desperate to keep the horrible room. Holly had a terror of sleeping on a shelter on the promenade wrapped in newspapers. Donald laughed shakily at her, but the nightmare persisted.

Until Thursday, they called what he had a cold, although he never blew his nose. By then her hands were dirty and stank of grease. There was no hot water in the lavatory where they washed and she had been in the habit of washing in the public bath-house which provided hot water, soap and towels for twopence, but since Donald had been ill she had stayed with him.

On Friday he woke with a frightful fit of coughing and then stretched out exhausted. His breath was sweetish, unpleasant. Holly tried not to come too close but he kept begging her to kiss him.

'Stroke my head, little love,' he said. 'Please Holly.'

She sat on the bed with one arm under his shoulders, stroking him until he fell asleep with his open mouth glued to her breast and his breath almost burning through her blouse.

At eleven-thirty she woke him for the midday show, but he fainted on the way downstairs. Holly hauled him back to bed, and rushed down to the amusement arcade. She told Herbert she would take Donald's part.

'I know the whole routine, backwards and upside down.'

Herbert reflected that Donald had not been singing, had not had what you could call a voice, for several days, and he couldn't get a replacement today, probably not before Monday.

'OK, my love, you have a little go, then.'

Holly did well. The crowd were intrigued by her way of singing and her 'good' accent was a novelty if nothing else. Holly sang with abandon and put in all the bits of by-play that went with each song. She *had* to do well to keep Donald in his job, so she crooned and quavered and made eyes as hard as she could. The manner sat peculiarly on her serious face, but that was part of the attraction. Herbert was satisfied for the moment.

She did all five shows on Friday and Saturday. In between she sat with Donald.

He slept for the most part. It was a sleep from which she could wake him only with difficulty.

The terrible thing for Holly was that his face became just a face, no longer a transparent mask for a Donald-Holly self. She watched his profile as a dog watches a master, hoping for a sign she knew. There was the hollowed cheek, the shut eye, the thin corner of a mouth sloping down, hair like coarse fur against the lumpy pillow. She observed a rim of yellow spittle on his lower lip for several minutes before wiping it away. It seemed to take all her resolution to do it.

But where has he gone? she thought. For *this* isn't him. Donald laughs and smiles and knows, always one jump ahead, as he says, waiting for me, and glad. His smile is like a window opening – it lets me in. This is the same body and face and brain behind it. So why am I shuddering when I go close? It isn't possible to find my husband repulsive. Well, not Donald – he's gone – his body. But I love his body. Can you fall out of love as quick as in? Or wasn't I ever?

I am despicable! 'I love you, I love you' one day and the next I'm thinking 'Who is this man?'

He says, Be honest. Never pretend.

This awful room. Well, clean it up then. The smell, I could never remove it, it's everywhere.

'I despise you Holly.' Would he say that?

This person can't say anything. He doesn't know where he is, he doesn't care any more. He's gone inside himself and shut the door on me.

Lots of people have much worse to put up with. Just get a grip on yourself. But I can't. I want to cry or to sleep. I want to wake up at home and all this not have happened.

No! Don't think that, not for one single second.

Would he ever say that if you were ill? Oh, never.

But he says, Be honest. Always.

Donald opened his eyes, he clutched her.

'Like a drink, Donald darling?' Carefully she supported him, and held the cup to his lips.

On Sunday night she knew she must call a doctor. She found a door with a plate round the first corner. He came most unwillingly.

'Why in heaven's name couldn't you have asked me to come in visiting hours if your husband's been ill for a week? Is this where you live? Up here? This building should have been condemned years ago. It's a disgrace. I'm not surprised people catch infections living here.'

He pushed the door which caught on the uneven floorboards and had to be given a shove to open fully, and saw the confusion – half-shut suitcases, clothes, paperbags of food, a dirty saucepan on a crusted gas ring, a carrier bag of refuse, empty unwashed milk bottles, patent cough medicine, peeling wallpaper looping down over the bed, a kimono over a chair back, a duffle coat on the sick man.

'Yes, he is very ill. We'll get him to hospital at once. He's thin – emaciated – what have you two been eating? Pleurisy, at all events.'

Holly went with Donald in the ambulance, shivery and frightened. Donald's stretcher was slotted out and put on a trolley, wheeled into a lift. A nurse held open the gates.

'Come along, Mrs Chisholm.'

In a small bedroom Donald was neatly undressed, re-dressed and put into bed watched by an old man in the other bed. Curtains were pulled round him with a lonely jangling. Only the bed's feet were visible.

'Go and wait outside, Mrs Chisholm.'

First she sent Fred a telegram, then sat in the waiting-room for the rest of the night. At six she was allowed to see Donald who was either asleep or unconscious, she wasn't sure which and dare not ask. The nurses were so quick and fierce. She had never been in a hospital before and it terrified her. She felt about six years old.

Donald had a tube going up his nose and another into his arm with a bottle of something that looked like urine but couldn't be dripping into him. Fearfully she touched his cheek, which twitched as if she were a fly.

Then a nurse with a grey face suggested she went home for a lie-down and something to eat.

'Have you told his parents that Mr Chisholm is ill?' asked the nurse in an accusing tone as if she guessed Holly would not have done.

Holly had never even thought of Donald's mother.

'His father is dead,' she said in a panicky voice and ran out of the hospital. The rubber edged doors whooshed behind her.

At the chip shop the owner was sloshing about with soapy water and a tattered mop. She had never seen him clean so much as the floor before, let alone the pavement outside. An angry swirl of water caught her feet and she hopped onto the bottom step of the staircase. The man barred her way up with the handle of the mop and told her she must leave. He didn't appreciate the remarks the doctor had made, opening his big mouth so all the customers could hear.

Holly ducked under the handle and went upstairs without replying. He shouted after her, 'Out on Friday, mind! You hear?'

She pushed some stale bread into her mouth and forced it down her throat with swigs of half-sour milk. Then she sat in a shelter on the promenade. She could not be sure if time was going slowly or unbelievably quickly. One or the other. It was not normal. She had been looking at a notice about being eligible for help with prescription charges which hung beside an orange curtain; now she was looking at the sea which had no horizon as a mist was flowing inland, its edge curling up on the oily grey water.

When she had dragged herself back to the hospital, Donald looked exactly the same. Only the level in the bottle was different. She stared hopelessly at the face she could no longer see into.

'How is he?' she asked timidly.

'No change, dear.' The dear was a grubby coin of no value.

Holly recoiled, and the nurse added belligerently, 'He is very ill. I hope you realize that.'

As it was time to go for the midday performance, Holly left the room, causing the nurse to huff and puff as she did things to Donald's inert body.

Very ill, very ill, very ill said her feet walking towards the stage. For once her talking head said nothing.

'This can't go on,' said Herbert when she appeared. He had been hoping young Chisholm would be back after the weekend. 'I'll have to ring for a replacement.'

'Donald's got pleurisy.'

'That's tough.'

'He's in hospital.'

'So I should hope. And about time too.'

Herbert appeared to sense she needed him to say something more. 'Well, I'm sorry kid, but that's life. You'll learn.'

'Don't get anyone else. Let me keep on, please!'

'Today you can and maybe tomorrow, but I'll have to get a fella.'

She began to pour out to him all the arguments for keeping her on, pointing out the circumstances and telling him how good she was. It was peculiar that she could not think, let alone speak of Donald being so terribly ill, but she could go on and on like this about the job, the pay being needed, the audience liking –

'To tell you the honest truth, kid, they don't,' Herbert interrupted. 'You was a novelty but that's gone off. You're not cut out for a crooner, are you?'

'What shall I do?' she whispered.

'Tell you what I think? Go back to your Daddy. He'll take care of you.'

Holly burst into tears, produced by treachery and relief, but quickly dabbed them away to preserve her make-up. She thought she would perform so exceptionally well that Herbert would be forced to keep her on. The two young men who accompanied her gave her nods of encouragement, but gloomily. She launched her body as well as her voice into the first song, seizing the microphone, wrapping herself round it. She watched this and heard her throaty low notes in a detached way, as if she were, perhaps, perched on the arcade roof, like that seagull who screeched violently and flapped off, wheeling into the mist.

Fred arrived in the town at two and went to the chip shop. Whatever he had dimly seen as Holly's down-at-heel lodgings with that fellow, this was inconceivably worse. One look, one horrified sniff was enough. He recognised the kimono and knew it was no mistake. The chippie sent him down to the arcade, to

Herbert's Happy Family Show, just after the bingo hall. Fred went.

The crowds were red from the sun of the day before, quite glad, really, of the mist to cool things down a bit; though, look, the sun was coming through. The opacity of the mist was becoming, minute by minute, curds of white cloud, yellowish where the sun touched them. The people were cheery from lunch, beer and double gins. They pushed and barged good-naturedly. Fred's jacket was daubed with a streak of candy-floss. In the distance he could hear the amplified sound of a woman's voice, coming and going in the chattering din. He had to thread his way through a queue waiting for a boat trip, a queue for icecreams, a queue straggling out of the women's lavatory. His steady feet carried him on.

Then Holly's face struck him like a blow and he stopped. For a moment he felt like turning his back and walking away. To see her stuck up there, swaying about with the microphone as if it were –
'God dammit,' he muttered.

Holly did not see him until her act was over, when she bowed and looked up and saw that one big face like a marker buoy among all the others, just blobs bobbing. In complete mindlessness, she ran at him, arms out. With a jolt he held her off.

'Take that stuff off your face,' he said, 'first.'

She went behind the curtain, avoiding the eyes of the two young men and Herbert. These three signalled to each other, wordlessly, with various facial contortions, then Herbert went breezily out to speak to Fred who blasted him.

'Look, matey,' said Herbert when he could, 'it's no affair of mine how my employees live. Chisholm is paid the usual whack for a student vac job – that's all there is to it. I didn't ask them to get wed. Nor more did you, I daresay. But what could I do? I bloody ask you. In all seriousness. What could I do?'

Holly came out with a clown white face, still wearing the blue dress, her hands and nails dirty. Fred was plainly embarrassed to be standing so conspicuously arguing with this fat fool, and his daughter looking like a washed-out tart. (Furiously he checked his thoughts.)

'Come on the beach,' he ordered her.

'I have to go back to the hospital.'

'Just for half an hour. It won't hurt.'

Neither of them wished to say Donald's name.

'My daughter's not coming back here. That's obvious,' Fred told Herbert.

'I sees that all right. Told her the very same meself only this morning.'

'Pity you didn't tell her weeks, months ago.'

'It weren't my business. I'm not a bloody child-minder.'

'So long as it's clear.'

Holly stood like a child in her father's shadow while the grown-ups settled matters.

'Goodbye Herbert.'

'Cheerio, kiddo. Keep smiling.'

She was led along the beach, a pace or two behind Fred, as if on a short, invisible lead, but she went willingly enough.

The high tide was trickling in its last few yards lifting scraps of litter and dry sand in its foam which turned a dusky cream. The family parties edged back against the prom wall, among the crackling fragments of old seaweed, like charred paper, where the sand was grey with dirt and smelt dry and sour. Fred and Holly picked their way between cramped groups of deck-chairs and sandcastles collapsing in slow motion. Eventually, at the far end of the beach, Fred sat on a rock and pulled her down. They were half a mile from the steps by the arcade.

When Holly had sat for a few minutes taking in where she was with slow, heavy awareness, she said to Fred, 'I have to go and see Donald.'

'What's he to you?'

This question made no sense, so she ignored it.

'Come on, answer me, Holly. I haven't come down here to put up with your obstinacy. What's the boy got?'

She thought for an instant, quick and striking as opening a shutter on a view of mountains, of Donald's loving face, his hands, his mouth, and an awkwardness crept into her.

'Eh?' Fred made the sound fierce and demanding. 'What's he to make you behave like this?'

Her sluggish brain was panicky now. If people went away and got *married* – Daddy must know! How could he pretend? When she ran away she had finished the argument. Surely? He must know. With painful reluctance she turned her body to face him. He was as large, solid, pink-fleshed as ever, and his round eyes reflected the water. On how many occasions in the past six years had she sat like this, a sort of tongue-tied prisoner, churning with resentment and with love, longing for his approval.

'Come on, Holly. You owe your mother and I an explanation.'

'Mother and me,' she corrected him, to express her contempt for him because he would not acknowledge she could love Donald.

'*What?*'

'Me not I.' Her heart was hammering. He was angry now. She dreaded his anger.

'For God's sake! I'm bloody well not taking cheek from you on top of everything else.' His polished shoes churned up the sand.

She was freed to say, 'I love Donald. We love each other.'

'Holly!' Fred wailed his exasperation. 'You don't know what the hell life's about. You can't just run off and marry the first man who asks you.'

'I have.' Suddenly her eyes were stinging with tears. She faced Fred helplessly. 'But I have, Daddy.'

'He's no good for you, darling.'

Delicately she put one finger on the back of his hand.

'You'll ruin yourself. Oh Holly!' he groaned.

Her chest was one box heavy with her thumping heart, her head another, buzzing, numbed. Her sandals were sinking into the sand saturated with water and cold. She lifted them out with a squelching suck and, flexing her knees, held her feet in the air. More and more she was a child in a fix, Daddy there to help. She was still crying feebly.

Fred shook out his spotless handkerchief and handed it to her in a bunch of folds.

'Donald isn't no good,' she said, when she had wiped her face. 'He tries so hard.'

'A man's no right to take responsibility for a wife until he has achieved something, got a standing in the community.'

'Is that what you thought up to say in the train?' she asked with juvenile cheek.

'I came by car,' Fred replied severely, but then he smiled at her.

Donald and all difficulties receded. She sat holding Fred's hand, her cheeks stiff from tears. The gulls' screams, the shouts and cries of children were heard again, and with apparent unwillingness the sea retreated with rearguard surges. The cleaned, dampened sand began to be marked by naked feet and the prong toes of birds.

Families, with due caution, extended their emplacements and the walking icecream seller had more room to get about. A red balloon marked ICES bobbed and strained over his head. Simultaneously Fred and Holly took deep, relaxing breaths, he to enjoy the seaweed tang, she in acceptance of her father.

'What about the hospital?' suggested Fred after a while, as if something had been settled.

'Yes, I ought to go.'

'Does his mother know he's ill?'

'No. I couldn't do anything.' She held out her hands as if physically giving the matter to him.

'Shall we send her a telegram on our way?'

'Yes please, Daddy.'

In the hospital at five o'clock Donald was asleep although he had been asking for Holly previously. She sat by his bed, sometimes smoothing the sheet which was already as taut, creaseless and starchy white as it could be. Donald with tubes in his nose and his arm did not look like someone to love.

Fred, on the other hand, who came in on tiptoe and sat opposite her across the bed, did. He sat four-square on the tubular chair, hiding it with his navy blue shoulders, one leg lifted on the thigh of the other. He retied the lace of his shoe, a flexible, polished leather shoe that in itself spoke of confidence and security; he brushed off some sand. He crinkled up his face at her gently as if he felt that in here smiles as well as movements should be quiet. Then he took out his pipe, unscrewed the bowl, tapped it, poked about inside, because he could not smoke in the ward and yet loved the feel of his pipe. Holly noticed his hands for the how-many-thousandth time, as pink as his face, the wrinkled backs marked by purplish grey veins, the edges smooth and thick, curving round to the palms now cupping his pipe, and the short, strong fingers. The length of the fingers was about the same as the width of his palm and each was furrowed across the knuckles. She knew they felt warm and secure, and smelt of lifebuoy soap.

Donald twitched under the napless bedcover, his nose beaked to the ceiling. Something in the tube gurgled, then all was still again. On the pillow, his face was dingy and between the coarse stubble spikes were red spots. His eyes were ringed with flesh so dark his eyelashes were invisible. He no longer smelt of sickness, but of hospital. Holly tried to imagine lying close in his arms and shuddered. The chaos and stink of the chip shop room had infiltrated all her memories and she had to go back to Lurgann, to lying in the grass there, to find her Donald and, of course, then he was only a boy, and she herself ignorant.

She glanced at Fred, who passed across to her another friendly, almost conspiratorial, smile. The longer she sat here the less real it seemed, and the less she felt. A sort of waking coma took her over. She expected Donald to die but no longer felt the terror of that, and was perplexed by her lack of knowledge. Would his jaw drop when it happened? Would his eyes open, or stay shut? How soon would the doctor take out the tubes? Where would he, would his body, go?

The mound in the bed was motionless, hardly human, apart from the head which was not Donald's anyway.

'I'll just go outside and have a smoke,' Fred said in a very low voice. 'Do you want anything. A cup of tea?'

The unreality of normal life with tea and tobacco threatened her calm for a moment. Tea! How typical of Daddy. But still, he only meant it to stand in for love. She shook her head.

The sound of the door closing caused Donald to open his eyes. Slowly, and apparently painfully, they travelled round and found Holly. She watched as knowledge, then pain filled them. When she had found his hand under the sheet, she stroked it, but the look in his eyes did not change and her heart began a rapid tattoo. A brownish tear dropped from the corner of his left eye and another pooled in the hollow beside his nose.

'Don't cry, Donald.'

She bent sideways and placed her head, very gently, against his chest, her cheek sliding on the glassy sheet. It was better, like this, not seeing him. She could speak to the man she remembered, not the tubed-up half skeleton, the colour of rags, who lay here and could not speak.

'I love you, Donald. I always will. I'll never forget you.'

How terrible death was! Making you want a person to be gone before they were.

'I'll hold you in my heart always.'

It became uncomfortable to keep her head just off his chest, so she sat up again. His eyes were closed. No more tears.

Then the nurse came in to take his temperature and fuss about with the tubes and bottles. She seemed more concerned than usual and left the room with a quick, one, two, three of her black laced shoes. She came back with the doctor. Holly observed his uncommunicative face, stood up and backed away. She supposed Donald was going to die now, and what she had sickened to imagine would happen before her eyes. Fred came back and stood beside her. She wanted to lean on him, but felt she owed it to Donald to stand apart.

The doctor was listening and feeling. Donald was awake, swivelling his head very slightly in Holly's direction. She creased her terrified face in a smile.

'Yes, yes,' said the doctor. 'He's on the mend.' He closed his stethoscope. 'You are a lucky young man. Close shave, you've had. Good.' He beamed at the nurse, then frowned at Holly.

'You are?'

'His wife,' said Holly, and did not believe herself.

The doctor shot a startled glance at Fred, who said staunchly, 'This is grand news.'

'Yes, well, he's a very sick man still. Shall we go outside?' He shepherded them into the corridor as he spoke. 'Yes, he's definitely on the mend, turned the corner. You are a lucky young woman.'

She gulped. The doctor's head was silhouetted against a silver rectangle of window.

'Can I take my daughter away for a few hours? She is very tired.'

'Of course. Keep her all night. The best thing. In the morning she'll see a big improvement. Now nurse – ' He turned to give the girl fresh instructions as Fred took Holly out.

She noticed they were driving out of Whitby.

'You need a change,' he said.

Somewhere in a moorland valley they stopped at a country house hotel and Fred took two rooms.

Still dazed, Holly wandered into her bedroom, a big square blue room. The carpet was soft, the bed cover, curtains and chairs all of the same glazed chintz with peacocks and sundials. Between the windows was a long mirror and Holly saw herself for a second without recognition – cheeks not flushed but spotted red on dirty white, hair matted and spiky, dirty dress, torn hem, blackened toes protruding from broken sandals. It was just one more awful fact to contemplate, and she sagged against the window frame. Outside was a rose garden.

Fred came in and put his arms round her.

'Have a bath, pussy. You'll feel better then. Look, I brought a case with a few of your old clothes. Mummy packed them for you. I think she put in some shampoo.'

Holly lay in the bath a long time, crying quite a lot and urinating every now and again as the warm water and the steamy air relaxed her. She felt used up and valueless. The future was a void.

At supper Fred took care to praise her looks, which were improved, but the girl still had a patina of something Lucille would have wanted to scrub out. Her hair pulled back in a band and an old dress she had worn for school did not entirely cancel out what was in her face. He hated to see the chipped varnish on her nails.

To be fair, Fred did his best to talk kindly about Donald's improvement, but Holly would not respond; so he spoke of the hotel and the food. Everything was extremely comfortable. A warm, sunny September evening made the most of the wide spaces, mirrors, bowls of delphiniums. Even a tank of angel fish was touched by the pink sunset flooding in. Holly smoothed the napkin on her knee. Its starch showed up the roughness of her skin, but pleased her all the same. She loved clean linen, glasses half filled with ruby wine, scrolls on the fork handles, candles whose gold shields of flame were unnecessary but pretty. She shuffled her feet in her shoes, glad to have nylons on again. She smiled at Fred.

'That's better. That's the ticket. A smile at last.'

'Oh Daddy.'

'There, there.'

Her face was pale but glazed under the skin with the flush of exhaustion.

'I'm not going to cry again, am I?'

He passed her another handkerchief, white, smelling clean, shaken out for her to use. Just the cool feel of its smoothness against her face was soothing and to blow her nose into its odourless crispness had once been a cure for all ills.

'Oh Daddy!'

She smiled at him, behind the sliding tears, until she felt her cheeks would crack.

'That's my pussy.'

After the meal she phoned the hospital and, while waiting to be connected to Donald's ward, imagined the muted noises there, the ether smell, the tinkling instruments in silver bowls, Donald's mud skin, his stubble, his breath.

'Your husband is sleeping soundly. You get a good night's rest too. He is completely out of danger.'

Putting down the receiver, she also put Donald aside and all the rest. What was 'all the rest'? she asked herself, but preferred not to answer.

She slept deeply and long. Fred arranged breakfast in her room. She sat up, wearing one of his shirts, but he was dressed in his usual dark trousers, and navy blue sweater, white shirt. He smelt of lavender after-shave and baby powder as he kissed her.

'Look,' he said, 'I went out to buy a paper and I found you some remover for your nails in the village shop.'

She hid them. 'Yes, they are nasty.'

'Before we go to the hospital this morning, we'll buy you some new clothes.'

'I like that old dress.'

'Smacks of school a bit, though? Now you're a married lady.'

She was too self-conscious to respond.

He took her silence for encouragement. 'Your mother and I do wish you had not rushed off like that, pussy. We'd have wanted to be at our daughter's wedding.'

'Not to Donald.'

He ignored that and drove on in his bulldozer way. 'It's a very special day. Your mother was very upset.' A tremor ran over Fred's face. Holly really did not care that Lucille had been deprived of the bride's mother's day, but she hated to see her father's features tremble even for a moment.

'It's you I care about, Daddy,' she said loudly in the voice of a startled child. 'Not being able to give me away.'

She was seeing Fred's face opposed to Donald's as both stood beside her at the altar and, in an overwhelming rush, realised her marriage had been disloyal. She ought not to have married Donald because it was letting Fred down. Then identifying the thought, she chased it into hiding.

'How silly,' she remarked aloud.

'What is?'

'Oh – people.'

'A bit on the erratic side,' he agreed, handing her coffee in a big fluted pink cup.

'It's nice here.'

'Not a bad place is it?'

He began to butter and cut up his slice of toast, then load each triangle with marmalade and insert it neatly into his mouth, held open, rounded, for the bite. Holly, to whom this sight of Fred feeding himself was thoroughly known, saw for the first time that he looked like a cherubic and clean baby, sitting there in his neat clothes, a white square of napkin spread on one knee and one splayed hand resting on it, while the other deliberately, precisely raised another golden piled morsel.

She lay back on the pillows, wriggling her clean toes against the sheets and gazing out of the window at fantail doves on the stable roof. She was sinking, sinking into her parents' world.

Fred had not chosen this hotel by design, he never plotted in any department of life, but he was glad enough to see how Holly was responding to it. It was better this way than any number of talks about her new way of life, how totally unsuitable it was and could not be allowed to continue. Fred detested talks and scenes, would do much to avoid them. From his earliest days he had borne events and hidden his feelings, but that had never meant he acquiesced. In spirit he still sat outside the door of his mother's bedroom, back braced to the unfeeling wood, determined to wait for her return.

'That was a pretty appalling room you were living in,' he said to Holly, leaping over the actual marriage.

'Yes.' She blushed. 'That was all we could afford.'

'Master Donald had no right to propose marriage without the means to support you.'

'He didn't propose. I mean, it was just understood between us. From when we were children, at Balchraggan.'

'Oh, come off it Holly! That's years ago. You hadn't met the fellow since the war.'

Fred was growing angry again. His feet were in a flurry of heel and toe taps.

'It's bloody calf-love, that's all.'

She was too tired for a battle. 'Don't say something you'll regret Daddy, and I won't either.'

He twitched and coughed, and noisily rearranged his body in the chair, while her mind lifted away outside and fluttered with the doves' wings in absent withdrawal. She could not reconcile the justice of Fred's concern for her with the interior rightness of

Donald's love, so she stopped thinking about it, which made an agreeable peace in her heart. She could rely on Daddy to keep matters on an even keel, and she rested against this assurance.

Eventually she had to get up, have another green soapy bath, then return to Whitby where Fred insisted on buying her a blouse and skirt – pink with tiny buttons and frills on the collar and the skirt pockets. Then it was midday and too late for the hospital so they had lunch. Fred took her, unknowing, to the same bay window where she had eaten on her wedding day and the same kids and mums dragged past the window, the same girls with dark glasses shot glances at her treated so tenderly by that handsome man. Holly's heart gave one or two violent pulses, aches for Donald, then quietened. She and Fred looked down on the beach and talked of Sandalcliff.

'I'm surprised you ever left the navy.'

'I'd had enough.'

'Of the sea?'

'Seeing men killed. It's a nasty business, war.'

'I'm sure.'

'There was a period,' he said, now she was married surely he could treat her like an adult, 'when I couldn't look at the water like we are now and not see dead bodies floating in it. Not nice tidy, decent ones either. Men who'd been turned into bits of charred meat by burning oil on the surface, head and arms handing in lifebelts with no legs below and guts trailing in the water like squid.'

'Don't!'

'Yes, well. It wasn't funny, I can tell you. Don't like to talk of it. Never think of it normally.'

Holly was well aware of her father's propensity for not thinking about things which upset him and for the first time she could sympathize, wish to copy him. She knew at this precise moment – 1.45 she saw on the sun-ray clock above the cocktail bar – that she should be going to the hospital, but was not.

'You like the sea again now.'

Fred smiled out of the window at the sealskin blue black of it. Yes, he loved every shade, movement, sound of it.

'It washes away the earth's impurities,' he said. 'I read that once.'

Where? she thought, amazed.

'And it's true, you know. All those poor dead fellows are gone now and the bitterness of it. The salt takes away the harshness somehow. I don't think it's too bad lying on the ocean floor.'

She imagined the dark, dark greenness, the currents wafting the hair, little striped fishes darting through the eye-sockets.

'As for all those guns and shells, they rust away to harmlessness. And the ships with men still at their action stations are drifted over with sand. It doesn't seem half as bad as burying someone in the muddy earth, with worms.'

'Daddy, you surprise me.'

'That makes two of us then.' His shadowless eyes challenged her. She should know she could not entirely escape his anger.

'It's time to go,' she said. 'To see Donald.'

At the hospital Fred waited in the corridor. Donald was a whole lot better, the nurse said, and Holly expected him to be sitting up watching the door, but he was still lying on his back, angular like a meccano man, with the tubes plugged in.

Holly kissed him. His eyes opened, flickered and hazily knew her.

'Holly,' he muttered.

She sat on the bed and began to talk in a flood of Fred's coming, where she'd been, what Herbert had said and the chip shop man. Donald did not seem to take much notice. His hand which she had taken in hers, escaped and feebly touched the new skirt she wore.

'Yes, new. Daddy bought it for me. Isn't it a pretty colour?'

Donald twitched his eyes away from her face.

'He's been really kind. The hotel we went to was so luxurious. I had two marvellous deep baths and there were doves in the yard, real doves, white ones, not pigeons. They are so pretty with their pleated tails.'

Donald managed a grimace, which she took for appreciation. She had the impression he wanted to ask something, for he looked carefully about the room as if searching for a clue to what he had to say.

There was nothing in the room but white walls, checked curtains and Holly, all pink. To Donald her brilliant eyes were sharp as jewels. He had the fancy they must hurt her, faceted like that.

'Don't cry, darling.' Not very expertly she wiped his tears

away. 'You'll soon be better. Then everything will be all right.'

When the nurse came in she said that Donald was worried about the digs.

'That's taken care of. I've told him. Daddy's looking after me. We'll fetch my husband's things and then, when you're better, Donald, we'll see. No panic, darling.'

She nodded at him and the nurse.

Donald, not able to think clearly and feeling very sick and weak, was sure, all the same, there was more to say. The world of his life was flying away, thrown out from the hospital as if by centrifugal force, leaving him isolated in this empty room.

'I'll go now,' said Holly. 'He seems so tired. See you tomorrow, darling.'

Even to Holly her movements and voice seemed too loud and sudden, as if she had been drinking. She bounced and floated away with Fred and they went back to the hotel.

He told her that evening that on Thursday he must go back to work. Three days were the most he could take off. The problem then arose of where Holly should go. She indicated to him that if he gave Donald and herself some money to pay the rent of a better room where she could live until Donald was well, that would be best. And then? asked Fred. It would be October, the season over. Had Donald a job in view? Holly might believe in his talents; no one else appeared to.

'Actors often have to rest,' she explained.

'Is he an actor then?'

'Well, a singer. He wants to work in opera.'

Fred had never seen an opera but to him the word implied, at the best, fat women in red satin, but more probably some sort of unpleasant, unnatural licence. There was no job in which he would have less liked to see a son-in-law. If you could call it a job of work – singing and prancing about in bloody, silly costumes.

Fred lit his pipe. He wanted to stay in control of this situation.

'It's not fair to judge Donald, Daddy. After all – '

'I hardly know the chap?'

'Not his work, no.'

'Work! Is that what you call it? And what will he do until he gets noticed by the management of the Windmill.'

Holly ignored this poor sarcasm.

'They rest. That means take jobs in bars and shoe-shops.'

The mention of a shop was enough to make Fred react violently. Into his resentful memory came the grocer's where he had been apprenticed – its smells and meannesses.

'Dammit, Holly! There's no future in that. And to think you might have been going to Oxford next month.'

There was a short, brooding pause. Holly had forgotten Oxford, and Fred's words flung her back into its sunlit grey calm and order, the thrill she had felt going up for the interview, the surprise that shops and buses had been the same there as anywhere else.

'Whatever happens,' continued Fred, 'I can't and won't have you living in some cheap room while Donald finds this work in a shop.'

A whiff of the chip shop room was superimposed on her dream of Oxford.

'It's that young man's job to sort his ideas out, find work, and get a decent place for the pair of you.'

She hated to have Donald called 'that young man', hated what her father was saying; agreed with it in her heart of hearts.

'Aren't I right?'

She gazed at him, mentally placing his face beside Donald's.

'Aren't I right, Holly?'

She nodded miserably.

'Until then – you come home with me.'

'Oh no, I couldn't possibly!'

She said it explosively but it was a little trick firework of opposition and had no conviction. Already she knew she would. She'd return to Carstead, to Lucille's clean and orderly house, her own claustrophobic bedroom with the single bed and the old Fido nightdress case drooping on the pillow, all his perkiness gone.

The hospital almoner eased her way. She agreed with Fred that it might be a practical solution of this temporary problem if Mrs Chisholm returned to her parents, as the patient was without means and would need quite a few weeks' convalescence. Perhaps a stay at a convalescent home along the coast could be arranged. She was right in thinking he had no means?

'Well, I suppose his mother might help. She's a widow,' said Holly, handing her married life over.

So it was his mother who visited Donald the next weekend, after he had had Holly's letter for two days under his pillow, all blotched with tears and crumpled with indignation. He loved her, needed her, craved the slightest touch of her hands and she had gone back home. 'Only till you're well, dearest, and have a job. I mean something permanent that will give us a fair way of life'. He supposed that was her father talking. What did he know about music? A Philistine by the sound of it, and a bore. Well, old man Tickener had made a mistake if he thought Donald Chisholm was settling for anything less than the career in opera that he wanted above all things. 'I came to tell you, but you were sleeping and looked so peaceful.' Yes, and you were afraid, Holly. 'It's only a brief goodbye, darling.' God! It sounded like some sugary novel.

'Think on it no more,' said Mrs Chisholm in her soft but cold Highland voice. 'The lassie's no for you, Donald lad.'

'This is only a temporary separation, Mother.'

'So you say now.'

She took him to the tiny flat she had in north London and he slowly recovered on a folding bed in the living-room. His chest mended quick enough, his spirits slowly.

Early in October he went to see his tutor at the College and they discussed possible jobs for him. There was nothing definite, nothing at the moment, at Christmas perhaps, or come the spring? The next day he received one of Holly's letters that he had learned to dread. They spoke most days on the telephone – he went to an outside call-box as Mrs Chisholm was touchy about her phone bill. Of course, she gave him the coins for the box, but that kept the cost in check. On top of the phone calls, Holly sent letters and these, although full of loving expressions, always carried some chilling news. This time it was that her bloody interfering father had 'been on to' (what an expression!) the college at Oxford where Holly had previously gained a place. The headmistress of her school had written, and one of her subject teachers, and the end result was that the college had agreed to let her start her degree course after all that year.

It was as if they'd never been married. Sometimes he wondered if they had, or if the whole summer was a sick dream he'd had in hospital. He handed the letter to his mother, with a hand almost too disheartened to move. She read it with pursed lips and just a tiny gleam of 'I told you so' – for which he could hardly blame her.

'Ay, that young lady knows how to look after herself.'

Donald had been leaning forward, now he flopped back.

'But she took no care at all of you, my lad.'

Always down-grading people was his mother.

'She just wants to wipe the slate clean, it seems to me. Is that what you want, Donald?'

'No. We are married.'

His mother irked him, as much as Fred irritated Holly. He resented her heavy handed, obvious summings-up. On the other hand, the boy Donald, still inside his adult body, relied on and appreciated her, just as Holly trusted Fred.

That evening when Holly phoned him, he would not go to the phone.

Two days later came another letter, from Oxford. Her plan, she wrote, was that he should find a temporary job in Oxford (they were ten a penny there) until musical work came up as she was absolutely certain it would. 'Darling Donald, I believe in you!' which was simple enough to write, as Mrs Chisholm commented.

Donald did not reply for several days. He was thinking it over between the long troughs of time when he thought of nothing, just lay on the sofa staring at the sky, the odd pigeons and starling flocks which crossed the wedge of it he could see between the tower blocks. He supposed he would go to Oxford. He wanted to be with Holly, of course he did.

She rang up. 'Please Donald, when are you coming?'

'Have you found anywhere for us to live yet?'

'Well, actually, now I've discovered that I absolutely have to live in for my first year. No exceptions, I'm afraid. It's silly, I know, very silly since we are grown-up enough to be married, but – there it is. I *am* sorry, darling. Next year though, well, from June really, we can be together.'

'That won't do,' he said with all the firmness he could muster.

'No. I was afraid you'd think so.'

'Well, will it?'

'No.'

'You can't think so.'

'No.' The line crackled. Then a silence.

'Do you?'

'No. But what else can we do?'

'You could give up this bloody course. You told me before you hated academic life.'

'Yes.' Her voice was growing steadily fainter. 'I do, sort of. But it means I can be independent.'

'What of? Of me, do you mean?'

'When you are out of work.'

'I shan't be all my life, Holly. This is just starting troubles. You know that. Or you said you did.'

'Yes. But Daddy says –'

'Oh Daddy!' He shouted at her. 'Don't tell me what he says. It was him persuaded you to leave me in the first place.'

'No, he didn't. Please, Donald, don't be angry.' She now sounded quite childish. 'He didn't persuade. I just saw –'

'Yes, that life at Carstead is much more comfortable. That's the truth isn't it?'

Her reply, after a pause, was so weak he could hardly hear it. 'Not just that, Donald.'

He put down the receiver; but knew immediately that he had little option but to go to Oxford. She was right, he'd find work there.

Then, without warning, at his lowest ebb, as such things do come, he had an offer of work in Glasgow, all winter and possibly a Scottish summer tour. His tutor had spoken for him. He filled up with hope and energy like a balloon expanding. His flesh almost visibly firmed, his drab hair stood up from his skull again like a new brush. Down to Oxford he rushed on his first real outing.

Holly was not in her room. Impatiently he waited for her, flipping through her papers and books. Then he saw her walking in the grounds, kicking up the piles of autumn leaves at the path edge and talking hard to another girl. Both heads were bent. It was clear something of absorbing interest was being discussed. He felt excluded, cheated even, and banged angrily on the window. Neither of them heard.

But when at last she came in, her face blazed with pleasure to see him. 'Donald!'

'Holly!'

They paused for a moment, then flung themselves together, and kissed thirstily. When he held her away from him he saw she was flushed with health and high spirits, her skin gleamed, her hair flew here and there as she questioned, answered, laughed.

'Donald! How lovely to have you!'

'Lurgann girl,' he said, stroking her face, kissing her eyelids. 'I was afraid you might not come.'

'How could I keep away,' he replied, biding his time. 'How do I look?'

She stood back, 'A bit peaky. Never mind. I'll soon make you well. I can cook for you here. See, I have a little cooker behind this curtain.'

She showed him her room – bed folding into the wall, useful cupboards, table in the window.

'This is where I shall work. It's nice to have an outlook. I think I'm going to specialise in dramatic literature.'

'I hope not,' he said.

She stopped dead, her hands splayed on the table.

'I hope you are going to come with me, to Glasgow.'

He told her of the operatic engagement there and, as he spoke, she sat herself slowly in the one armchair.

'Where shall we live?' was her first question.

'Oh, in rooms.'

'Not after Whitby.'

'That was exceptional. Digs can be OK.'

'Not in Glasgow.'

She had a horror of the city, based partly on what Bruce and Bob had told her of their tenement home with rats and bedbugs.

'Have you ever been there?'

'No, but everyone knows Glasgow is a dreadful place.'

'Don't be silly, Holly.'

She shrugged and suggested they had tea. She had some crumpets in her leather bag with her books, and took a stale-looking bottle of milk and a crushed packet of China tea from a drawer, cups from her bathroom. Donald scornfully thought it playing at being a student, but she looked earnest about it, and began to talk again about drama – 'specially the early ones, I'm interested in, like Dekker and Webster and Marlowe.'

'The Greeks were the earliest.'

'You know what I mean.'

He wanted to cross her.

'Why do you have China tea?'

'I like it.'

'You used to call it watery.'

'Now I like it. Any objections?'

'In any case, you should have lemon, not milk.'

'It's how you please. Serve to taste, it says.'

She had a child's brazen stare, then she melted.

'Oh Donald, be nice! I'm so glad you've come. I was so awfully afraid you wouldn't.'

He let that pass, and drank his tea in silence while she chattered on and on, never mentioning Whitby or Glasgow, or anything connected with the fact that they were husband and wife. His ring on her finger was the only proof he had, that and the foreboding in his wounded chest.

'Holly,' he broke at last into her talk, 'I have to take the job in Glasgow. It's a good one, better than I hoped would come my way so soon, even before I was ill.'

'Yes. You are good, Donald. I told Daddy so.'

'You agree?'

'Of course! You absolutely must take it.' She wiped the butter off her fingers with a tissue. She was nerving herself. 'But I cannot come.' She crumpled the tissue and rolled it into a ball before facing him, but she looked at his mouth, not his eyes.

'Because you can't face living in digs – with me!'

'Not just that. There's my degree.'

'You don't need a bloody degree! You never have until now.'

'Later on, if anything happened to you, it would be security.'

'That's what your father taught you to think.'

'Daddy has been very, very kind.'

'But you're my wife, Holly.'

'Yes.' She came out of her trance-like stillness and threw the tissue in the wastepaper basket. She looked at him boldly with bright blue eyes. 'But I don't really see what that's got to do with it.'

'Everything!'

She stood up and began to gather the plates and cups on to a tray, talking as she did so remarkably coolly.

'I don't see why. After all, plenty of couples stay apart for a bit. You have to get started. And it would be sensible for me to have the security of a degree, just in case . . . Perhaps, Donald, we did get married too soon. Maybe we weren't really ready.'

'You'd think it was a bloody business deal!'

'No, but we weren't very prudent, were we?'

Donald could not believe this was happening. A horrible inertia took hold of him. He sagged on his chair. There was so much to say in reply about love, and taking risks, and being together mattering more than anything else in the whole world, but if Holly no longer felt that – what was the point?

She came to stand behind him, placing her hands inside his open collar. She bent over and kissed his forehead. It occurred to him there was the best way possible to settle this nonsense.

But in bed she no longer felt right. She was loving and sweet, but like a child, as if she had forgotten all he had taught her. Her body was stiff with a sort of ignorance, or could it be dislike?

'Do you wish we weren't married?' he mumbled to her, keeping his eyes shut.

'Of course not, no. How awful.' She kissed him with something like passion, yet he was not deceived.

Afterwards they arranged the future as she wanted it. They would live apart for three years while she got her degree and he started on his career.

'Untrammelled by a wife,' as she said with an echo of her mother. 'In the holidays, of course, we can be together.'

'You mean you will actually come to live in digs with me?'

'Don't be silly, Donald,' she replied with a childish arrogance. She sat on the floor leaning against his legs.

'Why did you leave me?' he asked, and she knew he meant at the hospital.

It was not possible to tell him she couldn't have stood another day there, so she said nothing.

'All I could feel,' he said softly, 'was that your love did not count for much at all.'

She rubbed herself against his leg in feeble apology.

'I've tried to talk myself out of it but it keeps coming back, that feeling. You can't love me much.'

'I do,' she said. 'I always have. Please forgive me, Donald. I should have stayed.'

'I do forgive you. But not deeply enough.'

Not long after he went back to his mother's home and then to Glasgow.

He and Holly did not meet for the Christmas holiday because he was working flat out and she had some serious reading to get through, and his room was rather squalid, he admitted. At Easter he was on tour, and Holly went to a drama school in Wales with a girlfriend. They wrote to each other but his letters were more and more about his work and his theatrical companions, and Holly's letters became very short. She could not chatter to Donald any more. She thought it must be because he had said that about not forgiving her deep down.

When the summer came, Donald's show, a modern opera by a young Scot taken up by the media, transferred to America. This was a tremendous break for him. What young singer was offered a chance like this? as he wrote proudly to Holly. Fred called it a flash in the pan.

Holly avoided Carstead and occupied herself with various theatrical ventures, one of which was taken to the Festival Fringe. To her surprise, she discovered that she really was quite a competent actress. It had not been a case of a fond drama teacher's adulation. Fred and Lucille managed to bear her success with equanimity, for at least she was at University and not with that fellow.

Donald stayed in America all that second year because he found another job there. For Christmas he sent Holly a long, kind and patiently reasoned, quite final letter. Their marriage had been a mistake. He had thought so for a long time, but now he knew for sure since he had met someone else. He still loved Holly, but more as a brother. He would always have happy memories of her, of them, of Lurgann.

The pain was terrible, and the rage she turned on Fred. He had separated them! He had mocked Donald, denigrated him, driven him away, locked her up in this dead place!

'Oh for God's sake, I've had enough of this,' he shouted.

He jumped out of his chair and slammed down his book. The china ladies on the mantelpiece juddered slightly. Jaw tightened, neck thickened with vein cords standing out, forehead tight, mouth elongated and lipless he stood glaring at Holly with eyes so pale they were like water.

She faced him, equally angry but vibrating with guilt as well.

Stronger than anger he felt his wounds. For he had wanted nothing but the girl's good, would have been delighted to see her married to someone suitable, was even prepared to make the best of this singer chap. Yet all she could do, was blame him, be difficult, obstructive, plain bloody daft. For weeks she wouldn't look him straight in the eye, wouldn't answer, shrugged her silly shoulders and tossed her chicken head at him. He would like to hit her. Oh! many's the time. What she needed, had never been given, was discipline. She'd had life too soft. She should have had his childhood!

'You have ruined my life,' Holly said in toneless words, each separated by a quick breath. She left the room.

Lucille continued mending in the clinging silence which followed, while Fred walked from the sideboard to the window and back several times. He did not see the room he was in or the street outside – the roofs of cars passing, a bus, people's heads in woollen hats, the lamp standards springing into orange life – he was cocooned in a place he went to when things got on top of him. There was water regularly swishing near him, a blue-grey light, a wind inserting itself between his clothes, sun on his face, his back, his face as he paced. No one else was there. He was alone with the sea, and safe. He loved the firmness of the unresounding planking below his solid legs. Inside the wrapping of sea and air, he could let himself relax and then that place faded too, and he came at last in contact with a piece of green cloth, the extreme of softness and comfort. Without words he spoke to his mother, who did not reply but certainly heard.

Such moments affected him in two ways. They increased his self-pity, for she rewarded it with her own pity for his lonely motherlessness. They also strengthened his self-confidence, made him able to appear in command of himself again, affable and strong.

After half an hour he could stop pacing, sit down and take out his pipe. First he drew on the empty bowl to make sure no crumbs of old tobacco obstructed it. He liked the suck-suck noise it made. Then his squat hands cradled down his tobacco jar from its place below the lavender lady, and carefully, judiciously, with thumb and stubby forefinger pinched out just the right amount of the speckled, moist gold brown strands and tamped them deep and level in the pipe's bowl with a special brass tool he carried. Then the matches, the bright flare, the careful pull in, silent, smoky, and the first mouthful.

'She'll come round,' he said to Lucille, who had the dull face she wore nowadays.

'She'll have to, won't she.' It was not a question.

'Yes, yes. She's a good girl.'

'It's true what she says. You have ruined her life.'

He sucked and puffed, pretty unmoved by Lucille who had made too many scenes that came to nothing.

'No one's life is spoiled at twenty.'

'It can have been given the twist that puts it off the right path. You should know that.'

'Eh?' he said, picking up his yachting magazine.

'I do.'

'Well, well,' he said, making himself comfortable, crossing one leg over the other. 'We haven't done so badly, little flower.'

Lucille went upstairs. She could hear Holly crying in her bedroom but did not think she could do much for her. Later, she would try to help.

In effect, Lucille was as alone as if the house had been empty. (Hugh was out.) She had nothing to do but have a bath, change into her new blouse, go downstairs and make the tea. As it was nearly Christmas she would make mince pies. Hugh liked them. She smiled faintly at the thought of her son's pleasure, and a sluggish flag of domestic well-being flapped inside her.

She went downstairs into the square hall. The parquet floor smelt pleasantly of polish. In the kitchen all the paintwork shone.

7

FRED AND LUCILLE

In 1960 Fred was brought face to face with his wife. They had been living apart in number 4 for some years. When Holly graduated she took a job in a Repertory Company and at once began to have success. Hugh left school the moment he could and entered the insurance firm he was to be with all his working life. For a few years he still lived at home, but his parents saw little of him. He was a plump, cheerful fellow who liked good company and found it in the homes of his many friends. Invitations were showered on him – for a drink, for a meal, a weekend away, a night out – and Hugh accepted them all. When he was at home he made his mother laugh with his easy, joking manner. When he was out, the memory of her laughter with him made the house seem all the more silent. Eventually Hugh left home entirely and married.

Lucille saw what her life was and set herself to endure it. She made timid contacts with her neighbours and lived alone for the most part.

Two doors up The Warren lived a man who owned a prosperous shop in Carstead, originally a grocer's but lately expanded to sell wine, hardware, clothes and costume jewellery. Stan was a decent chap to whom Fred chatted in the pub at Sunday lunchtime. In the spring they swapped plant seedlings, in the autumn cuttings.

One Saturday morning Stan came into the Tickeners' garden by the back gate to find Fred pinching out his sweet-peas. Lucille, who was watering her tubs of petunias, whisked indoors.

'Hullo, old chap,' said Fred in his jolliest voice. 'How's things?'

'Fine, Fred, fine. On the whole.'

'Good, good.'

'Those look healthy plants.'

'Not bad are they?'

'Sweet-peas as ever this year?'

'I've always grown them. Lovely scent.'

'Can I have a word, Fred old chap?'

'Fire away, old man. Want a beer?'

'No, thank you all the same.'

'Come indoors.'

'No. Better stay here.'

For the first time Fred took in Stan's grave expression. 'Nothing wrong is there?'

'Well . . .' Stan hesitated and swallowed.

'Your wife poorly again, is she?'

Stan frowned. 'Just a friendly word, Fred old man,' he said.

'Right. Well, let's have it.'

'Your wife –'

'Lucille? She's indoors.'

'I think there is no doubt she has been stealing from shops for some time now.' Having delivered this sentence he had prepared, Stan took a deep breath.

'Look here!' Fred's feet trampled heavily on the soft soil. 'I should watch what you say.'

He wanted to punch the man, but they were hemmed in by sweet-pea stakes. In any case, what he said was beneath contempt. The phrase strengthened Fred. He glared straight at Stan.

'You had no idea?'

'It's preposterous.'

'Yesterday she was challenged by my manager. She had several items – not paid for.'

Silver and diamonds glinted up at Fred from Lucille's oval wicker basket. He firmed his mouth before asking, 'What items?'

'Well, there was a pot of Gentleman's Relish, some chocolate biscuits –'

'Food!'

'It's a bit of a facer, isn't it, Fred old man?'

'We are not poor,' said Fred helplessly. He suddenly felt like leaning on Stan, a man he hardly knew, and that made him full of shame.

'Oh, it's not usually lack of money,' explained Stan. 'Something else. Some lack, the head shrinkers say. Time of life, it can be. Is Lucille – '

'Over that. Over all that,' said Fred, clearing his throat vigorously. To discuss his wife like this was intolerable. He would much rather talk about the theft.

'If you let me know the value of what she took . . . Lucille! it's incredible. Are you certain? It was my wife your manager er, caught?' Stan nodded. 'Food! She hardly eats a thing.'

'I'm afraid that's not all. Your wife told him and the policeman he called in – he had to, old chap, his plain duty – she told them quite freely other things she'd taken over the past few months.'

'Months!'

'Or years.'

'What?'

'A blouse, ear-rings, little things for the house – '

'I'll return them all.'

'That won't be necessary, old man. We cover ourselves against these losses. Ladies of a certain age, as I say, do do such odd things. Personally, I have no intention of proceeding any further and I've told the police so. But, for the future – '

'Yes?'

'We did not make a lot of headway with Lucille.'

Stan did not want to tell Fred of his wife's outburst, how she had sat in the manager's office with her basket of stolen goodies and fairly blasted them with her scorn and unrepentant misery.

'She was upset, Fred, old man.'

'This is an appalling business,' remarked Fred in a more controlled tone. His first shock had passed, and his training in dealing with men was reasserting itself. 'Quite appalling. I'm most grateful to you for speaking to me like this. Most thoughtful of you. Most.'

'It seemed the best thing.'

'Yes. And you can rely on me. I'll have it out with my wife and it won't happen again. You can rest assured of that.'

'Right then. There's no more to be said. Thanks, Fred. Many a fellow would have blasted my head off.'

'No point,' said Fred succinctly.

'No, well, goodbye then. See you in the pub some time.'

Fred was sharply aware he would never go to that particular pub again.

Stan left him between the rows of canes, a ball of twine still in his hand. He flung it down. He swore. He ground his heels into the soft soil. He stood, irresolute, in an inward turmoil, like ice breaking on a frozen river, huge fragments jarring together. What a bloody fool Stan must think him! What a feeble failure of a man that couldn't keep his wife in order! How could she do it to him? And, dear God, *why*?

Fred who never observed himself or analysed others was being forced to do both.

How could the stupid little fool have pulled the wool over his eyes for so long? How long? Was it really years? At any moment for years might she have been arrested? Hurt and anger ran together in his bowels. Why had she done it? Didn't he give her all she needed? God! he spent himself at that hellish office for her sake.

One part of him wanted to charge down the garden and shake Lucille until her head snapped about on her shoulders. Instead, he picked up the twine and went on, as best he could, dealing with the sweet-pea sprouts. The flowers had always made him think of her, their fragility, her pale dresses. Now he hated them but went on patiently tying them in.

His fleshy pink body twitched under his shirt. He felt unclean. How *could* she? He was aware of a sour taste in his mouth. Of course, they were not as close as they had been once, but couples did drift apart, bound to, it didn't mean anything, they still loved each other underneath, just growing older, that's all.

Again he stopped work and stared towards the house, anger and incomprehension fighting within him. He could make out her sleek head bent over the sink. At one o'clock she called him for lunch, and he came treading down the lawn and into the house with a face of thunder.

'Was that Stan?' she asked, boldly.

'Yes.' He let a pause develop, but Lucille sat down and shook out her napkin as if nothing at all were the matter. 'Do you know what he wanted?'

'To tell on me, I suppose.'

Fred's jaw dropped. Never had he been so surprised as by her almost cheery assumption of guilt.

'Come on. Sit down, Tikki.'

She began to serve his food.

'Why did you do it?' Astonishment reduced him to this bald

question. He had been expecting denials, followed by floods of tears.

'Why in heaven's name not?' she asked in a bright, flat voice. 'Shopkeepers have only themselves to blame. They are so careless – pushing things at you. They deserve to lose some. And I'm quite sure they don't value them as I do.'

He had not remotely considered she might have a defence.

'Lucille! It's stealing!' He had the impression he was talking to someone who would not understand.

'Sort of. But not really. I mean – no one actually loses. I would never dream of taking anything that belonged to someone.'

'Did you never think of me?'

'What's it to do with you, Tikki? I only take things for myself.'

'Gentleman's relish?'

She shrugged this tiny item away.

'You are a thief,' he muttered, more to himself than her. His small eyes were hard and bulging like blue balls in his pink face.

'Have some more potatoes?'

'I haven't eaten these. How can I eat?'

'I don't see why not.' She was chewing as she spoke.

His anger was being shredded by bewilderment.

'To have that Stan and his manager discussing you!'

'Tikki, darling, do be sensible.'

With solemnity he said to her, 'I am terribly hurt, Lucille.' He had never accused her of hurting him before, though she had often accused him. It was a momentous step to take.

'Yes. I am hurt too – at this ridiculous fuss! What do you expect me to do. Put up with this dreary life for ever, I suppose?'

'I have given you the best years of my life,' he shouted at her, glad to be purely angry again.

'You may have. So have I. But you've not given me what I wanted. We could have had a life abroad. Twice you had the chance of it, but no! – all I got was Carstead.'

'Do you think I like it?' He jumped up.

She looked away, her face shut.

'Do you, Lucille?'

'You chose it.'

'For your sake! And the children's.'

'A fat lot of good it's done them.'

Her small face was ugly now with her anger.

'You never would bloody well understand,' he shouted.

'If you don't want your lunch, I'll clear it away,' she said, and did so.

Somehow the row had got off the question of shoplifting and on to older ground.

Fred went back to his garden and paced up and down the lawn. It was clear he could not keep his undertaking to Stan. He could not stop Lucille. What should he do? He felt sick with anger, and rudderless.

Then an idea came to him. Some days before Ida had written one of her infrequent, sparse letters in blue ink on violet paper. She had heard of a minor job in the coastguard service with a cottage nearby that was about to become vacant along the coast from Inverness, and she suggested that Fred left his city job and took this one. 'Just right for you. Think it over,' she had commanded.

At the time, Fred, after half an hour's happy thoughts of a return to the seaside, if not the sea itself, had dismissed the idea. Financially it would be too difficult. Now he began to tot up whether he could manage after all to live off a two-thirds pension, plus a little from the navy and what he could realise by selling number 4. The cottage that went with the job had a small rent, and was, by the sound of it, a good way from the village so Lucille would not have much opportunity for her fun and games. And, of course, he would be about more, would have to drive her to the shops when she went. It would be difficult to manage, but perhaps not impossible. And then – the sea!

He took one of his decisions – quick, cut and dried, no going back. He rang Ida, wrote to the Coastguard Offices, had an interview, resigned from his job, put the house on the market, all without a word to Lucille.

She knew he was furiously angry with her. For one thing, he went to sleep in Hugh's old room, and every night when he shut the door it was like a slap in the face. She knew too that he was up to something and this made her feel nervous, like a child with a punishment hanging over its head, but she had no idea what he planned until the estate agent's man came to fix the For Sale board on the gate.

When she did know, it was the final blow.

*

The cottage on the coast was small with thick walls and low windows which had bumpy plastered sills. There was nowhere to display Lucille's china ladies, but that hardly mattered as she never bothered to unpack them. Fred had to decide where the furniture should stand. He chose which cupboard was to be for the brooms, which for the glasses. She made curtains obediently from material he selected and watched in silence when he laid some linoleum she detested in the kitchen.

Fred was cheerful enough and seemed years younger. He strode about the cliff top and let himself in and out of the glass box that was the look-out station with the utmost good humour. He immediately established good relations with the other coastguard, who lived in a house a mile to the east, and with their relief who came out from Forres when needed. All were former naval men. For the first time in years Fred was enjoying the weather – rain on his face, hot sun burning the backs of his hands, the salt, damp smell of mist rolling in over the sea, and the gales that could not rock the solid cottage which crouched on the cliff with its smoke blown back right down to the ground.

Lucille sat most afternoons in her chair, her thin hands in constant motion, kneading, rubbing and clasping each other. Through the window she could see only a line of grass against the sky but this was of no interest to her and she never looked. Sometimes she was cold, sometimes hot. She had a pain in her stomach that gnawed away like a dog on a bone, except that she was the bone, she reminded herself. The thought caused her lips to tuck themselves in. For a year she thought over the past, becoming gradually more confused, and very likely to cry if Fred spoke at all sharply to her.

At Carstead she had gone over the past so often that it had taken on a life more real than the present, more real in fact than it had when it was the present. Her 'past' was for the most part her happy times, that is the days of her courtship with Tikki, some periods of their early years, the week's leave in Edinburgh and since then a few weekends and holidays, days out with Hugh. But after a year at the cottage her rehearsal of the real life past had lost its charm. Going over it was a ritual she was conditioned to by the simple state of being alone with nothing to do, but she went through the performance sometimes with downright disgust. This and the nagging pain was what made her weak eyes leak the tears that irritated Fred so. Even on her 'easy days', as she called the pain-free ones, her memories became unimportant to her, treasures handled until they had lost their patina, or photographs yellow and indistinct. Lucille had to peer to make out the details, and she had not the energy.

She sat in her chair, hands twisting and clasping, the right blindly feeling over and counting the fingers of the left, the left then rubbing the palm of the right round and round as if rubbing something in, or out, the knuckles smoothed and squeezed, then the finger-tips tapped together but without rhythm. All afternoon this continued, while her face was still and her worn memories were sorted, sifted, sieved. One day, without commotion or sorrow, with no sense of loss or abandonment, she put them aside for ever. Then there was very little that was coherent left in her mind. Her head was rather big and light. When she moved it she felt slightly dizzy. This frightened her and made her cry again. She could not remember what was outside the room she sat in, perhaps only darkness. This made her cry too.

One day in June, during their second year at the cottage, Lucille wondered whether she might scream, and go on screaming until Tikki came in. He would have to leave his little box, his binoculars and his telephone and come to her. He would kneel down beside her and ask what was wrong. Then she would tell him. But what?

That she did not like this cottage or the sea. Well, he knew that. So what should she tell Tikki when she had screamed and he had come in asking, 'What's the matter?'

That she hated Ida's interfering, the way she came with her cakes and her knitting and yattered for hours. But Fred took his sister's part as often as not. They chatted together outdoors.

So what should she say? That Holly did not care about her any more? Tikki did not like her to criticise his precious daughter. He spent whole evenings pasting clippings about her into his scrap album and never missed an opportunity to boast. Last autumn even the milkman had been told about her new play on Broadway.

Should she explain that it hurt to see so little of Hugh? Tikki would merely say that was to be expected. 'Chap wants his own life.'

What should she say then? Here he was kneeling beside her, his round eyes pleading. 'Tell me, little flower.'

She was not sure what to say, so really there was no point in screaming. No point in anything, which was something she had known for a long, long time. Out from her slack mouth wavered a soft, slow breath.

Then Fred did come in, unobserved. He watched her as she kneaded her hands. She was small and round-shouldered, her backbone permanently curved like an old woman's. She sat in the armchair like an embryo. He hated to see it. He felt pity for his wife, but why she needed pity, why she was 'like this', he had no idea. Dislike he felt more strongly, the instinctive dislike of the healthy for the sick, the powerful for the weak.

She turned slowly round to face him but then seemed not to know who he was.

'Yes?' she asked, with a pathetic echo of her social manner. 'Can I help you?'

*

In July she was still sitting in her chair, all day now, neglecting herself and the house, allowing Fred to cook. For the most part he prepared sausages or cheese rarebit which she could not stomach, so he gave her rice pudding. Ida, bustling over after a fortnight away, was shocked at Lucille's limp cloth face.

'Why didn't you get some help?'

'I can manage,' he said huffily. He had no wish for his lacklustre wife to be the talk of the locals.

'Of course you can't manage, Fred.'

She made him send for a doctor.

'You know I've no time for quacks. You can phone him if you like.'

Ida doubted if poor Lucille had much time to live.

In hospital there were tests and scans but from the very first doubtful, downcast expressions. Then Fred was told, none too gently, that his wife must have been poorly for some time. She had cancer and there was nothing to be done but ease her passage. Fred's anger at the doctor's uselessness covered any guilt he might have felt, and it took the edge off his pain too.

He had a nasty moment when he drove back alone from the hospital and had to let himself into the house, empty for ever more of Lucille. He poured himself some whisky and sat heavily with his hands planted on his knees, staring at the blank television screen. He remembered how he had carried Lucille over the doorstep of their first home in Mitcham and he could hear her laughter, feel her kisses. His feet began trampling fiercely on the floor as if pain made the soles red hot. Now she was that odd little creature full of hurt he could not ease. He poured another drink, then put on the television and turned up the volume trying to drown his thoughts. The speaking head boomed and lunged at him, making no sense, and he kept thinking he had heard someone come in so he switched the set off again, and moved his chair so that he could see the door. He glared at it combatively. No one came in.

Next day he rang Holly, by then back in London, and told her the news without preamble in an angry, distant voice. It was better that way – he would not break down and neither, with luck, would she. Her voice came warmly consoling. Tentatively, he hinted that she might come up for a while. It was only a hint for he could no longer be certain of her responses; but, yes, she said, at once and cheerfully, she'd be glad to. One thing though – she would have to bring someone with her.

He stiffened. 'For God's sake –'

'Yes?' Cool as you like.

'Do you have to, Holly? At a time like this.'

'I do actually, yes.'

He supposed it was Terence Burningham the actor she had been living with for several years, or perhaps she had some new chap in tow that she couldn't be parted from. It wouldn't surprise him. Wilful and thoughtless as ever. You would have thought with a mother dying she could have done without her – her man friend for a bit.

'Very well, Holly, have it your own way,' he conceded loftily and rang off.

Over his lunch he thought about Holly. He had spoken sternly to her because these everlasting strangers upset him. It was all part of the theatrical life she would insist on having. She had not been home much these past years but – never mind that now. She was his little prickle puss really! In trouble he knew she would come to him; and in moments of success she was likely to phone him. 'Guess what, Daddy?' she would say in a bubbling voice. 'I've no idea, pussy. Bought a new dress have you?' 'Oh Daddy! You old tease you.'

It looked as if she would never marry now. (Fred did not count Donald.) It warmed him to realise no one had been permanently preferred to him, although he paid lip service to the notion that a girl needed a husband.

He looked round the room which held emptiness like an enemy. Fred hated loneliness with every fibre of his stoical body. Tomorrow or the next day she would come.

In the hospital that afternoon Lucille murmured about Hugh. It had slipped Fred's mind entirely that he should contact their son. When he telephoned his daughter-in-law she said that Hugh was in Hong Kong tying up an important contract.

'Is Mum bad?' asked the girl in the south London drawl Fred hated because it reminded him of his youth. 'Is it terminal?'

'Not at this stage, no,' replied Fred gruffly.

'Well, shall I come up as Hugh's away?'

That was the last thing Fred wanted.

'I can farm out the kids. I could easily, Dad.'

'No, no. I'll keep in touch. Let you know how she goes on.'

'Right you are then.' Relief in her voice.

'Goodbye for now.' And in his.

*

A day after that he was able to drive into Inverness to meet Holly's train. She would not fly, she said, too much luggage.

Inverness station is windy and shaded by high roofs. There is a long bookstall facing across the waiting area to a cafeteria. Also a passport photo booth and benches, but not enough of these so that foreign hitch-hikers pile their rucksacks and sleeping rolls in steep mounds and lean against them, boots in the fairway. Despite the crowds of earnest tourists, the spinning postcard racks, the meaningless noise, the station keeps up an air of detachment, a certain haughtiness as if holding its head well up. The traveller feels he has arrived at a frontier.

The platforms are arranged out of sight of those waiting and engines come sliding round the curve with little fuss; and the first one knows of a train's arrival is a loose bunch of passengers wandering out, apprehensive, wind-flapped, raw. There are seagulls crying. Stout men in kilts, tall wives in tweeds stand almost at attention to wait. Their cars parked outside have petrol tanks full enough to reach distant glens. The passengers see a homely coat of arms on the station wall, then Marks and Spencer's, then a flat-topped mountain behind church spires, a stone forest of spires and towers. They feel somewhat disoriented.

Holly was at home. She came marching down the platform holding a small boy by the hand. He was absurdly like her, and like Fred.

'Here's Grandfather, Peter,' she said. 'Shake hands.'

The child solemnly shook hands with Fred who stood in a state of shock, responding automatically.

'Good God, Holly! I'd no idea.'

She grinned, but made no reply.

Then anger swamped Fred. 'Why didn't you tell me? How old is he? Three? Four?'

'Three.'

'Three years! Why was I kept in the dark?'

He stared at the boy who was regarding him with a comically similar expression. Peter had never had an old man with a pipe to belong to before. He smiled at his grandfather with friendly triumph. Holly squeezed her father's arm. 'We three,' he thought, but could not let himself give way so readily.

Holly had a trolley of cases and boxes and made a breezy commotion of having them trundled to the car and loaded into the boot, trying not to show how anxious she was about her father's reaction to her son.

Fred stood by the car while she and Peter waited for him to unlock the doors.

'Why didn't you tell us?' he asked again.

'No point if I wasn't coming home. Mummy would be sure to mind, to make a meal of it.'

'As far as that goes I –'

'You're far more broadminded than Mummy ever was.'

Fred took a breath and squared his shoulders.

'I've always been able to tell you things, Daddy.' It was flattery, but also truth in a way and she could see Fred loved it. 'Poor Mummy, she would have minded terribly.'

'You've got a point there.' Their agreement sealed his acceptance. He had always liked children and this boy was a sturdy little fellow. Fred fitted him on the back seat between a case and a box of groceries he had picked up on his way to the station, with a joke about sardines in tins. Holly slipped into the front seat, turned for a moment to see that Peter was happy, and settled with a sigh of content. Fred patted her hand with his freckled one, and she gave him a smile of pure love.

They drove along the coast road towards the east. To the right behind sloping cornfields rose woods, then rounded hills. To the left was the Moray Firth, tide out, gleaming iridescent in the evening light and on the far shore the green and russet cliffs of the Black Isle, small homely cliffs with caps of golding corn. The view was permeated with sky. Like a blue bag in washing water, it rinsed all the objects in glassy clear light, even sheep and the planing seabirds shone softly. Holly wound down the window and drew in deep breaths while her eyes drank too.

'Look Peter. Just look!'

'What's that house?'

'It's a castle.'

'Like in a story?'

'Better.'

'Can I stroke the sheeps?'

'They are shy. The lambs will let you.'

'Can we go in the water?'

'Mm. Tomorrow.'

'Rather you than me,' commented Fred. 'It's parky, even in July.'

'Clean though. You can hardly dare go in the sea in the south nowadays.'

'Good Lord.' He changed gear and turned off the main road towards the sea.

A large bulge of farmland stuck out into the Firth. A few stone farmhouses were visible, the lines of two roads, a grain silo, short rows of cottages with prim gardens set down here and there, then they were past even these buildings and running along a lane which aimed at the sky. Just at the end, set back in hedges, was Fred's cottage. It had two views, a narrow sideways one of the curving, empty sands and the pines beyond that clung to the tide's edge, dense and mysterious, and an open outlook to the Firth and the slate silver mountains shimmering ten miles off, hanging between water and clouds.

The cottage was a field's width from the shore where Fred's coastguard hut stood like a cube of glass. It was a nowhere point, a dot on the coastal path, a cross on the sailors' charts. Behind it was a square of garden where Fred raised his sweet-peas and some vegetables. The garden seemed to pin the cottage down; without it, there was no reason for it to be here rather than a mile east or west.

To Holly it was a satisfying place to come, to rest after years of effort, travel, grind and success. It wasn't quite Balchraggan, though on clear days like this she could see the divide of the Great Glen running inland and mentally pinpoint the village.

Perhaps she would stay. Her career, that gold balloon whose cord had both raised and supported her, was losing its buoyancy. Since Peter had been born and Terence gone she found the rewards less and the grind worse. She was a good actress and had developed the sort of pared down, almost empty face, with naked planes waiting for make-up and imagination to create other faces, of a good actress past her youth who has put on so many fleshly garments of emotion that her non-acting expression is neither plain nor beautiful but stripped, awaiting either, and with a rubbery mobility and pallor which exaggerated the always prominent, the faceted sapphire eyes.

During her affair with Terence she had ridden his wave and become nationally known. Without him and, all the more important, with Peter she had to work harder, not so much in the theatre (for she loved that, hardly counted it work) but out of it, over the PR things, going places, meeting people at the psychologically productive moment, and – really, she could, less and less, be bothered with it. Fred's phone call, coming as one production ended and another was yet to be finally decided upon, was a release, an opening to fresh air, an uncomplicated time.

The train going north had seemed to climb all the way, up and up. She and Peter had a first class carriage to themselves and after Perth she had him on her lap constantly pointing out to him this and that – heather, buildings, crouching and grey, humble, solid, and crags, waterfalls, dark glens twisting round mountain flanks, the tableland of the Cairngorms. The child had watched her more than the view outside which did not vary very much – just trees and hills, just green – but he had never seen his mother so shining.

When Fred had shown the cottage and stowed away their luggage, all three stood outside, looking seawards.

'Now,' said Holly firmly, 'tell me, how is Mummy?'

Fred flinched.

'Your mother is not very well at all, Holly,' he replied with a portentousness that covered pain.

'What does the doctor say?'

'Oh, you know what quacks are.'

She could imagine her mother languid and thin in one of her prettiest blue nightgowns with grapes on the locker and get well cards (from whom? well, Aunt Ida, certainly). Flowers and cleanliness decently hid sickness and suffering. Holly heard quiet footsteps on polished floors, saw silver basins covered with white cloths and Lucille's huge brown eyes in repose on a plumped pillow.

'When are visiting hours?'

'I sit with your mother whenever I'm not on duty. They like help with feeding her, you know.'

'Aren't you exhausted, Daddy?'

She could see in the low evening sunlight pouring across the water that he was.

'We'll take it in turns from now on.'

'Your mother may last for months,' he answered flatly.

Why, she wondered, did he not call her Lucille, or Mummy. Why this 'your mother'? Was it a sort of distancing, or a reminder of her solemn fate?

When she saw Lucille, Holly thought it was because Fred hardly knew her for his wife.

She entered the ward with an actress's presence, not noisily or flashily, but drawing eyes. On the pillows heads turned. Those propped up revolved their torsos. Momentarily, nurses paused. But from the bed by the window there was no movement. Holly drew back her arms holding her gifts, and felt her smile grow stiff. The phrases of greeting withered unspoken leaving her mouth dry.

Lucille was only just recognisable. Dark, creased skin clung to a face with fallen cheeks and lips, and the hair, neatly combed and held by a plastic slide, was dull grey, like much used fraying wool. Her eyes were dry with yellowed whites, and her hands were paws stripped of fur, not human at all.

Holly knew how to behave – the kiss, the quiet words, the silent, attentive sitting, the half-smiles at passing nurses – but it was more of an act than many theatrical performances. How to feel, she did not know at all.

When Fred came he sat at right angles to the bed, on a metal and canvas chair, profoundly uncomfortable. He wanted to hug and caress Lucille; he also wanted to hide this sight of foreboding behind the curtain. He tried to catch her few mumbled words; he also tried to shut her up in case she shouted and swore, as she sometimes did, causing him agony. He was convinced that the other patients and the nurses noted every single thing, every dribbling incoherence of the person he had loved.

Holly knew how her father felt because it was much the same for her. Neither could be natural in the face of illness. They vied with each other in bringing Lucille small gifts of flowers she could not focus on, fruit she did not eat, a bed jacket for when she sat up but she never did, and socks to warm her. The legs were not much larger than Peter's and were made of some cheap spongey rubber. Fred and Holly shared a shamed glance across the lower part of Lucille's body as they dragged on the socks.

One afternoon Holly took pictures of Peter. She had been delighted to see how fond Fred was of the boy and, while knowing she could not tell her mother the truth, still hoped some spark of happy understanding could leap the gap between her and the sick woman.

Lucille was having a good day, with two pillows behind her head and hands arranged tidily on the sheet, mottled hands, the wedding ring taped to her finger lest it slip off. Holly led up to the photos as best she could, speaking of Peter, my Petey, the little boy who's at home with Daddy and me. Then she produced one or two and fitted Lucille's spectacles on her nose for her.

'Yes dear, very nice,' said the thin, monotonous voice without even seeing the snaps lying on the sheet.

'No look, Mummy,' said Holly, holding one directly in front of Lucille.

Across the disintegrating face flitted an expression of anxiety. Dimly she sensed something was required of her. What? Like a beaten dog or a victimized child she drew back, fearing.

'Here is a picture of Peter,' said Holly, enunciating beautifully and in a gentle tone. 'Look Mummy, he's like Daddy.'

Then Lucille saw the picture. Relief washed over her, and a quick slyness.

'What a dear little pussy cat,' she said in a squeaky, thin voice, the ghost of the tones she had reserved for social encounters when it mattered you should be bright and on the ball. She squinted at Holly. That's right, isn't it? she seemed to ask.

'Yes, isn't he?' agreed Holly. She put Peter's picture away in her handbag, the clasp went home with a dull click. Of course Lucille could no longer share her life; all that remained was to enter somewhat into her mother's dying.

It was difficult. She took the canvas chair as Fred vacated it but had to break her vigil all afternoon by going to the window to stare at the small town square outside, or by chatting to other patients, those that cared for company. Holly fidgeted, against all her training and the discipline of years. She was anxious, afraid, ashamed, and bored. There was nothing to do or say.

This was not Lucille. A commonplace, but true. 'She isn't herself.' 'The sick man has changed his whole personality.' No. Not a change: an absence. This skinful of bones and diseased organs was without Lucille. She remembered when Donald had been so ill, dying she had childishly feared, how his face had become an object on the pillow, an object with no relation to her. Not Donald. Now her mother, who had been pretty and self-centred, so easily wounded or pleased, a lightweight person (she had thought) and deeply pitiable, this woman *was not here*.

Back at the cottage she slipped thankfully into ordinary things, spending much time on the beach with Peter. The boy was used to being apart from his mother and it was lovely for him to have her there, and the sea, and the sand, and the trawlers passing, the seagulls, flocks of little speckled birds at the water's edge, dead fish too sometimes, old boxes and footballs washed up by the slowly sucking, mysterious, rustling water. He played happily beside his mother, who reclined on her elbow letting sand run through her fingers in blowing threads.

In the ward there were many sounds but they were all small and controlled so that they merged into a clinking, rumbling, torpid half-silence soothing to the sick (one supposed) and inducing doziness in the visitors. Holly arrived invigorated by idleness beside the sea and was in some way reproached by the stifling quietness of the ward.

Over their meals Fred and Holly filled in the blank years. His resentment at her career was gone, indeed he argued forcibly that he had never opposed her, just thought she should have a degree first, but Holly saw no point in dwelling on the past. She had her memories. She knew. Scarves of affection clung to Donald all burnished by the sun of Balchraggan. Deeper and stronger was her love for Fred, sitting opposite now, his forehead rolled up like a desk top for Peter to ripple his fingers against, just as she had done.

'He's a fine little chap,' said Fred, when Peter was in bed. 'He likes it here.'

'Yes.'

She knew where remarks like that were heading.

'So do you, eh pussy?'

'It's home to me, this part of Scotland.'

'Well then?' he asked with an expression of joky slyness. 'Well, what do you say?'

'We must wait. I cannot make decisions as things are.'

'Ah.' He was recalled to his immediate future. The necessary grief to come shuttered down Fred's innocent face. After a few moments, he said, 'Your mother never liked it here.'

Holly liked it, more and more, playing at house in a cross-over apron, her bare feet in Scholls, her rings left by her bed. There was an ease and amplitude about life in the small house on the wide coast. Holly emulsioned the kitchen walls white and found some red cups and plates in a dusty corner of the ironmonger's; she picked montbretia to put in a jug on the table where it burned in the shadows of the cave-like room. The flowers grew on the cliff paths, and behind the dunes were michaelmas daisies, gone wild and drained by salt and sun to the palest mauve.

When lunch was ready she did not phone Fred but walked across to him with the dry grass pricking her instep, the wind gently battering, Peter running and shouting beside her. Even on dull days the coastguard glass hut was airless and dry-hot. Fred's face was tanned a deep brown and his bare arms were covered with freckles. He turned from looking out to sea to greet Holly and Peter with pale eyes which looked directly at them, keenly and kindly. His charts and papers lifted when the door opened.

'Quick, shut it,' he said to Peter the first few times. Then the boy had learned.

Sweat started on Holly's face as soon as she was inside. She flapped the collar of her blouse.

'It's an oven in here.'

'Yes,' agreed Fred, very pleased. He loved heat.

She wanted to go, but no, Peter had to be shown this or that ship out to sea. While this was done, Holly walked round the hut looking out of each side in turn, seeing the Firth, the pine forest along the shore, then inland the little town where the cottage hospital was, and finally the humps of cliffs running west.

The three of them walked back, arm in arm, hand in hand,

without hurry, each taking pleasure in being close together in the wide, windy landscape. In the cottage the rooms glowed in the sun beaming through the deep-set window like spotlights to pick out Fred's pipe lying beside his chair, or the tower of bricks she and Peter had built on the floor. If the day were warm enough, they left the back door open while they ate to the screams and swoops of the gulls.

Peter climbed on to a stool to wash his hands at the sink, and Fred helped, soaping his own at the same time. He made a ritual of it, then of the drying, the pushing back of quicks, and a quick dab of hand cream, 'the sort fishermen use, Peter old chap'. Fred loved these domestic rites, the more unchangingly they were performed the better he was pleased. In a few weeks Peter and he had established dozens of small daily habits.

Now, he was ready to eat, rubbing his pink palms together and wrinkling up his nose.

'Once more into the breach,' he said.

Holly discovered these phrases and rites of her father's no longer irritated her. They were rather endearing. She smiled at him with a broad happy grin.

However, as the time for his hospital visit came near, the atmosphere changed. Fred became self-consciously silent, as if pushing himself back into the grief situation, and also warning Holly that her mother came first, that all this pretty room, good food, fun, were poor secondary things. The trouble was that Holly could not help feeling that this was not how Fred really was, only how he thought he should be.

But she too was silent and gloomy. How would Lucille be today? Sick and weak, as she usually was, or crying and complaining? In any case, was it Lucille? And if not, where was she? Was it possible that people's spirits can depart before death? Perhaps the real Lucille was already free of that dreadful smelly bag of decomposing and proliferating flesh.

She and Fred took it in turns to go inside, the other staying with Peter in the town square or the park. But, whether Holly were pushing the child on a swing or sitting over a coffee while he had an ice, her thoughts were in the big, quiet ward, with its two facing rows of white beds like tombs. The visitors, intimidated by all that was unknown, all the busy messy things that happened when they were not there, sat like shadows attending shadows, murmuring sometimes. When it was her turn to go in, she passed Fred coming out with a slow, resigned look and slipped into the aqueous light of the blind-drawn hospital.

Sitting there, unbidden memories came to her – contradictory things, as if her subconscious were saying that her mother had been as mysterious and unknowable as any human being. She visualized a certain brooch made of leather in the shape of a flower, blue and maroon it had been with a hard button centre and a gold pin behind. Lucille used to pin this to her jersey before going down to breakfast at Balchraggan. Holly could see the chilblains on her index fingers and the determined look on her face as she fixed the brooch. 'It's important to keep looking nice,' she said bravely. Then Holly remembered her mother's tenderness for one of the twins when a cut on his leg had gone septic, and the tears she had shed at the dentist's because Hugh had been afraid. Once, sitting by the fire, Lucille had spoken of her own childhood. She had been an orphan; there had been an uncle who sounded dull, an aunt, cousins who were older. 'Auntie was a pet really. I had all the girls' cast-offs. And Nuncle would do as I wanted if I said the right things to him. At least he gave me a holiday once. But he wouldn't let me go to college.' What training Lucille might have wanted she had never told. 'Your father's a very clever man,' she often said. 'He knows more than I do. If he had stayed on at school – !' But then once she had cried out, 'I hate injustice worse than anything.' What injustice, and to whom?

Holly's strangest recollection was of the letter her mother had written to Fred and that she, jealous little Holly, had read and torn up. At the time she'd been looking for evidence of love, but it seemed she remembered something else. The written words hovered in Lucille's perfectly neat, rounded handwriting, then came clear. 'I am desolate. A dry wind is blowing in and out of my soul.' Something like that. Poor, poor Mummy! What must she have been feeling actually to mention her soul.

Holly opened her eyes to the grey face on the pillows. An acorn on a blind cord tapped against the window. An exhausted silence surged in and out of the ward as the doors swung and the nurses passed.

Afterwards, with what memory-laden sighs she and Fred shrugged away the afternoon. Holly kicked off her sandals in the car, Fred loosened his tie before starting the engine. It was six-thirty. The shops were closed, the pavements empty, cottage doors stood open, children sat on a wall sucking ices, the air was warm, the day tired. Fred drove slowly and a calm that was liquid ran smoothly over their hearts and minds.

At the cottage they sat in deck-chairs outside the door, with tea or gin. The short turf grew through sandy soil. Holly's nails probed down, exposing the rough white strings of roots, digging little earthy pits. She could so easily have begun to weep for her mother. If she once began, would she ever stop? Instead she fixed her eyes on the horizon. Out in the North Sea, beyond the corner of the mountain coastline, it was a hair line of sharp grey against a white sky.

*

One afternoon in the sunshine of August a summer carnival procession came past the hospital, float after float, with a band, then pipes. The noise rose up to the ward and the bright colours were reflected dreamily on the gloss paint of the ceiling. Lucille stirred. It was just the sort of occasion she enjoyed, full of gaiety and quick movement, a chance to wear a new outfit, and meet acquaintances looking her best. Through her drugged state could come no real knowledge of what was happening, yet still the agreeable atmosphere must somehow have communicated itself to her, for she opened her eyes, wide, wider until Holly could actually see half the pupil.

Cream and rose was gleaming above Lucille. Music. Was there dancing?

'Holly,' she croaked, 'is my dress ready?'

She knows I am here, thought Holly.

'Shall I wear my pearls or the locket?'

The words though indistinct were comprehensible and quite extraordinary.

'Holly?'

The head turned.

'I see you, Holly.'

A taut grin split the skeleton face.

'Are you ready?'

'What for, Mummy?' Holly faintly enquired. A principal feeling was amusement.

'To go, of course.' The thin voice conveyed impatience somehow.

'Yes, I'm ready.'

'Then what are we waiting for?' asked Lucille, querulous now.

'The taxi', replied Holly, still amused.

'Oh yes.'

The colourless face very slowly swivelled back to look up at the ceiling and the eyes closed. A long pause followed, during which Holly heard the trundly wheels of the floats and a few spatters of applause. Several flies were circling each of the hanging lights. Silent relatives sat beside the beds of other patients. What somnolent thoughts, wondered Holly, were aimlessly repeating themselves around these other heads.

'Hasn't the taxi come yet?' asked Lucille suddenly, quite clear, in her own voice.

'No.'

'We'll walk then.'

Amazingly, the sick woman struggled to raise herself, even to swing her stick legs in their huge socks over the bed.

'No, no, Mummy, lie down. You can't get up.'

'No-such-word-as-can't,' came in a rush.

From the street there was a burst of pipe music, the band come round again.

'You see! It's beginning. I love the reel.'

The face that was not Lucille's was contorted with will and excitement, the eyes that were not hers stared into the spaces of the ward as if between the couples in a circle searching for a gap to place herself in.

Holly firmly pushed her mother down and tried to cover her, but Lucille fought feebly, persistently to sit herself up, to get out of bed.

'Holly, what are you doing? Let me go.'

'No, Mummy, you must lie down.'

'Everyone is looking, Holly.'

'Just lie still and quiet, please.'

'Leave me alone.' She looked straight at Holly and it was, now, Lucille who looked, 'You are making a public exhibition of yourself, my girl.'

'You must not get out of bed.'

'I'm not in bed, you silly creature. Let me go.'

The timid but desperate struggle between the two continued.

'Lie down and rest, please, Mummy.'

'Holly!' said Lucille with almost her own piercing coolness, 'I will not put up with this behaviour.'

These words were Lucille's last. She swung back and down on to her pillows with uncanny slowness. The limbs relaxed, the jaw dropped. Holly was left staring at the absurd blue slide of love birds, beak to beak, which held her mother's hair back. She could still feel the clutch of fingers on her arm.

When Fred arrived a few minutes later, he took hold of Lucille's dangling hand, and stroked it.

'How timid and beautiful she was,' he said.

Holly's tears splashed down.

'Timid,' muttered Fred and looked enquiringly at his daughter. She nodded.

They had never been closer.

When the nurses and doctors came and bustled them about and were busy with screens and silence, Fred and Holly, shunted into a side office, were left to hold hands. In both hearts was an anaesthetising ignorance of what had happened to Lucille, and a tenderness for the other. Holly wriggled her hand comfortingly inside Fred's square grip which he tightened to show his understanding. Here was the father who loved and needed her – never more than now.

*

Then there was a wait of three days to be lived through. Fred slept little and got up in a bad temper. The shock of death had worn off and he suffered. His way out was to have the television on continuously and turn it up loud if anyone spoke to him. Thus isolated, he sucked his empty pipe and watched Holly reproachfully. Peter was pushed aside when he attempted to climb on his grandfather's lap.

'Not today,' said Fred, with heavy understatement.

Holly trod carefully, testing the ground. She and Fred really alone. How would it be?

'Mummy had not been happy for years,' she said, thinking to comfort him, but he flew into a passion of anger. How could Holly be so wicked, heartless and totally mistaken? What did she know – living in London? His little flower had been very happy in the cottage.

Her eyes widened with astonishment, and showed the shining, bluish whites, but she did not reply. It was as if Fred must play the

– 177 –

grief-stricken husband up to the hilt whatever he really felt, or perhaps because of it. The man by Lucille's deathbed, tender and unselfishly sad, vanished and the Bereaved took his place, heavily over-acting.

Hugh came up for the funeral, much to Holly's relief. The adult Hugh was fat and gregarious with a nervous laugh – he!-he!-he! Like his father, he never probed into any depths. A surface life was all he wanted and he trod water admirably.

Holly was amazed at how easily he handled Fred, so matter-of-factly. Their father never attempted his emotional coercion on Hugh. They chatted like two people who knew each other well, shared a liking for several aspects of life, and had absolutely no attachment. Fred began to smoke his pipe again rather than mouthing its empty stem like a black stained dummy. He went to the pub, and played with Peter.

Holly admired her brother's skill with Fred.

'How have you managed it?'

'With love,' he said at once, calmly. 'With cunning too, and silence, with absence when it seemed politic, and a booze up now and again.'

Hugh he-he-he-ed. Holly smiled wanly. Such a man's way was beyond her.

'Don't stay here too long,' Hugh warned her, 'or he'll have his hooks well and truly in.'

'I know.'

Already Fred had thrown her line after line. She knew it would not be easy to leave – if she wanted to.

As soon as the funeral was performed Fred suffered another sea change. He put on a muted joviality, as if relief and sorrow cancelled each other out. Brother, sister and father walked along the cliff top with easy strides, while Peter pattered ahead of them or ran back for a consoling handclasp. There were porpoises out to sea, and they took turns with Fred's binoculars to watch the gun-barrels of bodies rearing and rolling in the prussian blue oily surges of a slack tide.

'Marvellous brutes,' said Fred. 'Aren't they, pussy?'

She leant her head for a second on his shoulder.

Not only did Fred lay claim to her but the Highland landscape too. Also she had letters from London which made her disinclined to return in search of fresh work. Could she face it? Was it worth it

– the long hours, the exhaustion, dusty backstage rooms, tired costumes, quarrels, atmospheres, when she could have Peter here in the blue-drenched sea and mountain world, and Fred who needed her?

In late September the michaelmas daisies were making tufts of grey seeds but Fred's sweet-peas bloomed on, straggling up the netting with weedy, yellowing stalks and small, still sweet, flowers. She picked a bowlful of palest violet, rose, peach, greeny white and stood them on Lucille's round table. The flowers shone in the shadowing room.

'They're past their best,' said Fred disparagingly, but with the eye of pride. 'Must pull them up soon.'

'Yes, winter's coming. I must order some logs and start knitting Peter a thick jersey.'

This was her way of telling him she would stay.

He beamed. 'Mm. Log fires. And roasting chestnuts on dark nights,' he agreed. His thoughts leapt to a future that would repeat the best parts of the past.

'Not long now,' said Holly.

The pair exchanged a slow, exploratory smile over Peter's head.

8

TWO'S COMPANY

Life at the cottage had for a month the flaccid content of
convalescence when nothing is allowed near enough to hurt.
Lucille's feeble body had been laid to rest; Fred rested too, but
timorously.

After a week's leave he insisted on returning to his work and
carried out his duties with his usual conscientious thoroughness,
composing his face to a sternness that, when he thought himself
unobserved, dissolved into a vulnerable look of thaw. He and
Holly spoke little, each was content with the other's presence and
neither mentioned Lucille.

How she wished, later, that those early days after her mother's
death could have been endlessly repeated, but the process of
bereavement moves on inexorably.

Peter, who had never actually seen his grandmother, asked with
a nakedness the adults avoided, 'But where is Grandma?'

Holly, in the kitchen, heard this question piped to Fred and
froze.

'She has gone to Jesus,' her father solemnly and astonishingly
replied. Holly could not know that Fred in his embarrassed pain,
was repeating what he had been told as a boy.

'But what for?' persisted Peter.

'To be made better. Your grandma was very, very ill.'

'I know that. Mummy says it hurt her even to move – even ever
so little.'

'Yes.' There was a pause in which Holly sensed the child
preparing another question. Fred continued, 'Jesus makes people
better.'

'But then why,' asked Peter, using a favourite expression of his, 'but then why don't all ill peoples go to him?'

'They do in the end.'

Holly came to the doorway and saw Fred's pitiful look. The child was leaning against his knee searching his face with interest.

'Come here, darling,' she said.

'Me and Grandpa is talking.'

'Come here, Peter.'

She shut the kitchen door and drew the boy to her, trying to find words to explain.

'Is Grandma still alive, after all?' he persisted.

'No.'

'But Grandpa says – '

'He's just trying to be brave, to cheer himself up, Peter.'

'But then, but then who is Jesus?'

'Someone in a sort of fairy story.'

'Do mens read stories?'

'Sometimes, when they are unhappy. Shall we think of something nice to do for Grandpa as a surprise, to cheer him up? Shall we make some fudge?'

But Peter's questions triggered the next stage for Fred. A few days later, on a warm afternoon, he visited the rose garden near the crematorium where Lucille's ashes had been scattered by a kind and efficient arrangement with the undertaking firm. Fred paced up and down the paths and smiled with self-conscious mournfulness at the gardeners, who were quite used to elderly gentlemen with ram-rod backs and suspiciously bright eyes marching around the garden and merely nodded back without stopping their desultory conversation with each other as they hoed between the vermilion and lemon plants. Fred saw that many of the teak benches were inscribed with the name of a dead person. He sat on one, and thought in a detached, fleeting way of burials at sea, of flag-draped bodies and of the sheet pulled up over Lucille's face on the hospital bed.

About four o'clock when he judged it time for tea and got up to go, Lucille came with him. A slim girlish figure in a pale dress slipped into the passenger seat. He glanced sideways at her delicate profile outlined against the autumnal hedges as they drove home. There was no need to speak. They knew each other too well for that. He merely sketched a pat in the air over the seat where she was sitting with her usual and pleasing composure.

Naturally Holly could not see her mother, Fred did not expect that and to make up for it he began to talk about the Lucille he had resurrected. She was, it appeared, very beautiful, a great reader, she loved nothing more than a walk along the cliffs, she was a phenomenal swimmer and a tennis champion, a cordon bleu and the most intelligent person Fred thought he had ever known.

'Mummy?' cried Holly. 'She was lots of nice things, poor darling, but none of those!'

In her turn she began to tell contrary stories. Because she was a woman and had been with her mother in the war, there were things she knew about Lucille that Fred did not and was fiercely resistant to. She was also able to tell tales of her mother's childhood – things Fred had never heard. How Lucille had once been given a toy cabin trunk filled with tiny handmade garments, even gloves, to fit a doll. Her godmother, a well-to-do lady called Aunt Grace (but not a relation really, a former employer of the child's dead mother) who lived in Winchester had given this present one Christmas. When her mother died, Lucille had visited Aunt Grace and been taken to the cathedral where she had seen soldiers in scarlet tunics lined up at the door. Fred was as affronted by such reminiscences as Holly was by his idealizations.

She heard his voice boom out telling the relief coast guard or the baker's roundsman, anyone who came to hand, something of his wife, dragging her into every conversation by the hairs of her permed gold head, explaining how energetic, talented, beautiful, well-read, capable, independent and sought-after she had been.

'I was a lucky chap,' he said.

'Wasn't she good enough for you?' Holly challenged him. 'Why do you keep prettifying her?'

'No need for that,' he said with his dense cheerfulness. 'Your mother was as pretty as a picture – as you know full well, Holly.'

When his daughter said sharp things about Lucille reading trashy romances from the library van, or hating to walk in the fields because it meant taking off her smart shoes, Fred could have hit her. She was so infuriatingly strong and scornful standing in the doorway, blocking out the light. He marched off to his look-out box with a parade ground posture, and, safely shut inside with the scent of warm wood and paper, he gave himself up to the solace of Lucille.

The blue air and water filled three-quarters of the visible world, pressing against the windows of his box, and the sun soaked into his heart. His wife's presence came to him across the sea gently and sweetly like a sailing boat glides soundlessly and he entered a trance of happiness. She leant over his shoulder as he sat by the chart table. He could tip his head back against her soft breasts, or hunch his shoulder and rub his cheek against her hand placed there so lightly.

Sometimes in the heat and warmth and restfulness, he became confused and mistook her for his mother. Then his heart quickened its pace. If he turned and looked up at the face above, might he not see *her* – at long, long last? Instead he closed his weary and longing eyes, content with the sweet smell of woman all around him and the intoxication of his dream.

For the months of autumn he was sustained. His flower wife kept him company, and the rest of the world withdrew, some of the sting was removed from his loss and he gave an appearance of being normal.

But, like all obsessions, this one wore itself out. Try as Fred would to catch hold, the womanly presence became less vital. His grief was no longer powerful enough to summon it up. His bereavement became weariness. He then had an apprehension of hostility from the grey winter panorama of sea, sky and snow-spattered mountains. He ducked his head as if the gales whipping up the waves might loose shells at him.

The electric stove did little to heat the glass box. Fred sat with his overcoat on and a balaclava, rubbing his arthritic knees with his free hand. For the first time, his nautical work had little interest for him; he did not scan the water as regularly as he should, relying on the radio for distress signals. He could not allow himself actually to think, 'What is the point of all this?' but his ageing body thought it for him, and passed the message on.

Late one afternoon he returned from the look-out to find Holly and Peter were out, the cottage dark and cold. He hadn't the heart to light a fire, or make himself tea; simply sagged down in the living-room lit by the lamp in the passage. When he was used to the gloom, he saw that old Lucille was sitting in her chair kneading her hands together, her sunken eyes fixed on the wall.

Fred was placed at right angles to her. He put his trembling fists on his knees, and stared. He stared so unrelentingly that his wife's ghost disappeared, dissolved into shadows, left only the cushions pressed into the hollowed back of the chair. He leapt up and pummelled them into plumpness.

But from then on she regularly appeared. He was not afraid of her, but very angry at her for usurping the dream woman he loved.

He enumerated the tally of this woman's shortcomings. She had not welcomed him when he came in tired from the office. Because of her he had left the navy, twice. She had spent his money foolishly and refused to like his friends. She had been jealous of Holly, and spoiled Hugh. She had stolen from shops. In bed, she had often refused him, or, worse, made it clear she felt repulsion for him and the tacky mess he left on her thighs. In fact the ghost became one with all women, known and unknown, who had ever annoyed him, humiliated or tricked him, and he placed her with them against his mother, whom only he loved.

He took proceedings against her by sitting in her chair himself, or seeing to it that Holly did. (Peter was no good. The ghost once had the little boy sitting on her lap – or was it Hughie?) He stopped talking about Lucille, slammed the hatch cover on that part of life and took up his fatherly duties. He drove Holly and Peter out and about whenever he was free.

They went to the Black Isle, which has low red cliffs and arable farms, or they motored along the coast eastwards, rarely going inland towards the mountains because Fred did not like Highland scenery. He could not enter into Holly's passion for hills – great bare places, cold, uncomfortable and always the same.

'But that's what I like,' said she, 'the changelessness.'

Fred had imprecise but haunting recollections of hymns and psalms which equated hills in some way with eternity, even with the endurance of sorrow. He reacted against religious overtones as furiously as he dreaded the idea of eternal nothingness, which was all death could be and usually he shut both out of his mind. Hills with their immutable skylines, treeless and bleak, tried to force these ideas back on him. So he kept his face seawards.

'But there are no seasons at sea,' said Holly once. 'No spring or autumn, just water.'

'Don't you believe it!' Fred was secure in the sea.

'Go on! What happens then?'

'You put on white cap covers for one thing,' he said and laughed. 'No, there's every variation of colour, then tides, currents, winds, birds in the rigging, seaweeds drifting past – they are all different, changing with the time of year. I mean, summer storms are nothing like winter ones.'

Holly kept absolutely still. Her father rarely spoke of the sea which evidently meant so much to him.

'Yes. In a summer storm the sea has a huge roll, but confused and breaking in every direction and the wind lifts off the spray in clouds. When two waves bump into each other the tops can be pushed up above the ship and make a sort of spout. And if it's daylight somehow the sun penetrates, you see brilliant green like a flame in the water.'

'And in winter?' she prompted gently.

'The sea seems heavier, like liquid metal, it thuds over the decks. The hawsers are gloved in ice and lumps of frozen sea form on the stanchions, the guns. There are calms in winter too when you see seals basking on ice floes and the water is amethyst, or deep, dark pink in layers that shift as the ship moves on.'

He was looking at the sea as he spoke. They were sitting back to back, propping each other up, so Holly was looking at the moorland hills where Culloden was fought.

'Ah well,' she said, rubbing her back against his. 'We agree to differ about sea and hills.'

'That's it, pussy.' He rubbed against her in turn.

It was one of their good days. Fred had left the grey Lucille at the cottage. She never followed him out of doors. He could relax and allow himself to joke.

Such times were infrequent, and Holly tried to engineer his better moods. Her aim first thing in the morning was to get him dressed to the breakfast table. In a dressing-gown, with stubble and eyes watering, Fred was not pleasant, but in fresh white and his navy sweater, smelling of after-shave, the day could begin well. The sun channelled through the windows, marmalade gleamed, the fire blazed with a stack of clean birch logs beside it, Peter fired questions at a reliable grandfather, and her own affection and capability contented her.

She watched him wrinkle his forehead at Peter and realised that in her mid-thirties her father's good humour and approval was still desperately important to her. Almost, she had the feeling, more important to her than to him. He did not appear all that distressed by his bad moods; sometimes she thought he welcomed them, so easily did he slip into morose, weary bad-temper. She needed the indulgence of his approval, was betrayed and lonely without it.

The next winter, when Peter was five and at school all day, Holly experienced the full force of Fred's bad moods. She knew then, as Lucille had done, how total was his withdrawal into his own boundaries, how utter his refusal to let in another person on any terms. He would take meals from her without a word and made no effort to help in the house. He would sit a whole evening in silence with his yachting magazines. If she complained, he grew huffy and called her 'Woman!' – a term of abuse she found especially unpleasant. It was masterful and denigratory.

Holly felt she had been transmuted into her mother, at the very time that Fred was labouring to keep off the grey woman who huddled in her chair most evenings. He hardly heard Holly's conversation such was his concentration on repelling the ghost.

This creature once actually dared to come up the staircase with dragging steps and stand in his bedroom door, observing all he did. She pulled with her his guilt, like clammy ribbons of seaweed on a drowned man. He knew he should not have neglected her in illness and before; he knew he had failed her; he knew his judgements on her were unkind. This knowledge he hid away from himself, deep in the ravines of his eroded personality; therefore she stood in the door with it all night, while he twitched miserably under the bedclothes and wished dawn would come. She forced him to remember how once he had made her drunk. He had been so tired of her weeping, her complaints, her feeble ugliness. Longing for silence and rest, he had poured her some sherry in the middle of the morning. She did not cry for more than half an hour after drinking it. He had filled her glass a second time and then she sat up straight for the first time for months and smiled at him.

'Darling Tikki,' she said, with deep sincerity.

After the third glass she had laughed and fluttered her eyelashes and held her emaciated hands together in the way that had once been pretty, was by then grotesque. Her words slurred, she giggled. Fred sat coldly, like an experimenter, and filled her glass again. Blotches appeared on her stringy face. She laughed more and more, twisting and jerking in her chair. When he finally decided to cork the bottle, she wrestled with him, amorously.

'Another little one, please Tikki.' Then she stood up, unaided. 'And a kiss!'

She wound her old woman's arms round his waist and even, he gritted his teeth to remember it, seemed ready to clamber up him, twining one leg round his. Roughly he had given her a final glass, holding it to her mouth like medicine, forcing it down her in one gulp, then had left her, spluttering, to sleep it off.

This episode tortured him. It destroyed at a blow so many of his comforting illusions. To help himself, he turned to Holly. She was four-square and real, like himself. And yet . . . for minutes on end he could confuse her with someone else. He might call her Ida, or Maud, even Lucille.

'Just a slip of the tongue. That's what getting old does for you!'

'You are not old, Tikki.' This was her habitual answer to his habitual plea.

She had taken to calling him Tikki because Daddy seemed inappropriate now, and he said he liked Tikki – and really, what was a name? she asked herself, and tried not to mind when Fred slipped out a Maud in her direction. She saw that her father was in the process of type-casting her as the woman in his life, an amalgam of wife, sister, aunt and child. She feared the mixture might set as hard round her as a concrete mould.

*

Eventually, she decided it was time to leave the cottage. Fred must fend for himself, as most widowers did, after all.

That summer she worked for a season at the Pitlochry theatre, which was ideal because she could have Peter there on holiday and even drive up to see Tikki on the odd free day.

The following winter she went right back into her career, with a part in a West End play. Peter had to transfer to a London school and become used to the woman who kept house for the pair of them. He was an amenable, strong-minded little boy and managed well enough, but Holly knew it was not satisfactory. After the two years' break, she found acting more of an effort. Her notices were not all that stunning. Nor was she any longer sure she valued the prize enough to make the effort. She could have started an affair but avoided that; and, when the play closed in April, took Peter back to the cottage with a rush of joy that took her by surprise.

She, Fred and Peter had another honeymoon. The ageing man was rejuvenated, the weather superb. Huge hummocky clouds of bluish white with dusky centres came piling up over the mountains to the west but were scattered and dissolved by a dry wind as they sailed out over the sea. Only cottony wisps trailed in the sky over the cottage and the sun poured down through leafless trees day after day. The farmers harrowing their fields were enveloped in whirling dust clouds and the colour of the larch plantations turned from bronze to olive to acid green.

On the cliff top field Holly turfed out all the cottage furniture to scrub and polish. Even the carpet was dragged out and hung on the line to be thwacked by Peter in a torrent of excitement, which filled his dark curls with sandy dust. Fred rolled jauntily to his glass box and returned at cloudless midday to beer and cheese on the grass. He was full of old jokes, old facial expressions brilliantly lit by the clear, clean light.

Holly's heart filled with love, the emotion flooding into some cavity below her breast bone, like a cave, drained at low tide, fills up when the sea returns. She wondered how she could ever have left him.

Yet when, as inevitably happens in the Highlands, spring warmth giving way to a last gasp from winter, rain and sleet swept in from the north and east, and filled the cottage with chill gloom, turning the daffodils' yellow a bitter chrome, then Fred's sour temper and silences returned. Yet he needed her, even came near to asking her help. Once when she had got him out to walk in the spruce plantation he was able to ask why Lucille had 'gone a little queer', spent those hours rubbing her hands over each other. Gently, not to alarm him, she tried to explain in psychological terms her mother's withdrawal, but he flinched away.

'Don't give me that rubbish,' he exclaimed with a violent grimace.

'Tikki, don't be rude. I'm only – '

'I'll be what the hell I like.'

He stamped about the path, clumsily.

'Airy fairy nonsense!'

He wheeled to the right and plunged a few yards into the plantation until the sticks of dead branches held him up.

'Don't give me any of that.'

He tried to penetrate the wood on the other side, as if he must separate himself from her, but was again brought up by interlocking brown branches radiating out from each brown trunk. Some snapped off, and twigs adhered to his shoulders.

He stood among the trees and almost shouted at her, 'Because someone didn't have the right treatment as a baby, they steal Gentleman's Relish and silk blouses when they are fifty!'

So, she thought, he knows.

He came back to the path. She began to walk stolidly ahead after Peter who was running in and out of the broom bushes a hundred yards away.

'It's bloody ludicrous. Most people can't even remember their babyhood.'

'That's the whole point, Tikki.'

'What is?'

'That the subconscious is hidden.'

'Subconscious nothing.'

'Look,' she said, trying to be patient, and putting her gloved hand on his arm, 'you say you remember your mother but – '

'Say!' He was appalled, unbelieving his ears. 'Of course I remember her.' His features hardened, his eyes were blue marbles.

Holly persevered. As she picked a few twigs off his coat, she said, quietly, 'Not really, Tikki. You don't remember her. You couldn't. Not really. Mummy always said she reckoned you had no *real* picture of your mother.'

'She knew nothing about it. Neither do you. If I tell you – good God! They took me to see her the day Ida was born.'

'Yes. You've said. But, psychologically speaking, can't you see that – '

'No, I bloody well can't. Your precious psychology is an invention of about as much use as a flat bottomed boat and anyone who relies on it will come a handsome cropper.'

He moved his body out of her reach and smiled at her with malice. Then she called Peter and kept the boy between Fred and herself for the rest of the walk.

Having quarrelled once, they went on to other squabbles about trivial, pointless things like the best method of cleaning silver, the time of the last postal collection, whether or not to save scraps of string. Holly liked to do this, Fred called it cheese-paring. He was becoming a cantankerous old man. She said so during one row.

'Yes, but what is cantankerous?' asked Peter, interrupting the other two.

'Your grandfather is *angry*,' said Fred with dignity to the child. 'And with reason. I am not cantankerous.'

Holly countered his moods by taking up social contacts in Inverness, Forres and Nairn. Her uncle Hamish died that spring and she was drawn closer to Ida, by then a sick woman herself. She visited Balchraggan and met the Minister, a frail man with a sweet smile, and also a few friends from schooldays. Then, by a curious chance, she met Wishart Grant. He had been Chrissie's boyfriend when she was Donald's girl.

One sunny morning she and Peter were practising handstands on the beach, and she looked up to see a dark man with two dogs watching her. Recognition came to them at the same instant.

'Why, you are Holly Tickener.'

'And you're Wishart Grant.'

She laughed easily and Peter pranced with the dogs in the surf.

He had a swarthy, handsome, dignified face, a strong body expensively dressed, exceptionally clean hands with nails cut short, and a Highland voice, musical and deep. They sat on the sand and talked for a long time.

She liked him and so did Peter. They went out for drives and picnics. Wishart was an amusing and intelligent companion. He was a phenomenon – the local boy who stays where he is and achieves the polish and poise and money others travel the world to gain. Altogether he was a great relief as a companion from Fred, who had had an attack of summer flu which had turned to bronchitis and made him very bad tempered.

He never went back to full duties as coastguard. Holly had the impression that he was being gently eased out of the work. He had begun to be muddled sometimes in his thought; he dithered, then reacted with violent, misplaced certainty. He had never taken correction kindly, now the mildest check made the veins on his neck stand out, grey blue.

Peter was learning to be wary of his grandfather, which saddened Holly. She knew how loveable Tikki could be – how secure, serene, and full of fun when the real man shone through. She tried to wheedle good moods out of him.

Think I'm an old child to be jollied along, do you? his hostile expression said.

She sighed with a little humph of Oh! have it your own way.

Fred longed to reach out and grab her hand, pull her to him, to make up, but the chaining habit of other such moments missed prevented him.

Holly again took Peter to London for a winter play, again was dissatisfied with her work and could not find the right way to rearrange her life. Again she avoided forming a relationship with a man she met, and although Terence was in London, and took Peter out most weekends, nothing could come of that. She had burned that bridge as thoroughly as the one to Donald had been destroyed. In fact, she thought, I seem to have a way of denying myself access to the men I love. It's as if I punish myself for preferring them to Tikki. Only Tikki is left.

She went back in the summer. Several people besides Wishart welcomed her with real gladness. She was a gay person in company, happily intelligent, with good looks and a detached, ironic manner. Most of the men she met were attracted to her, and many women. She built up quite a circle of activities and that winter stayed at the cottage. Fred was not very well. Perhaps she had finished with the theatre. In her heart she would like to, but it was the only real life she had, which said little enough for her, as she rather bitterly reflected. My only life a thing built of pretence and illusion, needing make-up and tricks and 'business' to sustain. That's all I have to offer my son.

She stopped on the cliff path where she and Peter were walking, scarlet cheeked, wind battered.

'What is it, Mummy?'

He had the broad, open face of Fred.

'I love you, Peter.'

He looked away and shuffled his wellingtons.

'Yes, I know.'

'And what do I do for you?'

'Let's go back before that squall comes,' he replied.

The boy could read the weather. Scooting over the sullenly heaving sea was a drooping pall of cloud mingling with the water. They ran for the cottage, reaching it as the rain dashed water on their backs as violently as from a thrown bucket.

She rubbed his wet hair dry with laughter and chatter. They

draped their oilskins over the clothes-horse by the range. Holly put on the kettle. Peter took the sleepy cat out of her basket to nurse. When Holly went into the living-room to tell Fred the tea was ready, she found him looking stonily at the chair where Lucille used to sit. He did not turn when she spoke but got heavily to his feet and moved into the kitchen avoiding looking at her or Peter, but noticing all the same.

'How many times have I told you that if you fondle that animal you will get fleas.'

'My teacher says cat fleas are becoming rare.'

'Does she indeed! Tell her from me, will you, that she's talking rubbish.'

There was a silence while Peter diligently stroked the cat's knob of a head. He liked the feel of the rigid ears flicking upright when his fingers passed over them.

'Becoming rare! Have you ever heard such bloody nonsense, Holly?'

'Actually yes, I did hear something like that on the radio.'

Peter ignored both adults, stroking with concentration.

'Don't believe all you hear on that thing, or the bloody box,' said Fred for the several hundredth time.

The evening was settling into its routine.

Holly thought for a brilliant moment of the wind on the cliff. She flexed her arms inside her sweater sleeves. She felt strong. She must and she would shrug off her father. For Peter's sake, it would be right. And, after all, Tikki was powerless to keep her.

She craned her head until she could see her reflection in the mirror. Yes, a strong face and young enough. She attempted a confident smile to reassure her image, but the reflection remained impassive. It even had a look of warning.

9

HOLLY AND WISHART

The first time Wishart made love to Holly he was very happy. He had her at last and she was obviously as pleased as he was. The only bad moment was when she brought up the subject of her father.

She was lying on her back, relaxed, smiling at him, and Wishart, propped on an elbow, was smiling down at her. Her skin was pale, faintly gleaming on the cheek-bones and chin, and sweat had dampened the small tendrils of hair which escaped from the solid black loops. He fitted his hand over her face, thumb to little finger stretching from ear to ear. The faint menace in the gesture Holly liked. She had never known anyone do that, and it increased her belief that Wishart was someone different.

'Happy?' he asked her.

For answer she kissed his palm arched just above her mouth.

'You are a happy person,' he told her, flexing his hand lightly up and down. 'Aren't you?'

'In fits and starts.'

'Make it a start now.'

She smiled under his fingers and pursed up her lips to kiss him again. Then they remained still and quiet for several minutes, until she said, dreamily, 'I was happy as a child. With Tikki.'

'Who?'

'With Tikki, my father.'

Wishart immediately removed his hand and rolled on to his back; but he let the remark go by. Holly's father had no part in his plans. They never mentioned families when they were together.

They talked of the old days at Balchraggan and Wishart's various business interests, mutual friends, the theatre, and of Wishart's two passions – fishing and stalking. Old Mr Tickener was a sideline.

'Before the war,' he heard her go on, 'is like a shimmering bubble in my memory. Timeless. Just a few places, like the front room table, the golden rod clump, the end of my bed with velvet curtains and a toy hanging monkey on a stick – and Tikki, not so much a person, more an essence spreading through.'

'For God's sake! You make it sound like a religious experience.'

'I've never had one of those, so I wouldn't know. But Tikki was god-like then, yes.'

'And now?' he asked against his better judgement.

'Oh Wishart!' She reared up on her arms, the sheet slipping off her naked body, but said no more.

She could not be called young, he thought, but she had a suppleness that excited him. Her white skin lay over her bones like thick, soft leather. She was staring above his dressing chest at some prints of fencing positions which hung there. In these, lithe men in tight pants, mesh masks on their faces, thrust and parried with great elegance. The frames were scarlet.

'Where did those come from?' she asked.

'Uncle of mine,' he replied, stroking her shoulder.

His flat was full of rare objects which must have been collected with care, yet he never wanted to talk about them. It was as if he put them in their allotted spaces to forget them.

'Living with parents never works,' he said in his firmest tone. As she had brought up the subject of Mr Tickener, he was not going to let her evade it. Evasion would not be a propitious start. 'Tell me how it is.'

'Confused. Confusing. A nasty muddle.'

'Don't you get on?'

'It's not a question of that after – what? – the thirty odd years I have known Tikki. We love each other, but that's all so overlaid with irritations, bad habits, different tastes, the points of view that one clings to, quite pointlessly.'

'I don't find that with my mama.'

Wishart's mother, born Alma Calvatini, was blind and lived with an Italian maid in Inverness. Wishart visited her most days, listened to 78 records of Caruso and Gigli, drank Maresi, chilled, and ate almond biscuits specially imported via Jenners.

'No, well, Alma accommodates you, and you flatter her. You make her feel young and beautiful for half an hour every day. What a gift to give a woman!'

He pulled her down against him. They kissed. Then, not being a man to leave business unfinished even for pleasure, he tucked her against his side and continued in a ruminating voice, 'So, your Tikki – but what a name!'

'Rather twentyish, yes. Mummy thought it up. She was all for cocktails, cloche hats and the Charleston, I gather.'

'But the name suited?'

'It suited her, yes. She was never very real even to herself, let alone to Daddy.'

Wishart preferred the dated Tikki to Daddy.

'What did he do?' This was Wishart's key question, his way into every man he met.

What he himself had done was to develop his Italian uncle's chain of icecream parlours into a flourishing food shop business, picking up side-lines like estate agencies and a haulage firm on the way. At the same time he had taken over wholesale his Scottish father's musical voice, dignified manner and sporting tastes.

'Tikki's a sailor at heart,' Holly replied, and her heart swelled at the thought with primitive, childish patriotism.

'Dartmouth?'

'Good heavens no. He was a poor lad. Probably ran away to sea. He won't talk of his childhood, and my aunt I never thought to ask and now she's dead, as you know.'

Wishart did. He was handling the sale of Balchraggan farm and house, but he did not take up this remark. He was not ready.

'My brother, Hugh, always says Tikki did exceptionally well to become a captain from such a beginning.' Her fond pride was evident. 'Hugh did his national service in the navy and he says getting into the wardroom must have been one hell of a shock.'

'Mm.'

'Yet he left the navy. It broke him in a way. He took up trade and went underground.'

'Mining?'

'Only metaphorically.' She laughed. 'He had a city job. They like ex-officers.'

'Yes,' agreed Wishart judiciously, 'a few can be good for trade.'

– 195 –

'Then my aunt told him of this coastguard job and he was happier for a time.'

'Until your mother died, I suppose.'

'Before that. Some demon, or some worm of worry or guilt or – heavens! I don't know what it is that troubles him. It's as if there were a secret strata in his life. Whatever it is, he's become impossible, that I do know.'

'To you and Peter?'

'And to himself, I think.'

'The time I met you both in Robbie's Bar he certainly looked sour.'

This had been an awkward occasion. Wishart had come across the room smiling broadly at Holly and given her hand a stroking grip, so that Fred had picked up at once there was something between the pair. He also registered a man in the prime of life – fortyish, strong, healthy, with a confident face and obvious money. Wishart behaved as if the world were his to command, but he would not press the point just at the moment. Fred had become acutely conscious of what was never entirely absent from his awareness, his arthritic hip and knees, his failing left eye, the tiredness in his backbone, the bitterness of life passing on the other side of the street, or, in this case, the bar. All this vibrated in the air in the time it took Wishart to enquire about their drinks and order again.

Fred had sat between Wishart and Holly who chatted across him. Both extended their long legs, hers in silky tights and turquoise shoes, his in herringbone tweed and blue socks with a diamond pattern. They seemed at ease, but Holly was acting hard. She knew Fred's eyes were fixed on her like the eyes of a dead fish, pale blue with a watery glaze.

Of course, she had told Fred of Wishart Grant and how they had met on the beach after twenty years. Nevertheless guilt sprang up in her as she sat beside the two men. She tried giving her attention to Fred, looking directly at him, which was, by then, unusual, for she and her father had come to the point of spending whole days in silence except when Peter was home from boarding school and chattered for them. How this state of affairs had crept up on them, Holly could not explain to herself, let alone to Wishart; especially as she desperately pitied her father.

The word 'sour' which Wishart had used was fair enough for an outsider. Fred's face was stiff. The pouches under his eyes, the ridges of flesh ribbed along his jawbone, the tiny folds round his ears were carved hard by raw hostility. His hands usually gripped his knee-caps or the chair arms, on and off, on and off, as if a current were pulsing through his arms. Sourness to the onlooker, was agony disciplined to the initiated. Talking to Wishart he had tried to be his old hail-fellow, bar-easy self. Holly had quivered at the hideous effort it took.

'Tikki is a good man, deep down,' she said to Wishart, warm and cushioned in his bed. She could feel the fur of his chest against her lips tickling. 'He is a good man gone adrift. It's all too much for me. I give up.'

Wishart thought her insistent talk suggested she had far from given her father up.

He turned over the idea of Mr Tickener being more important to Holly than he had realised, seeing his way to accommodating that fact into his scheme. Wishart rarely took difficulties head on. He negotiated a way round. He tried never to say no, allowing time, silence and events to convey his negatives for him and in this way he had avoided much enmity. It seemed a much more civilised approach. Wishart linked the idea of civilisation with all the pleasant and soothing appurtenances of his life like well cut suits, old malt whisky, central heating, his fly rods, his mother's flat and his very large bank balance, chiefly the last.

'He has been good to you?' he enquired eventually in a gentle tone, his Highland accent suddenly noticeable.

'He was my life as a child. That's not good or bad – it's just reality.'

He had no more patience with remarks of that sort than Fred would have had. He squeezed her breast in his hand and said, 'Your public would not want you as Daddy's little girl.'

'Be damned to them.'

Holly had now been diverted from her father to her career. He could feel her inwardly debating whether to go on a tour with the RSC (recently and flatteringly offered her) or, as she had said the day before, 'to jack the whole weary treadmill in'. Her on/off theatrical life was becoming less and less satisfying. Wishart did not interrupt her thoughts, and in his own mind ran over again his plans for the future.

Then they turned to each other worldlessly and began to kiss. It was as if the long talk, full of pauses and diverging thoughts, had been a cloak under which the veins of desire had swelled and filled, electric, overflowing.

*

A week later Wishart told Holly he had a surprise to show her at Balchraggan. Something had kept her from visiting the village. She had not been there since Ida's funeral which had followed soon on Hamish's.

Winter funerals are by far the worst, especially when cold rain is falling, coursing mud and flinty stones into the open grave even as the coffin is lowered. Fred had stared defiantly at nothing while the wind blew about his spikes of white hair. He knew none of the many people crowding round in black, under umbrellas, and with rubber overshoes. He wanted none of them. They felt that. Leaving the graveside, he was introduced to an old minister who quavered about knowing Lucille. 'Your dear wife and I were tremendous buddies – that was the phrase in those times.' Fred stonily absorbed the Americanism and the liberty.

The farmhouse had seemed cavernous, echoing with the hesitant feet of mourners, all cold, all thinking unwillingly yet obsessively of death, their own in particular. Fred had marched back and forth from the chair where Maud had sat reading her Bible to the double china sinks where the land-girl used to loll cradling hot cocoa in the chilblained fingers which stuck out of her mittens like stiff red worms. Ghosts had come out from every corner.

Holly had been bemused by memories of the jinking dice in the red pot as they sat on the floor to play snakes and ladders, and Ida's apron taut across her barren hips. The kitchen, and the hall with its antlers were veiled in cobwebs, for Ida had been ill for many months. She entered the front room where Fred had spilled out the oranges and she had made a scene about being sent out of her parents' bed. Upstairs the treadle-machine was still in the back bedroom draped in a faded counterpane but the iron bed had given way to a desk stacked with farm account books, stock records. Bundles of agricultural magazines tied with twine were piled on the bare floor-boards which were stained for a yard round the edges. Even then she could feel the cold shine of the lino with the red lattice pattern that had been nailed to the floor. The tacks stood up with fragments of fibre adhering. From the window nothing was changed. There rose the timeless hill; there ran the burn, glimpsed through the door in the wall. Moss and lichen were crusted on the barn roofs.

When she arrived in Balchraggan with Wishart nearly two years later, autumn was at its peak of colour and warmth. All along the side of Loch Ness the sunlight flickered on the silver birch trunks and the silk rippling water. They drove right through the village, past the modern hotel, and turned eventually at the old Chisholm home by the track to the farm. Wishart drew up to roll back the roof of his car, and Holly, who at Ida's funeral had been drowned in sorrowful family memories and had hardly noticed the rest of the village, let her gaze linger on the window that had been Donald's, the tree where Chrissie had hung a swing. Her own name was still Chisholm. Wishart's dark face was intent on the business in hand, his large, black-rimmed eyes serious and calm as usual.

They continued up the lane and little primrose yellow leaves were blown in scurries from the birch trees. Some floated down the burn, others lodged in Holly's hair. The burn was brown, cream frothed with October rain.

'Why are we coming up here?' she asked.

'Part of my surprise.'

A local farmer she knew slightly was ploughing Hamish's big field in a following cloud of seagulls and crows, for the land had been sold separately from the house. As they came to the last bend beside the pines a lapwing soared into the sky from the sheep-fold and fluttered with wide wings, rising and falling in the light against the trees all shimmering with the sun behind them.

Holly prepared herself for the look of the farmhouse, its grey blankness after being empty for two years, perhaps vandalised. The Highlands are full of sad, half ruinous homesteads.

First she saw a fence of white palings, then a row of newly planted conifers beside the path to a front door of sparkling black. The windows had somehow been altered – she wasn't quite sure what was different – and the friendly yew that had pressed itself against the south corner was gone. Gutterings, slates, chimneys had all been repaired and straightened, as if someone had said, 'Stand up, stop slouching!' to the old house.

With movements expressing satisfaction and the expectation of more to come, Wishart opened the front door, grasping the brass knob in his leather gloved hand. She waited to see the stone hall, the run of doors, the stiffly turning bare staircase. She took a breath, anticipating the shut-in coldness that would strike her. But warmth surged out. Expensive rugs covered the flags that had been treated with some substance to give them a shine and reveal their grain. There were no antlers over the doors stripped of varnish; a huge modern mirror reflected a Chinese urn of chrysanthemums, her own astonished face, and Wishart's appraising one.

She found every part of the house had been altered, made warm, comfortable and apparently larger. One no longer felt the corner shadows creeping out to mist the chilly rooms. China, polished furniture, pictures, flowers, yellow patterned, red and jade green curtains, steel sinks, green bath suites, silver, mirrors, rich carpets, fires made the house not crowded but spacious and luxurious.

The most telling difference was in the kitchen, which had been made into the sort of traditional farm kitchen that never was, as Holly knew, all harshness done away with and convenience added. The windows had been over the sinks which had made it difficult for Ida to reach and fold back the shutters – Holly had an instantaneous picture of her aunt's straining body, awkwardly angled, leaning over – but now all sign of plumbing had gone and the windows had trapeze shaped seats with cushions and between them was a dresser filled with green plates in the shape of leaves. The old scullery where the pigswill tubs had stood and muddy boots, a harness or two, this was a neat, electric washing-up and laundry area linked to the kitchen by an arch with a rubber plant in a brass pot.

Wishart pointed out various features with a curious smile, half of pleasure, half anxious. She had never seen him look so young or exposed as he waited for her approval.

The house was not precisely to her taste, being rather too arranged and co-ordinated, approved by magazine. Wishart was not creative. She smiled at him and ran her finger along the curved back of a painted wood chair. On the other hand she would not even have seen the possibilities in the house, which was now comfortable and good-looking, even if it did smell of money. Nor would she have had the stamina to carry out such a unified scheme. She'd have relapsed into white emulsion and stripped pine. Her home-making was limited to such simplicities as artistic vases of wild flowers and draping embroidered shawls over uglier items.

All the many sets of rooms she had rented had looked approximately the same, had disappointed her, but not enough to spur her into activity.

For although Holly appeared to outsiders as an independent woman, fixing her own life up, this was merely the accidental fall-out of events. Her inner leanings were to having things arranged for her, so long as her freedom was guaranteed. This was something Wishart had been clever enough to understand. Even her career had flourished best under Terence's guidance and without him had fallen flat.

Wishart guided her back to the hallway where sunlight the colour of sauterne was streaming through the open door and his two labradors sat on the step as if conscious of their beauty. He asked her then, at last, straight out if she liked what he had done.

'Oh I do! I had no idea the old house had all this in it.'

He relaxed into a smile of revealing innocence – a boy in the approval of the women he loved. 'I knew you'd like it.'

'I do. Mind you,' she wanted to be honest, 'I liked it best before.'

He pulled a face.

'Probably that was because I was happy here as a child.'

His huge, soft eyes attached themselves to her, like moths. 'You will go on being happy here,' he said.

The moment froze. She became aware as if on a stage that her lips were slightly pouting, her hands gripping each other behind her back. She cried to herself, 'Fool!' She waited.

'Will you be my wife, Holly?' he asked. His eyelids covered his eyes. He gave the hint of a formal bow.

She managed to unclasp her hands and he took them in his, yet they remained standing motionless and wordless. Although they had been lovers all summer, Holly was taken completely by surprise, and saw at once how silly her surprise was.

What an extraordinary trick for life to play – a return to Balchraggan with Wishart Grant, of all people. She remembered him fleetingly as a child in this very house, eating her mother's angel cakes and teasing Chrissie. She liked him, he pleased her, they were amused and interested by the same things. It would be a very great relief to be on her own at last, not dependent on Tikki, not needing to work in order to support Peter.

She hardly thought all this. That came later as a rationalisation. At the time she stood close to Wishart and felt that, as life had sprung this surprise, she should accept it. Her spirit rose to the challenge.

'Please, Holly,' said Wishart softly.

Her sense of theatre made her, in turn, bow slightly over their clasped hands.

'Yes,' she said.

*

They were married by Christmas. Holly declined the RSC tour. Her career of acting that in adolescence had been a compensation for losing life at Balchraggan was allowed to sink away when the place was offered back to her. In her imagination she was re-entering her childhood.

She felt vibrantly healthy, sloughing off years of the cramp of cities. Her body grew thinner with exercise, her face and arms a little plumper so that she looked years younger than when facing her last audience. Wishart was an easy and exciting person to live with, and she found herself falling more deeply in love with him as they lived together – sleeping and rising, as the local expression was. She liked his thick hair rumpled by sleep, the way he pulled back the curtains with such an expectant and determined air, willing the world to go his way. Every morning his first real words, apart from mumbled endearments into her neck, were some positive comment on the weather. 'It will be fine by midday', or 'This rain is just what the garden needs.' It was happiness for her to spend a day in his company, outdoors, by the river or on the moor, preferably with Peter.

Wishart too was happy, and pleased with himself. He had what he wanted – a wife of sufficient beauty, much poise, good humour, intelligence and experience. He was deeply content when he watched her, as he did some mornings standing at the bedroom window before going into his work, start to climb the hill, steadily at a certain pace which she kept up right to the top where she disappeared from view over the rim to enter the mossy ride through the pine woods on the far side. When Peter was with her, he was even better pleased. Wishart had no great love of small children, but was more than happy to have a good-looking, bright, well-mannered lad of ten added to his household.

Having his home suddenly expand from a bachelor's town flat, where he rarely spent an entire day, to a solid farmhouse with a wife and a son, dogs, a pony, a second car, motor-mower, three telephones and possibly, he was mulling over the practicality, a sauna, was a matter of powerful satisfaction to Wishart who saw people and objects as largely interchangeable. Both had their advantages; the changing moods of one compensated for the static perfection of the other, and vice versa of course.

He had no real fear that Holly would cause him anguish. She was adept at muting her emotions and picking up hints, her training on the stage ensured it, and she loved him. He felt sure of that. Her sleeping morning smile so accepting and simple told him so.

Inevitably there were difficulties. Wishart needed her to entertain his business associates, men whom, on the whole, she did not like. Nor did she much care for Wishart in their company. He became cynical, even devious, with a hearty manner that set her teeth on edge. Equally, when her own friends came up from the south to stay, she was annoyed at the fuss they made about mud and rain and steep slopes when she took them about her heavenly land. Very few people came twice.

She let the landscape fill her days more and more, seeing it now with mature eyes and taking her pleasure from a mind trained in the appreciation of form and colour, knowledgeable about painting and the literature of the countryside; yet below was the stronger stream of childhood's passion, the delight that had burst open when she arrived from Mitcham and found Balchraggan. To pleasure was added that of being able to share it with her husband – a day by the streaming glassy river with his fly rod dipping below the hazels, or a long tramp over the moor past lochlans where water-lilies bobbed on wavelets the wind chased over the deep blue surface.

She and Wishart had one quarrel about her weekly visit to Fred. Since Wishart visited Alma every weekday Holly thought this unreasonable. She stopped drawing attention to her visits and Wishart half-forgot them, because he wanted to.

In fact Holly did not enjoy her days at the cottage. Her father seemed never to open doors or windows, and dank, cheerless air knocked down her spirits no matter how high she had raised them as she drove towards him.

He waited her coming with sour longing, fearing that when she came they would fight. He was a fighter, a man of activity, not one to accept the slowness of old age as a welcome release from duty.

But in this god-forsaken cottage what was there to fight? Only silence and emptiness. He was a fighter deprived of weapons and target, forced to act a resignation that his spirit totally rejected. It was this he blamed Holly and Wishart for most – that they had imposed resignation on him. It was the meanest trick: to make old people play along with their own nullifying.

He and Holly managed an hour or two of kindness and affection, when they spoke of the far past usually, of Sandalcliff in the early morning with the clear, clean sunlight on the sleeping housefronts, the idly swishing sea, and how Holly had taken cellophane wrapped biscuits from the slot machine, painted green and with narrow windows behind which the packets were piled. She would remind Fred of the hiss and the smell of the gas burner under the tea urn, and the way the soft tar between the planking of the jetty stuck to her shoes. He spoke of the purplish jelly-fish and the early glitter of the sea, still empty of boats. Sometimes, in memory, they strayed farther back to Mrs Willoughby's cat, and Holly pedalling her tricycle to meet Fred off the bus. He would take off his bowler hat to kiss her, and she then rode home with it on her own head. It smelt of damp leather and soot.

But always with weary inevitability some point of dissension arose. Fred's face hardened, he lifted voice, he clenched his hands on the chair arms, and jiggled his angry feet, making his slippers spring about as if alive. It was strange how his frustration found this outlet in his extremities, while his heavy body sat still.

She drove home fast along the coast road with the roof down, letting the wind blow her father away; but missing the deeper truth that love for him sprang in her inner core, like the underground meadows that cavers discover growing unseen and to themselves, unvisited, unpollinated, beautiful.

*

After a year of marriage Holly returned in distress from one of her visits to Fred. He was poorly, not fit to be alone. The next day she brought him back with her to Balchraggan, and Wishart found Tikki, as she persisted in calling him, in bed, the doctor just leaving. Mr Tickener had bronchitis rather badly.

Wishart accepted the situation with reasonable grace. He and Fred had established a wary but friendly relationship on either side of Holly, each secretly believing she was his. On that Friday, Wishart was touched by the weakness and pallor of the sick man, the way his bottom lip sagged showing the tobacco-stained teeth. He lay in bed for a week making no trouble. Then he got up, looking washed-out, and established his seat by the living-room fire, a big armchair with wings that Wishart liked but could hardly deny to a convalescent, who felt every draught. He solaced himself with the thought of spring coming, better weather and Fred going.

But Holly got it into her head that Tikki could not go back to his cottage.

'It's cold and damp. And now he doesn't do the coastguard work any more, what's the point?'

'The point is, surely, that it's his home.'

This annoyed Holly. She was sure Wishart knew what she was driving at. 'Well, and this is my home and I want him to stay here.'

'Do you indeed?'

Wishart left the room. He objected to the proposal all the more for its being made in front of his father-in-law who sat like an oversized baby between them, cocooned in a rug with a lumpy face.

'He'll come round,' said Holly to Fred as the door shut. 'You must stay here with me and Peter.'

Fred had been dreading the return to his cottage. He had learned to hate every part of it – the thick walls imprisoning him in dark rooms, the twisting stair so difficult for his arthritic knees to negotiate, Peter's toy cupboard holding only broken cardboard boxes and blunted colouring pencils, and the empty chairs with cushions all squashed and distorted.

'I will write today and resign your lease, then arrange to have your things brought over here.'

Both Fred and Holly liked to make these quick and irrevocable decisions. They'd both being doing it all their lives. He heaved himself straighter in the chair and gave her a piteous look of graditude.

'Poor Tikki,' she said, stroking his hand. 'Were you dreading going back?'

'It is a bit parky this time of year,' he said with an attempt at his usual manner.

'You won't miss the sea?'

His pale eyes avoided hers. He said nothing, afraid she was going back on her decision.

'We can can go over for a drive sometimes. Or you can. Visit your friends in Forres.'

She knew he had none, knew too he needed the fiction of acquaintances.

'Think I could have a smoke?' he asked, to show he was feeling better already.

She fetched his pipe, tobacco pouch and matches from his bedside drawer. The objects were redolent of her father, held in themselves his solid hands, steady gaze and kind manner to her. They were, she thought sadly, much more him than the feeble man in Wishart's wing chair.

*

Holly's precipitate action was the first unmistakable sign Wishart had of another side to her. Until then, from their first meeting on the beach, she had been compliant. It had seemed her nature to wish to please, to make smooth, to fall in with any plan once she had given her liking to someone; and liking for Wishart had flooded into her as they sat on the warmed sand watching Peter observe the waves creep up to the moat of his castle and eventually dissolve its walls, which did not crumble or fall, but slithered down in wet formlessness.

He, on the other hand, was adept at getting his own way without alienating others. He had decided, immediately it was suggested, that having his father-in-law to live at Balchraggan would not do. He was to be master in his home and would share it with no adult man. He was, after all, an Italian Scot. He laid plans, but said nothing.

Fred and Holly, unaware of schemes to disrupt their arrangement, were extremely satisfied, at least for a time. His release from Lucille's ghost alone made Fred's spirit buoyant, and his health improved with the spring weather. He and Holly basked in each other's approbation. He liked to follow her round the house, watching her at work, asking again and again the same idle questions, devised simply to keep her attention on him, and when she answered a little sharply as she sometimes did, even then, coming to the end of patience with him, and his cumbersome body getting in her way, he would grin to himself with pure satisfaction. He had always enjoyed her spurts of temper, the way her eyes flashed at him.

'Little prickle puss, aren't you?'

She couldn't do anything but smile back at him, allowing her mouth to express an edge of pique, knowing her childishness and feeling safe in it even while her adult mind analysed herself.

'Come on,' she'd say, 'let's have a sit down. I'll make some coffee.'

When Peter was at home they played rummy round the kitchen table and Fred cheated with a cheery, rosy face and roared with laughter when the boy challenged him.

'Grandpa! How could you?'

'He always was a cheat at cards, weren't you, Tikki?'

'I wouldn't say so. No. Not a cheat. Let's say a more than usually skilful player, eh?'

'No, a cheat pure and simple.'

'Ah well, pussy, no harm done. Families need the father to cheat at games.'

He and Holly smiled trustingly at each other.

With the warmer weather they spent time in the garden. Fred's arthritis prevented him digging, or kneeling to weed, but he paced about in a pair of old sea-boots and advised her, or sat under the apple tree half-asleep. Before she planted anything she would hold it up to him and he would raise his eyebrows and nod with encouragement. Whatever Holly did she needed to share in some way with her father.

The Highland summer was punctuated with long stretches of soft rain which chilled the air and darkened Fred's mood. He retreated into complaints and subterranean conflicts with Wishart about the central heating. Wishart and Holly made light of the weather and continued to walk and fish. Fred saw them coming down the hillside flushed and damp, talking and laughing, leaning together, apparently forgetful of him. He struck his palms on the window-sill and leaned forward like a bear.

When Wishart took Holly out for an evening, or to Edinburgh for the weekend, Fred was left to look after himself with the daily woman's assistance; and he had to learn the signs which meant that his son-in-law did not want him in the sitting-room, that he wanted his wife to himself. Fred did learn, but he could not accept it with any sort of grace. He felt strongly it was Holly's duty to be his companion. After all – he had nothing at all to do and she was active and free. Why could he not be included in her doings? He did not, perhaps could not, consider that an old man's slow talk, stumbling steps and repetitious opinions might sometimes be a drag even to his Holly.

She offered him new things to read, and talked to him of plays and exhibitions she and Wishart saw, she brought home catalogues from the Festival, and with the aid of binoculars and suitable books tried to get him interested in nature. It was useless. Fred grumbled he was too old for new tricks.

'Knowledge isn't a trick,' she said, but he saw exactly that it was. 'And plenty of people older than you do much more,' she added.

This was criticism, so he set his lips.

'In any case talking to our friends about their interests doesn't take any special effort, Tikki!'

In fact, it did. He found it increasingly difficult to follow conversations, drifted off down byways of familiar thoughts.

'Look at your father,' Wishart once exclaimed, 'sitting there sorting through his prejudices.'

Those Fred had in plenty and strong, confused emotions, but he had no resources. When he was in his prime, strong and active at work, this had not been noticed. In old age and ill health, his remaining strength was diverted entirely into his will to keep going, to be Fred. He was a power in a vacuum. He chose quarrels as a way of being active, of keeping his identity clear, and part of that identity was possessing Holly.

As she realised this, her pity grew. She thought his chances of reclaiming her were nil, and in his hopelessness she must humour him as much as she could. He, of course, hated to be humoured. It was belittling, and fed his sense of being at odds with all around him, even while he knew Holly was trying to be kind.

Old age is cruel. She felt it and so did Fred. Their glances handed the knowledge to and fro between them, though nothing was ever said. The man who had rowed whalers and hauled field-guns could not now carry his daughter's shopping basket and had to walk beside her like a child, following her wish to enter this or that shop, to cross the road at the lights or at the zebra crossing. Which room he sat in at the house, whether or not he smoked a cigar was at Wishart's whim to settle. Arthritis prevented him driving, and his blood pressure was a hazard that kept him artificially docile on many occasions when he felt like exploding.

Holly continued to set herself to please him and in this indulged herself too. Frequently they went to look at the sea. There were various hotels where he could sit in a window, smoke his pipe and watch the shipping and the tides. It was easy for her to launch him into reminiscences, which she enjoyed as much as he, no matter how often repeated – their happy time before the war, the sunlight, the strong young man, the child's hand. She would also tell him of her stage life, something she had until then kept private. Fred's eyes glinted with eagerness to know. He'd pick on a name.

'What sort of chap was this Burns then?'

'He was a terror where women were concerned, for starters.'

'Was he indeed?' She read this correctly as 'Tell me more', and spent half an hour building up for Fred a theatrical set, explaining the jargon to him. He smiled proudly, delighted to have her entirely to himself in this mood of revelation. She was equally pleased to have his total attention while she remembered aloud.

When they came out of the hotel they stood arm in arm for a few minutes, letting the wet wind buffet them, smoothing their features. She held his arm, but he leant slightly on her. Cool marine sunlight glittered on the car as they walked slowly towards it.

That evening, over supper, Fred returned to the subject of Burns, the actor, and his lady friends. Wishart made it plain he was not interested and firmly changed the subject, talking to Holly about some affair of his own. Fred knew he was allowed only a narrow foothold there. It was chancy to comment on Wishart's doings. You could be snubbed – a thing Fred hated more than most – so he withdrew into his wandering thoughts. He kept himself going partly with self-pity at this time. He began to sigh without realising it.

It was a habit he had developed to sigh to himself and mutter 'Oh dear' – an old womanish sound that irritated Wishart beyond bearing. 'Oh dear', as he sank into his armchair; 'Oh dear', as he was passed a plate of meat carved by Wishart; 'Oh dear', when Peter went to school; 'Oh dear', when shown Wishart's salmon, or his bag of grouse; 'Oh dear', at the business phone calls taken for his son-in-law; 'Oh dear', at the newspaper, the radio, the view; 'Oh dear', even at Holly working in the garden.

'Stop it, for God's sake,' Wishart commanded him.

'I'll bloody well say what I like.'

'Not to my wife, you won't.'

'She is my daughter and –'

'Please,' Holly slipped her arms round Wishart's neck, 'don't quarrel.'

They went into the orchard together. Fred thought he saw Holly drawing away from him, becoming Wishart's property. Peter clearly preferred his stepfather who took him out fishing and riding and helped him make model airplanes. Fred's fingers could no longer handle small objects. Anyway, why didn't the lad build battleships? He had seen in the toyshop some model aircraft carriers – cack-handed Yankee things with slant runways. What did these modern fellows know of the skill of his pilots who had flown in arctic gales from flight decks no bigger than a cricket wicket? If they came down in the drink they had three minutes to live, and you just try to launch a lifeboat and get to a sinking plane in those seas, under attack as well, in thirty minutes let alone three. Couldn't be done. God, they had been brave men! People like Holly's precious husband hadn't an idea of what things had been like. He thought he was clever to shoot some poor bloody bird out of the sky.

Fred, over the autumn, became as taciturn and gloomy as at the cottage, hardly speaking to Holly or Peter, though always making some effort to chat to Wishart because (he told himself) he did live in the chap's house and he enjoyed a bit of male conversation. In reality he was afraid of what Wishart could do. For a man like Fred to fear is the worst humiliation. To fear with no defence, no comeback except bad-temper which achieved nothing, not even his own release.

*

Wishart was pressing ahead with his plan.

When he had sold the farm he had kept back a strip of river-meadow, hill and wood. Not much wanted by the new farmer, they made a backdrop for the house and a piece of untouchable land if the Inverness commuters spread out to Balchraggan. Among the trees half way up the hill was the old croft, called Lurgann, where he and Holly had played as children, roofless still but with sturdy foundations, the stream to be piped and his own electricity cables passing near. Not long after his father-in-law's arrival, Wishart began to have Lurgann rebuilt and modernised. A small track was cut to it from the lane, half a mile from the farmhouse. He told Holly it was a speculation, purely a business venture. There was a demand for holiday homes and he hated to see a solid property go back for ever to brambles and nettles and the encroaching pines.

This was also explained to Hugh who came up for a short visit. Hugh greeted his father with reserved affability, brought photographs of his children and rum for Fred, a large box of cigars and new books for Wishart and Holly. He approved heartily of Wishart. From their bastions of finance the two men exchanged friendly salutes. Insurance and banking talk was swapped for trading and land deals with legs extended to the fire, while Fred did his best to join in, with the expression of a young boy wishing to break into a closed circle of more knowledgeable lads. Hugh he-he-he-ed in high good humour, easily picking up Wishart's references to committees and government reports only mentioned by acronyms. Fred could not keep up. He hunched forward in his chair, throwing in mostly irrelevant remarks, and heavy-handed, reactionary comments. He fulminated. He laid down the law. The two younger men nodded at him in parenthesis and pursued their conversation.

'It makes my blood boil,' he said, 'the way that Heath chap scorns the working people.'

'Yes, Dad. Well, he got his come-uppance.'

'That kind never do for long.' Fred's cheeks were dark red.

'How do you think the trade balance is shaping up, Hugh?' asked Wishart.

Fred allowed himself to rest back. He tapped out and emptied his pipe, then refilled it with an assumed air of calm. Inwardly he raged. He was intensely patriotic in the Isle-set-in-a-silver-sea style and half-choked to see a union jack break from a mast head.

Suddenly he inflated like a rubber life jacket and leant forward again.

'In the General Strike our ship was sent to Manchester,' he said, 'and I saw some shocking things. It wasn't right to ask seamen to do the dirty on the civilians.'

'I don't think we're in any danger of a general strike now,' said Wishart. The inference was that Fred had totally missed the point of his conversation with Hugh.

The television was put on to provide a diversion but the news, when it came, enraged Fred the more. He began to shout at Michael Foot who was being interviewed.

'Damned intellectual! Get off your high horse.'

'Are you a Tory then, Dad?'

'Good God, don't insult me. But I've no time for clever-clever reds.'

'Under the bed or anywhere else, eh?'

'What this country wants is a few decent, straightforward, grammar school patriots. There's far too many of your lah-de-dah public school twerps swinging the lead for my liking.'

'Dad's that great relic – homo right-thinkingus. He-he-he!'

'What's wrong with that? Churchill agreed with me.'

'Ah! The Dunkirk spirit rears its head.'

Fred saw he was being teased, and sank back like a tortoise, his heavy head nodding on his freckled, wrinkled neck.

These puppies! he thought. What do they know?

The following evening Holly heard Hugh he-he-he-ing in the orchard where he and Wishart were strolling before dinner. From her bedroom she caught mention of 'the old man'. She leant out of the window.

'You must watch your step,' Hugh said distinctly.

'Oh I will, never you fear,' replied Wishart and cast a quick look up at the window. His next remark was inaudible to Holly.

'My sister can be tricky where the old man's concerned,' warned Hugh who had not noticed her.

She went speedily downstairs, checked Fred was safely shut in his room on the other side of the house, and walked outside to challenge Hugh.

'What the hell do you mean – tricky?'

He laughed comfortably at her, not at all put out. 'You blow hot and cold over Dad. One minute he's everything to you, the next you're off to London again dragging that poor kid with you.'

Holly was so surprised she couldn't speak. Had Hugh thought that all these years?

'That's over anyway,' remarked Wishart, neutrally.

'You've said yourself he's difficult,' Holly found her voice.

'So I steer a steady course. He knows exactly where he is with me,' Hugh said.

'I can't just ignore him.'

'Who said ignore? Have some balance, that's all.'

'She is very, very fond of her father,' said Wishart kindly.

'But hasn't a clue how to treat him.'

'What absolute nonsense! We get on like a house on fire, you know we do.'

'And burn yourselves up,' agreed Hugh and laughed his gleeful laugh, putting his thumbs in his waistcoat pockets like any old man himself, she thought scornfully.

'I love Tikki, that's what you don't understand.'

'Of course I do, Holly. Don't be childish.' For once Hugh was sharp. 'Most girls are in love with their fathers. That's standard.' He added smugly, referring to his daughter, 'My Lucy adores me.'

Instinctively Holly put out a hand to Wishart who drew her close to him.

'You'll have to put that in the past tense,' he said. 'My wife is in love with me.' He kissed her.

The two easy men smoothed over the moment, making Holly walk under the apple boughs with them and explain her plans for the garden.

She knew some girls were in love with their fathers – she had acted such parts on the stage – but it was not true of her. Being in love was a pain like hunger, and bliss, whereas loving Fred was security. The touch of a lover set a current alive in her, but her father's hand was soothing. His presence used to be enough to make everything all right.

That was one of his phrases. 'Everything all right, pussy?' he would ask, pausing in a doorway or looking up from stooping over a plant, his round eyes bright. When she was sure of his love, everything was all right but at Balchraggan she was without this sustaining power for days on end. She forced herself to admit it: she was without it. Her father's cold face of self-pity pursued her from breakfast to bedtime.

No affection from Wishart could compensate for the loss of her father's. This was a secondary truth she made herself accept. She needed the assurance of Fred's love to make sense of her husband's.

The three of them lived a perilously balanced life which only came into healthful equilibrium when Fred was in a good mood and smiled with a real smile, not the false, living with my in-laws and making the best of it one.

For those twelve months Wishart himself was acting a part – that of a busy, preoccupied, but respectful and coolly affectionate son-in-law. He was not unaware of the cross-currents but ignored them. He liked the old man well enough; it was his effect on Holly that was unbearable. He felt his wife was obsessed with Fred. They could not go out for an evening unless the man were provided for like a kid.

'Good God, darling! Leave him to cook his own meal for once. Didn't he live alone before?'

'Poor Tikki, he hates loneliness.'

'Could we drop that ridiculous name? It doesn't suit him in the least.'

At that moment her father came into the sitting-room. It was clear from *The Scotsman* in his hand, the pencil and spectacle case that he was shuffling in to spend the evening with them, doing the crossword and discussing the news, although Wishart had provided him with a television and an armchair with wings in his heated room. Fred glanced from face to face sheepishly, raising his eyebrows until his forehead wrinkled in pink corrugations.

'Looks like quite a hard crossword today,' he said, in his jolly voice. 'Colin Parsons set it – always a beast for anagrams.'

Only his mouth's quiver indicated nervousness in case Wishart said peremptorily, as he often did, 'Mind if Holly and I spend this evening alone? We've something to discuss.' On those occasions Holly's heart hurt like a sea anemone touched and closing with a convulsive heave. Fred always replied too quickly, 'Right ho, old chap, quite understand,' but fingered the door handle before turning and shuffling out again. During these slow moments Holly noticed how baggy his trousers looked, how bowed his shoulders were in the fawn cardigan, pockets sagging with handkerchief and tobacco pouch. She could have cried aloud for the upright navy blue figure of her childhood.

But on this occasion Wishart asked, 'Coming in?'

Eagerly, Fred straightened, closed the door and marched forward. When he was seated Wishart announced, 'We were just discussing your name.'

Fred took off his spectacles and put on his quizzical grandfather face.

'Something wrong with it? "A poor thing but my own" as they say.'

'Tikki is just not dignified,' said Wishart to whom gravitas in all men, and especially elderly men, was necessary.

'Holly's mother thought that up.' It was several days since Fred had thought of Lucille at all, and for a moment he had difficulty in remembering what she was called.

'I have decided to call you Alfred. That is your name, after all.'

Wishart unfolded the evening paper and shook it out. He had stated his position.

Holly began a rambling thought about names – Christian, given, accreted, nick, pet, fond, derisive – and how they altered personality. A rose might well smell as sweet if called a lily, but how if Donald had been Cyril – a hateful name which made her wince, or Wishart himself an ordinary Ted? These thoughts helped her to avoid knowledge of her father's hurt. Quite why his face should have a look of pain she couldn't say, but there he sat like a child caught out in some naughtiness. He was hurt, afraid and furiously angry too, but kept it all in as he knew he must do as a guest in Wishart's house.

Alfred was the sacred name of his mother's love. In his dreams and fantasies she called him Alfred and he responded with clinging love. This fellow Wishart, this get-rich-quick Dago Holly had taken up with, knew nothing of his mother. How did he dare come into those closed places and throw his weight about?

Wishart lifted the lid of his cigar box and pushed it towards Fred. 'Have a smoke, Alfred?'

Fred could not help himself. He craved Wishart's excellent cigars, waited every evening for this moment. It was the cigar, more than the fire, the crossword or Holly's company, that brought him from his room. He fumbled a fat brown cone from the box. His hand itself took pleasure in the lightness of it, his ear enjoyed the faint, crisp sound. By way of thanks to Wishart who was eyeing him over the paper, Fred asked. 'What's wrong with Fred?' He felt he was betraying himself.

'Ordinary sort of name. Plebian.'

'Well, I'm an ordinary sort of bloke,' said Fred.

He did not mean it.

'You're not!' Holly told him at once, on cue.

Wishart considered the old man tiresome in his ordinariness, but merely said, 'Alfred was a great king, a law-giver. I'd be proud to have the name.'

'It just doesn't seem to belong to me, old chap.'

But it did, of course, too deeply and strongly belong.

From then on it was Wishart's inflexible use of Alfred, and

even Holly's slipping that way that was the principal element in the stirring up of Fred's memories.

It was Alfred who had been forced to sleep in his father's room, who had hated the snores and loathed the appurtenances of adult maleness hung and laid about the room – the collars, the brushes, the worn suit, the cracked shoes. As he grew older, terrible thoughts of married life had visited him there. The unutterable horror of imagining (in that instant before he stamped it down like the mouse in the packing case) his mother in the high, hard, creaking bed with Dad whose legs were skinny and yellow, and whose teeth, taken out, grinned in a tumbler all night. Alfred had suffered this.

Alfred had washed in the tiny bathroom with a skylight at the top of a funnel-like ceiling which never ceased to scare him, and there Alfred had once found bloody clothes soaking in the basin and fled in sick horror.

Alfred had endured eating gristle in gravy powder with dumplings in the dark back room with a glass cupboard full of gold-edged plates, never used; and he had been shut on Sundays in the cold front room with Foxe's *Martyrs* and feet frozen in pinching boots. Alfred had been despatched to the grocer's shop when he might have had a scholarship to real education; and Alfred had envied Ida the few caresses she received from Maud. He had pressed his face to the window, printing his cheeks with the net curtain's mesh, rather than look at his sister on the aunt's lap. Alfred had sat outside his mother's door for as long as he could, and then waited for her to return until the boys had laughed him out of it. Alfred had been clasped for one sweet moment in his mother's arms, his face to her green dress, feeling the rise and fall of her breast, infinitely safe.

Alfred, when he came to himself, found he was sitting in an unknown room with a wild hillside outside. A tall, upper-class woman came in and spoke to him. Painfully slowly his memories assembled themselves around her. She must be his daughter. There had been a wife – trouble, loneliness, the sea.

'He's going downhill,' said Wishart afterwards. 'Getting quite senile.'

'Don't be so crude!' cried Holly. 'It's just this long cold spell. He's had to be in so much. Stagnating. I'll get him out when some better weather comes. He'll perk up.'

– 216 –

She hated to speak of her father in this way, as if he were an object to be handled and managed, although she knew she was guilty of the same sort of thing. She chose her moment to mention certain contentious subjects, jollied him over awkward patches, treated him half like a child in the hopeless knowledge that his was an aged childhood in which no improvement was likely. He could not pass through this stage into one more convenient for everyone. Such thoughts made her squirm with self-dislike. He was her father, after all!

Fred, for his part, sensing their management of him, responded with sly misbehaviour. On one occasion when all three were out for a drink in Inverness he began to talk to the barmaid. He smiled at her, he touched her hand as she put down a glass, he called her 'love', all with an old man's slack flirtatiousness.

Holly could not believe her ears.

'Get us all a re-fill will you, love? That would be most kind of you.'

And when the drinks came, 'Many thanks indeed, love.' He handed her some money. 'Pretty little girl that,' he remarked to Wishart loud enough for the girl to hear as she returned with his change. 'Right ho, love, keep that for yourself.' With one hand he pushed some coins towards her, with the other he lightly caressed her bottom.

The conversation died away. Fred became aware that Holly's back was turned to him. She was on her high horse again, he supposed. In a few minutes, if he knew her, which he did only too well, she would say it was time to go home for supper. She and Wishart would sit at either end of the table with the damned silly candles she insisted on, whether it was dark or not, and the dish of floating flower-heads, and he would sit between them. She would go on about what she called 'the landscape' in her affected voice. Why couldn't she say fields and bloody woods and be done? But no, it had to be flood plains, plantations, drumlins, suchlike rubbish.

Wishart, who thought himself so smart, would mention this or that deal. Fred would just like to see the fellow in the London jungle. That would cut him down to size. Inverness!

They would discuss Peter, his emotional adjustment to his step-father, other claptrap. Holly might read aloud snippets from the boy's latest letter from school, pausing and selecting, obviously deciding what was fit for a worn out old grandfather to hear. Fred's blood boiled at the memory of these put-downs.

Yet, when Holly said 'About time we made a move', and Wishart reached for his coat, Fred obediently went out to the car with a 'Goodnight to you, love,' in the barmaid's direction and slid into the back seat, while Wishart and Holly installed themselves in front. Their backs were such a wall to him that he stared sideways, willing away the humiliating apprehension of dependence.

So much did it not seem possible that he had ever been in command of one of His Majesty's ships, that he sometimes caught himself thinking all that was still to come, his memories a vision of the future.

*

As the year passed, the cottage called Lurgann, or place of the stalks, was restored to habitation and Holly was glad. The architect had kept what he could of the old place – the sandstone lintels, window-sills and chimneys, and the brick-red front door – but the inside was gutted and extended at the back. The nearer trees were felled so that the windows looked over the woods towards the Monadhliath mountains. In the sloping bank in front where she and Donald had lain in the long grass, Holly planted new rose bushes. When she told her father he said, 'Why not have a fuchsia? They are lovely plants. I like them.'

'Do you?'

'When the flowers fall they make a rosy spot on the pavement. I like to see that.'

How had she known him all these years and not discovered that?

'I'm afraid we are too far north here for fuchsia out of doors.'

'Yes. Ah well. Just a thought.'

'If you like them so much I'll get one in a pot for your room.'

'I'd like that,' he said.

She sat down beside him. 'What's your favourite flower?'

'Oh, sweet-peas.'

'Of course. After that?'

'Roses, I think. What are yours, pussy?'

'I'm not sure. Something white. I like white flowers best.'

'Not a bit washed out?'

'I don't think so.'

They talked of flowers for some time. It was a moment of peace between them that gave her pleasure to remember for days.

Not long after, the cottage was finished, the rubble cleared, and Holly drove Fred up there to inspect it. She was full of joyful expectancy. It was as if a doll's house had become big enough to live in. She half believed she would find Chrissie inside with Ida's old teapot brewing up primrose wine; and Donald on the roof tree spying out the land. The cottage was hidden by the woods and the steep bank until you were almost on it, then popped into view like a small, neat face.

'What a dismal place,' said Fred without compromise.

'Oh why?' she was cast-down immediately.

'Backed into the trees. Damp for sure. It's bloody well swimming in trees.'

'It faces south.'

'And looks at a damn great row of mountains.'

'Come inside. He's done it nicely.'

From the small porch they went to the right through one front room and then round in a U through a kitchen and past a bathroom both built on at the back and into the other front room. Like all empty houses, it could be seen as either offering promise or confirming loneliness. The whole place was painted white.

'Like a hospital,' said Fred.

'Lovely big windows.'

'Too damn big – let in all the weather.'

'They are double glazed.'

'That's a fleabite against the cold up here.'

'Oh, you are being deliberately obstructive!'

She stood at the door taking gulps of sweet air blowing up from the valley over the resinous woods. Across Loch Ness, hidden in its trough, she could see the eastern bank like a green shelf dotted with toytown farms and counterpane fields, then the sloping rampart of brown moors rising to the grey tops of the mountains merging now with soft summer rain clouds.

Fred was stamping on the floorboards and tapping the walls, looking for faults to report to Wishart. Holly was struck by his appearance. There were the drooping shoulders and wrinkled neck of age, but the way he tapped the wood with loosely folded knuckles was a thing she had seen him do all her life. He did it with a young man's confident jauntiness. Her heart was cut by the unfair tearing apart that was age.

A few days later she happened to notice a furniture van turn up the drive to Lurgann. This surprised her as Wishart had said nothing of any tenants. She went up the old path through the wood, quickly, to discover what was going on.

No, no mistake, the van men told her and showed the delivery note. All ordered by Mr Grant and he'd sent along his secretary to help arrange it. A yellow car appeared and Wishart's secretary emerged with a sketch of the rooms and notes of where everything was to be placed. She even had curtains in the back of her car, made to measure in an Inverness shop. Scarlet linen. 'Cheerful. Do you not think so, Mrs Grant?'

Holly was unwilling to admit her total surprise. She chatted to the girl for a while and discovered she did not know who the house was for.

Going back down the hill, Holly realised the truth and came to a halt with the shock.

How stupid she had been! Of course, that was Wishart's plan, that was why he had been so good-mannered and accommodating to poor Tikki. Because he had this up his sleeve. How mean! How tricky! But then, he was merely repeating the trick that had worked with her – the *fait accompli* of a ready-made home.

When Wishart returned from work, he was met by a whirlwind. She came running down the front path at him, ear-rings banging on her neck.

'How could you! How *dared* you!'

The very worst thing to say. Wishart stiffened, carefully latched the gate. She pelted on. 'To do that behind my back. Conning me. And him.'

'If you mean Lurgann – you never asked. It was so obvious I thought you'd rather not know. If you had asked I would –'

'It's out of the question. I'll not have him there. It's outrageous of you even to contemplate it for a moment.'

'In fact,' continued Wishart when she drew breath, 'I felt sure you *had* guessed. Do you not remember saying a month or so ago that Alfred needed to be removed at spring cleaning time?'

She snorted. 'One casual remark.'

'We need our home to ourselves.'

'How can he live there?'

'How not?'

'He'd hate it. He's old and lonely, Wishart.'

'Being old is a fact of life we shall all come to, being lonely is due to your mother's death and his own nature.'

'Don't be such a blasted prig!'

'He's not ill, so why can he not live alone? Thousands of men his age do. When he does become infirm I shall pay for a resident woman to care for him. There are two bedrooms.'

'You will pay! Why should you?'

This assumption of responsibility paradoxically annoyed her further.

'It seems I took him on with you and Peter.'

She expelled her breath violently, unable for a moment to find words sufficiently contemptuous for this remark.

'You didn't *take me on*. Or Peter. We married each other, and I can look after Peter perfectly well by myself. Thank you.'

She stood quivering against the background of the housefront, her eyes sparking blue flints, her cheeks flushed. Wishart, in a corner of his mind, enjoyed the spectacle. Only in bed had he seen his wife so forgetful of herself.

'It's so unbelievably underhand,' she said.

That annoyed him. 'Openly to rebuild my own property?'

'And never say it was to bundle my father away in!'

'I could more fairly say it was underhand of you to smuggle Alfred in here under the excuse of an illness. You gave up the lease of his other cottage without a word to me.'

'It wasn't your business.'

'Even though it meant your father living permanently with us?'

'That's the right and proper thing. In Mediterranean countries old people always live with their children. You should know that.'

'My Italian mother lives in her own flat and is too proud to do anything else.'

Holly had forgotten Alma. She usually did.

'She's well off.'

'I don't intend to charge Alfred for living at Lurgann.'

'My God! I should hope not. Even you could not do that.'

'Even I?' he asked with sudden sadness. The fire went out of him. His dark eyes clouded. She felt half-ashamed and said, more peaceably, 'It was the shock of it, Wishart. That place means a lot to me. I always think of Donald climbing on the roof timbers.'

This was another mistake. He hated any mention of Donald or

Terence, had no wish to think of old lovers' ghosts round Balchraggan. He went into the house, and after a violent turn round the garden, zig-zagging among the bushes and young trees she had planted, she followed him.

Wishart was setting drinks out. From the faint scent of lavender as she came near him, she knew he had washed his hands in the downstairs cloakroom. He always did so, brushing his hair with an old silver backed brush he kept there and straightening his tie, eyeing himself with a smile hovering on his lips. Then he came to her for a kiss, and they drank a cocktail together. Alfred had been trained to leave them alone for that half hour. He had a whisky with them later.

This evening, Holly did not offer an embrace but stood by the grate where a fire shone pale because the sun was slanting in through the west window. Her foot rested on the brass fender with its cut out star holes, her elbow on the marble shelf. In dark blue with jade touches she was elegant and strong. Her face and half her looped black hair was reflected in the mirror along with sprays of wild cherry she was coaxing into bloom, shiny knobbly twigs sprouting green and white.

Wishart brought her a glass.

'Here, bellissima.' He held the drink in both hands, his face softened.

With a nod she indicated that he should place the glass on the mantelshelf. The tiny clink it made, expressed Wishart's renewed withdrawal from her.

'Don't play the grande dame with me.'

'That is such a cheap jibe! Can an actress not be allowed real feelings?'

The door opened and Alfred appeared with his cheeriest face.

'Reporting for duty,' he said.

'Come in. Have an early whisky. Holly and I have some news –'

'No!' cried Holly.

'– that I'd rather not keep.'

Fred, sensing discord for once not of his making, instinctively sided with Wishart.

'Right you are, old chap. I'd love a touch of malt, yes.'

Wishart handed him a drink and they chatted about the weather, the garden, the local Highland rugby team, both men fully used to circling a difficult issue.

'You know what all this is in aid of, don't you?' interrupted Holly in a combative tone.

'A nice little touch of conviviality,' said Fred gamely. 'Drink up, pussy.' He nodded at her untouched glass, then to Wishart, 'What happened over the business at Wick?' They had previously discussed a property deal there.

Now they went into further detail while Wishart poured more whisky. Holly wandered about her room, feeling unhoused, both scornful of male manoeuvrings and apprehensive. She drummed her fingers on the window. Wishart's softening up was exceptionally smooth and thorough, she had to admit, but the reason for it appalled her. Of course she would like her father gone, her home to herself, naturally she would – despite those Mediterranean extended families – that had been a silly remark, but she often forgot Wishart was Italian – half. All the same to condemn the old man to that out of the way place with a view of nothing but woods and mountains was cruel. She flinched from the thought of Fred's face when Wishart got round to telling him.

When she came out of her daydream, it seemed he already had. Fred was sitting extremely upright with a gauze layer of shock on his face.

'First class scheme,' he was saying, robustly. 'Just what was needed.'

'Daddy!'

'You two don't want me around the whole time. I can tell you Lucille and I would not have wanted to share our home.'

That at least was true, Holly thought.

'It's a well-built wee house,' Wishart said, his accent suddenly pronounced, 'and the central heating I've installed is an excellent system. I use it in all my important contracts.'

'I'm perfectly certain it is, old chap. Trust you, eh?'

It was Daddy's bar lounge voice: calm, steady, friendly and utterly false.

'And I've chosen furniture to fit in with what you like – a wing chair! That went without saying,' and Wishart's dark eyes twinkled at his father-in-law, 'a nest of tables, TV in a moveable cabinet – that sort of thing.'

'It's exceptionally good of you, old chap. Most thoughtful.'

'As for cooking –'

'I shan't do much for myself.'

'That's one of the problems,' put in Holly. 'You should eat proper meals.'

'It's all electric, simplicity itself. There's a little dishwasher too.'

'It's all most incredibly kind of you. Munificent.' Fred liked this word and repeated it. 'Munificent.'

'I'll not be wanting any rent. Just for you to pay the electricity and the rates and keep it all in order. I'll have my agent draw up a document. Best to have it on a formal footing.'

'Couldn't agree more, old chap.'

Perhaps his smile convinced Wishart. Holly knew it was only drawn on his face by self-respect.

'Let's drink to it.'

Their glasses were refilled. Holly sulkily took her tepid cocktail and tipped it down her throat.

'I'll see if supper is ready.'

'Can you possibly hold on?' Wishart asked coolly. 'I'd like to run Alfred up to Lurgann now. Just to tie up all the ends. Finalize matters.'

'At this time?'

'Why not? You don't mind do you, Alfred?'

'No, no. Fine by me.'

The three drove up to Lurgann in Wishart's car, the two men pally in the front seats, Holly in the back, shivering slightly in the early evening air and feeling completely up-staged by her husband.

She knew Fred's opinion of the cottage, but would never have guessed it from the way he extolled the outlook, the size, the simple colours, the big windows, everything was magnificent! And he sank with a slightly tipsy sigh into the mustard yellow chair.

'Suits me down to the ground,' he said. 'It's uncommonly generous of you, Wishart old man. I keep saying that, don't I? I'm an old fool.'

'Och, there's no need at all, Alfred. I hope you will be happy here, and, it goes without saying, come down to us whenever you feel like it.'

'That won't be too easy now I don't drive. My legs, you know.'

This was the first hint to indicate less than total agreement with Wishart's plans.

'You'll soon be active again, never fear. A touch of exercise on the terraces here, a bit farther down the path each day, you'll soon surprise yourself. Be walking down to lunch with Holly before you know what's hit you.'

Fred's face altered. His features slipped into each other as if his pink flesh was becoming liquefied. The blues and whites of his eyes seemed to have run together. His shoulders sagged leaving the cloth padding sticking up, and his hands trembled slightly.

To stop this he gripped his pipe and fumbled in his pocket for matches but he could not grasp them. All the time his gaze was fixed on the empty air over the ravine. Two buzzards came lifting up as if on invisible wires.

'Oh dear,' said Fred, agitatedly feeling in all his pockets for his matches, but still blindly, 'I must have left them behind. That's getting old for you.' He patted his thighs to feel if they were in his trouser pockets, and fumbled at his breast pocket, then stood up to see whether, against all habit, they were in his back pocket. 'No, no, they're not here. Must have left them,' he said to Wishart who was paying absolutely no attention, but looking at certain details in the room, checking up on his workmen.

Holly slipped her arm through her father's. His strangely marbled eyes avoided hers. She could not speak. She had not realized Fred could be this brave.

10

ALFRED UNDERWATER

Alfred walked as in his sleep from the wall to the big window at Lurgann and back again. He had moved the chair and table to give himself free passage. It was five paces. He held his arms folded behind his back, elbows braced, and looked ahead as if to some distant horizon.

He saw a submarine collage of split face and broken words, all scattered in the deep and saturated with pain. There were the dark rooms of his childhood and the stinks of the grocer's shop, a lad yodelling at him as he cycled by with the heavy delivery bike. There were naval barracks, his hammock, his ditty box, a smooth gun barrel, a deck white with scrubbing and sun. His infinite love for the sea in its power was with him, all the majesty and delicate beauty of the unending waters, but so also were the humiliations laid on him by public schooled officers, things that at the time he had swallowed and forgotten, but now stung like salt. He gripped his elbows more firmly and turned at the window.

There came images of Lucille in her striped dress under the fairy lights, Lucille holding baby Holly as if she might bite, Lucille violet with chagrin and temper. He saw fragments of his office life – a telephone mouthpiece wet with his breath, a gold pen tapped on teeth, a certain medallion on the carpet that had gradually worn thin and shown the jute backing, Margie's lipstick smile and casual slang. Weariness extreme, rather than pain, clung to these pictures. To shut them out he paced with eyes shut, five paces one way, turn, five back, turn, like some damned woman's knitting pattern, yet it did not help.

The oldest memories hurst worst – Maud's pinched mouth, her threats of hell, his father in long-johns using the chamber pot, Ida's crayons daubing his *Aesop's Fables*, his mother's bedroom door with one place where the varnish, too thickly applied, had run and set hard in a large tear drop. These things recurring every day, eternally clear, conveyed pang after pang to Alfred's heart, as if the tide had found a drowned harp and twanged its strings without mercy.

He tried to escape. He watched the television until shut down. He stayed in bed as late as possible, using the old sailor's trick of sleeping almost at will. He drank too. Holly would bring him only one bottle a week so he had a wine merchant deliver several crates and kept them in the shed. She never looked under the sacks there.

Every day she came carrying her pity. Inarticulately, in his secret depths, Alfred had no use for pity. He wanted his strength back and the power that went with youth. Pity categorised him, made him different, so that he hardly recognised the man Holly spoke to. He might have said to his daughter, I'm the same as I've ever been. Inside, I'm just the same. My feelings haven't changed a jot. Except that to say such things aloud would have troubled him acutely. A turmoil would have ensued in his heart as if a waterspout had brought dead things to the surface, things best unnamed, best forgotten; because Holly would have argued, given proofs, tried to show he *had* changed.

So when she came each morning with her pity, and little bits of food she cooked for him, and chatter he did his best to respond. He creased his face into a smile and agreed with most of her remarks. It would not do to quarrel with her, he was already lonely enough, and he was truly glad to see her, but . . . She went again so soon and there was the whole long day to get through. Well, she had her life, but he wished she would not try to manage him – always in the name of pity. He saw she avoided certain subjects as if he were a child, not that anyone had thought fit to shield him when he had been a child. But he was a man who had lived on the lower deck of a battleship. She chose to forget that.

Worse than this was the way she treated him like a juvenile. She had become inclined, since he had moved up to Lurgann, to say things like, 'How about a toddle along the forest path today?' Was he an infant, needing his hand held? Or, 'I'll make a nice little omelette.' What she cooked, of course, was the right size for one person. Or, 'It's about time we had clean underclothes, isn't it?' like a bloody nanny to a kid.

And she would keep on about the view. To his eyes it was always the same: fir trees like a hearth rug at his feet, over the top brown or green fields, depending on the season, then grey or white mountains, ditto, and finally the sky, usually featureless. Holly managed to see in it what she called 'infinite variety', which was pretentious, stagey nonsense. Now, give him the sea for variety!

He drew from memory one particular picture: a dull, crinkled sea with silver lights and sharp shadows, heaving sluggishly into spaced humps like the loose skin of an almighty creature. Then rain began, flattening the wrinkles and producing warts on the oily back of this animal. Alfred knew precisely and with love the look of the sea in such weather; and the chill smell, the heaviness of damp, salt air; the way the horizon made a dark pencil line, underscoring the sky. Few people he knew cared for the sea in such moods. They wanted azure calm or white-horses. It was the grey limitless rolling of the ocean that deeply moved Alfred, its pure wateriness, the millions of miles of wet levels, miles across, fathoms down.

He snuffed to catch the scent of it, and Holly asked, 'Have you another cold coming on?'

'Good Lord! Can't I sniff without you fussing?'

'Now don't be tetchy. I'm only concerned about your chest.'

'Tetchy!' He shuffled his feet violently and turned on the television so that Holly was forced to give up conversation. Tetchy! what a word to use to me, he thought, oblivious of whatever was on the screen. Anyone would think I was a cranky old man.

Soon after, Holly went home. Offended, he supposed. She had told him more than once that putting on the television was bad manners – never thinking what her own manners were like. Well, he couldn't care less how offended she and her precious Wishart were.

Yet he hated it without her. The unfriendly loneliness surged back, inexorably, smothering him. The woods took a pace nearer, another, and another. Their heavy branches drooped with rain. He could see water running down the central spines and dripping off to the branches below. The sky leaned in, dark with mist and rain, pressing on the trees and the house roof. Silence filled the small space around Lurgann and flowed into all the rooms until the tide was brushing against the ceiling and Alfred, drowning, was pacing again.

*

'How,' said Holly to Wishart, 'he can refuse to walk down the path to us when he must walk miles across that room every day, I just do not understand.'

'Obviously he does not want to come here. You'd better accept that.'

She stared stonily at her husband. Lately her broad face had worn a tight expression which aged her. Wishart was an alien who did not understand about her and Alfred. She had accepted Wishart's name for him, for it was more suited to his morose old age than the cheerful Fred or the whimsical Tikki, but she was damned if she'd accept his reading of Alfred's emotions.

'It's not that,' she said after a pause long enough for Wishart to eat a whole slice of toast.

He did not reply. He saw no point in inflaming Holly. He had what he wanted and could be relaxed about the situation now, even generous.

'He feels it's a total insult to be shuffled out of the way up there.'

'Hugh approves,' remarked Wishart peaceably.

'Yes!'

Her brother's attitude was a further irritation. Wishart had written to Hugh explaining what he had done and Hugh had rung up immediately to congratulate them.

'I had begun to think you might be lumbered with the old man for good. Well, for the very reverse of good. He-he-he!'

'No way,' said Wishart.

'Come the spring I'll be up again and take him out a bit. He can put me up at the cottage, I take it?'

'There's a spare-room, yes, but of course stay with us.'

'Hugh approves,' Wishart had said to Holly, replacing the receiver. She considered it despicable the way men arranged things between themselves.

Having eaten almost nothing, she began to fold her napkin. 'Alfred thinks he is not welcome here.'

'I made it perfectly plain – '

'Oh, you did that all right!'

'– that he was to come down for a meal and some company whenever he liked.'

'As if he would – having been turned out.'

'You mean, I suppose, provided with a rent free, warm and comfortable house?'

'He wanted to come into our lives, our hearts.'

'Don't be melodramatic, my dearest girl, and pour me some more coffee please.' She did so. 'In any case what you say is not true.'

'What do you know about him?' she asked feebly. Wishart's tone, his speaking where usually he was silent, impressed her.

'You go on and on, darling, about Alfred loving you – what it's meant to you, how it's felt, oh! how you do go on, Holly –' he smiled a kindly smile to reassure and disarm her, 'but for all that, it looks different from where I stand.'

'How different?' The wary words escaped her.

'Sometimes I think he is contemptuous of women, and fears them.'

'Not me!'

Wishart drank some coffee.

'Anyway, he adored my mother,' Holly said.

'But you've told me she couldn't love him fully, she sniped at him, she stole, in the end she went rather senile. He must feel let down in every way by her. Then his aunt who brought him up was strict and probably terrified of sex. His mother, of course, left him.'

'Oh, but he loved his mother, Wishart. That at least is certain.'

'Well, as to that – he probably had terrible feelings of guilt when she was ill, isn't that what happens? And resentment that she left him – feelings he drowned in the tears he refused to shed.'

'You've gone very Freudian,' said Holly, but mildly.

'You know how he treats you. He alternates bullying with sentimental affection, both of which amount to contempt. I tell you Alfred doesn't understand women –'

'Well, do you?'

'That's not what we are discussing. *He* doesn't at all events. He fears them and this comes out as contempt. Hidden, of course, from himself.'

'But crystal clear to you.'

He ignored her hostility. He smiled at her again. 'I can see that

– 230 –

with him love means possession and power. It has to because he fears its loss. When you, as a child, began to show aversion to being possessed, he began, in some sense, to dislike you, although he has no idea of it. He is merely aware you annoy him.'

Wishart was voicing thoughts Holly had come across in her own mind. She felt drained by them.

'If you'd say sorry and climb on his knee, he believes, bingo! everything would be clear sailing.'

'It wouldn't.'

'Of course not. I know that.'

'I've tried. It didn't work.'

'Of course not.'

She was crying, her fingers curved over her eyes.

'Holly darling, I am sorry. I do understand and I'm sorry.'

She dashed her tears away, rubbing with the heel of her hand. 'Not my side, you don't understand.'

'You love him much more sincerely and deeply than – '

Wishart paused and for a moment Holly thought he would say that she loved Alfred more than him. This was true but she did not ever want it said. However, after a glance at her, he ended, ' – than he loves you.'

She had built up her life on her father's love. He had always been there with his hand for her to hold. He had rescued the naked birds by placing them in the clump of golden rod, which had feathery stalks of flowers above her head and a sharp scent. The ground around its dozens of stalks, where Daddy had inserted the birds, was dusty, the rain never seeming to reach there.

She noticed with a start that Wishart was stacking the dishes in the machine.

'Wishart?'

'Yes?' He kept his back turned.

'What you said is your sort of truth. It's not mine.'

Ah well, he thought, a little progress maybe. Aloud he said, 'Does Peter's train arrive at 12.10? We must get a move on if you want to shop first.'

'All right.'

'Have you made his bed?'

'Of course. Everything is ready up there for him.'

'Right. We should leave in half an hour.'

'I've just time to pop up to Lurgann then.'

'Holly!'

'Just to make sure he's all right.'

She slipped on a garden coat which was kept hanging by the back door. It was bright blue and made her look eighteen.

'I won't be long.'

Wishart watched her run across the yard. The gate in the wall slammed behind her. She was like a girl hurrying to meet her lover, he thought heavily. He was disappointed in himself – a rare and unsettling experience.

Alfred was in his chair by the fire. She ruffled his hair, kissed him, went upstairs to make his bed. She did this every day, a chore she hid from Wishart and never mentioned to Alfred himself. It was tacitly understood that she would do this for him and that he would never admit he did not do it for himself. However, on this occasion, the bed was made. Then she saw from certain folds in the counterpane that Alfred had not slept in the bed. Was he ill? She clattered downstairs in her high-heeled shoes.

'Why didn't you go to bed last night?'

'Oh,' elaborately casual, 'I slept here on the sofa, pussy.'

'Whatever for?'

'Just felt like it.'

'No. Why did you?'

He assumed his brave face, which she actually found quite pitiful. Whether he was aware of this, she could never be certain. Sometimes she suspected him of trying to prick her conscience; at others she believed he did it unconsciously, sailing on automatic pilot as it were.

'My legs,' he said, apparently grudging the words, 'they're a bit too stiff for those stairs, you know. Damned steep.'

'Oh dear!'

'They are quite sore,' he added, patting his thighs.

'Well, why do you do all that pacing up and down, then?'

'Don't bother me, Holly.' He jerked irritably out of his chair and went to stare out of the window.

'You can't sleep on a sofa, that's for sure. That won't help your legs.'

'Slept in many worse places,' he told her in quite a warm, satisfied voice. He was treasuring her concern.

'Not aged seventy-five.'

'Well, what can I do?' he asked, swinging round to face her, half-fighting, half-pleading. 'I have to come down to the lav. several times a night. It's too much, Holly. I'm afraid I'll fall.'

'You should have told us.'

'It's not quite the sort of thing you discuss, is it?'

'Spending a penny?' She laughed. 'All of us have to.' She saw from his pained expression he did not want this sort of bodily talk. God help him and us when he gets really infirm, she thought. 'Are there other things you find difficult about this house?' she asked him gently.

He hitched his shoulders up and down and shuffled his slippers.

'I'm not used to electric stoves. Your mother always liked gas. I've left it on a few times, nearly set light to the teacloth.'

This hung on a hook by the cooker and she had noticed it once draped over the hotplate, then turned off.

'But I can manage,' he said in a deliberately stout tone. 'Just taking a bit of time to adjust.'

'Well, I have to go now to fetch Peter back. We'll come up this afternoon and bring your bed downstairs. All right?'

He smiled with a thin-lipped smile and his eyes were bright. It was what he wanted, her care for him; but he also hated being beholden to anyone, even Holly.

Wishart saw from the set of her shoulders as she came back that things had not gone well at the cottage. She shut the door in the wall with care as if fearing to wake a sleeper. She was stiff with pain.

That afternoon all three of them went up to Lurgann and rearranged things for Alfred. His bed was carried down to the second front room and the big table taken upstairs. They put the bedside lamp and Alfred's pile of yachting magazines on the dresser, making it a sort of bedside cupboard. A small table was brought from their own home to give Alfred somewhere to eat his meals. It all looked rather cramped, and Wishart felt put out by the disarrangement of the cottage over which he had spent quite a lot of careful thought.

Alfred did not look particularly pleased either, although he kept saying it was superb and just what he needed. A place to keep his clothes was a problem.

'Well, you will just have to go upstairs to the wardrobe,' Holly told him briskly. 'Take your time, and make sure the light's on.'

'Oh dear,' Alfred said. 'Oh dear,' in a sigh that was almost a groan, nearer still a curse.

He acutely disliked this bundling of his possessions to and fro, this fixing up of his world for him; yet he dismally knew it had to be so long as he was forced to live alone in this place. Why Holly didn't put her foot down and insist he came back to the farmhouse, he could not for the life of him make out. He glanced at her face which looked wary and gentle, then at his son-in-law who was expressionless – always a bad sign.

'Well, you'll be wanting to get off now. Don't let me keep you,' he said, hustling them out in his brusque, jumpy way as if he wanted nothing better than his solitude. If he could not have the life he really needed . . .

'Grandpa looks different,' Peter remarked as they walked down the wood path. 'His eyes have a white line round the blue bit. Why's that?'

Wishart and Holly revolved various replies in their minds, but neither answered. It did not trouble Peter long. He was too delighted to be home for the whole long summer holidays to worry over his grandfather's sea-change. Already Wishart had promised him a fishing trip to Sutherland, and even talked about buying him his first very own gun.

*

The summer passed. For Peter it raced, crammed with excitement and the pleasure of his mother's secure presence, towards September when he must return to school. For Wishart it marched on with steady days of business decisions and domestic enjoyment. He resolutely ignored all signs of disturbance. For Holly it staggered from happy times with Peter outdoors to desolate hours brooding on Alfred. Fits of worry over him took her when she least expected them. Out in a boat on a small loch once, with the water slapping regularly on the boards and Peter's reel whirring as he threw in his glittering spinner to catch a pike from the reeds, she was at peace with the world until the boy referred to the fish lurking to be hooked and jerked out to death as 'the old man'. Another time, plunging over bouncy heather, loosening puffs of pollen, the sun blinded her eyes so much that she turned her back to rest them, caught sight of Lurgann's chimney sprouting between the pines and felt a drag in the pit of her stomach. For Alfred each summer day was long for he had nothing at all to do. Nothing and no one, as he told himself silently each early morning, each midday, each evening when he stood watching the night come down on the mountains, jagged above the ranks of motionless trees. Yet, at the same time, the season raced faster for him than it did even for Peter because after the summer it would be autumn, then winter finally to close him up inside, to sink him. If there was nothing and no one now in the warmth and sun, openness of door and windows, the breeze in the pines sounding, Holly declared, like distant waves (but he did not hear it like that), what would there be for him when the forest invaded the cottage entirely and snow buried it?

An absolute nothingness, an absence so profound that Alfred feared he might dissipate in it. There would be nothing left of him but the small, bitter, searing, hard centre that was his abandoned self.

*

Gales hit the Highlands in October. Leaves were stripped still green from the sycamores, rivers overflowed, gardens drowned. Then came an unseasonable hard frost, and ice forced open knife cracks in the bare, unploughable fields. A thaw in November brought snow, wet, thick and clinging, pasting itself on walls and treetrunks, bringing down saplings, huge limbs of old trees and power-lines. In early December, a few weeks of sparkling weather, with frost, sun and sharp winds. The farmers went to work and gardeners were at last able to give their battered plants some winter protection, which was just as well because after Christmas tremendous storms from the east fell upon the mountains and corkscrewed into the glens, scattering the beasts to the shelter of walls and rocks, felling trees in swathes like feathers blown down, tearing at roofs. Snow continued for thirty-six hours piling ramparts round buildings, levelling hedge to hedge, then it froze hard and yet harder. Oak boughs split showing their foxy centres, waterfalls became grey, unmoving columns, houses were dens, hardly warm enough and pungent smelling.

Peter, home again for the holidays, was beside himself with delight, taking his mother and Wishart out to snowball, toboggan or climb the hills every day he could. They walked at an unaccustomed level, the fence posts were stubs to trip them up, the tree branches, looping down, disappeared into snow. Ice was humped on the east face of each trunk, as if a white stone pipe had been welded to the wood. None of the burns was visible. They had frozen over and were covered by snow. No sound came however close Holly and Peter bent over. The river did break through its crust in a few places – black in the white softness – but its movement was sluggish. 'It feels the cold too!' Peter laughed and picked up blossoming handfuls of snow crystals, which sparkled like some fairytale stuff in sunlight, and even in the moonlight. Peter would draw his parents to the door to see the amazing blue glints from the snow under the moon, lying in silent stillness, an undulating coverlet over the hidden garden.

In some ways it was a good holiday, but Holly felt strangely removed from it. She found herself sometimes going uncertainly about the house as if looking for something – she knew not what – or standing still for minutes on end to think about – nothing. Nothing at all. Or she would go out by herself to walk by the river, to rub her gloved hand over the birch bark, scaly red and silver, as if some message might be written underneath. A few fragments fell on the snow.

She clung to Wishart one moment, pushed him away at the next. One night almost at the climax of their lovemaking, her face twisted and seemed to Wishart to explode, its parts swallowed in three holes. She fell heavily on her back and burst into a storm of weeping. She lay with legs apart and sobbed with ugly tearing gasps.

Wishart begged her to say what the matter was, what had he done? In the end, he made out through her blubbered lips, the words, 'My father. He's so alone.'

'Oh God!' He rolled away from her, without sympathy. The ceiling above was as blank as his heart. This was the first time Alfred had intruded into their bed. In the morning he ignored her and went to work without a word.

On January 12th, when Peter had returned to school, she paid her morning visit to Alfred. He was out of bed, not dressed, standing at the window in his dressing-gown, pretending to be studying the mountains which were creamy rounded humps against a colourless sky, but in reality watching for Holly to emerge from the wood.

'Aren't the mountains magical this morning?' she asked. 'Like teacups upturned against a white wall.'

Alfred shuffled to his chair, dragging his slippers. He had

trodden down their heels and this gave his walk a particularly listless air.

'Have you had your breakfast yet?' she asked.

Alfred did not answer. He sat down in his chair allowing his body to fall heavily. This pained his hip but indicated his aggressive lack of interest in life, and the pain was almost a pleasure to him.

Holly went into the next room and made his bed, then put his day clothes ready for him. The cottage was very quiet and still. The hum of the heating only intensified this. As she observed her father staring into space, his lips in a thin line, the folds of white flesh on jaw and neck sagging, she couldn't help remembering, once again, his hopeful, youthful, happy face. As if sensing her mood, he said, 'I'm cracking up, Holly. The sooner the better.'

'Oh come on! You'll be lively again when the spring arrives.'

'I damn nearly passed out yesterday when I tried to walk a bit down the path.'

'You shouldn't have done that, not with the ice underfoot.'

'It's not the ice, it's my heart. I'm not what I was, Holly. I could go any time.'

'Of course you won't!'

'Be better if I did.'

He shot her a glance which she noticed and wondered again if Alfred put on some of his moods to get her sympathy. He would not do it deliberately, but unconsciously perhaps, going on automatic steering.

And why shouldn't he appeal to her? If you couldn't ask help from those who loved you, what a world it was! To him, she said gently, 'You are not ill, Tikki, not even crippled. You've still got an appetite and interests. Yes, you lost your wife but you had her for a good few years. You have a cosy home here, me to run errands for you. Peter. Memories.'

'I suppose you mean, I am better off than most.'

'Well, aren't you?'

'What are they to me?' he asked bitterly.

'Why must you be so bloody special?' Her anger spurted.

It was true, he did think he was unique. That was one of the roots of his despair. He, Alfred Tickener, special and different, had come to this dead end! Life was a cheat, with dreams unrealised and no time left. His hands clenched on his knees.

Fresh, strong pity welled up in Holly. Impulsively she knelt down by his chair and put her arms round him.

'I think I'm special too,' she said softly. 'I understand.' He turned full face to her and she saw his stubble and flecks of yellow at the corners of his mouth, which was trembling.

'We are two special people, you and me!' she reassured him.

He kissed her and she stayed crouching beside him for some minutes but already was thinking ahead of going home, a phone call she had to make.

'I'll get us a nice cup of cocoa.' As she moved about the kitchen she talked to him, asking first what the sea would be like in such weather. This launched him happily. He came over to lean against the door while she boiled the milk and made him some toast. His face was a better colour, he stood straighter. All he needs is company, she thought. As she carried the tray of food to the table, she said, 'I'll have to go back soon. There's a phone call I've to make for Wishart.'

'Oh.'

'You'll get dressed then, won't you?'

'Can't you come back afterwards?'

Where will that end, she thought, and said, 'Well, I've quite a lot to do.'

'Oh dear.'

'Jobs for Wishart, housework, a letter to Peter – you know.'

'You were my little Holly once.'

'Oh Daddy!'

'You were.'

'Yes.'

'My prickle puss.'

'I'm sorry,' she said.

'And so you should be – shutting me up here.' His temper flared.

'That's not fair! You're not in prison. You are free to do as you like.' His face tightened and hardened and paled as she spoke. 'It's unfair to Wishart to talk like that.'

'Damn that!'

'Drink your cocoa,' she told him calmly.

'Don't nag me, woman.'

Oh dear, oh God! she thought. I can be either his Holly or Wishart's wife. How can I be both?

'Well, make sure to drink it before it's cold.' She put on her coat and left.

Alfred watched her disappear down the path and then remained at the window for a period which passed as quick as a minute or lasted as long as a day. The wind rose and loose snow began to blow around Lurgann like flying mist. Eventually he dragged back the covers of his bed and lay down again on his back with his eyes open. Occasionally small tears oozed out of his reddened eye sockets and dripped to the pillow and dried.

*

When Holly had made her phone call she could settle to nothing. Peter's room was already cleaned, his bed stripped. She had written all her Christmas thank-you letters, and had no real need to write so soon to her son. None of her clothes or Wishart's needed washing or mending. Her friends could not come visiting because of the state of the roads. Wishart, because he had the will to work and chains on his tyres, was one of the few people locally travelling. She had finished her library books and put back all the dried flower arrangements removed for the festive season. The idea of spending a day with her knitting and the radio was dreadful in her taut and desperate mood. She said aloud to the uncaring furniture, 'Oh, what's the use!'

She decided to go for a long walk that would take all day. Wishart did not like her to go far in such weather – but, what the hell! She left a note on the kitchen table saying: 'Gone to Glen Livet to look at the falls.'

As she started out over the home fields towards the copse where the cattle were sheltering, she supposed that what she was doing was putting as much distance between herself and Balchraggan as she could without actually running away. She could not support the situation there any longer, torn between Wishart and Alfred, between her love and duty to them both.

Resolutely, she turned her attention to the countryside around. The oak trees beside the lane were frosted to the very top, like enormous white bouquets. The diffused sunlight crept in among the crumbly blossoms tenderly. In one tree two crows sat high up, three blackbirds half way down, a pink finch on the lowest branch, and there was a robin on the ground. It was like an illustration in a Book of Hours and comforted her briefly.

Walking awkwardly on the frozen ruts of mud and ice where

the farmer had driven the trailer to leave loose mounds of mustard brown hay for his beasts, she came to the birch copse. The drooping branchlets in ice casings clattered faintly in the wind. All through the wood the animals had scattered and trampled the hay among the tree roots. The Highland cattle's wispy hazel brown coats trailed delicately on the hard snow, and the whole herd followed her up the sloping track, determinedly, almost devotedly, lowing plaintively and nudging against each other's flanks. She was glad of their company as far as the young plantation of spruces which they were fenced out of. Long strands of cattle hair dangled on the barbed wire, furred white with frost, and broken trees had fallen across the wire in several places, burying their heads in snow drifts.

She crawled under the trunks, knocking snow down her back. In the plantation she found traces of deer. They had nosed down to the moss and dead leaves which were unnaturally bright in so much colourlessness. Beside the burn were old patches of trampled ice, a faint sound of bubbling water. Here a flock of finches scattered upwards at her approach like blown leaves, a hundred or more, quick and silent.

On the far side she came to the summer pastures, all the tussocks smoothed over by a white sheet, the pool a blind eye staring at the sky. Here the snow, exposed to intense nightly cold, had grown huge crystals, as big as soap-flakes, which rustled when she stirred them with her toe. All around were the woods of spruce and larch and pine, not green or black but grey and marked with arrow shapes like a vast plaid of herringbone pattern. A few sheep were there, pathetic creatures who had scraped away the snow and stood, each in her own gunnel, gnawing. Snow, piled on their curly backs, made their fleeces look grubby. Above was a sky like taut grey silk with a light behind it.

Then she was into the deep forest and no more living things. Instead a watchful hostility. Her feet creaked. Her breath's little clouds of frozen droplets drifted away, disowning her body. Between the black trees was grey monotonousness, gradually shadowing into undifferentiated distance. On every outcrop of rock among the silent, straight trees were placards of ice, and icicle fingers on monstrous hands. She imagined them forming over many nights in the utter quiet and solitude.

It was a relief to come out to the moor where wave upon wave of sculpted snow rose above her head in arrested movement. The sky was changing. Thick clouds, so darkly cream they had pink and brown in their recesses, came piling up behind the mountain called Mealfourvonie. Its domed brow was wrinkled with snow and rock ridges, its chin rested tight on the coverlets drawn over the heather. She thought intermittently of other times when she had come this far, of jokes made about the face of the old man mountain. The first time had been with Donald and his mother. They had had a picnic and swum in the pool below the waterfall. There had been other times alone and in company, all times of joy and beauty and fun, and all were now extremely remote.

Around the moor, shouldering up to Mealfourvonie, were the hills. For once they did not comfort her. She reflected that they are held in time as much as we are. They only seem unchanging because our lives are brief. The hills too pass, worn down by weather and rivers, and broken apart by convulsions from below. They have more permanence than man – that is all one can say; and in the great span of the galaxy's life and beyond that the exploding space-time of the universe, what did a little shorter or longer life signify? The massive humps of rock that had sustained her for years were hardly more long-lived than molehills, as much fleeting shadows as man.

Which threw you back, she thought, upon yourself, upon your humanness. As long as your heart beat you were permanent, and afterwards – what did all the mountain ranges in the world matter? We have to live in the cave of ourselves, changelessly alone. Her heart ached with sorrow for all humans, dumped here, clutching their consciousness to themselves, a parcel of awareness tied up by loneliness. Mostly she sorrowed for Alfred. He had been right to think the hills offered him nothing but sham comfort as he looked out from the windows of Lurgann or down into the depths of himself.

All this time she was walking steadily along the base of the mountain towards the cleft where the water fell.

The rocks for a hundred yards before the falls were coated two inches thick in glistening ice out of which emerged here and there the rust red pine trunks scabbed with snow. As she crossed the river at the foot her boots crunched down into layers of ice like shattered fragments of thin glass, loosely packed.

The water was rumbling faintly behind its frozen mask which

was not white but greenish yellow. Where the pool, for bathing, had been was a conical mound of ice rising as much as twenty feet and with a rough surface. Holly supposed it had been formed by freezing spray building up. Between this cone and the frozen falls themselves was a vaporous slit, chill with a watery cold. She crept into it. Above her rose the curved waterfall shockingly sheer and motionless. She put her hand on the grainy surface and even through two pairs of gloves, it struck cold. The silence was tense. Although nothing could move, pines, icicles, rocks and ice watched her. She was miles from any other human being, thousands of acres of frozen bog and ice-bound forest isolated her. No thought penetrated her brain now, only feeling.

What she felt was the terrible, long loneliness of her father.

Leaning back against the waterfall, she grew colder; feet and hands were numb. The pines might have been lead trees, the brushwood in the ravine tangled wires. Not even a raven sailed into the sky, which was beginning imperceptibly to settle on the land. Rock crests were disappearing, swallowed by nothingness. Gradually the trees above her and the curve of stopped water simply vanished as the mist drank the world. Still Holly remained concealed in the slit behind the cone, hiding, hardly knowing she was in danger. She hid from the life she had to go back and face.

Only when the snow began did she come out and hurry away, holding out her arms into the sticking, whirling flakes and opening her eyes as wide as she could to keep the narrow track in sight. It took her an hour to cross the moor. She was glad of the storm which released her from the necessity to feel.

She ran through the forest, panting, busy with the task of reaching safety.

Bursting out into the summer pastures, she found she had left the snowstorm behind and walked slowly in a patch of clear air between the curtains of snow behind and a mist rising from the valley. Flooding up from Loch Ness it infiltrated the wooden slopes above the village with a crystalline smokiness which, as the sun went down, became violet edged. She stood to watch the grey woods melt and the sky stain green. She was very tired. Slowly she realised what she had decided she must do.

When she came out of the young plantation into the home fields, the moon was up, the whole world black and white. Balchraggan hill, without trees on its top, merged with the white moon sky and did not exist. The cold was eating her bones, plunging into her lungs. Against the invisible hillside her home was an indistinct outline, blurred by snow. The oaks had a secretive otherness, austere, powerful, very old. When she put her hand on one for reassurance, she found none. Around the moon was a disc of blue edged with tarnished silver.

She went indoors and put on all the lights in all the rooms, systematically. On the table in the kitchen her note still lay, an accusing stare, and she stopped to think of Wishart, his face, his love.

'The hills are shadows,' she said aloud, her voice echoing strangely round the tidy room.

Then she went upstairs again and began to pack a small suitcase with her night things, some spare sweaters, underwear, toothbrush, and, a last thought, a book of poetry.

She sat down in the kitchen and placed her hands obediently on her lap: a child about to be taken on a journey of which the end cannot be imagined.

*

When Wishart arrived home to his home blazing like a beacon in the snowfields he found Holly sitting with her coat on and a suitcase beside her. He took it in with a calm glance and expressed only mild curiosity.

'Are you going somewhere?'

'Yes. I'm going to Alfred. He cannot be left alone.'

For a second or two Wishart considered offering his father-in-law shelter at the farm until the severe weather was over, but decided very quickly against it. Alfred was perfectly all right where he was, and it would not do to give in to Holly.

'Your being there at night won't make the least difference to him,' he said reasonably. 'I daresay he's made his supper by now and is in bed. Have him down to lunch tomorrow. It's in the day he'll feel being shut in more than the evening.'

'I do not mean that I am going for one night.'

Wishart had been taking off his layers of outdoor clothes, but stopped abruptly with his scarf half-unwound from his neck.

'I mean I am going to live permanently with Alfred. He is my father and he needs me.'

'So – do – I,' said Wishart gaspingly, and made an effort to put aside his scarf.

'You refuse to have him here.'

'Yes, I do! You know why? He separated you from Donald. But I intend to keep you for myself alone.'

'I am going, Wishart.'

Wishart took an immense breath. He felt it was dredging the very floor of his being.

'If you leave my house, Holly, I will not have you back.'

'I didn't think you would,' she replied, almost playfully, with a desperate little breath of laugh.

'That will be the end.'

'I know.'

'What about Peter?'

Her face quivered, then straightened. 'When the spring comes, we will see about him.'

'This is monstrous,' cried Wishart, willing himself to wake from what must be a nightmare – the house pulsating with light, Holly with her overnight bag. 'Absurd. Totally.'

'Yes, I do know that. But there's nothing I can do.'

'Of course there is! Don't be so – so – babyish! Unpack that damned case, sit down with me by the fire, and we will discuss how to help Alfred through the winter.'

'It's his life he needs helping through and his death.'

'Don't be so bloody dramatic.'

She stood up and belted her coat. 'Please don't be angry, Wishart.'

'That's cool, if you like.'

'I love you,' she said in a low voice, as if to herself.

'So I see.'

'I do, I do. You have been so good!'

'But Alfred is better? Is that it?'

She stood staring at him for the time it took for her eyes to fill with tears and brim over, then she turned and felt her way out.

From where he stood by the chair with his tumbled coat on, Wishart cried out, 'Remember Holly, if you do this I will not have you back.'

The door closed, she passed through the beam of light from the window. Her footsteps made no sound on the snow and he did not hear the blue door close, so that for a while he could pretend to himself that she was still in the yard, undecided, just about to return to him. He knocked urgently on the window pane, smiling pleadingly into the dark.

*

The narrow path was slippery and difficult to climb with a case. Her legs were weary after the day's walk, her heart sick at what she had done to her husband.

On the little platform in front of Lurgann she paused. The moon was now racing through white clouds with its burnished ring around it. All the lights in the farm were being put off. The cottage too was dark, the curtains undrawn.

She went in and by the moonlight saw her way through the porch to the switch.

On the table stood the drink she had made that morning untouched, covered with a thick skin. She pushed open the bedroom door.

Alfred lay in the bed with his dressing-gown on, flat on his back. He did not turn when she appeared but his eyeballs reflected the light.

'Daddy?'

'Yes.' He still did not move.

'I've come to stay with you. I am not going back.'

Alfred rolled over on his side like a heavy treetrunk set in motion.

'What?' He squinted up at her, his face squashed against the pillow.

She repeated what she had said. He hitched himself upright and sat on the bed's edge, feeling with his feet for his slippers.

He stood up, a giant in the shadows, and tied his dressing-gown cord.

'What did you say, pussy?'

'I'm here to stay.'

He came swaying towards her as if a ship's deck were beneath his feet.

'Ah Holly!' he said in a deep voice. 'That's better, my prickle puss.'

He was richly satisfied.

Outside the pines in a flurry of wind knocked their tops together and threw down frozen cones.